The Light Who Shines

By Lilo Abernathy

Bluebell Kildare Series
Book 1

COPYRIGHT

Title: The Light Who Shines
Author: Lilo Abernathy
Editor: Shauna Ward

Dedication

 or my parents, who taught me how to think, question, and learn about the world by reading. Thank you for raising me in a house with a huge wall of books ranging from *Horton Hears a Who* by Dr. Seuss to *Sherlock Holmes* by Sir Arthur Conan Doyle. And let's not forget the stacks of *National Geographic* and *Popular Mechanic* magazines. I will never forget falling asleep to the music enhanced soundtrack of *The Hobbit*.

You fueled my imagination with fantasy, then gave me the necessary critical thinking skills to discern fact from fiction. You taught me how to do for myself and make my own way in this world, while at the same time showing me how tremendously vast and interesting the world is.

Most of all, I thank you for giving me the foundation required to formulate my own opinions and for respecting them even when they diverge from your own.

TABLE OF CONTENTS

ACKNOWLEDGEMENTS

I would like to take a moment, or perhaps several days to acknowledge my long-suffering editor, Shauna Ward. If I knew how, I would curtsy to you, or better yet, bow, as curtsies just don't have the same elegant grace about them. Imagine me waving my arm in a flourish and bending at my waist, using my considerable dexterity to nearly touch the ground as the blood rushes to my face. I do this in acknowledgement of you. Let me just say . . . the phrase "that sounds a bit awkward" has been indelibly seared into my mind, but I'm a better writer for it.

I extend significant gratitude to Gina Fiserova for her excellent work in tightening the story. Your tutelage of me in the art of cutting will be a boon to my readers for the rest of my life.

And, Stephanie Shultz, without your final proof I would simply not be able to rest at ease.

My heartfelt appreciation goes out to all of my pre-readers for your fortitude in braving the variety of rough versions I presented and providing your honest commentary in return. The long list includes Jean Lombardo, Charles Lombardo, Eduardo Sampedro, Laura Ward, Evelyn Gauger, Ann Moynihan, Jennifer Blanton, and many others. You truly helped me improve and enrich the story.

I must also take a moment to thank Kristin Sallee, the gorgeous model for Blue, and Kirsi Salonen for producing the fantastic cover art.

Finally, I'd like to thank my readers for purchasing this book and beginning this journey with me. I very humbly present to you my first work and hope for nothing more than your true enjoyment of it.

PREFACE

The plot follows the investigation of the kidnapping, torture, and murder of a seventeen-year-old boy. The story opens at the crime scene and is written from the alternating perspectives of the two main characters: the primary inspector on the case and her boss. Love is in the air, even as villains abound.

The story takes place on earth, in a society similar to ours. However, some major events occurred about two thousand years earlier that caused a divergence from our reality. The prologue briefly takes us back those two thousand years to provide clues to some of the more mystical aspects that manifest themselves in the present day of this alternate existence.

The populace of this world primarily consists of several breeds of humans: regular humans as we know them, magically Gifted humans, and Vampires, who are essentially cursed humans. The story deals with a couple of our society's most ugly issues: prejudice and hate. Except that in this world prejudice is not between races but between breeds of humans. The story also confronts key questions about the nature of good and evil.

This novel contains a few scenes of vividly described violence and explicit sex. I consider it rated R and appropriate only for those at least seventeen years of age.

Prologue

Shaina

Winter, Year 1, Red Ages

I wake to the sound of pounding on the door and Mor's voice yelling, "Shaina. Shaina."

Sorcha wakes up crying as I rush to open the door. A bloodcurdling scream tears through the night, destroying any illusions of a peaceful return to slumber. I swing open the door with trembling hands and see anguish in Mor's eyes. The words that tumble from her mouth bring to the fore all the fears I'd been trying to suppress this winter.

"Shaina, Conor was found dead, killed by the bloodsuckers. Grainne and Aongus are calling you a Witch and gathering the town folks to burn you as one. Quick! We must run."

I start gathering my things together, but Mor yells, "There is no time. Grab the bairn. We must go *now!*"

Sorcha is wailing now. Tears streak her little cheeks as she grips her blanket tightly in tiny fists. I grab my plaid and wrap it around us both as I follow Mor outside.

"You must quiet her," Mor whispers.

I try to comfort Sorcha in a hushed voice. "Shh, Sorcha, you must be quiet. Shhhh."

Sorcha pays no heed and cries all the louder as she clutches me with her little fingers.

I hear the voices of the villagers coming now, yelling and screaming, "Burn the Witch. It was her husband who brought this upon us."

Aongus' voice rises above the rest. "Let her die too. Why should she be spared?"

Mor leads me past the blacksmith's shop, behind Fergus' cottage, toward the forest. I see their torches at my cottage now. A voice yells, "They're gone," and the villagers continue to chant, "Burn the Witch. Burn the Witch."

I cast through my mind wildly now, seeking a remembrance of a place to hide. My mind comes up empty, just as it did all winter when I feared a night such as this would come. I should have braved the cold and gone to the sea caves where the dragon tribe dwells despite the perilous winter journey.

Just then, Sorcha lets out a loud bawl, and I hear Grainne yell, "She's over there."

Mor and I run around Fergus' cottage and make for the tree line. The throng is following us quickly with the younger men in the lead. The woods are just up ahead—if only we could lose them in the deep of the trees. If only Sorcha would stop crying.

We reach heavy brush, and I hear the thunder of feet behind me. Just at the edge of the woods, my foot catches on a tree root and I tumble to the ground. As I land on the hard dirt, I twist to protect Sorcha from being crushed by my weight, and pain shoots up my leg. Fear strikes my heart as I realize I've a choice to make.

"Mor," I yell.

Mor glances over her shoulder and sees me on the ground. I try to stand, but my knee gives way. I see the torches through the dark coming swiftly closer.

"Mor, take Sorcha. It is too late. Run. Keep her safe."

Mor stands there, petrified. She looks at me, she looks at the woods in front of her, and she looks at the torches that are almost upon us. I thrust Sorcha out while warm, wet tears stream down my cheeks and fall unheeded onto the snow. "Take the bairn! It's me they want."

Mor grabs Sorcha and my arms, bereft of their lovely burden, fall uselessly at my sides. I stare hungrily after Sorcha for one last moment, and just as Mor and Sorcha disappear in the dark of the woods, the torches are upon me. First the young men arrive, their faces ugly with rage. I know each of them, grew up with them, broke bread with them, bartered with them, sang with them, but it matters not. It's fear that drives them this night, and no proclamations of innocence or fond memories will help me now.

Niall grabs my arms and drags me into the throng. I try to gain footing, but my right leg will bear no weight. Tadgh holds my other arm, and together they pull me to the center of town. The mob crowds around, cursing me, throwing sticks at me as I'm roughly tied to a large ash tree. The faces of my friends and neighbors swirl around me in angry confusion with rays of moonlight shining on a gaunt cheek here and a slashing brow there. The bindings are pulled tight, cutting into my wrists and ankles as I struggle, but I know it's useless. It's been useless since Torloch made his pact with the devil's handmaiden, Lilith. It's been useless since Torloch took my wee baby boy and returned home with his blood on his hands. It's been useless since Torloch became a bloodsucking monster and spread his disease through the village.

I look out at the faces of the crowd, and I see anger and fear. I see despair. It's a mercy they've let me live this long. I curse myself again for not leaving earlier despite the biting cold of winter. I hear one voice among the bloodthirsty yell, "Give her a Witch's Trial."

Another voice responds, "We'll give her a trial of fire. If she's innocent, let her be saved."

Bundles of dry oak twigs and sticks are piled at my feet. Oak, the tree of strength. I wonder if the oak will give me strength in my last moments of life. I think of Sorcha, the twin of my poor baby boy. I hope only that Mor got her away safely and at least one of our family will be spared.

Grainne walks right up to me and spits in my face. "You filthy Witch," she snarls. "Your monster husband and his kind killed my son. Shredded his neck." Tears run down her dirt-smudged face. "We are going to watch you burn for what you've done."

Una, who lost her husband to Torloch, grabs a torch and sets the wood at my feet on fire. The firelight reflects off her savage face, and I see months of grief and seething anger in the depths of her wild eyes. There is no mercy here.

I feel the heat rising, and it burns. I look at their faces, and even through my fear, I feel their sorrow and rage. I feel it in me as well. That has always been my curse: to feel others as myself. Their rage now feeds mine. The flames lick my ankles, and smoke fills my eyes.

I look up at the night sky and my fury overflows. Months of rage at Torloch, who took the life of our son to try to save himself. But most of all I rage at Lilith, who made him an empty promise and turned him into a monster for the price of our child. Tears stream down my face as I recall my own black pit of grief at losing my lovely little boy. I feel the grief and pain of everyone on this dark night.

I smell the smoke from the ash tree I am tied to mingling with the oak kindling about my body. My childhood learnings flit through my mind even in my last hour. While oak gives strength, ash is the bridge between Earth and other worlds. Good. Let it make a bridge to the Plane of Fire for me so that I might reach Lilith and pay her back in kind.

I shout to the blackness of the sky above. I call to the dark with all the rage of my soul. "Lilith, I call on you to hear me. By my blood, you will be destroyed. A light will come. A light that shines through your evil. A light that calls you to answer for your deeds. A light that binds you as I am bound and burns you as I burn. A light that rips you asunder and destroys your darkness."

The pain is so great. The flames sear my legs. I can't help but scream and convulse, though I know there is no escape. I writhe, trying to get away from the fire, but it just grows and grows as my calves blister and melt. A part of my mind wishes the fire were higher so this pain would end more quickly. The only escape now is death, and it fast approaches. The smoke is so heavy I cough as I scream. The fire has reached my waist now, and it envelops me in its excruciating embrace. I see the horrific faces of the mob, distorted and cast in red from the fire that consumes me.

I scream with all the strength I have, willing my voice to carry through the between spaces. "Lilith, hear me. I call to you. By my blood, you will pay for what you have done." I cough and hack, unable to get a breath of air. I thrash my head as the tongues of fire lick ever higher, melting my flesh, binding me to the holy ash tree as though we are one. The pain is so great now that I know nothing but the feel of it engulfing me. It seems to be all that was before me and all that will ever come after. I'm being eaten alive by the ravenous fire. The agony and the rage are the whole of who I am now.

I think one last thought, unable to even catch enough breath to scream it, unable even to work my mouth to speak it as the flames lick my chin. My dying thought sears into my soul and lifts with me to the Plane of Light. "Lilith, by my blood you will be destroyed!"

CHAPTER 01

DOUBLE DEPRAVITY

BLUEBELL KILDARE

MAY 26, 2022, RED AGES

he boy is stark naked, and dried blood streaks extend from the crushed area of his forehead down to the hollows of his eyes where they pool like small, bloody twin lakes. The lines of his ribs stick out so much I could climb them like a ladder. A stark white shaft of bone sticks out from his leg, gleaming against the bloody rupture on his thigh. A pattern of crimson, crossed lines decorates his crushed left hip. His skin is dirty and he stinks like crazy, but not from death. Not yet. More like a latrine.

Under this layer of grime is a layer of bruising, both fresh and old. His feet and toes are black. How he was able to stand on them, I can't imagine, as it looks and smells as though they are rotting. Calluses surround his ankles and wrists. He must have been tied up. Another pool of blood spills from under his head, spreading wide on the asphalt road. He looks sixteen to eighteen in age with the slightest bits of young facial hair growing about his chin. His body sprawls out on the street with his limbs twisted at awkward angles around him.

I'm going to catch the person who did this. I want to tear his heart out with my bare hands and squeeze it into a bloody pulp.

My fantasy of mushy heart muscle squeezing through my fingers as blood drips to the ground is unsatisfactorily interrupted. Dr. Nathan Perlman leans over the boy's hand with a pair of tweezers and carefully plucks out a piece of dark red thread snagged on a fingernail. It gets tucked away safely in a clear plastic evidence bag for future analysis. Realizing my hands are still fisted from my little fantasy, I release them, trying not to look like the vengeful murderer I momentarily wish I were.

Nathan looks up at me and says, "I'm ready to move the body. Can you step back?"

"Sure." I remove myself from the body, giving room for the

Medical Examiner and his assistant to hoist it onto the gurney.

While the men are in mid-lift, I take the opportunity to examine the boy's underside. With one hand squashing my hat to my head, I lean over until my hair drags on the asphalt. "Great Plane of Fire!"

Nathan's assistant stumbles at my exclamation and drops the boy's leg.

Nathan's fury overflows. "Holy shit, Patrick! Hasn't this boy been through enough?"

Four hands jostle the body until they manage to get it on the gurney.

Nathan's foul mood and abuse of Patrick is unusual. His typically jovial face is soured, and his smile lines twist in the wrong direction. My chest tightens at the pained look on Patrick's face. My heart goes out to both of them, really. I can feel the anger and pain rolling off Nathan. Patrick feels empathy for the boy and anxiety at having made a mistake on the job. I push their pains aside to focus on the matter at hand. Dealing with my own emotions is enough. Luckily I can't feel everyone's emotions all the time, just the stronger ones—unless I open up my sixth sense, that is. Then I feel it all.

When the body is safely enshrouded in clean white linen, I turn to Nathan. "Did you see the lacerations on his back?"

Nathan grimaces. "I hate to see shit like this."

I agree, and my heart squeezing fantasy transforms into daydreams of watching the perpetrator's flesh slowly disintegrate in a vat of acid. Propping my hands on jean-clad hips, I observe Nathan and Patrick load the destroyed body into the hearse.

Senior Detective Tony Gambino stands on the sidewalk next to the street where the body was found, spilling over with anger and determination. I can feel so many emotions at a murder scene where angst runs high. However, the job at hand requires I center on the victim.

"Gambino, can you give me a minute? I have questions, but I need some time here first." Why can't someone hanging around just feel guilty? My job would be so much easier.

Gambino nods his assent, and I admire how despite his abundant passion he looks the epitome of calm concentration.

I circle the taped off crime scene, stopping here and there, closing my eyes, feeling with my sixth sense for lingering signs of magic or strong emotion. A biting breeze blows by, sending a chill up my spine. The air, independent of the breeze, is awash with feelings. Coming directly from where the body had lain, a strong, sharp pang of pain mixed with duller threads of anguish hits me. My pulse escalates and my heart stammers as the agony and torment submerge me. I seek solace in slow, deep breaths, reminding myself this pain belongs to another.

Another emotion tickles my consciousness a few steps from the body. It's a small sliver of sensation, which indicates that it only lasted a brief moment of time, but it's intense. Confusion? No—it's surprise. I walk into the cloud of surprise only to be hit by another impression. My feet are positioned exactly where the shards of glass were scattered. The fine hairs on the back of my neck rise as I'm pummeled by a blast of shock and horror in one small space. This emotion is incongruent with the first because it comes with a different signature, a different resonance left in the air. There were definitely two parties here.

My feet carry me down the street a few steps where the signature shifts back to the first. I do not own these sentiments, but I certainly enjoy them. I sense liberation and triumph. Not the usual feelings one would expect to be haunting the body of a severely tortured young man. I discern something else warring with the feelings. It's a deep, primordial fear, the feeling of being prey. This boy was hunted or chased, or perhaps he was hiding from something terrible.

I stand still and further ratchet down my normal awareness, turning it almost completely off so I see more fully with my sixth sense, searching for any hint of magic. Emotions wash over me freely. Reaching past them, I look for something deeper and more elemental.

Something is coming from where the boy's body had lain. It's nothing more than a light tingling in the air, low to the ground, but I can feel its significance. Moving closer to stand outside the body outline, I crouch and fan my hands through the air close to the ground. A slight buzz zips through my hands, telling me the boy had a magical gift. The magic is clear, but its purpose vague. It's something basic yet powerful, and the reverberations don't speak to a specific gift. I sift my fingers through the prickly air. I can't feel that any magic was used, but rather just that magic had been there in the boy. Damn it! It's too elusive, and I don't have much to go on.

I straighten and open myself up to the world again. Gambino stands well outside the perimeter of my work area wearing a quiet, thoughtful expression. His fellow officer's face is full of wonder. Gifted sensitive work must be new to him. Well, at least it's curiosity and not fear that radiates from his expression. I shake off the lingering emotions and collect myself as I move toward them.

Most detectives work to blend in with everyday pedestrians, but Gambino is most at home dressed in a suit and tie with gleaming dress shoes. With his suave Italian looks, he wears it well. However, it only takes drink or anger to bring out the Irish side of his heritage, causing him to turn a signature shade of cherry red. Right now bright red spots highlight his cheeks, announcing his controlled anger to those who know him well. I know him well enough, but his freckled and fresh-faced companion is new to me.

As I approach, Gambino gestures to the crime scene clean-up van. Two men unload industrial-sized power washers and vacuum equipment, obviously preparing for an inefficient bout of manual labor.

"You know, Gambino, any one of a number of magic potions, powders, or spells would do the job more effectively," I say.

Gambino grunts. "Humph. You know the precinct isn't ready to use magic craft like that. You can't change the world in a day, but I'm working on them."

A familiar exasperation washes over me. It's the twenty-first century of the Red Ages, and the Gifted have helped keep the Norms safe from Dark Vampires since year one, but still they refuse to get over their fear and hatred of us. It's an old, festering wound I try to ignore. I turn my mind to the situation at hand.

"Okay, I've gotten what I can. What do you have?"

Gambino inclines his head toward his companion. "Officer Warren was exiting the Cock and Bull Tap with some guys from the force when they heard tires squeal. They saw the body when they turned the corner." Gambino indicates the corner where the Cock and Bull Tap makes its home.

I address Officer Warren. "Did you see anyone or a car?"

Officer Warren stands at attention, eager to divulge any detail that might be required. "No, Ma'am. We thought someone was just driving like an idiot when we heard the tires squeal. We didn't hear anything else. We didn't see the body right away when we turned the corner, because of those shrubs there." His sweeping hand takes in three medium-sized bottlebrush buckeye shrubs that grow a few feet from where the body had lain, positioned between the sidewalk and the street. The dense foliage could easily have hidden a body from view.

"It couldn't have taken more than a minute and a half for us to pass the shrubs and see him lying there. He was already dead, Ma'am. I ran to him right away and checked. No heartbeat, no breathing. The car was long gone."

"Did anyone move the body?"

Officer Warner's mouth tightens at the perceived slight to his professionalism. "No, Ma'am!"

I nix my next question, switching it to accommodate his pride. "Do you remember anything else?"

We seem to be on smoother ground with his next reply. "No, Ma'am. Besides that, it was quiet. No cars or pedestrians around. This is the end of the Warehouse District, and there isn't much between here and the river except the cemetery. Most first shift workers get off at three o'clock, and either head over to the Tap for a drink or head straight home. It was approximately 3:47 when we left the tap, and we found the boy at approximately 3:49."

My lips twitch in a smile. Officer Warren knew exactly what time it was. My guess is he's never anything even close to approximate. "Thanks, Officer Warren. You've been very helpful."

As he leaves, I see the forensic guys take down the tape and start closing up shop. I throw Gambino a look. "Did your guys find anything?"

Gambino's eyes shift over to the team before shrugging his reply. "Some paint chips, some glass. Nothing much. We may have enough to identify the car. The boy was pretty young, I doubt even eighteen. I hope he's on our missing persons list so we can identify him easily."

I hope so too. "I'll stop by tomorrow after I visit the Medical Examiner to check out his findings."

Just then, my chimerator tightens, so I flip open the lid and see Jack's countenance reflected in the dark, glossy surface of the black pearl. "It's my boss," I tell Gambino.

Gambino's eyes flick down to my ring, but unlike most Norms, he doesn't flinch at my use of it. A chimerator is an enchanted ring that projects the image and voice of a person contacting you. It also generally gives Norms the heebie-jeebies.

A smile ghosts over Gambino's lips. "Well, I'm heading out. We'll talk tomorrow."

As I watch Gambino walk to his car, I say "Hola" into my chimerator, trying to sound casual. My boss, Jack Tanner, is quite possibly the sexiest man alive. He exudes danger in a quiet, stealthy sort of way. I often think I should be frightened of him—quite possibly because he's a very old and incredibly strong Vampire. But I can't seem to muster any fear, even when he's in an obvious rage. That only makes me question my sanity. It's a constant struggle to feel casual, so I usually settle for sounding casual.

"Hi, Blue. So what's happening?" Jack asks.

Jack is not one for small talk, so I give him a quick rundown. "Well, an older teen boy, approximately sixteen to eighteen years old, was apparently hit by a car. Some off-duty officers were just leaving a tavern and heard tires squeal before they came upon the scene. The car was gone and the boy was dead when they reached the body two minutes later. Forensics picked up paint chips and glass at the scene, and the deceased has a large impact injury on his hip. The scene is located behind the Cock and Bull Tap at the intersection of the alley behind it and River Road. No other evidence was found, and no one else appeared on the street at the time of the incident. Unfortunately, I didn't sense any magic used at the site in the perpetration of the crime."

Jack asks, "So a standard hit and run?" He pauses a moment. "Wait, Blue, how did you see an impact injury on his hip?"

I scuff my boots on the sidewalk. "I wondered if you'd catch that. This is no standard hit and run. Before this boy was killed, it appears he was stripped, starved, beaten, tied up, and left to stand in his own excrement."

"Jesus Christ," Jack mutters.

"What's worse is that he felt free. I got the distinct impression of a feeling of triumph before he died. He thought he'd won. And then he got hit by the damn car and his brain was bashed in."

"For Christ's sake," Jack says. There seems to be an exceptional level of swearing with this case thus far.

"Although this looks like a standard hit and run and no magic was used at the death scene, the boy had a magical gift of some sort, and he was tortured, so I want this case. We're not going to let the boys in blue keep it for themselves." I say this last part with a level of confidence I don't feel.

"Who's working it from the precinct side?"

"Senior Detective Tony Gambino."

"It will be fine then," Jack assures me. "Gambino doesn't mind working with SIB. I'll file the paperwork."

"Thanks." I breathe a big sigh of relief, realizing how afraid I had been of losing the case on a technicality. The Supernatural Homicide Investigation Unit has limited jurisdiction, only working cases where death is caused by a Supernatural or the motive relates to the Supernatural. Supernatural hate crimes also fall into our ballpark. Unfortunately, there are far too many of those happening lately. A standard hit and run of a magically Gifted would not get us involved. It's regular work the police could do. But cases including torture of Gifted individuals have a statistically high chance of relating to the magical gift.

Jack voices a warning that brooks no argument: "Keep me updated on this one. I want daily reports. Whoever you're dealing with is a real gentleman." He practically spits that last bit of sarcasm out, and then his face fades from the surface of my chimerator.

I snap the lid closed and hook my thumb into my jean's pocket while I take another look around. All the police are gone. The sun is lower on the horizon causing me to shield my eyes to look west. Across the street sits a beige, corrugated steel warehouse with two tall loading docks and a discreet office door. Next to it sits a plain gray stucco warehouse with three steel loading docks and bright blue awnings over the office door and windows. I look northward, and more of the same nondescript warehouses line the street. Southward lies a stretch of unused land, and past that the street ends at Red Wood Cemetery and Half Moon River.

I look down at the faint stain of blood remaining on the asphalt. The subtle remnants invite me to reexamine the area with my sixth sense. With the crime scene tape gone, I decide it's best to work from the sidewalk; otherwise, I might end up joining the poor boy on one of Nathan's tables. It's never a bright idea to stand on the street while disengaging your five senses. My sixth sense is always active, but I only catch subtle impressions of strong emotions or magic until I shut off my other senses. I can also sense souls, but this boy's soul has already passed on.

I close my eyes, pulling my awareness in and tucking it neatly away.

I shift to my sixth sense, letting it grow and take the lead.

When it's fully engaged I open my eyes and scan the area for any magic or emotions that linger. My eyesight is dimmed, and I see the world in a different way. What normally appears in vivid color dulls to muddy shades of gray. And what I normally miss stands out in stark contrast. The feelings I track seem almost like visible scents that appear as elements lingering in the air without distinct form. Magic feels like vibrations similar to ripples through a pond.

My interpretation of souls usually comes in the form of colors and more solid characteristics defining the essence of their beings. Deeper than personality, it's more an understanding of someone's fundamental nature, which is greater than who they are in this lifetime.

I scan the street where the body had lain, looking for something previously unseen. Proceeding at an excruciatingly slow pace, I wrap my awareness around every inch of space in the vicinity. After a few minutes, I notice a faint trill of what seems like static electricity tickling the air around the bushes behind me. Like an eagle targeting prey, I center on the depths of the greenery. A deep, thrumming magic comes from the middle of the closest bush, something extremely subtle and very old. I try to focus in, but whatever it is . . . it's well hidden.

My full awareness springs to life again when I reengage my regular senses. Peering curiously at the bush, I wonder what secret it holds. I kneel and part the branches to view the shady center. When nothing is immediately obvious, I give the branches a good shake.

A glint of early evening light reflects off a metal object deep within the bush. With a fresh pair of gloves from my pack and an evidence bag at the ready, I push my arms into the bush up to my elbows and slowly feel around until my fingers run into something flat, hard, and circular. When I pull my hand out, a large, gold amulet is clenched between my slick latex-gloved fingers.

After carefully dropping the amulet in the bag and sealing it closed, I examine it through the clear plastic. Its face is smooth and decorated with a beveled jade triangle. The triangle has an eye-shaped cutout in the center with a circular hole that goes all the way through the pendant. A pattern of irregular ridges and grooves radiates out from the hole like rays of sunshine. Each ridge has a series of tiny, white beads dotting its edge at irregular intervals. A plain golden chain is threaded through the pendant, and it holds the greatest treasure of all: a small, dark red string caught up in the clasp—a fiber exactly the same color red as the fiber snagged on the boy's nail. The boy was naked, so where did this thread come from—or rather whom did this thread come from?

I put the evidence bag in my pack, heft it to my shoulder over my black leather vest, and hurry toward the Cock and Bull Tap.

CHAPTER 02

Slipped at the Cock and Bull Tap

Bluebell Kildare

May 26, 2022, Red Ages

The Cock and Bull Tap, otherwise known as The Cock and Bull Inn and Guest House by those with very long memories, sits on what used to be the main path out of Crimson Hollow. Of old, those passing over the Smoky Mountains by carriage would stay in the inn the night before their trip or seek its comforting embrace on their return. That tired path has long been paved over, and Cock and Bull's days of being an inn all but forgotten by most Crimson Hollow residents. The distinguished stone building sits behind a deep corner yard with its back against the alley. Between two tall posts hangs a huge, gleaming white sign painted with a red rooster and a blue bull in vivid, sweeping brushstrokes to welcome patrons both new and familiar. I wrap my hand around one of the ornate iron handles and heave the door open.

Firefly lanterns cast a soft glow on the tavern's interior. The tiny flakes of quartz set alight by magic, swirl rapidly inside the lanterns, glowing and twinkling. The gentle light reflects off the oiled and waxed oak furniture. Scanning the crowd, I see mostly hard-working men dressed in uniforms or jeans and flannels. Most are gathered in small groups at the long trestle tables, but a few lonely souls sit in isolation on stools facing the bar.

Dozens of pairs of eyes pierce my back as I move my long-limbed body toward the bar. I feel a few waves of lust flowing toward me from the bar patrons like a crimson breeze, but even more waves are filled with the dark and heavy emotions of disgust and hate and the sharpness of fear. Someone murmurs "Aberrant" under his breath, referring to my being Gifted. My back stiffens at the insult.

You can only tell when a person is Gifted if their mark shows. My mark is twofold. I have unnaturally blue eyes that could conceivably pass for simply extra vivid, but the streak of blue running through my hair is unmistakable. I don't have time to defend my pride today, so I just keep my chin up and proceed with strong strides.

When I arrive at the empty side of the bar, I make sure my Glock is visible to any onlookers by pushing my vest back as I retrieve my ID. A low murmur rolls through the crowd, telling me the gun is noticed. Good.

The bartender approaches, and I present my ID, which reads "Supernatural Investigation Bureau (SIB), Homicide Unit, Inspector Bluebell Kildare." He extends his large hand and introduces himself. "Hello, Inspector Kildare. I'm Steve Jamison. It's awful, what happened to that boy. Some of the guys told me what they saw on their way in. I'm happy to help if I can."

Well, he's congenial enough, and fortunately he doesn't seem to be a breedist. Steve stands medium height with a stocky physique and kind face. He's built well enough to keep people in line and seems empathetic enough to listen to their sorrows. I take all this in while his warm hand envelops mine in a firm handshake.

"Thanks, Steve. I'd like to ask a few questions. It shouldn't take long."

Steve tosses his bar rag into a pail behind the counter then turns his earnest face and ready ears to me. Taking his cue, I start drilling into my list of questions. "The incident occurred at 3:47 p.m. Do you recall anyone leaving the bar shortly before then?"

Steve considers a minute and then shakes his head. "Not that I remember. The first shift ends at three o'clock. The crowd is coming in around then, and the place fills up pretty fast. Some police officers with early shifts show up around two o'clock and have a drink or two before heading home. The officers who found him were the first to leave today. We have a few lushes who come in with the early lunch crowd, but they make themselves scarce before the officers start arriving."

My eyes skim over the room, searching for a point of reference. I spy the perfect thing on a shelf behind the bar. Pointing at a hand-carved and painted rooster, I ask, "Did you see anyone here today wearing an article of clothing matching that color red?"

Steve's gaze finds the rooster with a surprised look. "Yeah, I sure did. There was an older guy wearing a red cloak. He left out the side door just before you came in."

My head snaps back to Steve as his casual words register. Blast it! A potential murder suspect was inside the bar while we were processing the body outside.

I snatch up my ID and run out the side door with my pack jostling on my back. One sweeping look across the parking lot tells me none of the cars are occupied. I hope the man is still nearby. Flipping open my phone, I dial Gambino. He answers on the first ring.

Hoping he is still close by, I say, "Gambino, a man wearing a cloak that matched the thread found in the boy's fingernail was seen leaving the Cock and Bull Tap a few minutes ago. I'm searching the vicinity right now."

Gambino doesn't miss a beat. "On my way."

Holstering my phone and unholstering my Glock in one smooth motion, I step to the street. It looks still with nothing to indicate which direction I should take. I follow my gut and run to the right, set on checking the entire block. At the first intersection, I scan in all directions but see nothing. I round the corner and run down toward the end of the block with my boots clicking loudly on the sidewalk with each step. Cripes! I need rubber sole boots if I'm ever going to sneak up on someone.

When I'm almost to the second corner, I catch a flash of red disappearing behind a warehouse to my right. I cut across the lawn and run between two warehouses toward the center of the block. Just before passing beyond the shelter of the warehouses, I stop. Peering behind them, I assess my options. The building on my right has stacks of empty pallets in the shipping yard. The building on my left has an empty yard with only one large, stationary eighteen wheeler. Regardless of which side he's on, I will be wide open and an easy target while trying to reach either the truck or the pallets. I pull out my sixth sense, looking for a trace of a soul to guide me, but feel nothing. Shoot! Where's a little help when a girl needs it?

With my gun pointed ahead, I rush around the corner to the right. I place my back to the warehouse, feeling the rough bricks scrape my back through my thin shirt and vest. My thrashing heart is ready to burst in my chest. I strain my eyes, looking for the smallest movement. My sixth sense is still on high alert, then I feel a slight tug from the left. Turning, I notice a little spot of red under the truck. As soon as I swing my gun toward it, a loud noise blasts my eardrums. *Boom! Boom!* Chips of brick fly around me as two bullets narrowly miss my head.

I aim my gun at the red spot and shoot as I rush to the first stack of pallets opposite the truck. When I'm halfway there, I hear return fire. *Boom! Boom! Boom!* Three shots echo off the buildings. I dive through the air as the bullets fly around me. Curling into a ball, I land, rolling head over foot, but my backpack brings me to an ungainly stop. Just barely behind the pallets, I jump up sideways to take cover. Holy smokes, that was close!

Ignoring my scratches and bruises, I peek around the right side of the pallet stack. I want to get this guy so bad I can taste it. From this angle, I glimpse more of the deep red cloak behind the rear tires of the truck. I crouch, trying to identify the shooter, but all I see is the truck's shadow and the red fabric.

I fire two more shots under the truck. One bullet ricochets off the bumper, and the other tears a hole in one tire close to the spot of red. A sharp hiss fills the air, and the truck sinks slightly.

I pull several pallets off the top of the pile I'm hiding behind and position them on their sides in front of me to afford better protection. I aim my gun under the truck and shout, "Supernatural Investigation Bureau. Come out with your hands up."

Three shots whizz toward me, tearing up the pallets with splinters of coarse wood flying in all directions. I crouch down again, ready to aim carefully this time, but as I gaze across the space to the truck, I see Gambino coming from behind the vehicle with two officers following him. I quickly shoot two more tires on the right side of the truck, and the hisses tell me I aimed true. Unfortunately, the semi has eighteen wheels, so three flat tires lack the desired effect.

Gambino has his gun aimed at the red spot. Hoping to distract the perpetrator, I fire some shots wide into the ground to the right of the truck. The man returns one oddly wild shot back at me. It misses the pallet stack entirely. I aim for two more tires toward the rear, thinking that if I can get the back of the truck lowered, the man will be crushed or at least trapped.

Gambino yells, "Come out with your hands up."

I watch the spot of red cloth as Gambino gets closer. Targeting through my gun sight, I aim for another tire, but all of the remaining tires are behind the ones I've already shot. Gambino will have to finish the job. Right now he's even with the front set of tires, but obviously he can't crouch down to reach the man or he might come back up with a face full of bullets. If the man wanted to, he could easily shoot Gambino's foot.

After waiting a few tense seconds for the shooter to willingly surrender, Gambino gestures his men forward and they close in. Ignoring the wheels now, I fire two more careful shots, and I'm rewarded by the man's scream of surprise and agony. Gambino takes the opportunity to dive under the truck, and at the same time I see the spot of red disappear.

I hear Gambino yell, "What in the Plane of Fire? He's gone."

His companions surround the truck from both directions. One checks inside and another checks underneath, but both apparently find the area empty. Gambino climbs up the truck between the cab and trailer to inspect the top. I don't know how he thinks the man could have gotten up there. As he looks in the cab, another futile move, I begin to walk toward the scene, my gun still at the ready. I search the top of the warehouse and quickly sweep the entire area with my sixth sense, but I find nothing. Gambino gets out of the cab and holsters his gun.

"What happened?" I ask when I reach Gambino.

Gambino blows out a deep breath and looks at the truck. Then he shakes his head. "I know you hit him. He screamed, and I dove under the truck, but there was nothing there. It was just empty, not even a drop of blood. It's like he was a ghost." Gambino says this last bit while raising an eyebrow.

I sigh. Sometimes Norms just can't handle things they can't rationalize. "Maybe it was like a ghost," I respond, "but ghosts can't actually fire bullets, and I assure you those bullets were real."

"Did you get a look at him?"

I frown. "Unfortunately not. All I saw was a glimpse of red cloak trailing behind him as he ran between the warehouses. He must have dived under the truck, but I guessed he was behind the pallets, so I went that way." After I give Gambino the rest of the details, he and his men continue to search the neighborhood in case the man reappears. I hoof it back to the Cock and Bull Tap to finish my conversation with my friend Steve.

Still cursing to myself for being a minute too late, I reenter the bar.

Steve's frowning at my obvious disappointment. "We heard gunfire, but it doesn't look like you got him. Did anyone get hit?"

I shake my head. "The suspect probably got one superficial wound, but he got away from us. So have you seen him here before?"

Steve absently wipes down the bar as he answers, "Nope. I've never seen him before. We don't usually get his kind here. This is a working man's bar, and he was dressed in fancy trousers and a white dress shirt with a tie. He didn't even order a drink. I saw him snap open his phone and head into the bathroom. I assumed he was looking for a quiet place to make a call. He left out the side door, and you walked in the front door right after." Steve pauses to frown for a moment before adding, "I don't think he saw you coming. I think it was just poor timing."

I put my palms on the bar. "What did he look like? Did he have any distinguishing features or marks?"

Steve puts his thumb under his chin and thinks for a minute. "He was on the tall side, about six foot. He had a full beard and mustache, neatly trimmed. His face was narrow with a long, prominent nose."

"What color were his eyes and hair?"

Steve shifts his weight and frowns. "I can't say about his hair. He wore the hood up on his cloak so I'm not sure I saw his hair. But his beard was very dark brown, maybe black, with some gray in it. His eyebrows were the same, real heavy, you know. His eyes were dark brown or black. I'm guessing he was fortyish or early fifties." Steve glances at the firefly lanterns. "The lights are pretty low in here."

I agree that the ambiance is an issue and hand Steve my card. "If you remember anything else, please give me a call."

Steve says sincerely, "I sure will. Good luck with this."

I turn and leave, feeling the lust, fear, and hatred of dozens of strangers follow me out the door.

CHAPTER 03

The Wild Garden Grows

BLUEBELL KILDARE

MAY 26, 2022, RED AGES

I can't believe the perp got away twice. I adjust the heat in the car to ward off the evening chill, and my stomach grumbles. It's been a long day, and I'm too exhausted to cook. The Paco's Loco Tacos sign on my right lures me in. Not for the first time, I wonder if the tacos are crazy, if Paco is crazy, or if we are crazy for buying them. Well, I personally think a touch of crazy is one of the spices of life.

My car seems to have a life of its own when I pull up to Maud's house. I hadn't consciously decided to come here, but today just royally sucked, and Maud is my touchstone. The neighborhood is pretty with its modest, well-kept homes and old-growth trees lining the street. A covered front porch sweeps across Maud's small yellow Cape Cod, offering cool shade and ample breeze in the warm mountain afternoons. Her backyard is contained by a whitewash picket fence. I say contained because it is a tangled, wild land with flowering shrubs overhanging the fence, and wildflowers, grasses, and weeds peeking between the pickets. Snarled, riotous, and overtaken with native species, her backyard looks about to leap the fence and merge with the rest of the great outdoors.

It used to be a wonderland back there until Maud's husband, William, died two years ago. A glow stone foot path twined around a turtle pond, a bulb garden, and a vegetable patch, all interspersed with beautiful flowering plants and culminating in a wooden bench hanging from an arbor shaded with flowering vines. William built the swing by hand for Maud for their last anniversary. I don't think Maud has tended the back garden once in these last two years. But the front yard is neat as a pin with a bright bed of mixed zinnia lining the walk. I love the zinnia because they match Maud's personality—and her hair.

Maud opens the door, true to form in all her wild colored glory.

Her hair is bright fuchsia today, cut shoulder length and piled in a bouffant style. It lies around her tiny face like a fluffy, pink cotton candy cloud. She's wearing a sage green linen tunic and pant set with three long necklaces in a medley of pink crystal. Maud has large, green eyes framed in smile lines and a wide, vivacious grin. She is petite, thin but wiry and full of energy. Today she has a little blush of pink in her cheeks giving her a healthy glow.

I smile and hug her with one arm while handing her the tacos with the other. Maud is my dearest friend. We are like family to each other, now more than ever since William passed. Maud used to visit the orphanage where I grew up to read to us children. The joy her arrival at the orphanage inspired in me knew no bounds. More memories, unbidden and unwanted, take hold of my mind. Painful memories: cruel taunts, violence, unending loneliness. I force these memories away and consider Maud instead. She has always been a bright spot in my days.

Once when I was little, in my naïveté, I asked Maud if she would be my mom. She said she would love to, but she couldn't on account of William. He believed his job was too dangerous for him to be a father. I didn't really understand it then, and I don't understand it now. It seems a huge waste because Maud so wanted a child and I so wanted a mother, but I guess we sort of have each other anyway. I can't really hate William much because it was his reference letter that helped me get my job just before he passed. I let those bitter feelings slip away. Maud was there every afternoon for me while I was growing up, and now I visit her as much as I can since William is gone. Maud and me, we are quite a pair.

"Blue, come on in." Maud ushers me into the kitchen. "Do you want some iced tea?"

"I'd love some." I swing my pack down onto the floor by the kitchen table. This spot gives the best view of the backyard jungle through the sliding glass doors.

As Maud pours a beverage out of her curvy glass pitcher, she informs me, "It has raspberries today with a touch of lemon."

"Mmm," I murmur when I taste it. "It's delicious." Maud never offers much to eat, thank goodness. Cooking is not in her wheelhouse, but she sure knows her southern beverages.

Maud sets the table and opens up the bag of Paco's Loco Tacos. I could just refer to them as tacos, but the name is too fun. Maud finally settles down at the table across from me and asks, "So, how has your day been?"

Telling her about the shootout will only scare her. I blow out a deep sigh. "I got a new case today, and when I entered a bar to question someone, I was called an Aberrant. Then on my drive back this way, I passed a crowd of people downtown with signs protesting 'Aberrations' and 'bloodsuckers.' What do they expect us to do? Are they trying to rile the masses to burn us as Witches like they did before the Red Ages? Have humans always been this prejudiced against the Gifted?"

Wow, I had no idea I had all that bottled up in me. Maybe I need something stronger than tea.

Maud looks sad. "Maybe you need some liquor in that tea?"

I burst out laughing while in the middle of a sip, and it turns into a graceless coughing episode. Maud slaps my back until my throat clears. "I was just thinking that. But no, I'm fine." Maybe one day I'll tell her that slapping someone's back while they cough actually makes it worse. Really, I'll probably never tell her that.

Maud looks at me with a face dressed in sadness.

"When I was a young girl, it was pretty much as it is now, only not quite so bad. The Dilectus Deo are stirring the pot for a lot of folks. Some Norms have a lot of gall. They use firefly lanterns when they need to see in the dark, and herbal potions and charms, which have long proven superior to medication, but they somehow think they are better than the Gifted. They don't hesitate to accept a Vampire into the army, but goodness knows one will never be promoted up the ranks. It's fear, Blue. Even after the Gifted helped protect us during the worst of the Red Ages and the Daylight Vampires saved our butts, many of us Norms are just plain old afraid of any being who is stronger than we are."

I take another careful sip of tea and ponder this while watching the beads of condensation roll down my glass. Maud is a Norm, but William had been Gifted. They had been a mixed breed couple, so she certainly understands prejudice. The eternal wave of hate never stops.

Finally I say what's really bothering me, choosing my words carefully. "Maud, you would not believe this poor boy's body we found. He was Gifted. I can't give you details, but someone did terrible things to him. I'm hoping I don't find out this was a hate crime."

"Ugh," Maud grunts, throwing her hands in the air. "You are just like William, spending your days mired in the horrors of man." She shakes her finger at me. "Keep in mind that you see only the worst.

There are many good, loving people moving about their lives peacefully who you never run into."

"I know. Those are the people I'm protecting when I find these murderous idiots. I do it with them in mind."

"Yes," Maud says glancing at her patio door, "and speaking of idiots, I need to tell you about my neighbor Harry Pickets."

"Harry? Isn't he the widower who lives right across your backyard?"

"He sure is," Maud confirms as she stands up and stares out her sliding glass doors again. She moves about the kitchen in an agitated manner. The color on her cheeks heightens, making it obvious this is the reason for her healthy glow.

Maud alternates between opening her mouth to talk and pinching it closed, while her eyes shine vibrantly. Finally, the words start spilling out. "Yesterday, out of nowhere, I hear a knock on the door. I had just come home from the salon, you know, and I wasn't expecting visitors."

I interject, "Your hair looks lovely today, by the way."

Maud absently pats her hair as she paces. "Thank you, dear. Anyway, there is this man standing on the porch smiling at me with a wheelbarrow full of gardening tools behind him. I asked him if I could help him. I figured he was a neighbor needing to borrow a tool. He said he worked for Harry. He told me Harry sent him over to see if I wanted work done in my garden." She throws her arms up in exasperation. "Can you believe that? How insulting. As if I couldn't manage my own garden if I'd a mind to."

Maud is nearly rustling up a whirlwind in the kitchen with the rate of her pacing, and I am enthralled by the drama.

"So what did you say?"

Maud stops and covers her mouth as though she's afraid to say. "I was honestly speechless for a moment. Then I told him very sweetly that I appreciated the offer, but I didn't need his help. I asked if he could give something to Harry for me to express my gratitude. I gave him my beautician's card and my coupon for fifty percent off the next haircut."

I puzzle on this for a minute. "But Maud, Harry is bald, isn't he?"

Maud smiles her wide, mischievous smile. "Exactly."

An image rises to my mind of Harry standing at his front door, scratching his bald head with one hand and staring uncertainly at the haircut coupon he holds in the other. "Hairless Harry Pickets," I chuckle.

Maud laughs with me. She laughs so hard she snorts. Then we both laugh until our faces hurt and I'm afraid I might pee my pants.

"Oh Maud," I say. "You are a jewel, and you shine even brighter than your hair."

Maud beams as she fluffs her hair. Then she pats my hand before finally opening one of Paco's Loco Tacos.

CHAPTER 04

HIDDEN TREASURES

BLUEBELL KILDARE

MAY 26, 2022, RED AGES

I slip as quietly as I can through the bell tower door. The stone stairwell would be completely dark if not for the tall, narrow windows decorating each landing. I start the six-floor ascent to my familiar childhood hideout. The absent railing makes the winding stairway treacherous in the dim light. I trail my finger along the stone walls, enjoying the rough bumps and grooves as I move steadily upward. On the last landing, I climb a set of slim, wooden ladder rungs until my head bumps against a solid object. Shoving the hatch upward, I boost myself onto the wooden floor and stand to look around. The bell room has a stone half wall topped with four arches in keystone construction, letting in the cool air and the beautiful night sky. The roof is made of heavy oak timbers reaching up further to steeple heights. An elaborate brass bell works hangs from the timbers with the grand bell hanging in the center and extending down so passersby can see it through the arches.

I set my pack down by the south wall and plop on the floor next to it. The area is in deep shadow, so my fingers work blindly, counting the stones in the wall from the corner. One, two up from the floor and one, two, three to the right. I wedge my fingers around the stone and gently shimmy it out. It's more difficult than I remember now that I've grown and my fingers are larger. I deposit the amulet in an empty crevice behind the stone to the right of the one I removed and replace the block carefully. Even if someone were to remove the loose stone, they would not immediately see the evidence bag.

I stand to heft my pack to my shoulder, then take a moment to enjoy the peace of the evening. The stars are out tonight, though somewhat faded by the light pollution of the city. The city lights are sprinkled all around, concentrating in downtown Crimson Hollow. The lights spread out and up the mountains on all sides and dip down, disappearing between Black Mountain and Thunderhead Mountain in Shroud Valley. I can see the parapet surrounding the tar and pebble roof of the building I live in next door. Lights shine from my friend Alexis' apartment, but my windows are dark. Large, winged gargoyles decorate each corner of the roof as though standing guard against unseen enemies. I take a couple deep breaths of cool evening air, letting the stress of the day flow out, before heading back downstairs.

When I reach the bottom landing, I gingerly open the door leading back into the church. No matter, though, because Father O'Brennen catches me anyway.

"There you are, Bluebell. I thought I heard a mouse in my bell tower."

"You could hear me?"

Father O'Brennen chuckles. "No, I saw you slip through the door on your way up."

"Oh." I smile. "I didn't want to disturb you."

I've known Father O'Brennen since my orphanage days. We used to come here on Sundays for church. I've never been very religious, so I would sneak away from the housemothers before the sermon and spend the hour in the bell tower, pretending it was my very own home.

"You're not disturbing me at all," Father O'Brennen says. "Why don't you join me? I was just getting a snack in the kitchen. You can tell me how your apartment is doing."

The building next door is a defunct school belonging to the church. It's mostly used for storage space now, except for the top floor where the nuns' living quarters used to be. Some renovations have been done to make it suitable for a few modern apartments. When I was of age and ready to move out of the orphanage, Father O'Brennen offered one of the apartments to me rent-free until I found my first job.

Well, I suppose, there is no polite way to get out of a conversation with Father O'Brennen, so I decide to make the most of it. I need some answers anyway. "Do you happen to have any cookies left over from the church ladies?"

Father O'Brennen chuckles again. "That's exactly what I was after myself."

We walk down the hall to the roomy kitchen. It has beige tile counters, dark oak cabinets, and a slate floor. It's lit by electricity as this is holy ground, so no magic works here. Father O'Brennen pulls two glasses out of the cabinet filling them with milk from a pretty glass decanter. Then he loads two plates with fresh gingersnaps, bringing the container of cookies with him. I arrange the plates and milk on the counter island. It feels as though we're sneaking a forbidden midnight snack.

Father O'Brennen stands medium height with deep-set, dark gray eyes. His salt and pepper hair is mostly salt now, and is crowned with a shiny spot, visible when he leans forward. He's quick to laugh but otherwise has a quiet, wise look about him. I do like Father O'Brennen, and he's always been particularly kind to me. I'm just not a fan of God since he has never gone out of his way to make my life easy. So I usually avoid the kind of deep conversation with Father O'Brennen I'm about to embark on. However, I'm twenty-three now, and it's high time I get some answers about my family.

"How's your apartment doing?" Father O'Brennen asks.

"It's fine. It kept me warm all winter and I expect it will keep me warm all summer as well," I say with a grin.

Father O'Brennen leans back and laughs a deep, throaty laugh. "Well, that's what the terrace is for."

I pause for a moment and crunch on a gingersnap, thinking of how best to approach the topic of my family with him. Then I ask, "Father, I think you told me once that you knew both my parents, didn't you?"

"I did, certainly. They were wonderful people."

"You were also the one who brought me to the orphanage."

Father O'Brennen nods in confirmation.

"Well, the housemothers told me my parents were killed by Dark Vampires. Several of the children were orphaned in the same manner, so it wasn't unusual. But none of the other children still had family alive. I know this because the mothers told them. But when I asked about my grandparents, they told me it was a story best left till I was older. Every time I tried, they shut me down. Well, I'm twenty-three now. I've been on my own for five years. For the last two years I've been capturing murderers for a living. I think I'm old enough to know now, and I'm asking you this time."

Father O'Brennen, sober-faced now, heaves a great sigh. "I guess you are old enough."

"Are my grandparents still alive?"

Father O'Brennen nods with a sad look and the strong feeling of empathy flowing from him. "Yes, as far as I know. They used to be parishioners of mine, but they haven't been for quite some time now. The last I heard they were all still living, but that was many years past."

Wincing at this news even though it's what I expected, I look to the side to blink back the tears. It's not that I was alone in the world; it's that I was unwanted. The cold reality seep into me. I ask through the thickening of my throat, "Do you know why they didn't take me in when my parents died?"

Father O'Brennen sighs again. "Your grandparents were very devout people, but . . . they were afraid of the Gifted. When your mother's gift started to show, her parents, due to the nature of her gift, felt it was unholy, and they disowned her. Your father asked his parents to help, and in the course of doing so, he revealed that he himself was Gifted. His parents threw him out as well. I tried to counsel your grandparents that God doesn't hate, and he loves all his children. But they saw the gifts as an unholy thing and an affront to God."

My sadness turns to anger at the cruelty of my grandparents. "So both my parents were made homeless when they were just teenagers?"

He nods before elaborating. "Your parents clung together during this hard time, and a strong love grew between them. I married them myself as soon as they were of age. After your parents died, I approached both sets of your grandparents to ask them if they would take you in. Your grandmother on your mother's side seemed willing to relent. She did grieve for your mother. But your grandfather, her husband, would not. When I visited your father's parents, I knew by the way they talked about your parents, who hadn't even been buried yet, that it would be wrong for me to allow you to stay in that house. I'm afraid you would have come to great harm.

"After that, neither set of your grandparents came to this church anymore. They knew in no uncertain terms I felt their choices were wrong. I'm sorry to say I don't think any of your grandparents ever came to repent over their deeds, except perhaps your maternal grandmother."

I feel a rush of rage at those faceless people for rejecting me and my parents over their antiquated beliefs. Then I think about how my parents must have felt to have known their love and then lost it.

I ask, "What were my parents' gifts?"

Father O'Brennen pours me more milk, obviously needing the time to consider his words. "Well," he says, "your mother was able to see ghosts, the souls of those who have died but have not yet passed on. She could see them when they were passing or if they lingered. She was a very religious woman, your mother. I was worried she would cast the Church aside because of the behavior of her parents, but even as her gift separated her from them, it strengthened her connection with God. She couldn't deny what she saw with her own eyes. She saw souls passing to the Plane of Light and occasionally in the other direction." Father O'Brennen looks down at the floor with that last statement.

This shocks me. "She saw souls going to the Plane of Fire?"

"Yes. She said she could, and I believe her. Now, your father was a Gifted Healer. He could direct his energy to heal the flesh. Whenever there was a patient who was particularly sick and your father thought they might not make it, your mother would go with him. She said it was so she could be sure their soul made it safely to the other side."

The argument breedists always use is that if gifts were from God, magic would be able to exist on holy ground. Since it can't, they believe it must be evil. "So, what do you think of Gifted people, Father? Do you think the gifts are from God or that they're evil?"

Father O'Brennen looks at me kindly and asks, "Has anyone ever told you the story about your birth?"

I shake my head, feeling as though something momentous is about to be revealed.

Father O'Brennen takes a deep breath and looks me directly in the eyes as if to give me strength and says, "Bluebell Kildare, you were stillborn, born with the umbilical cord wrapped around your neck. You were as blue as a bluebell, so I've been told. The midwife pronounced you dead and handed you to your mother. Your mother cried and said she could see your soul in the room.

"Your father rejected your death. He grabbed you and performed infant CPR. He sent healing energy into you through his hands. Your mother called for you, trying to get you to come back. She said that your soul drifted back into your body just a moment before you opened your lungs on your own and wailed."

Father O'Brennen pauses a moment, then says, "You know, even Healers are not supposed to be able to breathe life back into the dead. I don't know if it was your mother calling for you or your father's healing that brought you back. Perhaps it was a combination of both."

I did know that Healers weren't supposed to be able to bring life back to the dead. I'm flabbergasted and can't seem to speak due to the thoughts racing through my head. I was dead and brought back to life. My parents obviously loved me to reject my death so strongly. That thought is a treasure I will always hold dearly. I fold my hands on the counter, drop my forehead to them, and close my eyes. I let that thought settle. My parents really loved me. My parents truly loved me! After a minute of letting that soak in, I lift my head again waiting for the rest of the story.

Father O'Brennen says, "Now, I wasn't in that room, and even if I had been, I wouldn't have seen your soul drifting toward the Plane of Light and then reverse direction. Nor would I have seen healing magic flow through your father's hands into your body, restoring your life. But you were dead, and now you're alive. That I would have seen. When your grandparents heard about this, they assumed it was greater evidence of the evil nature of gifts. But I don't believe a soul would be excused from the Plane of Light without our Father's permission. I believe all gifts are from God, and I must assume he approved of the use of your parents' gifts on that day."

Father O'Brennen pauses for a moment and offers more cookies. I take them, mostly to keep myself busy while my brain processes what he's told me. It's more information than I'd ever heard about my parents, and I treasure every word.

Then Father O'Brennen says, "That's not the only reason why I feel gifts can be used with the blessing of God. What have you been told about the day your parents died?"

I stand up, stretch, and walk to the window. I tell him, and my words seem to echo hollowly in the kitchen as if in accord with the loneliness I feel inside. "I was told that a group of Dark Vampires came upon them in an alley when they were on their way home. I was told they were killed in bloodlust."

"Yes, that's true, but it's not the whole tale."

I lean against the window and bow my head, unable to watch Father O'Brennen tell this story anymore because the emotions I feel are already too intense. "I'd like to hear what you know."

Father O'Brennen asks, "Did you know you were with them that day?"

"No," I murmur. I'm almost beyond surprise at this point. I suppose I might be in shock.

He continues with his tale—my tale, really. "You were barely three years old and wrapped in a carrier on your mother's back. It was very cold that night, so she'd thrown a blanket over your head. Your father had been caring for an elderly woman, and because of her age, your mother accompanied him. So there you all were, walking home late at night through an alley. When the Dark Vampires attacked your parents, they pushed your parents against some buildings. Your mother landed in a corner where two buildings joined, so you were protected from the impact. Your parents were dead in seconds, but the corner you were wedged in kept you out of sight for a moment. A Daylight Vampire was hunting Dark Vampires that night and came upon the alley just as the Dark Vampires were feeding on your parents. You started crying, and one of the Dark Vampires stopped feeding, pulled your mother away from the corner, and uncovered you.

"The Daylight Vampire approached and was about to intercede when the entire alley filled with a bright light. The Dark Vampires shrunk from the light, and their skin sizzled and burned black as though touched by the sun. They tried to run, but the one who had killed your mother was too close to the light and instantly turned to ash. The Daylight Vampire picked you up and brought you to me."

Father O'Brennen pauses for a moment and then drops the real bomb. "He told me the bright light that drove the Dark Vampires off and killed one of them was emanating from inside of you."

I am astounded. I peer at him sharply to assess his truthfulness before remembering who he is. The tale is so outrageous I can hardly believe it.

He forges on. "The light coming from you burnt the Dark Vampires like they burn when they touch holy ground or when they're exposed to the sun. When Daylight Vampires give in to bloodlust and become Dark Vampires, Lilith calls their soul to her, and their bodies are simply unholy shells of who they were. Lilith operates them like puppets filled with the endless need for blood and death. Since all good is gone from them and only evil remains, they cannot stand the touch of that which is pure, good, and holy. Your gift forced them back and even killed one of them. So I believe your gift must be from God."

"You think my aura holds my gift? And that's what hurt and killed the Dark Vampires?"

"Yes, but I don't believe an aura is some miscellaneous light wavering on the outside of your skin, Bluebell. I believe an aura is the part of your soul that extends beyond the boundaries of your skin. I believe the light from your soul hurt and killed them."

I stand now and pace the kitchen in front of the window. So many thoughts swirl in my mind. "But what of this Daylight Vampire who saved me? He wasn't burned. So then it follows that Daylight Vampires aren't evil, right?"

Father O'Brennen answers as though he has pondered this very question for untold hours. "My heart tells me no. I believe Lilith has her mark on Daylight Vampires to entice them to do evil and give in to their bloodlust. I don't think the Father allows her to truly claim them until they actually do evil. Like all creatures that still have souls, they have the will to choose. It's more difficult for them, and it takes more willpower, certainly. They can drink blood from people in a humane way by keeping their bloodlust under control and getting consent. I don't believe it's a sin when the blood is freely given. After all, they require sustenance as you and I do. It's when they give in to their bloodlust by killing during the process that they do evil. Then they choose their path, just like you could choose a path of evil."

I respond heatedly, "Well, it's clearly unfair that they can't die without Lilith claiming them. They have no chance to go to the Plane of Light. Their only choices are to live here endlessly, denying their bloodlust, or give in and go to the Plane of Fire. They have to be good for so much longer than we do with so much greater temptation."

Father O'Brennen affirms my feelings. "I know," he says. "I don't have all the answers, Bluebell. I wish I did. Just remember that as long as Daylight Vampires are able to walk in the sun, they're defying Lilith's enticement, so in my opinion, all Daylight Vampires are to be respected in that regard."

Just when I feel good and angry at Father O'Brennen for representing a God who gives inequitable graces, he goes and says something that makes me see him as human, fallible and wise all at the same time. I feel shame for my outburst now, and think about what he said while I help him clean up our plates.

As I bid him goodnight, I swallow back the heavy emotion I feel thickening my voice and glistening in my eyes. "Thank you, Father

O'Brennen. Tonight you gave me more knowledge about my parents and my own history than I've ever had before." He smiles at me and grips my forearms in a warm embrace. I turn and walk the short way home.

CHAPTER 05

OF SMOKE AND SHADOW

BLUEBELL KILDARE

MAY 27, 2022, RED AGES

I draw back the lilac shower curtain surrounding my claw foot tub and step onto yesterday's towel. Nuns aren't exactly big on vanity, so I'm grateful they installed a mirror when renovating the space. I use the corner of the towel I'm wearing to wipe the fog off the gold baroque mirror to brush my teeth. My teeth are smallish and straight, and I like to keep them a nice, bright white. My face is framed with dark brown hair that looks black when damp except for the one-inch wide blue lock that hangs from my forehead. It's a pale blue, almost like a tinted white. When I was young, I tried to dye it dark brown like the rest of my hair, but the color wouldn't take. It remained stubbornly blue. Sigh. At least it matches my eyes.

My eyes are vivid blue, the color of bluebells, or so I've been told. I always thought that's why I was named Bluebell, not because I turned blue when I died at birth.

As I assess my reflection, the bathroom light flashes on and off and on again. I hear a roll of thunder and wonder if the apartment will lose power today. A good storm is brewing. I shake off my ruefulness and decide to stick with the original story of my name. I glance at the birthmark on my shoulder in the mirror and release a deep sigh as I turn away. On my way to the bedroom, I peek out at the terrace and see an ominously dark sky dropping sheets of rain. It's going to be a dreary day.

I enter my bedroom to dress. Calling it a "room" is perhaps giving it grander airs than it deserves. It's more of a three-walled nook or an alcove for the bed. Sheer curtains do their best to separate it from the living room. It does have a nice, long closet running the length of one wall, which I barely fill with my meager wardrobe. My apartment is small, but it's decorated nicely in bright jewel tones, and it's my first real home.

Sitting on the edge of the comforter, I start rubbing a mixture of coconut oil, lavender, and mint on my skin. I rarely wear make-up, so this is the whole of my beauty routine. My phone, which is still sitting on my nightstand, interrupts my calm with an annoying ring. I give it the evil eye, but it ignores me completely and keeps on ringing. I answer it begrudgingly with my oil-free left hand.

"Hello?"

"Blue? This is Jack." His deep voice washes through me with all the richness of a fine brandy.

"Jack, I know it's you, on account of the fact that the phone says 'Jack' when you call. Plus now that I've been working for you for two years, I can finally remember the sound of your voice," I tease.

How nice of him to use the phone instead of the chimerator at this hour of the morning. Then again, maybe he thinks I look hideous before I've readied for work.

"Blue," Jack growls in warning, his voice becoming impossibly deeper, making my insides thrill at the tone.

"Sorry," I apologize, trying to suppress the image of his strong body from rising in my mind, "but you called me early. What can I help you with?" I suddenly notice my right hand has begun sensually massaging the oil into my thigh. I shake my hand as if to erase the action. Bad hand! Oil and the sound of Jack's voice do not mix.

"The M.E. is ready to give his preliminary report," Jack says.

Suddenly my mood is brighter and I'm able to concentrate. "Great. I'll head down there first thing. Actually, I'm glad you called. After the forensics team left yesterday, I found a piece of evidence at the scene. It's an amulet with some sort of magical capabilities. I'll hand it over to Gambino as soon as I can. The amulet has a piece of dark red thread caught in the clasp matching a thread snagged on the boy's fingernail. I checked with the bartender at the Cock and Bull Tap, and a guy wearing a cloak of the same color had just left as I entered."

Jack says, "Really?"

"Really, and that is not all." I relate to Jack the events that followed after I left the bar, and to say he is unhappy would be a gross understatement. As I finish the tale, Jack's voice is thunderous.

"Why didn't you send an alert to me? Why am I only finding out about this now?"

"Jack, you didn't know any of the details of the case, and Gambino couldn't have gotten far. He was only gone five minutes."

Jack orders, "Next time, send an alert. Absolutely no excuses. Your safety is my responsibility, not Gambino's."

I give Jack the only response possible. "Yes, Jack."

Jack is not finished yet. "Let me make this absolutely clear. Anytime, ever, you are shot at, the moment you have cover, if not before, you *must* push the alert on your chimerator. Is that clear?"

I swallow dryly. I know he's right. "Yes, Jack," I repeat.

"Okay," Jack says gruffly. "See what the M.E. has to say, and we'll speak when you get into the office." He hangs up abruptly.

He really should learn how to properly end a call, but this is probably not the time to mention it.

I finish my modest beauty routine, comb my hair, and rifle through my dresser for some fresh underwear. I select a pair of bright fuchsia, French cut panties and a matching push-up bra, both decorated with tiny, black satin bows. I look at myself in the mirror and approve. My body is slim and long with modest curves, but curves enough. Maybe one day someone besides me will appreciate my lingerie. I frown at this thought as I hide my treasures with dark blue, straight leg jeans and a crew neck tee in a gray toned camouflage pattern. My outfit is finished off with boots, a black leather underbust vest, my gray pageboy cap, and, of course, my Glock and holster. My work clothes are dismally boring with the only exciting part remaining my secret.

I grab an umbrella and bolt out the door. My boot heels click down three flights of stairs, reminding me to replace them with rubber soles. As I reach the marble tiled entryway, I'm stalled by a yellow sign blocking the door. "Caution! Wet paint," it warns. Shoot, I have no time for this. I fly down the hall and out the back alley door.

Not more than a few steps into the alley, I feel a presence behind me. As I whip my head around, I feel an iron clasp on my arm. I'm jerked backwards into the chest of a man. I catch just a glimpse of a black mask with two narrow eyeholes.

I jerk my body forward in protest with my other hand reaching in back for my gun. A man's voice scornfully laughs "too late" as he tosses my gun on the ground in front of me.

I push violently backwards, then quickly pull forward, trying to break free from his grasp, but the cold edge of a blade at my neck stops me.

"Be very still and very quiet, or I might enjoy myself too much," a voice hisses in my ear.

I immediately still my body, but my mind is racing. His arm tightens across my chest like an iron band, keeping my arms still at my sides. Rain pours down on us, but I hardly feel it. I glance to the left and see he's pulled me into a corner so we can't be seen from the street. To the right is the long alley, blocked on either side by a tall row of brick buildings. That way lies disaster. If I'm to get free, I must go left toward the street.

I quickly assess my options. With my gun lying useless on the ground and my arms restrained, I have only my mind and my gift to aid me.

I push out my sixth sense and physically flinch away as I feel the evilness of his soul, but the sharp prick of the knife slicing into the skin of my neck stops my forward movement. A small stream of blood trickles down my neck, intermingling with the rain. Lightning flashes, followed by the low rumble of thunder. I can sense the man is high with excitement, enjoying his power over me.

I whisper, "You don't want to do this. I'm a Homicide Inspector with the Supernatural Investigation Bureau. If you harm me, trust me, you will be hunted down."

I feel for his response, but the fear or surprise I expect to rise in him are woefully missing. He knows exactly who I am. My dread increases. This is no random attack.

He chuckles. "Oh yes, I want to do this very bad, in fact, but you know what they say: business before pleasure." The sick, seductive tone of his voice makes me cringe. He digs his fingers into my arm and demands, "Yesterday you investigated a crime. Tell me what you found, and then I'll let you go."

Those are his words, but the malice I feel from him belies those words. He has no intention of letting me go.

He presses the edge of the knife in a little harder. I feel my heart stutter as visions of his gruesome work on the boy's body rise in my mind. I know exactly what he's capable of. I blink to flush away the vision, and out of the corner of my eye I see a flicker of movement in the shadows of the alley. Does he have a cohort? Or is it someone who might help me? Best to keep talking until the hidden is revealed.

I know the man is referring to the amulet, so I avoid giving him this information. I whisper, "We found the body of a boy who had been hit by a car and damaged severely. Was that your handiwork?"

A sneering voice responds, "Yes, you are a genius. So clever . . . "

I see shifting in the shadows along the buildings closer to me now. Whoever is there is trying to stay hidden, and the overcast sky is helping. If the man gets distracted, I could grab his knife arm and twist it or get out of his grasp and run. I could wrench away and use my umbrella as a weapon. My hands tremble at my sides with the force of my desire to fight. It's almost unbearable to stand here waiting at the mercy of a man who has none.

I need to discern if the third party in this alley is friend or foe. I push my senses out, trying to penetrate the gloomy alley in the direction of the flitting shadow. I feel a wild, predatory rage coming from that direction. It feels both savage and unflinching. I'm suddenly unsure of an imminent rescue and wonder if something more dangerous comes that way. I could alert my abductor to the danger and perhaps get free, or I could bide my time hoping to escape when the distraction arrives. Beads of sweat form around my hairline, blending with the rain as I war with my options.

The masked man digs his nails cruelly into my arm, and I realize I missed something he said. He repeats himself. "What of the amulet?"

I lie, "I didn't find an amulet."

He hisses and jerks me farther back into the corner. "I don't believe you."

Just then, I see the shadow separate from the side of the building and shoot into the air right at us. The masked man sees it as well, and his grip on my arms relaxes. I feel the knife blade back away from my neck just a smidge. I lift my left hand to grab on to his forearm, pushing with all my might to further the distance between my skin and the knife blade while swinging my right arm back and ramming the metal point of my umbrella into what I hope is his gut. Letting go of the umbrella, I bring my right arm up to push his knife away. I feel him recoil from the umbrella impact. I twist my body away, gripping his forearm with both hands, then let go and spin out of reach.

Time moves in slow motion, and the creature from the shadows appears suspended in the air. I see long claws and huge, gleaming fangs in a gaping, hungry mouth. The masked man brings the knife up to defend himself against the new threat. I see the glowing green eyes of the creature and hear a vicious snarl as its fangs wrap around the man's knife arm.

I am all but forgotten, so I run toward my gun on the opposite side of the alley. When it's safely in my hand, I pivot, turning it on the man—only he seems to have disappeared into thin air, leaving the creature to snap and snarl savagely at the empty space where he had been. Now that the creature has four clawed paws on the ground, I see he is in fact an enormous gray wolf, and blood is seeping from his side.

I can't believe I was just saved by a wolf. He seems to sense me watching and lifts his keen eyes to me. I curse my stupidity for staying around and aim my Glock at him instead. I back up slowly toward the street, not wanting to shoot, but the wolf starts running toward me at full speed. I should shoot him, really, I should. He just ripped into a man's arm—but he also saved my life.

My hands, aiming the gun straight ahead at the wolf, shake at the force of my indecision. Before I can make up my mind, the wolf has already reached me. He slows his pace, circling around me, sniffing and yipping quietly. Then he puts his forepaws and head down right in front of me and sticks his rump in the air, wagging his tail as though he wants to play.

Rain still pours down on us, water runs in rivulets through my hair, but I pay no attention. He is huge. And beautiful! When he stands again, I'm amazed that the top of his withers reach my waist. His coat is long and thick, fading from a charcoal color on his back and nose to silver around his flank. He has touches of brown throughout his coat and around his eyes, which have now changed from a glowing green to a pale, icy blue.

I reach out slowly with my left hand. He sniffs at the proffered hand, then puts his head under it like he wants a pet. I comply and slowly scratch him about the ears as I slide my Glock smoothly back into its holster.

The two of us are drenched in rain, standing in the alley, greeting each other. What a strange life I lead. After a moment, when I think he's used to me, I gently feel deep down in his neck fur for a collar. His fur is so thick I can't be sure, but I don't think he has one. He appears to have traveled a long and difficult road and looks too dirty and skinny to be a pet anyway. I squat down to examine the gash on his side, but the blood and rain obscure the wound.

"What am I going to do with you, shadow-walker?"

He looks up at me with questioning eyes and I am lost to them.

I put my hand on my hip and say, "You had better come with me."

He walks by my side to the car, seemingly oblivious to his wound, and waits patiently while I pop the trunk. I pull out a blanket and arrange it over the back seat. When all is set, I wave the wolf in. He immediately leaps in the back seat of my car like he's been doing it all of his days. He takes up the entire back seat when he lies down.

I slide into the driver's seat and wrinkle my nose at the stench of wet, dirty animal. Reaching over, I spring the latch on the glove box pulling out a granola bar to feed him. I think he eats it, though it's really hard to tell because it disappears so quickly. He certainly didn't taste it, and there was absolutely no chewing action going on. A bath, medical care, and food are in order. I definitely prefer my wolves well fed.

CHAPTER 06

HERBAL ETCETERA

BLUEBELL KILDARE

MAY 27, 2022, RED AGES

I pull my car up in front of the shop my neighbor Alexis owns. It's located in the middle of Dunnwell Street, a thriving business community in our neighborhood. The storefronts are well kept with old quality craftsmanship in their design. Alexis Demetriou's storefront is painted in sage green, burgundy, and cream. Whimsical stenciling on her large front windows announces "Herbal Enchantments" with smaller print below that says "Amulets, potions, charms, etcetera." I'm here for the etcetera.

I let the wolf out and look at him closely. He looks smaller now, about the size of a large dog. I shake my head and wonder if I'm going mad. My state of panic surely played tricks on my mind.

As I walk in with the wolf pushing in front of me, the door chimes merrily announce our arrival. Alexis has her back turned toward the door as she places little bottles of potions on a shelf. She's wearing a neatly pressed, pale blue pantsuit that makes her dark chocolate curls stand out beautifully.

The store is filled with bottles of all shapes and colors with neatly printed labels. The colored glass sparkles even in the dim light filtering through the clouds and the large storefront windows. Aside from the shelves of potions, there are walls of charms and several amulet trees. The place is in pristine and orderly condition. I don't blame the place at all. I wouldn't get out of line either if I were Alexis' store.

Alexis is tall and fit, but curvy in a generous way—as opposed to me, who is curvy in a barely noticeable way. I like to think that her generous bosom reflects her generous personality. She has brown skin, large brown eyes, and beautifully thick hair. She also has a lot of sass. It seems like when she's not pointing her finger, she's crossing her arms, putting her hands on her hips, or raising her eyebrows. And look out if she starts shaking her head at you.

Alexis turns around and her eyes widen, showing an extraordinary amount of eyeball, but in a good way. "Great Demon of the Abyss!" she exclaims. "You have a wolf."

She rushes forward, but a few paces away from him she seems to remember he is a wolf. She stops, offering her hand slowly. He sniffs it and gives it a perfunctory lick. Then he cases the shop, sniffing fervently at the abundance of scented goods.

I spit out in one breath, "I was attacked in an alley behind our building this morning—a man from a case I'm working on, but don't worry, I'm fine. This wolf appeared out of nowhere and tore into him like an avenging angel. The guy disappeared and got away. I don't think he's dangerous unless he's threatened." I pause for breath.

Alexis puts her hands on her hips, clearly outraged. "What do you mean you don't think he's dangerous? He jumped you in the alley, and you have dried blood on your neck."

I widen my eyes and grab my neck. "Shoot, I forgot about that. I meant I don't think the wolf is dangerous. I'm going to keep him. The man is definitely dangerous. The wolf got cut by him, and is in far worse condition than I am."

Alexis' eyes flit to the wolf and then back to me. Then she immediately springs to action, her healing nature taking over.

She squats down informing the wolf, "I'm going to touch you gently by your wound, and you are going to remain calm and stay still."

She tentatively parts the bloody hair on his left flank, and he abides her orders, standing still through her ministrations. I watch carefully for signs of aggression but see none.

Alexis looks up at me, and I feel her relief as she says, "Thankfully it is not that bad. His fur protected him a good deal, and the rain seems to have helped. It looks like the knife nicked some surface blood vessels, but the wound isn't deep."

Then she looks at the wolf and starts cooing, "You poor thing, you look so starved. Let's get you something to eat and take care of that cut."

This is not an unexpected response. Alexis does two things very well. She can cook up herbal potions like no one's business, and she also does her best to feed everyone in sight. I personally agree feeding him before taking care of the injury is a wise idea.

Alexis leads us to a back room equipped with a small commercial kitchen decorated in a mix of stainless steel and country charm. She mixes most of her potions in this comfortable and efficient space. Alexis' assistant, Penelope, is busy ladling some mixture into bottles with a funnel. She turns to Alexis and immediately drops the ladle back into the pot with a plop when she sees the wolf.

Alexis smiles and says, "Penelope, we have a patient today. Do you want to mind the front while I take care of him back here?"

Penelope is a pretty, young girl with rosy cheeks and curly hair, which frequently escapes her bun. She's usually hardworking but a little silly. Right now slack-jawed most adequately describes her as she stares, mouth agape, at the wolf. The wolf, in return, is utterly ignoring her. Eventually Alexis' words seem to penetrate Penelope's temporarily addled brain because she wrings her apron in her hands and promptly runs up front.

I hop up on the edge of the butcher block island as Alexis pulls things down from the cabinets. She opens a purple bottle and pours a green substance on some gauze pads. Handing them to me, she instructs, "Dab this around your injury while I care for the wolf. What are you going to call him?" She turns her back to me and starts pulling things from the fridge.

I consider her question for a minute. "Well, the only real memory I have of my mother is her telling me a bedtime story about a wolf. It's hazy, only a wisp of a memory really, but I think she called the wolf Varg. So that's his name."

Alexis turns around to look at me as I tell her that story. Her eyes go soft and warm. Then she turns around again and starts briskly heating things in stainless steel pots on the red porcelain stove. "Varg is the perfect name," she says.

"So, do you have any remedies for fleas and worms handy as well? I think he's been traveling a long way without any care. I also need a strong soap for his coat."

Alexis looks up thoughtfully. "I usually don't sell veterinary supplies out of the store. I do make them when I get requests. I'll have to make some from scratch."

"Do you mind? I'll pay of course."

"I don't mind. In fact, I insist. But it's going to take a little time." She turns to me with narrowed eyes. "And I'm not going to let him go wandering around town when he's full of potions. Even though they're natural, they take a lot out of a body. He's hurt, and he'll need protection against viruses and diseases as well. We don't know where he's been, but here in the city with the dog population, he's at risk. And good Lord!" She sniffs. "He needs a bath." Alexis finishes this with a nod like it's all decided now.

She turns back to the stove and handles the long wooden spoon like a master while I hop down to rummage through her cabinets. I locate a large, green glass bowl, fill it with cold water, and set it on the brick floor. Varg laps the water up with a terrific thirst but stops when Alexis puts down another huge glass bowl filled with rice, ground beef, and garlic.

"Wow! Just wow!" I say as we watch him move over to that bowl and devour it like it's nothing.

Alexis crosses her arms and says, "Yeah. He'd better stay with me today. I'll get him in shape."

I give Alexis a big smile. "Thanks so much. I've got a new case, so I'll be running around all day. I'm glad he doesn't have to wait to get fixed up."

"Of course he shouldn't wait with that injury. Now, don't worry about him. I'll see you when you get off work. If the shop is closed, you know where to find me."

Then she wets a paper towel and leans over me to dab at my neck. "There, you're all clean now."

I hug her and affect a serious tone. "Now I owe you one. If anyone ever murders you, remember, I'm the one you should call."

Alexis laughs and pushes me toward the swinging door. "Go, get, scoot."

I start to leave with a smile on my lips. Then I remember something, so I spin around. "Hey Alexis, If you wanted to learn more about a certain magical artifact, where would you go?"

"Easy. The Dragomir Magical Artifact Shop. Make sure you speak with the owner."

"Thanks again," I shout, running out the door on my way to the Medical Examiner's office.

CHAPTER 07

EVIDENCE OF ANGUISH

BLUEBELL KILDARE

MAY 27, 2022, RED AGES

I think to myself how ugly the new Medical Examiner's building is as I eat up the sidewalk on the way in. It rises out of the mountainside as a cement and steel square oddity in discord with the rustic countryside. Hopefully it was gentle on the taxpayers' pocketbooks because it certainly is no asset to our architecture.

By now the rain has stopped, and a steady, cooling breeze blows my hair across my face. I tuck it behind my ear as I enter the building.

Inside, the receptionist accepts my ID and gives her reluctant assent for me to proceed to the autopsy room. I gather by the way her mouth sours on sight of me that she doesn't care for my kind. I don't care for her kind either—the breedist kind.

Pushing past the steel door, I enter the heart of the operation. Dr. Nathan Perlman, with a two-day shadow on his chin and a clipboard in his hand, stands over a body. He seems tired and worn. He looks up, and forces his usual affable smile. "Good morning, Bluebell. I was expecting you."

He covers the body with a white sheet and pushes the table through a cooler door while whistling. I think the whistling is for his benefit more than mine. He pulls out another table, maneuvering it toward the examining area. "This is our boy."

"I'm afraid to ask what you've found."

Nathan nods solemnly. "The only good thing is I know you're going to find the person who did this. That thought has been my saving grace today."

I say softly and firmly, meaning it from the bottom of my soul, "I promise, Nathan. I'll do my very best."

Nathan nods and pulls back the sheet. He picks up another clipboard then starts his report. "This is a summary of my preliminary findings. The cause of death appears to be due to blunt force head trauma caused by a vehicular collision." Nathan points to an area on the front of the boy's skull. "The frontal bone was crushed on impact, causing fracture contusions on his brain, massive hemorrhage, and immediate death. Fragments of glass were found in the wound area."

Nathan points to the back of the boy's skull. "The occipital bone was also fractured, causing brain contusions and additional hemorrhage. Abrasions on this injury site have fragments of asphalt embedded in the wound."

Nathan pulls the sheet down further and points to the boy's hip. "His left pelvis is crushed, and his right pelvis has multiple fractures. This pattern of contusions appears to be from a car's grill." He points to a crosshatch of bloody stripes on the boy's skin extending from his left hip down over his left thigh.

Nathan pulls the sheet down further still and points to the lower left leg where the bone protrudes. "His left tibia and his left fibula both have complete fractures and several incomplete fractures. The tibia on his right leg has one incomplete fracture. Green paint chips were found embedded in his thigh."

Nathan pauses and looks at me. "These injuries indicate his death was caused by impact with a passenger vehicle driving at moderate speed. It appears the car hit him at a slight angle from the left. His leg was immediately broken by the bumper, and his hip and thigh hit the grill at an angle. His forehead hit the windshield, causing instantaneous death. At that time, I believe the driver braked and the boy's body was thrown onto the asphalt where the road impacted his skull again leaving asphalt in the back of his head. His back side is covered in contusions and embedded with asphalt."

I feel nausea and tension building in my stomach. What Nathan has told and shown me so far isn't too much. I've been doing this for a while. It's that I know there is much more to come and it's a lot to handle at once. I ask, "Can you give me a minute?"

Nathan nods. "Take as much time as you need." He gently covers the boy's body again with the sheet.

I turn my back on the table and walk away. I begin to pace briskly, but the sound of my heels clicking on the cold cement floor reverberates through the room and agitates me more. I halt, turn toward the opposite corner of the room, and close my eyes. Tension fills my body, and horror reels in the back of my mind, threatening to overcome me. I roll my neck and do some slow, deep breathing to contain it. When I finally restore some calm to my body, I return.

"Okay, Doc. I'm ready. What else do you have?"

Nathan mercifully keeps the sheet over the body and says, "During my internal examination, I found the body well hydrated, but the gall bladder is distended, and the stomach and intestines are empty. The total body weight is 112 pounds, with a height of five eleven, giving the deceased a BMI of 15.6. This information combined with his labs tells me this boy was dangerously undernourished."

"Can you tell how long he was without food?" I ask.

Nathan replies, "He did not have food recently, but it's unclear if his malnourishment came from having no food for a short period or inadequate food for a longer period. The amount of time a person can survive on little or no sustenance depends on their starting weight and basic metabolic rate. I can say the extent of his other injuries prior to the collision would've increased his energy requirements significantly."

"Okay," I say, taking that in. I cross my arms over my chest as if to shield myself from the information. "What else do you have?"

Nathan draws the sheet aside to reveal one hand and points at the boy's wrist. "Both wrists are encircled in calluses about two inches wide. Bruising and contusions encircle the base of his hands."

He points to the upper arm and shoulder. "Behind the shoulder, the teres major muscle is torn on both sides, and the ligament tissue connecting the long head of the triceps brachii muscle to the bone is torn. Both ankles show similar calluses and contusions. The injuries and bruising on both the ankles and the wrists show all stages of healing, which means the wounds were continuously inflicted over at least two weeks."

Holding my hand up for a pause, I probe, "Is it possible he was tied with a rope or handcuffed?"

Nathan's face turns into a deep scowl. "It wasn't rope, there were no fibers embedded. The skin is clean as though it was metal encasing his hands and feet. But handcuffs are too narrow to provide the wide grooving and callusing I see here. These injuries are more consistent with having feet shackled and hands shackled over the head."

Nathan moves to the end of the table and gently folds back the sheet that covers the boy's feet and lower legs. A foul odor fills the air, making my stomach roil in protest. I reluctantly join Nathan at that side of the table.

Nathan points to the bottom of the boy's feet, which are black, wrinkled, and covered in sores. "This boy had a condition commonly known as trench foot. This is evidenced by the wrinkled skin on the bottoms of his feet and the blisters and open sores on the bottoms and sides of his feet."

He points to the black, rotting toe and says, "Fungal infection and gangrene had set in. This stage of trench foot lasts from two to six weeks. Additionally, I found evidence of human fecal matter and urine on his feet. Trench foot occurs when the foot is in damp and cold but not freezing conditions for an extended period of time." Nathan steps back covering the feet again.

Nathan sighs. "I have one last area of injury to show you." He gently rolls the boy over on his side and lifts the sheet to show his back. I see wounds and bruising extending from his waist to his neck. "First of all, he has a mark, a green circle on his lower back. I assume it's a magic mark, but you are a better judge than I. As you observed at the scene, this boy had lacerations and bruising covering his entire back. They're in various stages of healing. Because the wounds are deeper in this area," Nathan explains as he points to the boy's mid-back where the skin is stripped away and muscle is exposed, "I estimate this healing took place over the course of three to four weeks. The forensic report will take some time, but I found fibers in these wounds that appeared to be conditioned animal hide. Preliminarily, I believe these injuries were sustained from a leather whip."

I step back, turn away, and clasp my shaking hands as I fill with insurmountable rage. The sound of my blood pulsing through my body fills my ears with a wild rushing noise as my head buzzes. I try to regain some control, but the image of the boy is vivid in my mind. I see him starving, chained, and shackled in some cold, dark place. I see him being whipped day after day until his flesh peels away like the skin of an onion. With great effort, I push the image into a corner of my mind. I need to carry on. My job is to find the monster who did this. I will find him.

With my back still turned, I ask, "Anything else?"

Nathan answers, "No. But I did check for sexual assault and am at least relieved that there are no signs he had to endure that indignity as well."

"Thank goodness for small miracles. Our perpetrator is a real saint, isn't he?" Spinning around to face Nathan and the body again, I inquire, "Did you send the preliminary report over to Detective Gambino?"

Nathan smiles wryly. "Yes, about an hour ago. I included images and measurements of the grill pattern."

I tip my hat to Nathan, bowing slightly in gratitude. "Thank you so much, Nathan, for doing what needs to be done. Call me if you find anything else significant or when the pathology and forensic results come back."

"Certainly. But can I ask you a personal question?"

I nod my assent and Nathan asks, "Why do you insist on coming here for the preliminary results rather than just accepting my report? Wouldn't it be easier to take in writing? I see how much it affects you."

I look Nathan directly in the eyes to divulge my logic. "There are two reasons. First, I'm a Sensitive. While I can't feel anything from a body when the soul has left, by looking at it, and hearing and seeing what happened, I get a feel for the shape of the evilness that possessed the perpetrator. When I encounter a soul capable of that sort of evilness, I sometimes see a potential match. My sense can't be conclusive, but it can tell me if a person could possibly be the perpetrator. I can also rule people out. The second reason is I need to feel the pain. That drives me to find the perpetrator. I'll remember today countless times when I'm frustrated or at a loss, and because of today, I'll keep on."

Nathan looks at me with understanding dawning on his face, and I feel his empathy wafting toward me. "I can't imagine what it is to feel the soul of a person who does things like this."

I accept his empathy with a nod. Then I walk out, remarking over my shoulder, "In case you're wondering, you have a good soul, Nathan." He has a very good soul.

CHAPTER 08

The Dragomir

BLUEBELL KILDARE

MAY 27, 2022, RED AGES

I decide to swing by the Dragomir Magical Artifact Shop before heading to the precinct. As I turn onto Windsor Avenue, I consider what Father O'Brennen told me last night. Is my aura the reason I've never encountered a Dark Vampire? Even though most people go their whole lives without running into a Night-Crawler, I work in the Supernatural Homicide Investigation Unit, so I should have by now. Ernesto is our resident Night-Crawler expert at the office and leads the hunts. Still, there has been many a time I've been called out for a homicide in the wee hours of the morning just to find the call was reported incorrectly and was actually a case of death by Dark Vampire.

And who was the Daylight Vampire who saved me? I didn't think to ask Father O'Brennen. Is he still around? Is there more he can tell me about that night?

I stop my musings as the Dragomir Magical Artifact Shop comes into view. It's a corner store made of flagstone and favored with a rare parking lot of its own. I park and walk around to the front entrance.

No merry bells announce my arrival here. Solid oak shelves covered in thick layers of dust fill the dimly lit store. The dust is so thick it seems to swirl around me, gathering in glittering pools and eddies that hang in the air.

I wave it away from my face and look at the shelves adorned with a wonderful assortment of magical items: scrying mirrors and a looking glass fountain to keep connected with loved ones, firefly lanterns to light your house, and glow stones to brighten your garden. One entire wall is devoted to glass-covered shelves stacked with aged books on every magical subject imaginable. Another case is dedicated to gorgeous parquetry safe boxes. These special boxes are made of tiny geometric shaped veneer inlaid over interlocking pieces of wood. They require a magic word to open. When you close them, their designs rearrange, disguising the opening.

As I take in my surroundings, a few rays of sunlight peek from behind the clouds shining through the windows in bright streams, lighting up the whirlpools of dust still filling the air. It makes me want to twirl around like a little girl. I immediately love this store, musty dust and all.

Behind the heavy oak counter, the clerk is studiously ignoring me as she reads a book. Her reading glasses have dropped to the tip of her nose, and a mess of wavy, brown hair has fallen about her face. I wait for her to look up, but she seems oblivious to my presence. I stand in front of her to get her attention, but still she keeps her eyes pinned down on the book. I am obviously three feet in front of her, yet she pretends I'm not here.

This is extremely vexing, and just as I'm about to say something rude, I notice a sign that says, "Please ring bell for service." Next to it sits a large brass bell. I ring the bell, and a high pitched sound reverberates throughout the room. I resist the urge to ring it five times in a row to annoy the clerk. Then, wonder of wonders, she lifts her glasses to peer at me through the lenses. How glorious it feels to be acknowledged.

Even more astonishing than her new realization that I exist is the way her face lights up in a beatific smile transforming her into a very arresting mature woman. With her head lifted up, her hair now looks like a riot of soft waves framing a face dominated by deep-set, warm brown eyes that flicker with golden light.

"Hello," I say a little uncertainly. She has definitely put me at sixes and sevens.

She answers with a deeply melodious voice, "Hello, what can I help you with today?" Her voice is so strange. It's like ten voices speaking at once, or like the strumming of a harp with notes overlapping one another. It is simply musical. I tilt my head to hear it better.

I realize she is sitting there waiting expectantly for me to answer. I pull myself together, remembering I have a goal to accomplish. "I'm looking for Mr. Dragomir," I respond.

Her smile immediately turns chilly, and her voice sounds like a dozen angry people speaking to me from different directions. "Mr. Dragomir is not in." Then she points her eyes toward her book again.

Darn, I lost her again. Beginning to catch on, I ask, "Are you Mrs. Dragomir?"

She looks up and says with great power, "I am *the* Dragomir." I feel unaccountably humbled and apologize.

"I am sorry, Dragomir, for my error. My friend Alexis from Herbal Enchantments referred me to you."

Looking slightly mollified, but still a little snippy, she says, "Please call me Dragomira. Now, what can I help you with?"

"Excuse me for commenting on this, but your voice is the most remarkable I've ever heard." Then I pull out my ID for her. "My name is Bluebell Kildare. I'm with the Supernatural Investigation Bureau. I was wondering if you could answer a few questions."

Dragomira ignores my statement about her voice and my ID, looking unimpressed with both. "It depends on the nature of those questions."

"I'm looking for information on a particular amulet. If you can give me a piece of paper, I'd like to make a sketch."

Dragomira, still exuding a markedly severe demeanor, deigns to retrieve some paper and a pencil from a nearby drawer.

Undaunted, I sketch the amulet, drawing the triangle within the circle and the cutout in the shape of an eye. My sketch includes the hole in the center of the amulet and a depiction of the back including the ridging and beading.

As I sketch the amulet, Dragomira's eyes become riveted, and I swear they start glowing amber. When I finish, she puts her hand up and her chorus of voices whispers, "One moment. This conversation requires no audience."

She goes to the door of her shop, turns the heavy brass deadbolt, placing her "Closed" sign face out.

When she returns, I say, "I take it you know this amulet. Should I pull out my privacy charm?"

Dragomira laughs softly and says, "My dear, this shop is so well warded the Gods themselves would have trouble entering. Perhaps I know this amulet. Tell me, what it is made of?"

I look curiously around the shop, then point to the sketch and answer, "The amulet is gold. The triangle looks to be jade. The grooves on the back are gold, and the beading is some sort of white metal, perhaps white gold."

"It's platinum," Dragomira says crisply. "Yes. I know this amulet."

"What can you tell me about it? Why would someone want it?"

Dragomira leans her arms on the counter, and her warm brown eyes betray her worry. She shivers. "Ah, Illustrissima. That is the question. What would someone want with the amulet? I am afraid of the answer."

"This amulet has two pieces. What you drew here is only one part. The triangle is made of jade, the stone of wisdom. Its significance is that it's part of a key used to unlock a book. The missing part, the center, is in the shape of an eye. The iris of the eye, carved with the circle of life, is made of sugelite, a purple stone, which issues dire warning."

Dragomira jabs her long, elegant finger repeatedly at the center of the eye in the drawing as she speaks. "It warns of the end of humanity. In the center of the eye is a pupil made of amber, used for its properties of attraction, to help you find that which you seek with the book. The eye fits into the hole in the center and has grooves and beads of its own. The two pieces, joined together, form the symbol for the All-Seeing Eye, which sees across planes and into the Underworld."

When she finishes with her explanation, Dragomira assesses my reaction in a way that makes me feel somehow inadequate.

I forge ahead anyway. "What book does the key open?"

"Ah," Dragomira says heavily. "You plunge right in, do you not? It opens the ancient *Grimorium Cantionum Spiritualium—The Spell Book of the Spirit and Soul*. It is a book that contains the knowledge to call demons and spirits from other planes, including the Plane of Death. It is a very powerful book, and those who have possessed its knowledge have done massive damage to those who live in this world."

I shift uneasily as this case is much more dangerous and complex than I'd originally thought. "What sort of damage?"

Dragomira gestures toward a stool at the end of her counter. "I will tell you a story. Please sit down."

I drag the stool over and sit, listening avidly as her hypnotic voice weaves a picture of a bygone era.

"In ancient Ireland," she begins, "a talented sorcerer's apprentice came to possess the *Grimorium Cantionum Spiritualium*. We now know this apprentice as Patersuco—'Father of the Vampires.' Patersuco was deathly ill from a blood sickness and desperate to save his own life. The learned now speculate he suffered from leukemia, but that matters not to this story. Patersuco was a selfish, greedy man, so he sacrificed his first-born infant son and used the knowledge of the book to summon the greatest demon of the Plane of Fire, Lilith, second only to Lucifer.

"When Lilith arrived, Patersuco tried to bargain with her for immortality. Lilith asked what he would give her in return, and Patersuco said the sacrifice of his son was his gift to her. Lilith laughed at him and said the sacrifice was nothing. She said the baby's soul was innocent, so it went to the Plane of Light, and all she received from the sacrifice was a blood gift. She taunted him, telling him instead of killing his son, he could have simply slit his flesh and dropped some blood on the altar."

Dragomira sees the shocked look on my face at the idea that a man had so easily sacrificed his own son. "This was just before the Red Ages, and the earth was still wild and untamed. Man also was wild and untamed. Human sacrifices were not uncommon, as wrong as they may be. But even then, sacrificing one's own son was unheard of."

I interject, "I think Patersuco was foolish to think that Lilith would trade a mortal life for an immortal life. Isn't it immortal souls that are collected on the Plane of Fire?"

Dragomira raises her eyebrows at this. "Excellent observation. Indeed, a mortal life has no value to Lilith. Nonetheless, Patersuco, in his foolishness and arrogance, was enraged that she made so little of his sacrifice—but he was determined to achieve his goal. So he offered to give her his soul when he died. Lilith laughed at him again and pointed out he had killed an innocent in cold blood, his own living flesh, even, so his soul was already destined for the Plane of Fire. She also reminded him that since he was asking for immortality, she would have to wait a long time for that prize."

"Lilith sounds highly conniving. Apparently by sacrificing his son, he had given her his own immortal soul. But Lilith didn't recognize this as part of his payment to her."

Dragomira says, "She is second only to the Prince of Lies, the Prince of Thieves, the Master Bargain Maker. She is indeed skilled, and instead of taking his bargain, she offered him another."

By now I'm sitting on the edge of my seat, waiting for Dragomira to spin the rest of the tale.

"She said she would cure his blood disease, but it would require he drink the blood of other humans to survive. She said to make this easier, she would make him desire blood. She would give him strength and resistance from disease, but he would always carry her mark. He'd live a long life and be difficult to kill, but the only immortality she'd grant him would be the same all mortals achieve: through creating more of their kind. He could not conceive new life; he could, however, fill others with his blood, and they would carry the same gifts she gave him. But she gave him a warning. If he killed in bloodlust, his soul would immediately belong completely to her."

Dragomira suddenly stands up and tilts her head as though listening to the ceiling. Then closing her eyes she recites a string of words in an ancient-sounding language, painting patterns in the air with her hand. She seems to be in some sort of trance. I sit silently, unsure how to respond.

After what seems like forever, she opens her eyes. "Excuse me for that," she says. "I felt a disturbance in our wards. Someone was trying to enter uninvited. All is well now." Then she sits back down continuing as though nothing had happened.

"Patersuco, unwise as he was, accepted this offer. Thus, Lilith created the first Vampire. All Vampires are descendents of those turned by Patersuco. All Vampires carry Lilith's mark. All Vampires are doomed to the Plane of Fire. Because of this bargain, Lilith ensured many more generations of souls would come to her."

"So she pretended to give Patersuco what he wanted, and in return she got over two thousand years of an ever-increasing number of souls. Patersuco offered a very cheap price for the boon he ended up giving her in return."

"Exactly. He was a selfish, greedy man and a lousy bargainer. Lilith gave Patersuco the ability to create new beings, each of whom has the temptation of bloodlust, and eventually when they give in to that bloodlust and kill, their souls go to her. When their souls go to the Plane of Fire, their flesh is left on Earth to continue to ravage humans, and ravage they do.

"The mark she left on Patersuco was a dark smear on his soul, and every child he created carries this mark. The mark ties the soul to Lilith, and when it's finally released from the body, it returns to her like a homing pigeon. So, even if a Daylight Vampire never kills in bloodlust, their soul joins her in the end."

I hold up my hand at this. "I understand how Patersuco could bargain away his soul, but how could he bargain away the souls of the people he turned? He didn't have the right to them, and until they kill, they are still innocent."

Dragomira raises her eyebrows. "I'd never thought to wonder. But you are correct. I've never heard of another story of someone giving away souls that do not belong to them. Perhaps when a person is turned into a Vampire, their soul is forfeited to their maker somehow. Not all attempted turnings work, you know, and some humans die. Perhaps those are cases in which the human will not relinquish ownership of their soul."

I am dissatisfied by this response. If humans give up their souls at the time of turning, at least one Vampire would have mentioned it by now, but I keep my silence to let Dragomira finish the story.

She steps off her stool to stretch her back. Her entire back bends like a bow, her spine cracking fiercely as she moves. When she straightens, she glances out the windows with a flick of her eyes, then brings them back to me with solemnity.

"As you know, the birth of the Vampire brought on the Red Ages. Around 1500 R.A., Dark Vampires, those who had already killed in bloodlust and lost their sanity, almost wiped out humanity. It is said in the time before the Great Pact, the very ground wept blood and the rivers flowed red. It wasn't until humanity was at the brink of extinction that the Daylight Vampires, who were still rational, realized once all humans were gone, they would perish as well. Without a blood supply, they would be forced to turn cannibalistic and eventually wipe out their own breed. So the Daylight Vampires made a pact with humans to hunt Dark Vampires. People agreed to give blood donations to the Daylight Vampires, and the Daylight Vampires agreed not to feed without consent and to keep their numbers under control. With this pact, people were once again able to live without the constant fear of being hunted, and a sense of balance was restored."

I nod at this. "Yes. We learned that in our ancient history lessons in school as that was the beginning of the Reconstruction Period. But we learned nothing of the book. So basically what you're saying is with this book, Patersuco was able to summon the demon Lilith from the Plane of Fire, and his bargain with her nearly caused the extinction of all humanity on Earth. I assume the other things this book teaches are also a double-edged sword. Do you know where the book is?"

Dragomira shakes her head emphatically. "Absolutely not. After the birth of Vampires, the leaders of each breed held council on what to do with the book. Some wanted it destroyed. Others wanted it saved. Some accounts say attempts to destroy it failed. In the end, it was decided to lock the book and make it impossible to find. They designed the key and made it so only with the key could the book be opened. The key was then separated into two pieces, and they hid all three items in separate places: the amulet, the eye, and the book."

Ignoring my panic at the significance of what I hold in my possession, I inquire as nonchalantly as possible, "Does anyone know where the pieces of the key are?"

Dragomira looks askance at me and says, "I've researched the subject thoroughly and have never read an account of someone knowing where any of the three items are."

What was the boy doing with the amulet, and where did he get it? I'm glad it's hidden on holy ground because magic and evil can't penetrate there. I came here for answers and ended up with more questions. So many questions swirl around in my mind, and I can't make sense of them. Instead of asking them, I simply say, "Thank you, Dragomira. I appreciate the information."

Dragomira puts up her hand and says, "It is I who must thank you, Illustrissima. Thank you for listening to a favorite tale of mine. It's rare I get an audience these days. It is so rare, in fact, that I'd like to give you a gift."

This surprises me. When did Dragomira change from an arrogant and aloof woman to a woman giving gifts?

"That's not necessary at all," I assure her.

Dragomira ignores me and lifts up her arm. She says a word in that ancient language again, and a metal object flies from another room straight to her hand. She catches it deftly and stabs it down into the wooden counter in front of me. It's a gorgeous, gleaming knife with a sapphire and diamond encrusted hilt and a double-edged blade of about seven inches long. I had no intention of accepting a gift, but I find myself entranced by this knife. My eyes slip enviously over the blade and my hands twitch, longing to wrap around the hilt.

I look up at Dragomira in awe, and she says, "Its name is Curator, or Guardian in English."

I say softly and regrettably, "I can't take this. It's clearly precious."

Dragomira insists, "You must take the knife. These are dangerous times, Inspector Kildare. Just moments ago, someone was knocking on my wards looking for you."

My eyes go wide. The masked man from this morning must still be after me. Of course he is—he didn't get what he wanted. How foolish of me to think otherwise. My hand flies to my neck as I think of his blade there just hours before. Dragomira's gaze flits to my neck as well, her eyes knowing but her mouth quiet. Without saying another word, I grasp the knife in my hand and pull it out of the wood.

Dragomira laughs softly and follows me to the door. As she unbolts it, she says, "Remember, his name is Guardian. Stay true, Illustrissima."

I'm left wondering why she keeps calling me Illustrissima as the door closes softly behind me.

CHAPTER 09

EVERY DAY ENMITY

BLUEBELL KILDARE

MAY 27, 2022, RED AGES

I enter the precinct headquarters and step into the sallyport, conscious of the knife tucked in my waistband. It's not the knife that makes me uncomfortable, but rather how improperly sheathed it is, which I find shameful.

The officer at the front desk invites me past the sallyport and asks me to wait in the general station room while he calls Detective Gambino. The room has scuffed, stark white walls and gray linoleum floor tiles that could use repeated washings. Outdated metal desks pressed against each other give little privacy or work ambiance. A few officers writing reports and doing paperwork glance at me in mild curiosity. I stalk the open area by the doorway, anxious to finish at the precinct so I can get to my office. It's already been a long and exhausting day.

As I wait, two officers walk in from the back. One officer, heavyset, with short, thin hair plastered in small wisps to his oily face, leers at me. Lust rolls off him, filling me with disgust. I know the other one and hold no love for him either. His name is Detective Dean Schmidt. He's tall and broad-shouldered with coarse blond hair. He's built like an athlete who's gone slightly soft in the middle. His hazel eyes are a bit too wide-set for his face, and his thin lips rest in a permanent sneer when he looks at me. He's holding a box of Ma Farina cookies in one hand and a cup of coffee in the other. Ma Farina is the best bakery in town. What a waste of cookies. He stops when he sees me and snarls with disgust, "What are you doing here, Aberrant?"

Internally I cringe. You would think I'd be used to insults by now, but they still sting. Instead of outwardly reacting, I use the skills I learned in the orphanage and put on a brave front. "What's your problem, Schmidt?" I spit out Schmidt's name like it's a curse word.

"You're my problem. I just arrested one of your kind, and I come here and you, another Aberrant, are in my building."

His buddy interjects as his lascivious stare rakes me up and down. "But she sure is hot. I wish they all looked like her."

I ignore the buddy and say to Schmidt, "Listen, Slick. Why don't you put your little snack down and get Gambino for me. I don't have time to listen to your prejudiced idiocy. I have a murder to solve."

Detective Schmidt moves his hand toward me like he is going to hit me and his box of cookies falls to the ground. The lid of the box opens during the fall, and cookies roll around at his feet. One cookie rolls in circles, around and around, before spiraling to a stop.

I back up. Maybe being on the offensive was the wrong tactic.

Schmidt looks at his cookies, and his mood turns even blacker. I can't blame him, really; those are darn good cookies. He takes a step forward with his fist raised. I look around for help, and I see two wide-eyed officers staring at us with mouths agape. No help there.

I move to a defensive fighting stance. Schmidt is well-trained and much larger than I, so I don't stand a chance, but I am not going to take his abuse lying down. I feel comforted that I have the knife, but I won't be the first to pull a weapon.

Gambino's voice suddenly cuts through the room in a tone brooking no argument. "Stand down, Schmidt!" An avalanche of protective rage from Gambino warms me. It's nice to know he feels that way.

Schmidt steps back.

Gambino says with a calm that is remarkably contrived, "Inspector Kildare does excellent work. She has solved more homicides in two years than you have in the last ten, Detective Schmidt. I expect you to treat her with respect when she comes to this office."

Detective Schmidt's mouth is closed in a white line of fury, and if looks could kill, I would be pierced with a million shards of glass.

Gambino looks at Schmidt's buddy and says, "Officer Randall, she is not a piece of meat. Get your dick out of your hand and get back to work."

Officer Randall turns bright red all the way up to his ears while I struggle to maintain a straight face.

Gambino turns to me. "Right this way, Inspector Kildare," he says kindly but firmly.

I follow him to his office with as much dignity as I can muster. Gambino shouts over his shoulder, "And pick up those damn cookies, Schmidt."

"I'm sorry you had to deal with them," Gambino says once we're safely in his office. "There are many good men on the force, but a few fall short in certain areas. We're working on it."

I nod in acceptance of this apology. Prejudice is rampant these days. The Gifted are human, just like Norms. The only difference is we have a gift, a magical power of some sort. Some, like Dragomira, are Gifted in spell casting. Others, like me, have a special strength in one specific area. Prior to the birth of Vampires, the Gifted were hunted down as Witches and burned. But once the Vampires were born, the Gifted often helped protect the Norms. Due to this help small pockets of humans survived until the Great Pact between Daylight Vampires and humans was made. Since then, many of the Gifted have stayed in public service positions like mine.

Unfortunately, there are still those who are subject to selfishness and greed, and a percentage of us, just like humans, do immoral things. Being Gifted allows those so inclined to take greater advantage of Norms. Even when we don't, many Norms are fearful simply because the Gifted are mysterious and unpredictable to them.

Because they keep the Dark Vampire population down, Daylight Vampires are generally well tolerated in society, except by the more extreme hate groups. During the worst of the Red Ages, Daylight Vampires struck an agreement with humans. Each human, Gifted included, provides a pint of blood to the blood banks every three weeks, and in turn they do not hunt us. They also agreed to keep their populations down, and police this rule strictly amongst themselves. Anyone who makes too many children is using too much of the blood supply and is hunted down.

There are many hate groups, particularly among orthodox religions, who would like to see all Vampires and Gifted wiped out. The requirement to give blood every three weeks is considered by many as inconvenient, and this alone causes plenty of resentment.

Due to the nature of the prejudice that permeates our society, I am not new to hate rhetoric. Still, it hurts.

Doing my best to brush off the encounter, I ask Gambino, "What have you found out about our boy?"

Gambino opens a folder on his desk. "The boy was on our missing persons list. He was seventeen years old and was missing for twenty-eight days. The investigating officer thought he was a runaway, but the parents claimed there was no reason for him to run. We have already notified the parents, and they identified the body at the Medical Examiner's this morning. The boy's name was Jason O'Connell."

I stand up and pace a little in Gambino's tiny office. My blood is still high from the incident with Schmidt, so the office feels confining. I hardly take three strides before I have to turn. "Please don't mind me," I say to Gambino. "I can't stand to sit still too long. Continue, if you would."

Gambino nods, obliging me. "The M.E. faxed over the grill pattern they found on the boy's skin. We're searching for the model car it belongs to. We also have paint chips from his skin and glass from the scene at forensics. Hopefully between these three pieces of evidence we'll get a match on a car registered in the area."

"Have you read the preliminary report from the M.E. yet?"

Gambino taps his folder in disgust. "Yes. I'd like to nail the asshole who did that to a seventeen-year-old boy. Our perp is a real sicko."

"You and me both. Do you have any persons of interest?"

"Well," Gambino pauses as though reluctant to reveal what he must. "There was some trouble in the family. The parents have been estranged for about four months. The mother is Gifted, and she hid it from her husband for almost twenty years. When Jason's gift came to light and his father rejected it under no uncertain terms, his mother revealed her gift and stood by the boy. The father left home when this happened. We've talked with both parents, and I don't see any evidence pointing to either of them, but maybe the father was so ashamed he decided to off the boy."

Gambino pauses for a moment and shakes his head. "I just don't see a father who loved the boy for seventeen years, turning around and doing this kind of work on his own son."

Gambino points to a photo of the boy's back with the lash marks highlighted under a bright camera flash. It is a gory photo, not nearly as impactful as what I saw hours before, but I get his point.

"He doesn't seem like that type of man, and has no history of violence," Gambino continues. "But for now, that's all we have."

I offer, "Well, there might be something else going on."

I reach into my pack, take out a small glass vial, and place it on the table. "This charm will prevent others hearing what I'm about to say, and I need you to stop taking notes."

Gambino looks at it curiously. "What's in it? Sand?"

I laugh because it does look like sand. "It's filled with dried, ground worms as they are one of the few creatures that can't hear."

Gambino makes a noise, clearly expressing his distaste.

I defend myself. "It could be made of octopus or squid, but they are out of my price range. This is just as effective."

I can see by his face that he's unsettled but accepting, so I continue with my news. "After your forensics team left, I did another search with my sixth sense and found an amulet in the bushes. After some research, I learned it's an ancient piece with significant powers. I have it in an evidence bag stored safely for now. What's interesting is the piece of dark red thread caught in the clasp. Do you want us to keep it, or do you want to store it in the evidence locker?"

Gambino looks up. "That's very interesting. The preliminary report from the M.E. said a red thread was snagged in the boy's fingernail. I'd like to see it, so if you could bring it down, that would be excellent."

I nod. "You can start taking notes again."

When he lifts his pencil, I go on. "I went back to the Cock and Bull Tap to question the bartender about the man in the red cloak, and got the following description: in his forties or fifties, about six feet tall and thin with a long nose. He has a neatly trimmed, full beard and mustache. His facial hair is dark brown to black and slightly graying. Eyes are dark. Head hair could not be seen due to the cloak's hood. He was well dressed in trousers, a white dress shirt, and tie."

When I stop speaking, Gambino stops taking notes. That's what I like about Gambino. He's professional with good attention to detail.

"Does that description match anyone in the family?"

Gambino says, "It doesn't match the father, and no other men lived in the household."

I pause to think for a moment. "Do you know what the boy's gift was?"

Gambino leans back in his chair, stretching his legs out. "That was one of the strange things. Neither parent seemed to know. It makes sense from the father because he wanted nothing to do with the boy after finding out he was Gifted. But the boy's mother stuck up for him, and I would have thought she would know. All she said was the gift was kind of crazy and would interfere with other magic. That's all she knew for sure."

I try to give this information some context for Gambino. "Sometimes when a child has a gift, it takes a while for them to figure out how to work it. The gifts usually show themselves around puberty, so this boy may have been a late bloomer, gift-wise. I struggled to understand my gift. Since a child's gift is often nothing like their parents', even a Gifted parent can't guide their child in understanding their gift."

Gambino's eyes reveal a new understanding when I finish. Then he asks, "Do you have anything else?"

"Yes and no." I fiddle with my hands as I say this next part. "This morning I was disarmed and held briefly at knife point while a masked man asked me about the amulet."

At this Gambino stands up and curses. "Jesus, Mary, and Joseph!"

His protective streak resurfaces, and I wait patiently for him to sit down and reassume his mask of calm. When he does, I go on.

"I didn't see anything new or helpful beyond the description the bartender gave me, but the man could have fit that description. Obviously because he was masked I can't identify him. I was able to get away, but when I reached my gun and turned around, he was gone. He did his disappearing act again."

Gambino raps his fingers loudly on the desk. "The disappearing man," he muses. "Is there anything else I should know about?"

I give him a wry smile. "No, not at this time. I do want to talk to the parents myself though. Can you send their information over to my office?"

"Sure. Let me see you out, then."

I pick up my privacy charm, and Gambino escorts me back to the sallyport.

As I walk to my car, I notice Officer Schmidt and his cohort are standing by a patrol car talking. They're standing in profile and must see me, but make a point of ignoring me.

As I hop in my car, my chimerator pulls tight. I flip the lid and see

Jack's face reflected. I answer the call, "Hola."

Jack growls, "Blue, I told you I wanted daily reports. Are you alright?"

"I'm just leaving the precinct. I'm on my way over."

"Well, hurry up." Jack disconnects.

Cripes! He really needs to learn some manners.

I turn on the ignition, and with my arm stretched over the back of the passenger seat, I slowly back up. A crackling and popping noise followed by a slow hissing sound emits from my tires. Just my luck.

Heaving a huge sigh, I slide the transmission back into park and climb out of the car. Both rear tires are as flat as pancakes. I get down on my hands and knees to carefully feel around on the pavement under my back tires. Sure enough, I pull out a handful of sharp nails, all the same size and all shiny new as though fresh from the box. I shield my eyes with my hands and look into the sun toward the direction of Officer Schmidt and his accomplice. I can see they are laughing and taking sidelong glances at me.

I kick my tire in frustration and look up at them again only to see they are still laughing. I could go over there and accuse them, but they'll surely deny it. I could threaten to hex them. I wonder if they'd believe it. That would be funny but a bit childish. Unfortunately, I think my revenge will have to wait until an appropriate opportunity presents itself.

Leaning up against the side of the car, I flip the chimerator open and chime "Rubalia." Rubalia is our office assistant extraordinaire. The chimerator works its magic, and a few seconds later, she answers.

"Rubalia speaking."

"Rubalia, I'm at the precinct and I have two flat tires. Can you send a tow truck?"

Rubalia's reflection shows her glasses slipping down the bridge of her nose as she peers over them. "Two flat tires. That's quite a coincidence, and at the precinct too . . . "

"It's no coincidence, as you darn well know. Please tell Jack I've been held up and will be in as soon as I can."

Rubalia purses her lips and furrows her brow. "Of course. I'll get someone out to you right away."

Chapter 10

The Office

Bluebell Kildare

May 27, 2022, Red Ages

Two hours and too much money later, I'm on my way to the office again. As I navigate downtown, I pass yet another group of protestors wearing yellow robes outside the Mayor's office. I press my fingers to my forehead to ward off the headache they're about to give me. The Dilectus Deo, or Beloved of God, as it's translated, are a cult of Norms who believe that all Vampires and Gifted should be eliminated and that ungifted and unturned humans are the true children of God. I personally think the Dilectus Deo are more frightening than Dark Vampires. They appear to be peacefully protesting, but the signs they hold are anything but peaceful. One reads, "Kill the leeches." Another reads, "Aberrations should be put down," as though we are animals.

What really makes me mad is the mom out there with her daughter who can't be more than eight years old, shaking a sign that says, "Get the Aberrations out of my classroom." It appears they start the hate training early. The kids who are taught to hate early rarely have enough strength to break away from a family culture of hatred. The girl has little chance to develop an independent mind because she can see with what vehemence alternate thinking will be treated. I sigh deeply and keep driving.

When I arrive at work, I walk toward the Supernatural Investigation Bureau building. It rises up, a sleek glass and steel structure, three stories high. This is the central office for the entire Smoky Mountain region, though our unit concentrates on the City of Crimson Hollow. Crimson Hollow is the capital of the region and spreads out over the most scenic, mountainous areas of the Smokies surrounded by smaller outlying suburbs. It's divided by districts with each district covered by a different unit.

As I approach the building at a fast clip, I see my reflection in the shiny glass. Maud's saying that "good posture makes the woman" flits through my head when I notice that I'm walking with a straight back and my head held high. She would be happy to see that.

The air thickens and buzzes around me as I walk through the wards just beyond the entrance. The entire building is ensconced in highly specialized wards, and only those who work here can walk straight through.

When I exit the elevator on the third floor, I follow the arrowed sign that reads "Homicides." I am newly amused each time I read it, as it seems to invite me down the hall to be murdered.

As soon as I walk through our department door, the inviting reception area surrounds me with the comfort of home. I love this office and I'm proud to be a part of it. The room glows with the warmth of oak furniture and dark brown leather upholstery. Fresh flowers on the tables and cheerful paintings on the walls bring color to the room, while the sunlight filtering in through the floor-to-ceiling windows brings the whole setting to life.

I remember two years ago on my first day, the office seemed so professional and grown-up, and I felt like neither. I was sure that before long, my inadequacies would be revealed and Jack would send me packing. No one was more surprised than I when it turned out I was actually good at this job. It's probably because I truly believe in what we do.

The goal of the Supernatural Investigation Bureau is to maintain interbreed peace and security. Our unit is a small but vital part of the machinery that makes that possible. We use our skills and our strengths to keep the peace and ensure the balance between the Norms, the Gifted, and the Daylight Vampires. We do this by bringing Dark Vampires to the sun, and prosecuting the Gifted and Norms who commit homicide against each other for reasons relating to the Supernatural. The regular police are simply not equipped to deal with these crimes. Our strength and special powers give us advantages.

Reigning queen over the reception area stands Rubalia, but she is far more than a receptionist. She is a brilliant research assistant, an office manager, and, I sometimes think, a goddess. Rubalia has deep brown skin and black shoulder length hair styled in big waves with flippy ends tipped in gold. She wears ruby red cat eye glasses trimmed in marcasite as her crown. Her robes are elegantly fitted skirt suits, and her weapons are dangerously sharp stilettos.

The gold tips in her hair are her magical mark, but I'm unsure of what her gift is. Some gifts are very personal or simply frivolous, so it is considered rude to ask. I could check with my sixth sense, but that's rude as well. It would be equivalent to men comparing phallus sizes in polite society. I speculate her gift is to be creative, or to find information, or even to keep order. When my mind is being extremely wicked, I imagine our uptight reception commander is really Gifted in pleasures of the flesh and lives a secretly lurid lifestyle when she leaves the office. Go Rubalia! Sometimes imagination is more fun than reality. She would probably slice and dice me with her stilettos if she had the faintest inkling of my imagination. Some things are best kept to one's self.

Rubalia simply will not allow anyone to be disorderly in her space or in the processes relating to the office. She allows us to be messy in our own offices as is evidenced by our office mate Xavier Ramsey. But woe be unto us if we forget to pick up our messages or don't properly charm our papers blank when we're done with them. If we miss an appointment, Rubalia is not shy about giving us a dressing down that we will not soon forget. This is a professional office and "by God" she is going to make sure we behave like professionals.

I now know the real reason I succeeded at being a professional when I started was simply that Rubalia wouldn't allow me to be otherwise. One day I should thank her. That is, if she will allow me.

Right now Rubalia is speaking with Ernesto Ramos-Delgado who is asking for a map of this week's Dark Vampire sightings and incidents. Rubalia plots the sightings, and Ernesto uses the map to target his hunts. He's primarily responsible for eliminating Vampires who kill while feeding, thus turning from Daylight Vampires into Dark Vampires.

Not only does Ernesto keep tabs on Daylight Vampires in our vicinity, but he also watches out for Dark Vampires who matriculate in from other areas. He calls on Jack for backup in more extreme cases. Jack is very old, even by Vampire standards, and thus extremely strong. Ernesto is also relatively old, and he is a skilled fighter in martial arts and swordplay. Of course he can use a gun too, but guns are useless against Vampires. He does use a compound crossbow that shoots oak stakes as an effective means to eliminate Dark Vampires.

Essentially Ernesto is an executioner—or an exterminator, depending on your outlook. A Daylight Vampire must kill in bloodlust to turn into a Dark Vampire, so the very existence of a Dark Vampire is proclamation of guilt. Because of this, no trial is required, and they are free game to be killed. The only way a Dark Vampire can be killed is by an oak stake to the heart, Holy Water, exposure to the sun, or being thrown on holy ground. Even if you decapitate them, you had best throw Holy Water on them or hold them down until sun-up; otherwise their bodies continue crawling around searching for their heads. Finding their heads and placing them back on their necks will revive them, thus the name Night-Crawlers.

Since they are pure evil, the only thing that ends them is something purely holy. I am not sure why a wooden stake is purely holy. I must remember to ask Father O'Brennen.

When Ernesto finishes speaking to Rubalia, he lifts up his arm, waving it down again in a graceful flourish while bowing low to me. My face heats up in a blush. I've always wanted to respond to his bows with a curtsy of my own, but I don't know how. It would be utterly embarrassing anyway. Right now I clutch my cumbersome backpack as an excuse.

"Good afternoon, Señorita Blue," Ernesto says.

Ernesto must have been turned in his mid-fifties. He has light brown skin and short, dark hair with a sprinkling of gray. His elegant, swooping mustache is the perfect accent to his tall, lean form.

I smile at him and respond, "Good afternoon, Ernesto."

I feel Ernesto's eyes sweep over me, then keenly scan my neck for a moment. I breathe a sigh of relief when he chooses to ignore my injury, instead flashing an easy smile as he walks away.

I drag my pack up to the counter in front of Rubalia's desk and lean over it, hoping to keep the cut out of view. "Good afternoon, Rubalia. Are there any messages for me?"

Rubalia hands me a small stack and pins me with her eyes like I'm an errant teenager. "Good afternoon, Blue. Jack has been highly agitated because you didn't contact him today. Next time we would all appreciate a chime sooner. He's responsible for everyone in the office, you know."

I accept my comeuppance and apologize. "I'm sorry, Rubalia. It was a very busy day. I'll try to do better in the future."

Rubalia holds her mouth in a stern line and says, "Don't try. Do."

I nod with chagrin and walk straight back to Jack's office,

wondering what I'll see when I arrive. I start to knock, but before my knuckles touch the wood Jack calls me to come in.

Jack sits with his arms flat on the desk, leaning forward while tapping a pencil against the wood top. I had expected anger, but I see warmth in his gaze as he takes me in. Jack is a good boss. He's fair, and he gives good advice, but he lets each of us run our own investigations. He primarily acts as support and backup, but he does seem to pay extra attention to my work.

Realistically, I am physically the weakest of my comrades. My gender limits my physical strength. My gift isn't helpful in a physical confrontation. I'm a non-Vampire, and I'm relatively young, and inexperienced compared to everyone else.

Thankfully, Jack doesn't hold me back; he just keeps tighter tabs on me than he does my counterparts. Sometimes I wish it were because he had feelings for me, but there are too many practical reasons for his overprotection to conclude that.

Jack Tanner is a dichotomy of a man. He wears impeccably tailored suits and mixes with the upper echelon with charm and ease, yet when in his comfort zone his manners can be rough and quite abrupt. While his attitude is often cool and distant, his nature is protective and his actions show he's caring. He has incredible strength and speed and can be a warrior when needed. All in all, he's an excellent man to have on your side and would make for a fearsome enemy.

I stand in the middle of the room, simply because I prefer standing to sitting, but with Jack's gaze on me, I feel awkward. "I'm sorry I didn't get into the office until now. It's been a really busy day."

Jack's eyes look concerned, then I see his nostrils flare. He stands, and in the blink of an eye he's right next to me. I always find it disconcerting when he moves so fast, especially now because he's standing in my personal space. He slowly moves all around me, circling me like a jungle cat, assessing me, close but not touching.

When he comes around to the front of me again, he asks in a low, growling voice that rolls through me, making my abdomen clench with an ache, "What happened today? Your neck is injured and you're shaky."

Jack is so close I have to tilt my head back to see his eyes. It's challenging to stand this close to him and not reveal how he affects me.

"What do you mean I'm shaky?" I ask, ignoring the more obvious question. I try not to notice the strong line of his jaw close enough to my lips that I could lean in and trace it with my tongue. I try to ignore the deep, musky scent of his skin that makes me want to inhale deeply. I fail on both counts.

He reaches his hand out to my arm but pauses torturously a hairsbreadth from my skin. He drops his hand, instead saying, "Your aura is thicker today. Thicker and shaky."

My mind wars with the urge to touch him or step away removing temptation entirely, but instead I stand immobilized within easy reach.

"How do you know what my aura looks like?" I ask.

Jack shifts on his feet, lifts his hand toward me, and then drops it again. He mercifully returns to his desk, at human speed this time, sitting down. What would he have done if I had reached out for his hand and caressed it? Too late as the moment has passed.

Jack says, "I never told you? That's my gift. I can see auras."

"No. I didn't know you had a gift. I don't see a mark. In fact, I didn't know Vampires could even have gifts."

I move to sit in the chair across from him. I was a little unsteady just now, and it seems safer in the chair.

Jack frowns. "We were human once, just like you, Blue. Some of us are Gifted."

"Oh. I guess it was wrong of me not to consider that." He's piqued my curiosity now. "So, what does my aura look like?"

"Beau . . . " Jack cuts himself off. I swear he was about to say "beautiful."

He continues. "It is a white light with a faint tint of blue. The tint is the same tone as your eyes, blue with a touch of violet, only much lighter. Hardly blue at all. Usually it's only a hazy outline, but today the margins are much thicker. It comes out almost three inches, and it's wavering like a flame."

"Hmm. Well, it must be because I had a challenging day." I tilt my head and squint at Jack. "So, Jack. You must be an expert on auras, since you are one of the few people who see them."

Jack looks a little uncomfortable when I make this declaration, but he nods. "I do know more than most."

"Well, have you ever heard of someone having an aura strong enough to scare Dark Vampires away?"

Jack starts coughing very hard, and his color turns a little gray before he turns his head away. When the coughing subsides, he finally looks at me and asks, "Where did you hear this?"

I try to sound nonchalant. "Oh, Father O'Brennen and I were talking, and he mentioned hearing that happened once."

Jack is my boss, so I really don't want to get into the whole died at birth, chased Dark Vampires away by the age of three, and was rescued by a mysterious Daylight Vampire thing. It seems a little heavy. What I want is for him to think of me as a capable professional.

Jack seems to have recovered from his spontaneous coughing fit and says, "As a matter of fact, I think there was one case I recall, a long time ago. I prefer not to go into the details, though."

Then, in an obvious attempt to change the topic, he demands, "You're injured. You have been avoiding telling me about it. I need to know what happened."

I retort, "Like you are avoiding telling me about auras chasing Vampires away?"

Jack smiles smugly. "Yes. Exactly like that, except you work for me. Tell me what happened."

Jack leans back in his seat and his hair, which is full of dark gold curls, catches the sunlight from the window. He keeps it long enough so you can see the curls but not long enough for them to be ringlets. He has vivid green eyes and a disturbingly sexy five o'clock shadow. His broad shoulders look magnificent in his light gray suit. I'm not sure what make it is because I don't shop in those stores myself, but it is very elegant. His charcoal gray tie hangs loose, and his top shirt button is undone, both uncharacteristic of him. I wonder if my late timing made him that upset or if it was something else. His eyelids droop lazily as he leans back in his chair, looking the picture of ease, but I'm not fooled. He's watching me intently.

I take a deep breath, gathering the courage to tell him about the incident with the masked man. Since no out presents itself and I see no way to further delay, I fold my hands in my lap and say gently, "As I was leaving my apartment building today, a man grabbed me from behind in the alley, disarmed me, and held a knife to my throat."

Jack doesn't move a hair, but the air in the room immediately fills with a violent, thrumming energy. He, who is usually so hard to read, is pouring deathly rage into the room to such an extent it seems the very air is becoming pressurized to the point of explosion. Outwardly I see only his eyes tighten at the corners and turn into two black, bottomless pits. His mouth is fuller, a sign his fangs have extended, though he keeps his lips tightly sealed. His absolute stillness feels indubitably more dangerous than a thousand men attacking with knives. Others might not notice anything wrong if they walked in this room at this moment, but with my gift, I feel it. I'm almost overcome by it.

I lift my chin a degree and brave the threatening explosion. "The man was wearing a mask and had me from behind, so I can't give a good description. He was about six feet tall and thin, with an obvious beard beneath the mask. That matches the description from the bartender at the Cock and Bull Tap of the man wearing the red cloak. There was no red cloak today, though. He was wearing a gray cloak and dark pants with a white top. He was asking about the amulet, but I didn't tell him where it is."

Jack moves his hands slightly, gripping the edge of his desk. Despite seeing his knuckles turn white and hearing the wooden desk groan beneath his fingertips, I finish the tale.

I drop my voice to a whisper, knowing full well he can hear me clearly but hoping to calm him slightly as I recount the entirety of the events. When I finish, Jack's eyes are still black pools, but he has relaxed his hold on the desk. The intelligence has returned to his eyes, and they flicker as he internally calculates all the possibilities of what happened, what could have happened, and what might happen. I'm afraid of his conclusions, but even this is preferable to the mindless black rage I saw a few moments ago.

Jack finally leans forward and appears to regain his voice. Through clenched teeth he snarls, enunciating the key words, "You *took* an *injured wolf* that was about to *kill a man* . . . in your car *with you?*"

I've learned when Jack is snapping like steel to remain strong like silk.

"When you put it that way, it doesn't sound so great. But it was really fine. I went straight for my Glock, but I didn't need it." I decide not to tell Jack I couldn't make myself pull the trigger. He doesn't seem in the mood to hear it, and I'm not above omitting teeny tiny, irrelevant facts such as that.

"And where is this wolf now?" Jack inquires.

"He's with my friend Alexis getting cleaned up, cared for, and fed."

This seems to settle Jack down slightly, but still he probes, "And he showed no signs of aggression toward you or Alexis?"

"None whatsoever, nor toward her assistant. I'm sure his aggression was directed solely toward the man."

Jack settles back a bit more.

"So, as I was saying, I dropped the wolf off at Alexis' so this put me behind. Then I went to the Medical Examiner's office."

Jack nods his head and says, "We'll get back to the masked man in a moment. But tell me, what did you find out from the M.E.?"

I hand Jack a copy of the preliminary report. Jack sits quietly for a few minutes, scanning through it. He flips through the pages, and I watch his face as it goes through several degrees of disgust and rage—not quite the degree of rage I saw a few moments ago, but rage nonetheless. When he finally looks up, his mood is black.

"It was pretty bad," I say.

Jack's mouth presses in a tight line. "I see it was."

"I also stopped by the Dragomir Magical Artifact Shop and got a little history on the amulet."

Jack looks curious. "Did you speak with the Dragomir herself?"

I raise my eyebrow. "Yes. Do you know her?"

Jack's lips twitch slightly, and I can see immediately he does know her, perhaps personally. I feel more than a little angry about this and try to school my face from forming the scowl it wants to. I remind myself he's my boss, and even if he were interested in me, it would not be wise to pursue any type of relationship. He's goodness knows how old, so I must seem terribly immature to him. He probably has some stunning Vampiress I cannot possibly compete with keeping him company at home. This thought does not help with my scowling problem.

Jack says, "Yes. I've known her for some years. She's an expert on certain topics."

I scowl despite myself. I bet she's an expert on certain topics.

Jack gives me an assessing glance and asks, "How did your interview with her go?" I contemplate how much to tell him. I stand and pace a little as I speak, feeling restless for some reason. "She gave me a hard time at first, but when I showed her a drawing of the amulet she was very forthcoming. She told me the amulet is part of a key. There are two parts: the amulet and an eye that fits in the center. The eye is missing from the piece I have. Both together serve as the key to the *Grimorium Cantionum Spiritualium.*"

Jack sits up straight. *"The Spell Book of the Spirit and Soul?"*

I nod slightly, watching his reaction.

Jack demands, "And where do you have it stored?"

"I have it hidden in the wall of the bell room in St. Michael's Church. I thought it best to stash it on holy ground."

"That was a good choice," Jack says. "So, did Dragomira tell you the history of the book?"

"Yes. How did you know about it, though? It sounds like it was kept pretty secret."

Jack frowns and looks out the window, obviously considering what to tell me. "Years ago I did some research on the Birth of Vampires. That's how I met the Dragomir. I've never seen the book, of course; no one has. I've only read some of the history."

Something has been bothering me about the story, and I bet Jack knows the answer. "How come this story isn't well known? It was obviously pivotal in our history."

Jack stands up and appears to be concentrating on something outside the window before he angles toward me. "The book itself is too powerful for many to know of. But remember it took some time for the Vampire population to grow and cover the globe. It wasn't until about a third of the way through the Deconstruction Era of the Red Ages that knowledge of Vampires was widespread, and the incident with the book had long passed. People just knew that Vampires were. The further civilization deconstructed, the harder communication and learning became. Then, during the Bloody Era of the Red Ages, all humans were in hiding."

Jack walks close to me, standing in my body space again. His eyes implore me for something. "Even though I was turned during the Bloody Era of the Red Ages, I am not proud of who we were and what we did. I know most Daylight Vampires feel the same. We are ashamed of how we treated humans and how we looked away as Dark Vampires destroyed your breeds."

My mind reels. Jack has just dated himself to before the Reconstruction Era. That makes him over five hundred years old. Jack's eyes search my face, and I feel he's seeking some sort of absolution from me, a person who had not even been born at that time.

"Jack," I say, "you are only responsible for your own actions, and what you do today speaks to who you are now, not what your people did five hundred years ago. Civilization is a thin veil over our savage selves, easily lifted by some for personal glorification. Look at the Dilectus Deo if you want an example. We fight to hold on to our moral values and maintain civility between breeds. Regardless of what your people did in the past, Daylight Vampires did make the peace pact with humans that brought on the Reconstruction Era. Today you keep us safe from Night-Crawlers, and today, that is what matters."

I can see his eyes lighten, and he steps back, leaning against the wall of windows behind him. Then he looks sharply at me. "So someone's trying to get the book now. It is a dangerous book, Blue. It would be an interbreed disaster if it gets into the wrong hands. It could destroy the peace we've fought for during the last five hundred years."

"I know," I say. "I also learned a few more things today, but before I get into that, I want to show you this." I reach behind my back and pull out my knife.

Jack's eyes light up. He holds out his hand and asks, "May I?"

I give it to him hilt forward and watch him caress it with his thumb and eyes. "It's beautiful," he says.

"Dragomira gave it to me. I wasn't sure if I should take it. It's obviously very valuable. However, after the incident this morning, I couldn't say no."

Jack looks up at me with a question in his eyes, then he seems to answer it for himself. "You should keep it," Jack says. "Do you have a sheath for it?"

I shake my head.

Jack takes it to his closet and steps inside. I see some ammunition belts and swords hanging, but Jack's broad back blocks my view. He rummages around a little, then closes the door. Turning back to me, he places the knife in a beautifully embossed black leather sheath. He hands it to me. "A weapon this special should be housed properly."

I smile from ear to ear as I run my fingers over the exquisite craftsmanship.

Jack says, "Now, about the other things you learned. Please tell me everything." He's back to his feigned nonchalance again, crossing his legs gracefully as he leans against the window.

"After the M.E.'s, I went to the precinct. The boy was on the missing persons list for twenty-eight days. His name is Jason O'Connell. He had a magical gift, but it's unclear what it was as he'd just come into power. His mother is Gifted as well, and she hid it from her husband for their entire marriage. When the boy came out, the mother came out as well, and the father split. He is obviously a person of interest, but Gambino isn't feeling it."

"You plan on questioning them?"

"Yes. I'll do that first thing tomorrow. I should be in the office before noon. By the way, can I share openly with Gambino about the book?"

This must be an important question because Jack raps twice on the window behind him in his thoughtful way before answering. "I think we need to tell him a powerful and dangerous book is involved," he says, "but I don't think we need to give him details or the history. Furthermore, you shouldn't tell him where the amulet is. The fewer people who know, the better."

I nod at this and contemplate it awhile. Jack seems to understand my pause, because he says, "Don't worry, I'm not asking you to lie. It's sensitive information and we have a right—no, a responsibility—to keep it confidential. Tell him it falls under the category of privileged information." I nod again, this time feeling a lot more comfortable.

Then Jack asks, "So, what are your theories on the murder so far?"

I think for a moment. Many theories have run through my head, some more viable than others. "The boy was hit by the car at an angle. It seems to me if someone was purposely running him down it would most likely have been head-on, though not necessarily.

"It's possible the murderer is not the same person who had the amulet and tortured the boy. I doubt it was the father, because what would the father who hated magic be doing with an amulet? Could the boy have gotten the amulet on his own? I don't know. I think the amulet is the key to finding out what really happened. I'd like to know more about it."

Jack says with hooded eyes, "Tomorrow I'm going to the Glenwood Charity Gala. They have a silent auction of magical artifacts. Everyone who is anyone in the magical community will be there, including the most knowledgeable of collectors. Why don't you accompany me?"

"Isn't that Gala to support the Green Tree Orphanage?"

Jack nods imperceptibly, and I wonder if he knows I grew up at Green Tree.

"I don't know," I hedge, more than slightly embarrassed. "I'm not used to mixing with that crowd."

Jack smiles warmly. "You'll be fine. I'll guide you in anything you need to know. The invitation is exclusive, and the timing is kept confidential, so only share this information with those you trust. Dress in evening attire, and I'll pick you up at eight."

"Okay," I say, because it's an excellent opportunity to meet a collector and gather more information on the amulet. After all, it's never wise to collect all your information from one source.

Jack becomes serious as he gestures to his guest chair. "Now sit down. We need to discuss the masked man in detail. First of all, why did you leave through the alley entrance rather than the front door?"

I sigh. "Because the front door had a wet paint sign on it. I assume he put it there to direct me to where he lay in wait. I should have been alert, but I was in a rush. Inexcusable, I know."

Jack ignores my self-berating and says, "A murderer obviously knows where you live, so we must keep an eye on your place. We could have a man there to try to catch him. Is there somewhere else you can stay for a while?"

I give Jack the evil eye, which I hope speaks louder than words, but just in case I vehemently insist, "No way am I going to cower down at someone else's house. Nor are you putting a stranger in my place. If you want to have someone drive by, fine. But remember I can sense souls. The only reason I was surprised was because I was in a rush. I won't make that mistake again."

Jack looks dubious but says nothing further, so I excuse myself.

What does it say that the question most unsettling me as I leave is what in the world am I going to wear to the freaking Gala?

CHAPTER 11

BEGGING FOR REPRIEVE

JACK TANNER

MAY 27, 2022, RED AGES

When Blue leaves my office, I listen to her footsteps all the way down the hall. Holy shit! I can't believe Father O'Brennen told her what happened with her aura and the Night-Crawlers in the alley.

As soon as I hear her enter her office, I pick up the phone and dial. When a woman's voice answers I announce myself. "This is Jack Tanner. Is Father O'Brennen available?"

"Please hold. I'll check," says the voice. The phone goes silent, and I try to calm down because I don't really know what he told her. It seems like she would have said something different to me if she really knew.

I drill my fingers on my desktop until finally a calm, warm voice answers, "Father O'Brennen speaking."

"Father," I say, "this is Jack Tanner."

"Well hello, Jack. It's good to hear from you. It's been ages since we've seen you. Not since Blue reached her age of majority, I believe."

"Thank you, Father. I'll stop by next time I'm in the area. But today I'm calling for a specific reason."

"Sure, go right ahead."

"Blue was in my office today and asked if I'd ever seen someone with an aura strong enough to chase Dark Vampires away. I didn't know what you'd told her, so I didn't know how to answer."

"Yes," Father O'Brennen says. "Last night, Blue paid me a visit. She asserted that she was a mature adult and should no longer be protected like a child. She thought she had a right to know more about her family and her past, and frankly, I agree. I told her the story of how a Daylight Vampire found her the day her parents died, but I didn't say it was you."

I breathe a huge sigh of relief. "Father, I'd never ask you to lie.

However, if the question should arise and you can avoid telling her it was me, in a way that doesn't offend your sense of morality, I would greatly appreciate it. I'm not sure she's ready to hear that."

Father O'Brennen protests, "She does have a right to know you were the one who brought her to me. Nor am I sure I understand why she wouldn't want to hear it was you. The best I can do is promise not to broach the subject unless I see great need."

"Thank you, Father. I appreciate that. I just need a little more time."

"Jack," he says kindly, "I think you should come down to the church sometime. I'd love to catch up with you, and it sounds to me like you may need a little grounding."

I laugh softly. "Father O'Brennen, I need a lot of grounding. I may take you up on that offer soon. Thanks."

"You are welcome, Jack. I look forward to seeing you soon."

I hear the soft click of the phone and hang up my end. I press my forehead into my hands. Thank the Light she doesn't know yet. How am I going to explain this mess to her?

Chapter 12

Lessons on Wolves

Bluebell Kildare

May 27, 2022, Red Ages

I park my car down from Herbal Enchantments. As I walk toward the entrance, the hairs on the back of my neck prickle. I pivot to look behind me. Nothing seems out of place, and I don't feel any strong emotions, but the prickle is followed by a shiver down my spine. A man and a woman sit at an outside café a few buildings down enjoying their meals. An older woman sweeps her stoop on the opposite side of the road. The street looks quiet otherwise.

I see the air shimmering by the curb where I parked my car. Could the sun still be evaporating the rain from the street? My uneasiness increases, and goosebumps cover my arms. I keep my senses open and quickly close the distance to my destination.

The cheerful noise of the door chimes wipes away the last vestiges of fear. I notice Penelope's blond curls are further rebelling from her bun. She says brightly, "She's in back with the beast."

I chuckle and let myself in the kitchen. Alexis is ladling some minty-smelling potion into a large, green glass bottle while watching the news on a small under-counter TV. Varg runs up to me placing his forepaws down and his rump in the air. I bow to him in return. "Hello, Varg."

Alexis turns and smiles at me in greeting.

I smile back. "How was he?"

Alexis dips down into a partial squat to watch the potion line as it rises in her bottle. "He was perfect, but the customers were a bit frightened so I kept him back here. We just got back from a walk a few minutes ago."

"Well, he looks beautiful."

Alexis nods as she continues to ladle the potion into the bottle. "I gave him a bath as best I could with the hose in the alley. He's way too big for the sink, so I sprayed him down and used my soap to scrub his fur."

Alexis pulls the ladle out of the glass jar, apparently satisfied that it's properly filled. "I also brushed him as gently as I could, avoiding his cut, of course. He was getting matted."

I get down on my knees and give Varg a face rub. He sniffs at my face and in turn, I sniff the air around him. "He smells wonderful."

Alexis puts the ladle in the sink and pops a cork in the bottle. She gestures to the bottle she just filled. "This is the soap I used. It has tea tree oil and mint in it. It's charmed too, of course, but both of those repel pests naturally. I also gave him several potions to internally fight fleas and disease. He may be tired tonight as his body gets rid of the toxins."

Alexis pops a label on the bottle that reads "Dog Shampoo."

"He ate three full bowls of food throughout the day. I shaved around his wound and put a salve on it. It isn't too deep and should heal in no time. I think it is best to let it air dry."

I take a look at the underside of Varg's flank and see a shaved strip of about four inches, but there is no cut to be seen. "Um, Alexis. Where is the cut?"

Alexis looks over at me, frowning. "Right in the middle of the shaved area."

I shake my head. "No it's not."

Alexis squats down by Varg. She looks up at me with wide eyes. "The salve was charmed, but I'd have expected it to take a few days to heal. Maybe it works better on wolves than on dogs."

I'm dubious, but I let it go.

Alexis shrugs, then stands to grab a bag from a hook on the wall. She starts filling it with things and explaining their purposes. "This is the shampoo you should use to bathe him. It's gentle on the skin. Once a month should be sufficient. Any more than that will dry him out. This bottle is for getting rid of fleas. Give him two tablespoons a month. Pour it on his food, and it will taste like gravy to him. This is the salve for his cut. Obviously you don't need it anymore, but keep it in case he gets injured again. You should swab it on twice a day until the wound heals. He'll lick at it, which is normal. If the wound is more than a quarter inch deep or wide, he needs stitches. I'll drop the de-worming medicine off in a few days. I was out of a few ingredients."

"Do you really think he has worms?"

Alexis raises her eyebrows. "Does a tree have ants?"

"I'll take that as a yes. Thank you so much, Alexis." She's such a good friend.

"My pleasure," she replies. "Have you eaten? I have some leftover Chinese."

"Now that you mention it . . . "

Alexis laughs. She pulls the food out of a hot box. A hot box is a wooden box similar to an old time breadbox but charmed to keep food warm without spoiling it. It sort of keeps it in stasis. I select the remainder of the General Tso's chicken and hop on the island counter to eat with gusto. Varg lounges at my feet with a hopeful look on his face.

"So," I say, between bites, "did you know in the beginning times after Vampires were just born and there weren't that many, people went hundreds and hundreds of years not believing in them?"

Alexis says, "Yeah, we talked about that in my magical history course in school."

I sigh jealously. "You were so lucky to go to magic school. Do you ever wonder if any of the other myths have a basis in truth? Like fairies or trolls?"

Alexis thinks about it and says, "Actually, I've never thought about it as an adult. As a kid I always wanted fairy tales to be true. Just think about how for thousands of years we Gifted had to hide our identities. It is possible there are other beings in hiding."

"Do you think there might be wolves with special powers?"

Alexis looks at me, raising her eyebrows again, then looks down at Varg. She puts her hands on her hips and returns her gaze to me. "What did he do? Besides healing quickly, that is."

I study my box of chicken very closely, poking at the pieces that are stuck to the side. "Well, I can't be exactly sure, but he might have grown a tad bit and then shrunk again. It could be my imagination." I look up at her. "It was a really stressful situation. But I swear his withers came to the height of my waist before, and now he looks like a large dog."

Alexis smiles broadly. "Very interesting. So is there anything else interesting I should know about?"

"There might be."

Alexis puts her hands on her hips and demands, "Out with it."

"Okay, Jack asked me to go to the Glenwood Charity Gala with him tomorrow night."

Alexis turns her full attention to me now. "Jack? Your boss?"

"Yep," I say casually to tease her.

Alexis crosses her arms under her chest and commands, "Spill."

I smile because I love to get her worked up. "Actually, it's for work. I need to get more information on that magical artifact I'm researching, and he thinks there will be knowledgeable people at the Gala."

"He's right, but still," Alexis says brightly, "he did invite you. He could have gotten a name himself and given it to you afterwards. This means he doesn't already have a date, and he wants you with him. What are you going to wear?"

I give her my biggest blue-eyed look while clasping my hands together to beg her. "Do you have something I can borrow? I don't have time to go shopping, and you know I don't have anything because I never go anywhere."

Alexis cocks her head and thinks. "Actually, I do. I have the perfect dress. I'm a little bigger upstairs, but this dress is a halter so it won't matter." She looks at me closely. "I think our waists are about the same. It's a light blue dress with black piping. It will be stunning on you."

"Thank you, thank you, thank you!" I give her a warm embrace.

Alexis hugs me back. "You have to tell me all about it, though. That's the price I charge."

"I promise." Then I ask, "Alexis, if you had a totally hot boss who was very protective of you and generally a great guy, would you consider, you know, being with him?"

Alexis' eyebrows draw in as she ponders this seriously. "I don't know. Having a fling with a boss is a big no-no professionally. So if it were me I'd take it slow to see if there are real feelings on both sides first before I screw up my career." Then she adds with a sly wink, "But then again, that depends on how hot he is."

I laugh at that. He is pretty darn hot.

I gather my things to leave, and Alexis turns back to the news. She holds up her hand to halt me. "Hey, you better look at this."

She turns up the volume on the TV to the sound of the newscaster speaking. "Three bodies were found on the Upper North Side in the quiet neighborhood of Rowan Park."

A grisly scene flashes on the screen of a woman and two children, ripped to shreds and lying in a massive pool of blood. Their bodies are next to a building, and blood is splattered up the wall over twice the height of the news reporter on the scene. Some cardboard boxes next to the bodies are soaked in blood and strewn with what appears to be gory chunks of pulpy flesh. Large hunks of flesh are missing out of the bodies. The smallest body is almost unrecognizable as human. I can't believe they are showing this on the news.

"Residents in the neighborhood are staying inside after dark as this is the third night in a row bodies have been found. There is significant Dark Vampire activity in this area. The police say they are working closely with the Supernatural Homicide Investigation Unit and are doing everything they can to bring the perpetrators to sunlight."

"Cripes!" I say. "Jack didn't tell me we had a problem in this area. No wonder he was upset today."

I turn to Alexis. "Why don't you let me follow you home?"

Alexis' eyes are wide and fear drips off her. She nods. "Sure. I was just about to close up shop anyway."

CHAPTER 13

HOMECOMING

BLUEBELL KILDARE

MAY 27, 2022, RED AGES

I let Varg into my apartment and drop a huge bag of dog food on the floor in the kitchen. While he inspects the premises, I fill the water and food bowls. Looking skeptically at the kibble, I wonder if that's enough for a wolf. Probably not, but Alexis fed him so well today, it will do for now. I'll have to supplement his diet with real meat.

"Well, Varg, this is your new home."

My living room is small and consists of a sofa facing the sliding glass doors to the terrace and a small TV in the corner. Two tall bookshelves are filled to the brim with my used book collection. I grab my laptop from the coffee table to scan the news.

"Varg, Dark Vampire attacks have been increasing citywide. What do you think of that?"

Varg growls.

"Yeah, that's what I think too. It has to stop."

Varg agrees with me by walking over to the rag rug and curling down in its shag depths. He twists a few times and then gets up again. Suddenly, his body tenses and the hairs on the ridge of his back rise. With a pounce, he's growling at the sliding glass doors to the terrace, and it's a vicious, teeth-baring growl. He doesn't stop there, though. I know something is out there when he starts barking and snapping savagely at the glass doors.

"What's the matter, Varg?" I go to his side and peer out into the dark, but it's no use. I can't see anything out there. I shiver a little bit, and my heart starts to thud in my chest. Whatever is out there can surely see me just fine.

I pull away from the doors and turn off the lights. Then I peer through the glass doors again. Varg is still growling, but I can't see anything. Opening up my sixth sense, I feel through the wall for a soul. Something, something menacing, seems to be in the far back corner of the terrace. As my eyes adjust to the darkness, I see a faint movement in the shadows.

I pull my Glock out and throw open the door. Varg rushes past me toward the movement. Flipping the outside light on as I follow him, a quick glance tells me nothing seems to be in the corner. I turn in a slow circle, checking all around me and up at the roof, but still see nothing. I hear a faint creak by the corner where I'd seen the shadow, so I move to examine it more closely. A sick feeling curls in the pit of my gut when I realize my rocking chair is rocking slightly, seemingly of its own volition. I lick my finger and lift it up but feel only the slightest breeze. Varg is still in that corner sniffing and emitting low, unhappy sounds.

I thought I'd sensed someone briefly as we walked onto the terrace, but the sense of them was gone in a flash. Worrying my lip with my teeth, I think about the disappearing man. Well, whoever it was, they're gone now. Consideringly, I look down at Varg. If it was the disappearing man, he probably wasn't happy to see the wolf with me. Good.

"Varg, let's go inside."

Varg looks up at me as I hold the door open, and he reluctantly follows me in. I check the bolt and pull curtains across all the windows.

Unsure of what to do now, I pick a book from my shelf and curl up on the sofa again. Varg comes up to me and rubs his massive, furry head on my knee.

"You did a good job, Varg. Thank you for telling me something was out there."

Varg wags his tail and curls up by my feet. We relax like that for a while, but I can't get into my book as I think of all that has happened over the last couple of days.

My grandparents hated me, but my parents really loved me, so I guess I can live with that. I might not be named Bluebell because of my eyes, but rather because I was blue and dead at birth. I ended up alive, so I guess that's alright. Apparently my aura saved my life, but I sure wish it had saved my parents' lives. If only they hadn't covered me up. Honestly, though, I'm not sure I buy the story about me killing the Dark Vampire. Then some mysterious Daylight Vampire rescued me from the alley and brought me to Father O'Brennen.

I also noticed a few interesting things. I was able to feel Father O'Brennen's feelings briefly while in the church, which is not supposed to happen. Gifts shouldn't work on holy ground, so that is peculiar. I hope I'm the oddity and not the church, since the amulet is hidden there. The other thing I've noticed is with Jack. I can hardly feel his emotions. Occasionally I get a whiff, but not often. Today was an extreme exception. My gift doesn't seem to be playing by the rules.

Jack, now he's a puzzle. I wish I could get a read on him and his feelings about me. He's good to me and takes extra care with me. He lets me be independent while showing his concern. But is he attracted to me the way I'm attracted to him? Does he have feelings for me?

And how do I feel about him? He's tall and broad-shouldered with a rock solid powerful body. His eyes are a sensual, ever-changing kaleidoscope of green that I have to keep tearing my eyes away from so I don't get lost in them. How many times have I imagined twining my fingers through his golden curls? While most people would be afraid of him, I see his rage as simply the way he expresses his protectiveness. I don't believe he'd ever hurt me or anyone he considers a friend. He gets angry for us, not at us.

But I don't know anything about him. He's lived for hundreds of years, for cripes sake! Is his house decorated in modern décor, or does he like antiques? What are his political affiliations? What does he do for fun? Hah! I can't even see him having fun. What is fun for Jack? Somehow I think his fun is killing Dark Vampires.

Now how about Dragomira? What is she? With her voice and the little routine she did when the wards were disturbed, it's clear she isn't a Norm. She's not a Vampire, that much is also obvious. She must be Gifted. She owns the best magical artifact shop in town. But what about her voice? Would a Gifted person have a voice like that? Maybe her voice is her gift.

As if these aren't enough questions, I am trying to find a murderer. Plus, I've taken in a wolf who might have the magical ability to grow and shrink.

I glance over at Varg, who is lying with his head on his paws watching me. I jump up and grab the leash. "Varg, do you want to go for a walk?"

Varg looks like he understands me and stands up. He goes right to the door and waits patiently while I hook the leash on.

As we start traipsing down the block, I chuckle to myself. Because of his size I can't drag him an inch in any direction he doesn't choose to go. The leash is ridiculous since I know who is really walking whom. Luckily, Varg is well behaved and apparently likes walks, as he leads me quite well. I keep my Glock and my new knife on me and pay close attention to the neighborhood as we pass. Varg growls at shadows a few times, but I see nothing that poses a threat. After about a mile or so, Varg starts leading us back home.

When we get home, I shower and slip under the fluffy comforter on my bed. Varg jumps on the bed and looks at me with mournful eyes, begging to join me. He is so cute in a vicious, wolfy, fangy sort of way. But I don't want to sleep with a wolf. I put my hands around both sides of his head and give him a vigorous rub. His eyes close as he thoroughly enjoys the massage. Then I throw back the covers and grab another comforter from the closet. I fold it into a nice bed and place it on the floor next to me. Varg seems to understand this is his spot, and settles into it right away.

I slip under the covers again and soon drift off, thinking how nice it is to have Varg in the apartment. I've been alone for so long, and he makes me feel safe.

CHAPTER 14

The Hunt

JACK TANNER

MAY 27, 2022, RED AGES

After getting the latest report on the Rowan Park area murders, I flip open my chimerator and chime Ernesto. His face appears on my polished onyx stone. "Good evening, Jack."

"I just got the report on the murders. I'll meet you at the water tower in ten. We're hunting together tonight."

Snapping the chimerator lid closed, I gaze out of the windshield, trying to calm my rapidly increasing pulse. My fangs are already fully elongated. A rage fills me and quickly escalates to boiling point at the threat of the Dark Vampires daring to move into Blue's neighborhood. A deep, undeniable primal instinct to protect pervades me.

There is no question. They will be eliminated tonight.

Ernesto arrives just after I do, wearing a loose-fitting black linen pant set. During the day, he looks like a gentleman of leisure in his white linen suits, but at night he wears black and looks the picture of lethality.

We've hunted together so many times during the last hundred years we know each other's minds. Ernesto knows I have a special interest in protecting this vicinity. He's never indicated he understands why, but he's no fool.

I've already started climbing the water tower, and Ernesto follows closely behind. Pulling myself up the pole on the side of the ladder hand over hand, ignoring the rungs, I quickly attain the lookout position. Circling the tower, surveying the neighborhood with eagle sharp eyes and sniffing the air, I search for the smallest hint of Dark Vampire presence. My gaze is so precise I can see a mouse from miles away. The joy of the hunt is on me.

Ernesto does the same, moving in the opposite direction.

"Nothing," I say. We climb down and run to the schoolyard on Washington Street. At our fastest speeds, our movements appear as blurs to the human eye. I ascend the school building via the ridges in the bricks. My nostrils flare and I scan, watching, listening, scenting. We circle the building but are disappointed once again as only the smell of children lingers here. With silent leaps, we drop off the edge of the school to the playground beneath.

Ernesto and I know Dark Vampires hide close to humans. We know all the tall structures in each neighborhood, and have memorized our route. We meet at our third rendezvous point, St. Michael's Church. We scale the building silently, climbing the steeple. The smell of something foul, rotting blood and flesh, comes from the northeast. I indicate my discovery to Ernesto by a whisper so soft it's less than the fluttering wings of a gnat.

Ernesto nods almost imperceptibly. He moves closer to my position, and his nostrils flare as he catches the same scent. We scan the area but see nothing.

I descend the building to follow the scent and close in on my prey, my senses sharpening all the while. The world is a glitter of brilliant light to my eyes even in depths of the night. The disgusting aroma of rot assails my nostrils. From the scent I can tell that there are at least two Dark Vampires, and they turned at least three days ago.

I shift from shadow to shadow, tenaciously stalking them, interminably closing the distance. With a motion for Ernesto to take position and guard the escape route, I circle around them.

We are just five blocks from Blue's building.

I am aware of the slightest breezes and circumnavigate around them, keeping the Night-Crawlers upwind. This means I have to travel further from Blue's place. My fury fuels my blood to a hot rush, and my blood vessels strain against the confines of my skin, but I keep myself in rigid control.

I smell three now.

A dog barks, filling the night air with his unheeded warning. Still the Night-Crawlers move a block south, closer to Ernesto and closer to Blue.

I'm two blocks away from them now, coming from the north like an iron machine; I cover the distance in a second flat and stand still under a large oak. Scenting the air, I know I'm right on them now, and I smell human in their vicinity. I hear them stalking their prey just as I stalk mine, but their mindless evil knows little caution.

I whip around the corner of a three-flat building. A woman sits under a porch light on her balcony on the top floor, oblivious to the danger of the Dark Vampire climbing the deck post below her. A second Dark Vampire, female, hangs upside down from the beams that support the deck. Her long, greasy, blond hair that was surely beautiful just days ago hangs down in clumps, and saliva drips from her desperate mouth as she relishes her future meal. The third Dark Vampire's position is unknown.

I quickly scale the post behind the first male. He sees me and jumps to the second story balcony. His eyes glow red, and his fangs further extend as he hisses, frustrated at being deterred from his quarry.

The woman screams, and I hear the opening and closing of a sliding glass door. It's little protection from the terror awaiting her outside.

I pay no attention to my prey's warning, and with lightning speed, circle him, reaching for a stake in my ammunition belt at the same time. He twists to the side, trying to escape, but I grab his shoulder with my left arm in an unrelenting grip. Bringing my right arm down in an arc, I impale his heart through the muscle and bone of his back.

As my first prey falls to the deck floor in a shower of ash, I turn to the second without pause. Instead of fleeing, she's leaping over the balcony toward the woman's sliding glass door. Her savage mind has apparently obscured her ability to recognize the threat of imminent death. Her foot dangles for a diminutive space of time as she goes over the balcony, intent on her victim.

I reach up to grasp the bottom beam of the balcony and leap for the top railing with my other hand. Glass crashes. It must be the door to the apartment. With a push of my arm, I propel myself over the balcony. Kicking off the railing, I leap onto my prey as she moves through the entrance. I straddle her back, crushing her against the shards of glass still attached to the door frame. The woman's scream carries from the back of the apartment. With my hands wrapped around my prey's head, I twist until the satisfying crunch of fragmenting bones rewards me. With one more swivel and wrench, muscle, sinew, and flesh shred, until her head separates from her body.

I stand above her with my foot on her back as her body continues to writhe. With a flick of my wrist, her head flies backwards over the balcony. Then in one continuous movement I bring my arm back, grab another stake, and bring it down between her shoulder blades, through her heart.

The smell of the woman's fear wafting from the depths of the apartment commingles with the scent of burning flesh from where the stake entered the malevolent being. The body of the Dark Vampiress disintegrates into another pile of ash, and only a remnant of scent hangs in the air marking her previous existence.

When I stand and scan my surroundings for the third Dark Vampire, I sense him too late. He jumps from the roof onto my back, and we both sail over the balcony. I land on my feet, with evil still attached to my back and clawing at my neck. His nails puncture my neck, and his putrid scent fills my nostrils. With a mighty push of my thighs, I leap fifteen feet in the air as my enemy rips a hole in the side of my throat. The pain is incredible, but of little consequence in the moment. With a twist backwards in midair, I position my prey so he is crushed beneath me as we land, then I immediately rock my body forward. The impact loosens his grip, but he maintains his clasp on my neck. This Dark Vampire is strong, but not strong enough.

I wedge my hand under one of his and using both hands, I snap his left wrist, making it useless for the moment. At the same time, I hear a whirring of wind behind me as a blade slices through air, then flesh. I roll forward, and the Dark Vampire's remaining hand loosens as his head rolls off his neck and onto the grass below. I jump up and turn in one movement. Ernesto is calmly wiping his blade on the grass.

With a swift kick to the head, I send it far from the body, which is still squirming and grasping uselessly where it lies. I rip the bottom of my shirt and tie a hasty tourniquet around my neck, though the wound is already healing. Turning to Ernesto, I smile. "Mi amigo, thank you for watching my back."

Ernesto smiles in return as he reaches over his shoulder, sliding his sword into his scabbard. "No hay problema. That one was like a leech, stuck to you, trying to suck your blood."

I chuckle, then restlessly look up to the night sky. The moon is obscured by a cloud, and the stars shine brilliantly. "Do you have holy water on you?"

"Sí, señor, claro. You have places to go?"

My rage toward the Dark Vampires and my fear for Blue have subsided into a restlessness I know will not ease until I check on her.

With a sigh I turn to Ernesto. "The woman will need to be calmed down, and the body needs to be eliminated. Can you stay to finish this up?"

Ernesto smiles gently. "Of course. Go do what you must."

I pat Ernesto's shoulder in thanks. Thanks for his help, his understanding, and his silence. Then I give into my burning urge and run toward Blue's apartment. As I leave, the sizzle of holy water meeting Dark Vampire flesh and a soft poof fill the air, telling me the body has disintegrated into the final pile of ash.

In no time, I arrive at Blue's apartment and do a patrol around the building. The man I've placed to watch her apartment sits quietly in his car across the street. I scale the stonework on my way down from inspecting the roof. As I hang from the small ridges in the stonework, the wolf smells me, and I smell him through the wall. He growls warning at the scent of a fellow predator. I chuckle softly. Perhaps this wolf will be useful after all.

I catch Blue's even, slow breathing from her bed and place my hand on the wall between us, yearning for what I cannot have. At least I'm satisfied her slumber is undisturbed. I climb down and head for home and the lonely meal of bagged blood that will sustain me.

CHAPTER 15

A NONE TOO GENTLE

REMINDER

BLUEBELL KILDARE

MAY 28, 2022, RED AGES

I am awoken by my phone's blaring *ringggg, ringggg!* I extend my arm and thump along the nightstand, searching blindly for the blasted thing. After encountering what feels like my keys, a glass of water, and a candle, I admit the necessity of opening at least one eye. Squinting, I flip the phone open and mumble, "Hola."

"Blue?" Gambino says.

"What do you want?" I ask, not even attempting to hide my irritation about the early morning call.

"Someone broke into the evidence locker, but the only evidence box opened was the one for our case."

This not only requires both eyes to be open but also that I remove myself from my inclined position. Irked at the need, I sit up.

Gambino continues, "What's strange is nothing was taken."

"They want the amulet," We both know it, but it must be said.

"Do you still have it?"

I weigh my answer and settle on, "Yes. It's well hidden."

"Good. Now listen, there was no sign of forced entry."

"Hmm." My interest is piqued. "Did you catch anything on camera?"

My mind starts spinning through the magical capabilities that would allow someone to steal something in a protected room without breaking and entering. There are a number. Someone could locate the object and dematerialize it. But nothing was missing. The guard could be hypnotized so they could enter. They could break in with skill, stopping the cameras like my coworker Xavier Ramsey does. Or someone could portal in and portal out. That would fit with the rapid disappearance of the man under the truck and in my alley.

"Negative. The cameras are located on the outside entrance of the room. No one came in that way," says Gambino, "and the exterior walls are well warded. We don't know what this is. It could be an inside job or someone working magic. Given the situation, if you're sure your hiding place is safe, it's probably best for you to hold on to it."

"Wait, Gambino. How did you know someone had broken in?"

Gambino's gruff voice answers, "The heat sensors inside set off an alarm. We know someone was there, we just don't know how they got in or out."

"Well, at least we know it wasn't a ghost. I'll ask Jack to file the paperwork to keep the evidence in our possession." I breathe a sigh of relief because I couldn't give him the amulet anyway, given its capabilities. Feeling accomplished at avoiding that discussion, I move on to the next topic of the day.

"By the way, I'm going to question the O'Connells this morning."

Gambino says, "Let me know if you find anything interesting, and I'll let you know if we get anything on the vehicle. Sorry to wake you so early."

"No problem," I lie. "Thanks for calling," I lie again.

I flip the phone closed and slide back down under the covers, rolling over in their cozy warmth. Then I feel a weight dip the mattress down toward the floor. I roll back over and glare at Varg, who's looking at me hopefully.

"Okay, okay," I say. "I'll take you out."

Reluctantly, I swing my legs over the edge of the bed to start my day.

At seven o'clock sharp, I pull up to a curb in the neighborhood of Talon's Grasp in front of Jason's father's residence. Squinting through the morning sun, I see a mundane, brick row house that looks about right for a middle-aged, middle-income man who still supports a family in another house. I imagine he's no longer required to pay child support, but Jason was almost eighteen, so that's probably irrelevant.

I close the door on Varg, who looks at me unhappily through the window. The cool mountain air still hugs the earth from the night before, so he won't overheat in the small space of time I'll be away. As I walk up to Ian O'Connell's townhome, I prime my sixth sense to get a candid look at his feelings.

A man quickly answers the door wearing a pair of tan tweed pants, loafers, and a light sweater. His face is unshaven, and his dark, thick hair is rumpled. Bloodshot eyes framed in dark circles stare back at me. I glance inside, but it's difficult to see beyond the wide shoulders blocking my way. I deduce this is Mr. O'Connell because I feel huge gray waves of grief flowing from the man.

"Mr. O'Connell?" I ask.

"Can I help you?"

I show him my ID. "I'm Inspector Kildare with the Supernatural Homicide Investigation Unit. I know you've already answered questions from the Crimson Hollow Detectives, but do you mind if I ask you some questions as well?"

Mr. O'Connell glances at my ID and twists his lips in a bitter parody of a smile. "Yes, it's ironic how you police people are all so interested in my boy now that he's dead." His voice is heavy with anger and pain.

He waves me into a living room just beyond the entryway and says in a resigned voice, "Come on in. I'll tell you what I can."

I step over the tile entry and into the sad living room. It's furnished bare bones with a blue plaid sofa that's seen some wear and a cheap glass coffee table. A small, outdated television sits in the corner on a spindle leg bookcase. It looks like he did his shopping at a resale store, which is not unexpected given his situation. Aside from the eclectic décor, the place is comfortably lived in but not overly messy.

We sit at opposite ends of the sofa, and I dive right in so he doesn't have a chance to prepare himself. Making sure my face and my voice are laced with all the empathy I'd feel toward an innocent man, which he may be, I slowly and softly say, "Mr. O'Connell, first of all, let me tell you how very sorry I am for the tragic circumstances under which you lost your son."

I see tears spring to Mr. O'Connell's eyes before he turns his face to swipe them away. The emotions I feel from him are coming in robust waves. The strongest feeling is of huge loss and deep grief. Tinges of anger, guilt, and fear lace through the grief, and my job is to figure out why.

Mr. O'Connell says, "Thank you, Inspector. You can call me Ian."

I look at him gently and ask, "Ian, do you know anything about where your son was on April 28?"

By the way Ian is looking down at the carpet and furrowing his brow, I see he struggles with how to answer this. Guilt floats in the air around him in accord with his averted eyes. "I'm sure you heard I'm separated from my wife."

I say, "Yes, I'd heard that," keeping my voice free from judgment. I hope he is about to reveal the reason for his guilt.

He continues quietly with a faraway look in his sad eyes. "Because I moved out, I wasn't up to date with what Jason was doing on a day-to-day basis. I was out of touch. The detectives confirmed he was at school that day, but he just didn't come home. They thought he'd run away, but Sandy and me, we didn't believe it. I can't say more than that." His voice falls off at the end of his answer, and he takes a deep breath.

I wonder if the source of his guilt is that he'd been out of touch with his son. It could be. In his eyes, he may have failed Jason in his hour of need.

"Can you tell me what he usually did? Who his friends were? Where he usually hung out?"

Ian sighs and turns his gaze on the blank TV with another blast of guilt permeating the air. The corners of his mouth turn down in a frown. "Jason was a serious boy. He kept to himself most of the time. Maybe it was because of the magic stuff." When Ian says the last, I feel a spike of fear coming from him.

He continues. "He had a hard time making friends. The only person he really hung out with was a boy named Tim Pulgowski. They would hang out after school. I don't know where they went. My wife always kept up with that stuff."

"Do you know Tim's address?"

Ian looks at me directly now and says, "Sandy will have it. Have you talked to her yet?" Suspicion is coming from him now. He's fishing to see if he's the only one being questioned.

"I will be speaking with her next."

Ian nods, and his shoulders relax a little.

"Ian," I say, "I know this has been very hard on you, but I need to ask. What brought on your separation from your wife?"

The force of guilt is now so overwhelming I feel it inside of me and have a desire to confess and beg forgiveness. However, I also feel righteous indignation that I imagine keeps him immobilized. His face becomes stiff as he tries to hide it, answering in a scratchy voice. "You know, my wife is an Aberrant. She kept it hidden from me for almost twenty years. When I found out that Jason had it too—" He says this like it's a disease. "—and my wife had been lying to me all those years, I just couldn't deal with it."

Sadness weaves heavily with guilt now as he looks down at his hands. "I know a lot of people are prejudiced against Aberrants, and I guess I'm one of them."

That was a confession of guilt. My respect for Ian, previously practically nonexistent, goes up a notch. It takes strength to recognize your weaknesses. It's the first step toward mending them.

Then a roll of violent rage rises up, and he looks directly at me as he points his finger, punctuating every word. "You find the bastard who did this. Whoever did it is a monster. I don't care if it was prejudice or not— no one should hurt a boy like that."

Then tears start streaming out of his eyes, and I feel only loss and grief. "Not my boy. Jason was a good boy. It wasn't his fault he was an Aberrant."

Ian turns his head and tries to hold back his sobs in a manly way. It's astounding how quickly his rage melts under his profound grief. He covers his mouth, and the sounds come out in short, heartrending bursts. He tightens his neck and face, trying to stop it, but it refuses to be caged. His grief is real and inconsolable.

I came here feeling so angry at him for his prejudice toward his wife and his son. But now, I feel only pity. Still, I can't leave without addressing his prejudice. I should ignore it. It isn't my job. But the idiocy of it burns me up, and this man is the perfect example of how much harm prejudice does. It destroyed his family as it destroyed mine.

So despite my better judgment, I put my hand on Ian's shoulder, which is still shaking from his sobs. I speak softly. "Ian, I know you are mad at your wife for hiding that she was Gifted for almost twenty years. I get that; anyone would. But remember she loved a man for twenty years even though she knew he would hate her if he found out she had a gift she couldn't help having. She may have hidden it so she could stay with you. If that is the case, she must have loved you very much. You may not realize it, but a gift is a wonderful thing. Even so, she suppressed it to be with you. It sounds like the only thing that caused her to risk her relationship with you was her need to support your son through his transition."

Ian lifts his head from his hands and looks at me with wide eyes. I see a small flicker of understanding before he turns his face into his hands again and starts sobbing anew, unabashedly this time.

With that I stand, "Thank you, Ian. You've been very helpful."

I quietly let myself out while Ian continues to weep on the sofa and waves of grief, sorrow, and regret curl around me, accompanying me through the doorway as if trying to escape.

CHAPTER 16

VAPOR

BLUEBELL KILDARE

MAY 28, 2022, RED AGES

 walk out of Ian's house, and Varg is inexplicably waiting for me on the stoop.

"Varg, did I leave a door open?"

I walk to the car and check. Nope, no open door. I look up and down the street, and the only person I see about is an older lady with gray hair tied up in a bun, dressed in a beige, ankle-length skirt and a pretty floral blouse. She's sitting on her front patio two townhouses down, enjoying a beverage. She looks approachable enough, so I walk up to her.

"Hi, Ma'am, I'm sorry to bother you, but did you happen to see anyone near my car?"

She replies in a snippy voice. "No. I didn't, as a matter of fact. I only saw that wolf of yours. I was scared out of my mind. It almost gave me a heart attack when he suddenly appeared from the other side of the car."

I frown at this. "Oh, I'm so sorry he scared you, Ma'am. I left him in the car and was wondering if someone let him out. I wouldn't have left him wandering. How long were you out here?"

She says in a slightly appeased tone, "Since you got here and well before that."

"And you would have noticed if someone walked up to the car?"

Now she snaps some very intelligent brown eyes at me, "I'm old, not blind, Missy. Of course I'd have noticed."

I smile at this. "Of course. I meant perhaps you had your head turned."

"Humph."

I smile wider. "Thank you so much, Ma'am. I really appreciate it."

Goodness, I love older people. When you get to a certain age, you can say exactly what's on your mind. How nice that must be.

Varg and I walk toward my car, I cock my head and peer at him keenly. "Varg, did you open the door by yourself?"

Varg does his little happy dance, which looks completely undignified on his predatory form. Then he jumps away with a yip and does it again. Well, if he's guilty, he's certainly not contrite.

As we settle in the car, I contemplate my route from Ian's house to his estranged wife Sandy's. Her house is located in the neighborhood of Whispering Falls, a solid, middle class neighborhood with excellent schools and low crime. Talon's Grasp, where I am now, is a lower middle class neighborhood, a little rough around the edges, with a lot of character. The fastest route between the two is to go through Shroud Valley.

Shroud Valley is another story entirely. Officially, because it is east of Crimson Hollow city boundaries, it's policed by the Misty Rivers unit. Unofficially, it's policed by no one.

Three large rivers, the Great Oak, the Weeping Ash, and the White Thorn Rivers, pour through the Misty Rivers mountainside, giving the suburb its name. The three misty rivers flow into Shroud Valley, pooling deep in its center where the mist condenses into a deep fog that billows out over the valley. An odd crosscurrent blowing between the peaks of the surrounding mountains keeps the fog from rising completely even on the hottest days.

Today is not the hottest day, but my schedule is full, and I'm not above jaywalking through another unit's territory when expedience requires.

A few miles down the highway, I take a right onto Widow's Pass and promptly hug the center line. It's the main thoroughfare around the lake, traversing the rivers in a series of covered wooden bridges. The road is narrow with steep grades and winding curves that are impossible to see around, making it easy to guess the origin of its name. A few miles from the first bridge over White Thorn River, a gentle mist covers the landscape, hanging in the crevices of the mountainside and drifting over the trees. As I drive on, the mist thickens until a full fog envelops the car in a white netherworld. I keep my headlights low reducing my speed to accommodate the limited visibility.

I see the two main portal posts of the first covered bridge come at me quickly, and the rough wooden floor of the bridge replaces the smooth asphalt road. My world of white is transformed into a world of darkness.

I hold my hands like steel bands on the steering wheel to prevent the unevenness of the wood planks from taking the wheels in an undesired direction. The river is below me, but it's a great distance beneath and would be no comfort in the event of a fall. I drive steadily toward the center of white in front of me, grateful as it expands larger and larger, until all at once I am thrust back into the white abyss again. Something about being on this side of the bridge always gives me an eerie feeling.

I flip the defogger switch to clear my view and soldier on. The road dips down a steep grade bringing me deep into the heart of Shroud Valley. Ghosts of houses line the mountain edge, but fog clings densely to the land making their individual forms indistinguishable. I know the homes are painted in vivid hues, but the whitewash covering them turns their merry countenances into nothing more than pastel smears.

As I reach the bottom of the valley, the road levels and straightens out a bit, giving me a chance to relax. The fog is even thicker here, and my defoggers aren't working well, so I resort to blasting the heat. Still the fog condenses, and my only remaining option is to unroll the windows. I do and am greatly relieved to see the white patches on the windshield diminish.

As the window clears, I see the fast approaching portal posts for the second bridge spanning Weeping Ash River. This time I'm prepared, and while my hands are still gripping the steering wheel with white knuckles, inside I'm much more at ease. I see glimpses of white through the gaps in the planks that cover the bridge as I travel through. My car makes the familiar thumping sound on the wooden boards, and I feel a sense of accomplishment as I approach the exit, knowing I've survived yet another of Shroud's dreaded bridges. I glance at my clock and notice I'm running later than expected.

Just as I lift my eyes to the road again and breach the tunnel exit, I see a pair of headlights aimed straight at me. Holy Mother! I jerk the steering wheel quickly to the right in a desperate attempt to avoid the car. My fear of collision is immediately replaced by terror at the thought of going off the edge of the mountain. I straighten the wheel as the car zooms right past with the curve of the road. My car angles down off the road and rides at a tilt on the soft shoulder. I apply my brakes to safely slow the car down.

Thank goodness I survived that. With my white knuckles gripping the wheel, I decide the angle of the shoulder isn't unmasterable, so I continue, looking left to merge back onto the road. Just then I hear a piercing scream and terrified wail coming from an area of homes on the right. What in the world?

Varg growls from the backseat, and I bring the car to a gentle stop on the shoulder. I slip out the driver's side, and Varg jumps over the seat to exit with me. His hackles are raised as he races toward the noise without encouragement. I take off after him, knowing full well he's a much better tracker than I. Tracking becomes unnecessary as the screams continue guiding our way.

I jog up a side road and through a small copse of trees, trying to keep Varg in sight. As I exit the shelter of the trees and reach the edge of a clearing, I see a woman screaming, clutching a small, wailing baby in her arms. Something on the ground near the woman writhes around, and my heart stutters in fear.

Varg arrives on the scene in advance of me and positions himself next to the screaming woman. I reach into the small slit of my leather belt and pull out a clear glass vial. Then I approach quickly, knowing there isn't much time.

Fifty feet away, I clearly see the woman holds a long wooden stick— oak, I hope. She wields it toward the slithering mess before her.

Varg growls and snaps furiously as he seeks to herd it away from the woman. At twenty paces away, I see what I had expected: a debilitated Night-Crawler thrashing his prostrate body in an attempt to squirm forward. I quickly glance up, and though it's mid-morning, the fog is so thick here no direct sunlight touches the land. The woman clutches a diaper-clad infant, trying to spear the pathetic remnants of the ruined Night-Crawler.

Once a Day-Walker has killed in bloodlust, the crazed, soulless remains have a limited survival time depending on their original strength. Some last for decades while others last only days. If they are not eliminated, their own irrationality will eventually do them in as their crazed minds increasingly lose grip of reality. In their demented ways, they do reckless things like running in front of cars or crawling about midday in the fog. Though the sunlight isn't direct, even the diffused power of sun reflecting off the billions of droplets forming the fog is enough to slowly eat away at their flesh.

This creature's mouth is hanging open, and his eyes are bulging out as he's slowly devoured by sunlight. His skin is melting and sloughing off in places, and dark patches of burns and gaping holes litter his naked form. His mostly bald head is covered in blisters with just a few strands of long, stringy hair hanging on. The flesh is completely gone from the bottoms of his feet, and only the gleaming bones help him propel his body. Still, with his insatiable bloodlust, he continues creeping forward toward his prey.

The woman's back is against a tree, and behind her ascends a steep wall of mountain too difficult to climb with a baby in hand. She could dart to either side and probably outrun the rotten lump of melting flesh advancing through the mud toward her, but one look at her eyes tells me she's incapable of coherent thought. If her eyes didn't tell me, then the feeling of stark terror flowing from her in abundance and the piteous, continual screams emerging from her throat certainly would.

I ready my vial of holy water, unstopping the cork and stepping up to the creature. Varg's hair is raised from his forehead to the tip of his tail as he snarls savagely at the Night-Crawler.

As soon as I become the closest source of warm blood in the crawler's vicinity, he snaps his red, glowing eyes on me and pivots on his belly in my direction.

Exactly what I'd hoped and dreaded.

I shout, "Come on, you slithering sack of putrid flesh. Come and get it."

He follows my voice and starts slithering toward me. I hope I'm the only one who knows I'm using false bravado because even in the throes of death, his grip, once on me, would be unbreakable.

I slowly back up, bringing him further from the terrorized woman. Her screams have turned to soft whimpers now, and hoping she has regained some rationality, I call out to her. "When I say 'run,' I want you to run toward the house as fast as you can."

She looks up at me with seemingly blank eyes, but I see a slight nod of her head.

"Hold on to the baby tight," I shout.

Holy smokes! All I need is for her to drop the baby. The horrible image of the bloodsucker ripping apart the baby sears my mind.

I have my finger over the opening in the vial now, careful not to let the precious liquid spill onto the grass. I take a few more steps back, and the putrid remnants of the Vampire follow me.

I look up at the woman and see she is watching intently. Good.

"Run!" I yell.

The woman lifts up her skirt with one hand, clutches the baby tight with the other, and runs toward the house.

The Night-Crawler snaps his head toward her, his attention snared by her sudden movement. He gives a sickening hiss, and lifting himself up on his elbows and knees rapidly moves in her direction.

Cripes! I run toward him, determined to reach him before he gets her. Varg moves around him in a circle, snapping his fierce jaws and heading him off. The Night-Crawler hisses his rage at Varg, saliva dripping down his own fangs, then whips his body back in my direction.

His sudden turn brings me immediately within his grasp. He sticks his slimy, rotting hands around my left leg, jerking me forward toward his gaping maw. In the same moment that my brain shrieks with disgust, I realize his grasp has unbalanced me and I'm falling backward. I know full well that reaching the ground at his level, regardless of how close his eventual demise is, will result in certain death for me.

I uncover the vial and throw the holy water in his direction mid-fall.

My backside lands roughly on the hard, wet ground, I see Varg fly through the air at the Night-Crawler and land on nothing but a puff of vapor rising up from where he had lain. A small scattering of ash lies at my feet. I push myself up and gather a handful of grass to wipe the muck from the Night-Crawler's scummy hands off my boot.

"Disgusting!"

Varg sniffs around the pile of ash, and looking satisfied, he comes to my side, sticking his head beneath my hand.

"Good job, Varg," I say. "If you hadn't cut him off he might have reached the woman."

Looking up, I see her stumbling on her front steps, desperately trying to get inside. I resolutely walk toward her, knowing she's in no state to be taking care of a baby right now.

She's fumbling ineffectively with her door handle.

"Miss," I say to get her attention.

She looks around wildly at me.

"He's gone. I eliminated him with holy water."

She glances back over the yard, and the gleam of terror in her eyes lessens but doesn't disappear.

"Miss—" I join her on the porch. "—what is your name?"

She looks at me with the veiled eyes of a sleepwalker, and I know she's in shock.

I repeat myself softly. "Miss, what is your name?"

She answers in a raw, unsteady voice. "Maggie."

I smile at her and say, "Maggie, do you have family around here?"

Maggie only nods dumbly.

I look at her kindly and say, "Maggie, the Night-Crawler is gone. You did a great job saving your baby. Was the stick you were holding made of oak?"

Maggie's eyes get a little clearer as she nods at that.

"That was great thinking. But you've had quite a shock, and I think it would be best if you had family come stay with you. My name is Blue, and I'm with the Supernatural Investigation Bureau. If you give me someone's number, I can call them for you. Would you like me to do that?"

Maggie nods again.

"I'm reaching for my phone now, and I'm going to open it up." I slowly reach for it, careful not to startle her, and flip it open.

"Who would you like me to call? A sister? A mom? Or a husband?"

She softly whispers, "My mom."

I nod and smile at her. "I think that's a great idea. What's her number, Maggie?"

Maggie struggles for a moment to sort out her confused mind, then slowly gives me a number.

I dial it up and a woman's voice answers, "Hello?"

"Hi, I'm with your daughter Maggie right now. My name is Inspector Kildare, and I'm with the Supernatural Investigation Bureau. I want you to know that your daughter is physically fine, but she had a shock due to a run-in with a Night-Crawler."

I hear a low gasp on the other end of the line, and the woman says, "And little Jonas?"

"The baby is fine too, but I think Maggie could use your help here today. Like I said, she's had a shock and isn't herself."

I glance up at Maggie and see tears in her eyes as she listens to me, but she doesn't protest. She knows she's in no shape to take care of her baby. She gently kisses his head and rubs his back as he whimpers softly in her arms.

The woman says, "Thank you, Inspector. I'll be right there."

I turn to Maggie. "Maggie, do you want me to come in and get you a cup of tea?"

Maggie's eyes latch onto mine, and she says in a desperate whisper, "Yes. Please don't leave me alone."

I smile gently. "I promise I won't leave until your mom arrives."

I turn to Varg. "Please guard the house." He steps off the porch and loops around it. It's remarkable how he always seems to understand exactly what I say.

I reach around Maggie's shaking frame and twist the doorknob open, pulling her inside with me. The door opens to a small living room with a comfortable red armchair by a fireplace.

I suggest, "Why don't you sit down, and I'll make that tea."

Maggie walks dazedly toward the chair and sits down, setting her still whimpering baby on her lap.

A few moments later I have Maggie and baby Jonas tucked securely under some blankets on the chair and am locating teacups when someone rushes through the front door.

Maggie jumps up with a start, but sits back down when she sees her mother. She is a middle-aged woman with her hair in a bun and an apron, still dirty with flour, tied around her waist. The woman rushes forward hugging Maggie and the baby. Maggie embraces her back numbly. The woman steps back looking at her with great concern.

After a moment, the woman directs her attention to me, stepping forward with her hand outstretched. "Hello, Inspector. My name's Mary."

I smile and grasp her hand in return. It's a small, calloused hand, familiar with hard work.

"I just made some tea. Why don't you come with me into the kitchen and I'll tell you what happened."

Mary follows me in and I quietly explain what transpired.

Mary asks, "That was your car I saw on the side of the road?" I nod.

She says with gleaming eyes, "Well, thank you for all you did today. I've no doubt you saved their lives. I'm a widow, and Maggie is my only child. If there's anything I can ever do for you, you just let me know."

"Just stay here and help her out. If she doesn't seem herself by tomorrow, you should probably call an herbalist. A small potion may help her immensely."

Mary nods in agreement, then says, "Well, you'd better get going because your car is in a dangerous spot. When people leave the bridge they're somewhat blinded by the change in light."

I couldn't agree more. I hand Mary my card, then say goodbye to Maggie and Baby Jonas as I make my way out.

Thankfully, my car is fine when I arrive. I can't believe I just saw—and eliminated—my first Dark Vampire. Well, I guess that answers the question of whether I can kill a Dark Vampire with the light of my aura. I wonder how much more of the story of my parent's death is fiction. And I wonder why a Daylight Vampire would lie to Father O'Brennen.

It's interesting how much the Night-Crawlers reek, and though I've heard talk of how mindless they get, I hadn't grasped the severity of it until now. I couldn't sense any soul in the creature's presence, but now I know they can't easily surprise me because the one feeling they exude in massive quantities is a bottomless pit of hunger. I store the memory of that feeling away for future reference.

With my mind full of scenes and feelings from the events that just passed, I make it through the rest of the Shroud Valley hardly even registering the bridge over the Great Oak River.

CHAPTER 17

THE BITTER TRUTH

BLUEBELL KILDARE

MAY 28, 2022, RED AGES

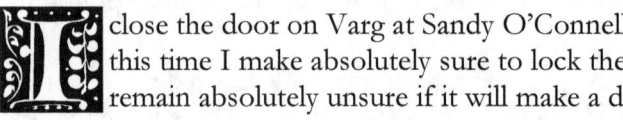 close the door on Varg at Sandy O'Connell's house, and this time I make absolutely sure to lock the doors. But I remain absolutely unsure if it will make a difference.

Sandy lives in a pretty, yellow house with a perfectly manicured lawn and trimmed hedges. I knock on the door, and an older woman, looking tired and drawn, appears in the doorway. She has mostly white hair done in a tasteful pixie cut, and holds herself in a dignified manner.

"Hello," she says with a weary voice.

I feel tendrils of sadness coming off her, but from beyond her, I feel a blast of gray-black grief so deep and abysmal I feel as if I'm being sucked down an endless pit of darkness.

The woman in front of me is too old to be Ian's wife, and I imagine the greater wave of grief is coming from Jason's mom inside, so I ask, "Is Mrs. O'Connell home?"

The woman answers curtly, "I'm Sandy's mother. Who are you?"

When I show her my badge and introduce myself, her response is to curl her lip. "Sandy doesn't want to talk to you."

"Ma'am, I know this is a hard time for her, but it's important I speak with her. I won't take much of her time."

Sandy's mother draws herself up and shouts at me. "Why, you people have a lot of nerve acting like you give a shit when we all know you don't."

I take the beating and respond by looking at her gravely. "Ma'am, I promise you I care very much. And the last thing I want is for whoever did this to strike again before we stop them."

Sandy's mother snaps, "Well, you should have thought of that before."

Then a soft voice comes from inside the house. "Mom. Let her in. It's okay."

Sandy's mom drops her shoulders in defeat and steps aside to let me pass. I go in the direction of the voice and find a handsome woman with straight blond hair sitting at the kitchen table. She's wearing blue jeans, a loose t-shirt, and a drab gray sweater wrapped tightly around her small frame. She, like Ian, has deep circles under her bloodshot eyes and looks utterly desolate.

A feeling of such tremendous loss and pain rolls off her, I feel it through my entire core, and it's practically paralyzing. This woman loved her son with all her heart, of that I have no doubt. I push through the waves of grief to find myself again. Sometimes it's hard to separate other people's feelings from my own when they're that strong.

Sandy's mother says, "Sandy?" Sandy looks up at her slowly as if she's under water. "This lady is an inspector and is here about Jason. Are you up to talking with her?"

Sandy moves her eyes to me and says, "Yes. Please sit down." She speaks slowly as though every word takes a grave effort to push from her mouth.

My heart goes out to her. She is engulfed in despair and I hope she recovers. I also want to get out of this house as soon as possible to avoid this terrible, bleak feeling. I feel guilty for thinking it, but the black waves of sadness are so strong and so profound, I feel myself being dragged into the abyss with her.

Resolved to see this through, I introduce myself. "Mrs. O'Connell, I'm Inspector Kildare from the Supernatural Homicide Investigation Unit. I'm investigating your son's case. I know this is a very hard time for you, but I have to ask you some questions. I'll be as quick as I can."

Sandy nods.

I continue slowly, trying to take it at her pace while doing my best to ignore the huge grief welling up inside me from Sandy's emotions. "On April 28, the day your son went missing, do you know if he was planning on doing anything after school?"

Sandy says, struggling now to speak at a normal pace, "I don't know. He never said. He wasn't with his friend Tim. No one knows if he tried to go straight home or if he went somewhere else."

Then she looks at me a little more sharply and says, "He didn't do it, you know. Ian was angry, and he hates us Gifted, but he would never hurt his son." Then she mumbles more to herself than to me, "He would have come around eventually."

"I believe you, Mrs. O'Connell."

She looks at me and recognizes I tell the truth. She nods in acceptance of that.

"Do you have Tim's contact information?"

She looks at her mother. "Mom, would you get my address book? It's on my desk."

Sandy's mother leaves the room, quick to help. I ask, "Can you tell me about your son's gift, Mrs. O'Connell?"

She says with some effort, "Just Sandy, please. I'm not sure what his gift was. It sort of interfered with other magic. He didn't yet have it under control or understand it himself, I don't think. When other people would do magic, just his presence would mess it up. Maybe it was a gift of interference." A puzzled look crosses her brow, and then she continues trying to explain.

"Last year at his younger cousin's birthday party, a clown was levitating for the kids when Jason walked in the room. Suddenly the clown shot up in the air and rammed his head into the ceiling. We had to call an ambulance. Another time I was lighting a candle while Ian was still at work. I have the gift of fire, you know. Jason walked in from school, and the flames shot up two feet high. I had to get the fire extinguisher to put them out. Luckily, the candle was on the stove so it was easy to contain. I told Ian I had a grease fire . . . " She trails off, obviously stuck in the memory. A different sense of sadness and loss permeates the air now.

Sandy's mother returns and gives me a slip of paper with Tim's address written in a delicate scrawl.

"Thank you, Sandy. I really appreciate the help. Can I ask why you didn't want to talk to me at first?"

Sandy looks at me bitterly and pins me with her angry, gray eyes. "You know, we told Officer Schmidt he wasn't a runaway. I called the precinct every single day telling him to take this seriously." She slams her fist down on the table in a show of energy I didn't think her capable of. "He wouldn't even take my calls anymore. If you'd paid more attention to us then, maybe my son would be alive. Maybe you could have stopped some of the torture he went through."

Tears well up in her eyes and stream down her face, but she keeps her eyes directed straight toward mine as she drills her pain and grief into me. I feel the full impact of her anger and bitterness at us, at all law enforcement officials, and I truly can't blame her one bit.

I don't shrink from her accusing gaze. Instead, I pull out my card and place it on the table. "Sandy," I say, "I'm so sorry for your loss, and I understand your anger. But this I promise you: I will not stop until I find the person responsible."

Sandy looks away from me now and stares at the wall while cupping her chin in her hand. I know I can't give her what she really wants. She wants her son back, and she wants the terrible pain he went through to be undone. The bitter truth is she is right. If Jason's disappearance had been treated like a kidnapping, he might be alive today.

Sandy's mother shows me out.

CHAPTER 18

MAKING AN ENTRANCE

BLUEBELL KILDARE

MAY 28, 2022, RED AGES

When I step out of Sandy O'Connell's house, I am still reeling from how Officer Schmidt treated the case like an adult walk-about. He disgusts me to the nth degree. I wonder who to report this to, Gambino or Jack. Jason was a supernatural, so this case should have been the Bureau's to begin with.

I take a moment to relax and breathe. My lungs drink in fresh air, and my shoulders loosen up as I leave the pain in that house behind me.

It isn't until I reach the car that I realize Varg is quietly following behind me. I give him a sharp look. Well, isn't this interesting? I wonder how he does it.

When we settle back in the car, I notice a missed call from Gambino, so I ring him back.

His deep voice rumbles, "Gambino."

"This is Blue."

Gambino discloses his news. "The forensics report came back. The glass fragments were not helpful, but the paint chips and the grill pattern were. They come from a 1968 Meteor Shockwave in Pewter Green. Only three are registered within a hundred mile radius."

"Excellent." Luck is with us that it's such an old car.

Gambino says, "I'll send profiles of the owners to you. I'm heading out to question them myself. But first, I'll stop by to speak with the bartender and see if he recognizes any of them."

"Let me know how it goes."

Gambino agrees, "Sure thing."

I say goodbye, then point my car in the direction of the office to update Jack.

A few minutes later, I enter the office with Varg pushing ahead of me into the space that Rubalia commands. Xavier is pulling a document out of a printer with his back to us. He's medium height with the face of a model and the body of an ox, all of it muscle. He keeps his head shaven, and his skin glows a rich sable all the way down to his wrists. His hands, however, are a pure, matte black, the manifestation of his gift.

Rubalia is busily typing away on the computer. Her gold-tipped hair is full and fluffy, and her specs have slid to the tip of her nose. She looks up to greet me, but her smile freezes on her face. She points her finger at Varg and says between thinned lips, "Good morning, Blue. I'm glad you made it in earlier today. What is *that* doing in my office?"

Now, I've already contemplated how to handle Rubalia. I have a plan, and I cross my fingers that it works.

"This is Varg," I tell her. "I found him in the alley behind my apartment building. He saved my life from a dangerous assailant. I decided he'd make an excellent guard dog since I'm often dealing with shady characters. I'm sure you've heard of the Dark Vampire murders in my neighborhood lately?" I glance at Xavier, who is listening avidly, and on impulse I add, "He seems to have a talent with escaping locks that requires additional investigation."

Rubalia rebuts, "Jack and Ernesto already eliminated the Dark Vampires." She opens her mouth to say more, but Xavier comes to my rescue.

"What do you mean he can escape locks?" Xavier asks. I knew he'd be interested in this since he is our office guru on illegal entry, and his talents are not purely academic.

"He appears to be a master escape artist. He escapes locked car doors with no perceptible evidence of how he does it."

"How remarkable," Xavier muses, stepping forward to get a closer look at Varg, who is now investigating the premises.

I turn to Rubalia, trying to keep her distracted. "Have any documents come in for me from the precinct?"

Rubalia is onto me and is having none of it. She snaps, "Nothing yet. And if that creature pees in this office, I don't care if he's a descendent of God Almighty Himself, he will be out!"

I let this slide. I've learned it's best not to confront her head-on because the humiliating truth is I will lose.

"Is Jack available?" I ask.

Rubalia looks at his phone line. "Yes. He appears to be free now."

As I head to his office with Varg trailing beside me, I hear the fading sound of Rubalia muttering under her breath and Xavier chuckling good-naturedly.

Before I even knock, Jack calls through the door, "Come in." It always surprises me when he does that because I forget about his incredible hearing.

I walk in with Varg pushing ahead of me as usual. Jack looks neater today than he did yesterday, which I take as a positive omen. He's wearing a pale, bluish gray suit with a matching vest that makes his hair look all the more golden. I try not to stare as I slide into the chair opposite him.

Varg stands next to the desk with his eyes trained on Jack, his purpose clear. Jack watches Varg watch him and chuckles. "It is good to see he takes his job seriously."

He slowly puts out his hand to Varg. Varg sniffs his hand then lies by my feet, still alert.

"His name is Varg."

Jack leans back in his chair and looks me over coolly, inquiring, "So, where are you with the case?"

I dive in. "Forensics came back on the car and Gambino has three hits within a hundred mile radius. He's sending me the owners' profiles shortly. He's also questioning them and the bartender today. I met with both parents this morning. Neither is involved as far as I can tell, nor can they confirm the exact nature of Jason's gift. The mother is Gifted, and her best deduction is he had some sort of interference power."

I relate the mother's stories to Jack about Jason's effect on magic.

"Interesting," Jack says. "Follow up on that please."

"I intend to. The mother gave me Jason's best friend's information. I'm headed to see him soon."

Jack appears to approve of this, so I go on to report about my early morning phone call. "Gambino informed me the evidence locker was broken into last night. It's heavily warded, there's no sign of entry, and the exterior cameras caught nothing. The only box opened was for our case, and none of the evidence was removed. Gambino and I think the perpetrator was looking for the amulet. He suggested I keep it where it is for now."

Jack rubs his forehead and frowns. Then he glances at me, still frowning. I wait patiently because he is clearly deep in thought. "So our perpetrator is still hot on the trail. Have you had any more encounters with him?"

I glance at Varg and say, "Varg did hear a noise on my terrace last night, but when we went to investigate we found nothing."

Jack nods and goes on. "If the amulet gets into the wrong hands, the consequences would be disastrous. If someone used magic to locate it and can use magic to get past wards, then holy ground is the best place to keep it. I don't like that you're a target for them, but I don't see a way to rectify that immediately. I'll file the paperwork to keep it in our possession."

"Thank you." I'm thrilled that Jack hasn't made more of a stink about putting a constant guard on my place, but my relief is short lived.

Jack nods, then sits down and says very smoothly and calmly, "I also think you should let me do a nighttime protective detail on your apartment for the duration of this case."

"What? No way." I shake my head vigorously. "Just no. Capital N-O. No. Thanks for the offer, though."

Jack draws his eyebrows together in consternation and a scowl forms on his beautiful face. Just as quickly it disappears, and his face relaxes in a half smile. He has obviously just thought of something, and I don't trust him one little bit because that was way too easy. But there's little I can do. I can hardly ask him what nefarious plan he's plotting to protect me.

Moving on. "I saw the news about the recent Dark Vampire murders in Rowan Park. Rubalia told me you and Ernesto eliminated them last night. But I have to be honest; I don't care to find out from the news something my own office is dealing with. It makes me look and feel like an idiot. What is the situation with Dark Vampires right now?"

Jack looks taken aback by this statement, then surveys me appraisingly, like he's meeting me for the first time. He answers carefully, "I didn't mean to make you feel excluded. We're not sure if there is a situation. Dark Vampire activity has increased twelve percent citywide in the last month compared with prior years. It could be a temporary anomaly. The numbers are still in the range of normal variability. We're keeping an eye on the stats. If it doesn't reduce soon, we'll have to look at possible causes. I'll keep you updated if we have any major status changes either way."

I lock my gaze with him and say firmly, "If it continues, I can help work the cases." When I see Jack has received my message and accepted it, I drop another bomb on him. "I killed a Dark Vampire today."

Jack shoots out of his chair, sending it slamming back into the wall. "What in the Plane of Fire happened?" His eyes are turbulent green, and his dark gaze sweeps me from head to toe.

"I'm alright. He was expiring already. I heard a woman scream as I was passing through Shroud Valley, and when I investigated, I saw the Dark Vampire crawling on the ground, bleeding out from the fractured effect of sunlight through the fog. I just splashed him with holy water. That's why the Bureau supplies me with it, I assume?"

I add that last comment to remind Jack it's not entirely unexpected for me to run across a Night-Crawler. Jack has got to see me as a strong member of this team and not as a novice to be protected.

Jack runs his fingers through his hair and looks up at the ceiling for a moment. I imagine he's counting to one thousand at Vampire speed, hoping to get his blood pressure down. When his eyes finally meet mine again, they look calm and unexpectedly tender. He walks over to me, standing close enough for me to feel the electricity ripping through the air between us. He lifts his hand and gently pushes a strand of my hair back out of my eyes. "Did it touch you?" he asks.

I keep my voice pert in an attempt to break the tension. "It grabbed my foot when I got very close, but I threw the holy water on it immediately. It didn't have time to bite me, if that is what you want to know."

"Which foot?"

"For goodness' sake, it was my left foot. I had my boots on. I am fine. He didn't even touch my skin."

Jack looks down at my left foot, and I get the strong impression he's fighting the urge to examine it. Thank goodness he doesn't because if he knelt at my feet to check me for an injury, I just might melt into a puddle on his carpet, professional relationship be damned.

Jack says, "Be sure you restock and carry several vials at once. They often hunt in packs." He turns back to his desk. Taking advantage of the apparent dismissal, I spin around and walk toward the door.

Jack adds smoothly as I leave, "Don't forget, I'll pick you up tonight at eight o'clock for the Gala."

"I'll be ready."

CHAPTER 19

A GRAIN OF SALT

BLUEBELL KILDARE

MAY 28, 2022, RED AGES

I stand at the counter in the office of Tim Pulgowski's school right before the end of the school day.

The administration clerk, Trudy Babbith, jabs her bony finger in the air toward Varg. "Dogs aren't allowed on school grounds."

Thankfully Varg is his small self right now. I flash her my ID and say, "He's a police dog."

Trudy looks skeptical as she reads the ID. "Isn't he supposed to wear a jacket that says 'police dog' on the side?"

Darn, I forgot about that. "His jacket got torn up in the last drug bust."

Disbelief is written all over her face. "You work in a drug unit and homicides?" obviously referring to the title on my ID.

Double darn, she's sharp. "My dog's skills are used in a wide variety of situations, and we help where needed." I can tell she doesn't buy it, but lets it pass anyway, which is good because I feel as if I'm about to be sent to the principal's office.

I lean forward on the counter while tapping my foot. "Anyway, is Tim Pulgowski here today? I'd like to ask him some questions about Jason O'Connell."

Trudy looks a little more sympathetic to my cause. Her thin face contorts in a frown, and her drooping eyes sadden. I decide Trudy is a good nut after all. She sniffs and says, "Please take a seat while I call him down."

I sit on a hard, orange plastic chair, the same one that's adorned high school waiting areas everywhere for the last few decades. It hurt my butt in high school, and it hurts my butt now. I restlessly pace the eight by ten foot waiting area while Varg sits dutifully next to the chairs. He appears a far better student than I. A bulletin board on the wall draws my attention. Oh, look, chess club meets tomorrow. I was always a fan of chess club.

As I'm examining the flyer, a boy about Jason's age walks through the door. When he sees Varg, he exclaims, "Whoa, awesome! That looks like a Canis lupus. Only like way smaller."

"He's my police canine," I say trying to distract Trudy.

The boy looks at me sideways with that statement but nevertheless asks, "Can I pet him?"

"Sure."

He sticks his hand out slowly. Varg sniffs his hand and wags his tail a little. The boy gently touches his back, and encouraged by the fact that he's still alive, he gives him a few small strokes. "Wow. He's beautiful."

I beam like a proud mother.

Trudy, who's standing at the counter, clears her throat and jerks her head to get his attention. Her sagging jowls shake a little when she does this, which gets my attention.

The boy stands straight and hands her his slip. He says dutifully, "I was called down to the office."

The clerk nods in my direction. "Inspector Kildare from the Supernatural Homicide Investigation Unit would like to speak with you."

Cripes! That woman is good. She got that from a one-second glance at my ID. We should hire her at the office, bony finger and all.

I turn to Tim and notice his shoulders slump and his back hunches slightly. "Hello, Tim. I'd like to ask you some questions about Jason. Do you have a few minutes?"

He looks a little stricken, but says, "Sure. What do you want to know?"

"Why don't we step outside so we can discuss this privately."

I turn to Trudy. "We won't be more than fifteen minutes." When she assents, we leave.

As soon as we leave the building I ask Tim, "So, what is a Canis lupus?"

He says, "Dude! It's a gray wolf. This one doesn't have any hybridization in its features, though it's smaller than I'd expect."

"You certainly know a lot about wolves."

Tim shrugs. "I like animals. It's kind of my thing."

"What do you think the chances are that Trudy is not looking up Canis lupus right now?"

Tim laughs at that, a short, amused chuckle. "Zero chance. She totally is."

"That's what I was afraid of."

I move us toward a bench in the schoolyard so we can speak undisturbed. Tim perches on the edge of the bench while scuffing his feet on the ground. I settle next to him to help put him at ease. Tim is mid-height for a boy his age, a little on the skinny side. He sits nervously, playing with his hands and avoiding my eyes. The feelings I'm getting from him are anxiety and sadness.

I turn to face him. "I understand you were close to Jason."

Tim looks like he'd rather talk about wolves but is trying to man up. While still fidgeting, he says, "He was my best friend."

"How long were you friends?"

Tim pulls the unfastened zipper on his sweatshirt up and down. "We met in honors algebra our freshman year, so almost three years ago. Jason was the smartest kid in class. I was kind of struggling because biology is more my thing, and Jason helped me out."

Coming from this kid, saying that Jason was the smartest in the class means something. He's obviously very bright himself. "Did you guys spend a lot of time together?"

Tim looks askance at me. "I'm not a suspect, am I? Because if I am, I want a lawyer."

I smile at Tim. He's a sharp boy, no doubt. "No, Tim. I'm just trying to get to know a little more about how Jason spent his time. Since you were his best friend, you probably know better than anyone."

Tim looks much relieved, and I sense a lot of his anxiety dissipate. "Okay then. Well, we had honors classes together a lot, and so we had the same lunch period. So we usually sat together with the other honors students."

"Did you guys do any extracurricular activities after class?"

Tim shrugs. "We both took a robotics class after school in the science lab. That ended before winter break. We haven't done anything since."

"Did Jason do any activities that you weren't in?"

Tim shakes his head and starts picking at his fingernails.

"Tim, I know it's probably really hard to think about him right now. I'm sorry I have to ask you all these questions."

Tim says, "That's okay." But he keeps picking at his nails. I know it's so not okay and this really sucks. Varg comes around the bench and puts his head on Tim's lap. Tim breaks a small smile and starts entwining his fingers with Varg's fur.

"Did you and Jason ever do things or go places after school that were not school related?"

Tim is more at ease now that he's petting Varg. I should have told Trudy he was a therapy dog. Tim's eyes flick to mine now, and I see a well of loneliness.

"We walked home from school together a lot. We could have taken the bus, but sometimes we just wanted to be outside. You know, the break is nice before you have to do homework and chores. Sometimes we would stop off at Fizzy's for malts on the way home. You know, the usual."

I ask, "Can you tell me, did Jason have any problems with any of the kids at school?"

Tim sniffs and looks down at his hands in Varg's fur but doesn't stop moving them. "No. He didn't have a lot of friends, but that was because he was pretty quiet around most people. No one had a problem with him, though."

"How did the kids feel about his magic?"

Tim looks at me sharply with that question. "No one knew, except his parents found out a few months ago. But he never told anyone at school because a lot of the more popular kids would have harassed him. That sort of thing doesn't go over too well at our school."

"So you think he would have been bullied?"

Tim studiously weaves his fingers through Varg's thick fur, examining the effect as he talks. "Well, Jason was in pretty good shape, but he wasn't super big. I don't know that anyone would have hurt him, but they'd have bothered him. And you know, he was into his studies. He just didn't want to mess with that."

"Did it bother you that he had a gift?"

Tim looks up now with a smile. "No, Ma'am. I thought it was awesome."

Hmm. I'm not too happy about being called Ma'am. But what is really frustrating is I feel I'm getting nowhere.

I try a different angle. "Tim, can you remember back to the last day you saw him? Did anything unusual happen that day?"

Tim looks at nothing in front of us, and I can practically see him scanning his memories of that day. "I saw him in school that day, and he seemed totally normal. We ate lunch together. I had to stay late in the library after school, though, so I don't know what he did afterwards."

I frame the next question carefully. "I understand Jason had some trouble with his magic. Was he seeing anyone to help get control over it?"

Tim looks at me like I've lost my mind. "Jason didn't have any trouble with his magic. He was in total control."

Well, that sounds definitive. I chastise myself as I've made a gross error in not taking the perceptions of Jason's parents with a grain of salt. They are parents, after all.

"Hmm, I'm sorry. I must have been given incorrect information. I was led to believe he was still struggling with some control issues. Can you tell me about his gift?"

Tim seems happy to correct me on this point, explaining with a certain amount of pride in his friend, "I guess he did have some trouble controlling his gift at first. But he practiced and was awesome at it. He just didn't share it with his parents because they were all freaked out about it and stuff. His magic was sort of an amplifier. He could make anyone else's magic stronger."

I need to confirm what he means, "So for instance, if someone had the gift of lighting fire, he could turn a small flame into a large flame? Something like that?"

Tim says, "Dude! I mean dudette! Exactly! Except that he could turn a small flame into a bonfire! He was practicing with magic fireworks so he could audition for the Sun Flare Celebration Fireworks Show. It was awesome."

"Could he do this with any kind of magic or just certain kinds?" I inquire.

Tim smiles. "As far as I know, he never ran into anything that didn't work."

"So how did his audition go?"

Tim thinks back for a minute, and suddenly his eyes go wide. "I don't know. He never told me. It was coming up soon, I know, but I don't remember exactly when."

I try not to let this small bud of hope flare up prematurely, "Do you know where he got the information about the audition?"

Tim nods. "It was on the school bulletin board. They were looking for volunteers."

"Thanks so much, Tim. You have been a great help." I hand him my card and say, "If you remember anything else that happened that week, please let me know."

Tim nods and rubs Varg's head a few more times before standing up to go.

I stand up with him and say, "Tim, I'm going to do everything I can to bring whoever did this to justice. I won't stop working on this case until that happens."

Tim looks up at me, and I see something click in his head as he understands I mean it. I feel that somehow I've righted something for him. A sense of heaviness falls off him. It must be scary to be a kid and have one of your friends die unexpectedly. Hopefully it makes him feel better to know people care and Jason will not be forgotten.

Tim nods at me, "I promise I'll call if I think of anything else."

I hold out my hand to shake Tim's, and he takes it while looking me in the eyes for the first time. I think he understands the handshake is more than a goodbye; it's a promise.

Varg and I run into the school again and burst into the office. Trudy is standing with her hands on her hips when I check out the bulletin board. Trudy starts giving me a death glare, but I ignore her as I scan for the flyer. Well, I'll be. The flyer is old, but it's still there. It reads:

Seeking Volunteers for the Sun Flare Celebration Fireworks and Magic Show

Talents of Interest: Fire, Fireworks, Illusion Magic

Great opportunity. Gain valuable experience for your résumé and give back to the community.

Auditions will take place on Phantom Island across from the library.

Thursday, April 28 at 3:00 p.m.

Sponsored by the Rotary Club

Chapter 20

Fertilizing the Flowers

Bluebell Kildare

May 28, 2022, Red Ages

As I walk up to Maud's house, I wonder what in the world possessed her to replace the zinnia with marigolds.

Maud is holding the door open impatiently. "Would you hurry up, chicky? Hot rollers take a little time, you know."

I quicken my pace and leap up on the stoop with Varg following behind.

"Maud, this is Varg. Varg, this is Maud."

Maud raises her eyebrows, making them look like golden arches under her sherbet colored hair. The fuchsia appears to have faded to a soft pink, and new streaks of gold have been added. Her subtle peach kimono style dress perfectly complements her hair, and both do wonders for her complexion.

Somehow, I'm hardly shocked at all when Maud responds to a wolf in her home with a practical, "Well hello, Varg. I'm sorry I haven't any steak for you."

Then she proceeds to ignore him completely, glaring at me instead. "I have the rollers heating up. Why in the world aren't you wearing your dress yet?"

"I'm changing here." I dash into her bathroom, dress and bag in hand.

A few minutes later, I emerge wearing a blue satin confection, trimmed about the waist and halter straps in black piping. I swish my hips, and when the full skirt twirls around my thighs, I give a delighted peal of laughter. "I haven't worn a dress in ages."

Maud looks at me with narrow eyes. "That is your own fault, chicky."

I protest, "It is not. I never get asked out."

Maud throws back her head and laughs throatily. "You have it all mixed up, Blue. First you wear the dresses. Then you get asked out."

Hmm, she might have a point there.

Maud pulls out a chair by the hot rollers. "Well, let's get to this." I obediently sit down as she starts rolling my plain, straight as a board, dark brown hair.

"So, you're going with your boss, Jack?" she asks.

I knew I wouldn't be able to avoid this conversation. It figures she waits until I'm pinned underneath her agile fingers to drill me.

"It's just a work thing."

Maud tugs a little harder than necessary. "Uh huh. Men don't let themselves be seen with a woman at a social event unless they think she's beautiful."

I ponder this for a moment. She might have another point. However, in an effort to deflect her questions, I make a point myself. "Maud, do you honestly think marigolds are an adequate replacement for zinnia?"

Maud jerks my hair this time as she gathers the strand for the next roller.

"Ouch!"

She goes a little more gently now. "Sorry. You just brought up a sore subject. I did *not*, let me repeat, *not* replace my zinnia with marigolds. It was that damn Harry Pickets again."

I flinch under another strong hair tug. "Ow! Really? How do you know it was him?"

"Be still, girl. Beauty is pain. I know because I caught his gardener this morning as he was finishing up. He gave me a message from Harry," Maud says as she deftly sections another portion of my hair.

I clench my teeth through the next few tugs. "What was the message?"

"Your hair is an inspiration," Maud says as she rolls another section up.

I huff in exasperation. "What do you mean my hair is an inspiration? It has got to look ridiculous in these rollers."

"Not your hair, chicky. My hair. That was Harry's message."

"Ohh. He must have meant that your hair looked like the marigolds

Maud, maybe Harry has a thing for you. What did you say to that?" I flinch again as she nears the tender hair at my neck.

Maud clicks her tongue with annoyance. "I decided one favor deserved another. So I paid the gardener to dump a load of manure in Harry's yard."

I bust out laughing.

Maud chuckles softly. "The gardener thought it was a great gift. I do hope Harry gets the message behind it."

Maud circles around me and leans back to appraise her work. She nods in satisfaction and says, "Now we wait. So tell me about this animal of yours."

Maud and I chat while the rollers cool. I tell her all about Varg's adventures and his potential magical abilities. Maud is enthralled. She has a thing for strays, me included, I think.

When the rollers are cool, she pulls them out, and her green eyes soften. "Hold on. I have the perfect things to go with this."

She runs to her bedroom and returns moments later with her hands behind her back. She says in a sing-song voice, "Now close your eyes."

I obey and can feel her placing barrettes in my hair, a necklace on my neck, and some clip-on earrings on my ears.

"Okay, you can open your eyes now. Go look in the mirror."

I walk to the mirror in her foyer, and holy smokes! I look spectacular. Black crystal barrettes glitter in my hair, holding the waves in elegant swoops. My blue streak is tucked in a wave down the side of my head. The necklace has a large, black, pear-shaped crystal dangling just above my cleavage. It's surrounded by smaller crystal beads alternating in glistening blue and black. The earrings are matching blue drops hanging from a black crystal flower clip. The colors tie in perfectly with the dress. The dress, the hair, the jewelry—I don't even look like myself. I don't even feel like myself. I feel luxurious and beautiful.

Maud stands to the side, admiring me. "You look stunning. Any man who had you on his arm would be lucky."

"Oh, Maud!" I throw my arms around her in a big hug. "Thank you so much. You are so good to me."

Maud hugs me back, then slips some money into my hands. "That's for the auction so you can try to win a little something for yourself. Don't worry about paying me back. It's for charity."

Her small gift means so much to me. She's on a fixed income, so I know money is tight. I look at Maud, still clasping her hands and smile at her. I kiss her on both cheeks and she smiles back.

"Go on, get out of here. You'll be late for a very special occasion." She ushers me all the way to the door and nudges me out.

CHAPTER 21

SHORT DRIVE DOWN

MEMORY LANE

JACK TANNER

MAY 28, 2022, RED AGES

I bound up the steps toward Blue's apartment at inhuman speed. Coming to a halt inches before the door, I listen for a moment to the soft sounds of her movements within. Varg knows I've arrived, and his scent and the sound of his padded feet move closer to the door. I knock before he alerts Blue to my arrival.

"Coming!" Blue yells through the door.

A few moments later, the door swings opens and my eyes drink her in. She's a vision in a blue silk halter gown that molds perfectly to the curves of her breasts, narrows with her tiny waist, and flares out over her hips. Sparkling crystals gracefully adorn her ears and neck. But it's her skin that holds me prisoner. It smells of coconut and lavender, and it shimmers under her aura, giving her an ethereal glow. Large expanses of her beautiful skin are visible, from the tantalizing curves of her breasts to her long, graceful neck. Crystal pins catch her hair in elegant waves. The blue streak of her hair is pulled in with the waves and brings my gaze up to her eyes. And finally, her soft, pink, rounded lips are lightly glossed and slightly parted as she takes in my attire with rounded eyes.

I suppress a smile as she seems to realize herself and wraps her shawl more tightly around her shoulders. I inquire, "Are you going to let me in?"

"Ohh!" she stammers nervously. "I'm sorry. I just have to grab my purse. Come on in."

She steps back and quickly retreats behind the sheer curtain that separates her bedroom from the rest of the apartment. As she moves, I admire the soft swishing of her skirt around her hips and the beautiful bare legs stretching from her strappy black heels to the hem of her skirt. I suck in my breath at the long expanse of bare skin on her back, as desire hits me hard.

She picks up a tiny, black beaded bag hanging from a silver chain and returns. I drag my gaze from her enticing form to examine her apartment. It's a small but comfortably furnished space, her feminine touches are pleasant without being overpowering. I frown as I ponder the sliding glass doors to the terrace. Anyone could break in there. Maybe I should have Xavier assess her apartment for security. How could I legitimately approach her on the subject?

When I've finished pondering her security and perusing her abode, I allow my eyes to settle back on Blue. She squirms a bit under my gaze and asks, "Am I dressed alright?" She looks too perfect for words.

I say, "Turn around."

She slowly spins around, and her skirt flares out, lifting slightly and then settling back down around her thighs like a gentle mist. She is so beautiful, I can feel myself hardening just from looking at her across the room. I catch her eyes with my gaze, and her lips part slightly again. Christ! I'm acting like a schoolboy on his first date.

I quickly move to her patio window and look outside to rein in my lust. I check my emotions so she can't tell how she's making me react. When I've wrestled my feelings down, I respond as coolly as I can, "You'll do nicely."

Blue looks down at Varg. "I might have a problem with him. He's gotten out of my car twice by himself, even when I know the doors were locked. I'm afraid he'll try to follow us."

I look closely at Varg, who has his gaze fixed on me in return. I walk toward Blue while looking directly at Varg and put my arm around her shoulders, leaning in close. I try not to think of her soft skin beneath my hand as I firmly say, "Varg, Blue is with me. I'll stay by her and keep her safe. You stay and guard the place."

Varg looks away and walks toward the sofa to spread out on the shag rug. With that, I pull Blue out of the apartment, reluctantly dropping my arm as soon as we close the door.

I let Blue into my car and watch her settle comfortably before closing the door. She takes a moment to look around and lightly runs her fingers across the leather seat. She takes in a deep breath of air, obviously enjoying the aroma of leather surrounding her.

I put my eyes on the road and move to a neutral topic. "Did you learn anything else about the case today?"

She takes a minute to respond, her eyebrows furrow and her upper teeth bite gently into her lower lip. It drives me crazy when she does that.

"I'm chasing some information that Jason's best friend gave me."

This statement is woefully slim on details, leading me to assume she doesn't want to discuss it right now. I nod at this and repeat my new mantra: eyes on the road, eyes on the road.

Blue angles herself toward me in her seat. "Do you do a lot of charity events like this?"

I look at her quickly, then remembering my mantra, I return my eyes to the road. "I try to."

"I didn't realize you were so philanthropic."

Yikes, I don't want her to imagine me as some prince charming and forget who I am. "You know, Blue, I am a Vampire, and that means I drink blood to survive. It is always donated freely, but it doesn't always come from a bag."

Out of my peripheral vision, I see Blue wince at that last part. Good. She needs a dose of reality.

"I carry Lilith's dark mark on my soul, and my craving for human blood will never go away. I've had many Daylight Vampires friends, living perfectly normal lives, drinking only donated blood, who suddenly give into their bloodlust. I don't know why they stopped fighting the desire, but they did. So while I'm still in control, I want to do as much good as I can. I'm not a saint for doing good things. I am simply trying to make up for the inevitable."

She stares at her hands quietly for a minute, thinking about this. Then she asks in a small voice, "Do you ever feel out of control?"

I can feel her gaze on me again, and I frown slightly. "I've been alive for hundreds of years, Blue." I let this fact settle in her mind before going on. "There are times the bloodlust rises stronger, times of passionate emotion and rage or times of physical need. Yet I'm in full control of the choices I make, and I hope if after all this time a situation hasn't happened to cause me to lose control, it's not going to happen. I assume it's the same with other Daylight Vampires. The only time it seems giving into bloodlust is not a conscious choice is when a Daylight Vampire has been harmed or starved to the point of mindless thirst."

Ever the inspector, Blue asks, "Do you have any guesses as to why Vampires suddenly give into bloodlust?"

"I don't know for sure, but perhaps they are tired of being in control. Certainly the fact that the Plane of Fire is an inevitability for us plays an important role in the decision to give up the fight. It would be better if we could die an honorable death and go to the Plane of Light. However, I'm in no danger of giving up any time soon."

I look over at her to judge how she's taking this news. She shocks me by briefly touching my arm. Her elegant, thin fingers are as light as a butterfly on my forearm, which she caresses in one long motion. Jesus Christ, she's soothing me! She should be scared out of her mind, but instead she's soothing me.

She returns her hand to her lap and says, "I trust you, Jack."

My chest is oddly tight as I keep my eyes firmly on the road and press my lips together.

She apparently decides a change of subject is in order. She suddenly says, "I grew up at the Green Tree Orphanage. Did you know that?"

Now my chest feels even tighter and I nod slightly. I know very well that she grew up in that orphanage.

"The housemothers were mostly kind, but when I was younger, the kids were not. They called me a Witch, and were afraid of me. I learned what you are isn't the same as who you are, Jack. I learned who you are is more important."

Right now, my heart feels like it's going through a vice. I can't believe she just told me that to make me feel better about being a Vampire. I glance at her, and she seems lost in thought now. I'm glad because I don't think I can speak without my voice cracking. I keep my hands on the wheel and try to ignore the presence of one of the kindest and most beautiful people I've ever met who is sitting inches away from me, slicing my control into ribbons with ease. Focus on the road, focus on the road.

Just then, in the middle of a commercial area downtown, traffic slows to a stop. A small crowd of Dilectus Deo march in front of a blood bank, protesting blood donations.

As we drive by, Blue says in a sad voice, "That man's sign says 'Purify the human race.' We spend all of our time trying to protect these people, and half of them hate us."

For me, human hate means little because I know what it was like before the Great Pact, and I understand humans have no chance against Vampires if the bonds of the Great Pact are broken. Suddenly, though, I want to know how it feels to someone who's Gifted and doesn't have our strength.

"Blue, you said the kids were cruel to you at the orphanage. What did you mean by that? How were they cruel?"

Blue takes a deep breath and replies in a soft voice, hardly a whisper. I keep my eyes on the road, this time to afford her privacy as she tells her story.

"I was playing on the jungle gym one time and noticed one of the girls, Melanie, standing on a platform looking over the edge. I could feel she was very sad, a feeling of deep desolation. I went up to her and asked why she was so sad. She looked at me in anger and denied it. She was lying.

"One of the older boys, Billy, was standing nearby, and when he heard her he got in my face yelling, 'Stay away from her, you freak. You're making her sad.' Then he shoved me hard. I lost my balance and fell off the platform, down about eight feet onto the grass."

I draw my breath in sharply, and my heart feels pressed again. I knew about her fall from the reports I'd received, but I had no idea the event was surrounded with so much hatred.

Blue continues. "I cried and cried, but none of the kids helped me or called the housemothers. I lay there for what seemed an eternity with blood flowing from my nose and sticks stabbing into my back. When I was able to stand and made it inside, the housemothers called the doctor. He said I had a mild concussion and was lucky not to have broken my neck.

"Later I learned Melanie was sad because a family had come to pick a child to adopt. She was one of the girls they were thinking of adopting, but they picked another girl instead. She was mad at me because I knew how heartbroken she was, and she didn't want anyone to know."

My heart beats wildly as I think of Blue as a little girl and how hurt she must have been. Knowing Blue, though, she didn't tell me the worst of it at the outset. So I prod the wound with a hot poker, determined to learn the extent of the injury. I ask as casually as I can, "Was that the worst thing that happened in the orphanage?"

Blue sighs and looks out the window at the houses running past us.

She says in a small voice, "No."

Just as I suspected. "Would you tell me about the worst of it? I know it's personal, so you don't have to." I struggle for a reason she'll accept. "It will help me understand how the Norms' hatred of the Gifted impacts their lives. That's important for me to know."

She sighs again, "Okay, Jack. I'll give you my worst story, but please don't share it with anyone. The kids hated to play hide and seek with me because I could sense their souls, so I always knew where they were. I would join anyway. One time I ran up the attic stairs to find where Becca was hiding. I had found everybody else, and there was nothing left to do except find her, so I ran upstairs to her hiding spot. She was standing at the top of the staircase on the landing to the attic. When I reached the top of the stairs she was furious I'd found her. She said, 'Get away from me, you Witch,' and she kicked me. Her foot caught my shoulder, and I lost my balance."

I hear the creak of the steering wheel and realize I'm in danger of ripping it off the car. I relax my grip and unclench my fingers.

"I rolled down the long flight of wooden stairs, breaking my arm in three places. My bone was sticking out of my forearm and blood was dripping everywhere. Becca walked right over me, not caring at all that I was hurt. To her I was just a thing, less than a thing, really. In my heart I know had I died on that fall she would have just walked right over me and kept playing the game."

The fury within me is enormous, but it's easily eclipsed by the sea of my own guilt. If it weren't for me, Blue never would have gone there. I should have found her a loving home. How stupid I was to imagine her safe.

"By then I knew better than to expect help from the other children. I didn't cry despite the pain, though I definitely came close to chewing a hole in my lip. I lay there on the third floor landing for a while with blood gushing out of my arm until I had the courage to move. I twisted around because I was too faint to stand, and I scooted down on my butt to the second floor landing. When I reached it, I called Anna Marie, my favorite housemother. She and the other housemothers got me into bed and called the doctor. The doctor set my arm and had a few private words with Anna Marie about it."

I can just imagine the scrappy little girl Blue had been, lying on the stairs too proud to cry as she fought for the will to move and get help.

It's been so long since I was a child that I have only the vaguest memories, but I had no idea children could be that cruel. Dreading her answer, I ask in a voice that does not seem my own, "And that was the worst of it?"

"Well, there were countless times when my few possessions went missing and the kids all denied taking them. I would always know who lied, so I would accuse them. That only made things worse because they would call me a Witch. When I tried to play games with them, they'd either flat out say no or they'd break up the game. If they were stuck doing chores with me they'd loudly complain about having to work with 'the freak,' 'the evil one,' or 'Satan,' it was pretty bad in general during those early years."

I feel like a knife is ripping through my chest at this point, and guilt lies so heavily on my shoulders I'm surprised the car can keep pulling the weight. I should have watched her more carefully. I don't have the words to comfort her. I don't know any words that could erase that sort of pain, but I must say something. "Blue, I am so sorry you went through that. It must have been a very hard childhood."

Blue's laugh is brittle. "Yes. It was hard, but it did get better. Shortly after my arm mended from the fall, Anna Marie took me on what she called a field trip. We went into the forest next to the orphanage, and she asked me to sit inside a circle she had drawn in the dirt. I remember sitting cross-legged in the center while she chanted a bunch of songs in a foreign language waving her arms beautifully. She said they were holy songs, and I was so young, I believed her. Now I know she was performing some sort of ritual or spell, though for what, I don't know. I certainly felt magic in the air, but I wasn't afraid because Anna Marie said she was singing a special song to help me.

"I remember it was a chilly fall day with the ground covered in fallen leaves, and the trees were bright splotches of fiery color against the clear blue sky. We were out long enough for my nose and ears to get cold when the other housemothers came and made a big fuss. They yelled at Anna Marie before grabbing me to take me back to the orphanage. They told me Anna Marie had kidnapped me, but I didn't believe them, and I yelled at them to leave her alone.

I don't know what she did, but after that, the kids were nicer to me. They were not kind and friendly, but they weren't so afraid of me or cruel to me. Anna Marie never came back to the school after that, and I never found out what exactly she did, but whatever it was, it helped."

I glance over at Blue, who is staring out the window with an unseeing gaze after finishing her story. The scars of her troubled past are clearly etched on the planes of her face and in the gleam of her bright eyes.

What did Anna Marie do? I need to do some research on her and find out. That incident never showed up in the reports I received.

I lean toward Blue and whisper, "Here we are. This is Glenwood Mansion."

CHAPTER 22

GALA MAGIC

BLUEBELL KILDARE

MAY 28, 2022, RED AGES

I hear Jack's low voice breaking into my thoughts, and with a shake, I extract myself from my remembrances. Looking out the window, I see Glenwood Mansion, a softly glowing apparition emerging through the curtain of night.

A valet takes Jack's car, and we approach the entrance. I admire the softly glimmering firefly lanterns illuminating the trees hovering over the glow stone walkway. I steal a surreptitious glance at Jack again, hoping he doesn't think less of me for the embarrassing truths I revealed about my childhood. His face looks a study of angles in stone, immovable and unreadable. He's wearing a black tuxedo with a champagne embroidered waistcoat and a gold tonal silk cravat. As we step through the entrance, the party lights dance through his gilded curls. A man asks if he can take my shawl, but I decline, tugging it close about my shoulders, eternally conscious of my birthmark.

Mr. and Mrs. Glenwood greet us just through the entryway. Mr. Glenwood is a balding gentleman with a standard tux and bow tie and a nonstandard twinkle in his eye. He takes my hand warmly and bows over it with his sparse white hair flopping over in a bow of its own. He kisses the back of my hand as if I'm royalty, and my face heats in a blush.

Mrs. Glenwood is dressed impeccably in a black lace surplice gown with a full skirt overlaying a golden sheath. The gold goes beautifully with her caramel hair which surely must be dyed or charmed to match her color of youth. Her eyes are intelligent and observant as she takes my hand in a firm embrace and glances over at Jack.

Jack introduces me. "Good evening, Valerie. This is my good friend Bluebell Kildare."

It's an odd way to introduce me, but perhaps it's wise not to announce he's brought a work associate in case it puts people on edge.

Apparently Mrs. Glenwood thinks it's odd too. She raises one eyebrow and says, "How unusual."

I wonder what she finds unusual: that Jack brought a friend or that he brought a date at all. Perhaps it's me she finds unusual.

She looks at me again and smiles making the little lines around her eyes crinkle up in pleasure. "Welcome, my dear Bluebell. Any friend of Jack's is a friend of mine."

Despite a compulsive urge to curtsy to her, I resist and thank her instead with a smile of my own. "Just call me Blue, please. Thank you so much for having us."

The line behind us presses us deeper into a soaring foyer, ending the formalities abruptly. In front of us, a wide, curved oak staircase leads to the second floor. Jack tucks my arm under his, and we walk through the cavernous hall and enter a room via an archway on the right.

On the other side of the archway spreads a two-story grand ballroom with an expansive, gleaming parquet floor. Tall windows draped in white and gold brocade curtains line the exterior wall like soldiers at attention. Gilded frames holding bold classic and contemporary artwork adorn the interior walls, and the ceiling is made of hundreds of squares of glass held together by cream-colored steel beams. The ceiling is aflame with thousands of small firefly bulbs set in three massive, tiered crystal chandeliers, giving the room a luminous ambiance.

The far end of the room is a wall of paneled glass, and the ceiling is tall enough that a pair of weeping fig trees easily stands in the corners with plenty of room for growth. The second floor balcony surrounds the other three walls of the ballroom, and I see people milling about, elegant dresses and stylish suits moving effortlessly in and out of doorways.

On the wall opposite us stands a long row of tables and counters where the silent auction is showcased. To the left is a refreshment table mounded with hors d'oeuvres and overflowing with fresh fruits and desserts. Servers weave through the room tendering copious amounts of champagne to the guests.

My eyes are absolutely delighted with the ballroom from start to finish, but my insides are assaulted with the cacophony of emotions that fill the room. Usually I only feel emotions when they are strong, but the pure mass of people in this room assails me with a dizzying array of sensations. It's so confusing because people are mixing, and I can't pin feelings to individuals. Hundreds of signatures swirl around me in dissonance.

Jack leans close to my ear, I imagine because the room is buzzing so loudly. "You look pale. Are you okay?"

I pinch my brows together and look down a minute. Then I catch a lively tune I'm unfamiliar with. I lift my eyes and see it comes from a small orchestra playing between the fig trees. Suspended over a small black stand in front of the orchestra, a magic baton cuts the air, moving left and right, up and down in a wild dance. I smile in delight as I watch the magic baton direct the orchestra. It eases me greatly to listen to the sound of the music instead of my sixth sense.

I stretch on tiptoe to lean close to Jack's ear, and when my lips are almost brushing his lobe I feel my cheeks heat in embarrassment. I remember he's a Vampire and can hear me despite the noise. Jack's lips twitch slightly in repressed humor as I settle back down and say, "I'm alright. There are a lot of people, and I'm getting all their impressions at once." Then I look questioningly at Jack. "What kind of music is this?"

As he replies, his breath brushes my ear and causes my entire body to tingle. "A minuet." Then he asks, "Would you like a refreshment?"

I shake my head no. "I'd like to go to the auction first. Maud gave me a little money to spend, and I want to find someone who can further my knowledge of the object in question."

Jack nods and puts his hand on the small of my back, guiding me forward. Again I puzzle—am I a friend? Am I a date? Or am I an associate? As usual I can't read Jack, so he remains an enigma. I decide to stop worrying and see what happens.

When we approach the tables and distance ourselves from the throng on the dance floor, the onslaught of emotions eases and is instead replaced with the deep, thrumming vibrations of magic. A fine tremor runs through the whole of my body from the force of the power in the vicinity. Many of the individual items are weak, but in large quantity the effect is quite strong. The cases are framed in oak with thick, cream-colored velvet interiors and lit from within like cases at a fine jewelry store. Heavy oak tables are set up to exhibit some of the larger items.

I stop briefly in front of a fountain with a sculpted Grecian boy peeing water into an enormous clamshell. A thin flow of water lifts itself from the clamshell and flows upward, twisting around the boys leg and torso before finally entering through his ear. It's listed as a "magically operated pumpless fountain." I laugh softly. If I were ever in the market for a Grecian peeing fountain I would prefer one that didn't require a pump to operate. For now, I think I'll pass.

Jack holds my arm tucked neatly in his, and I revel in the feel of his muscles beneath my fingers. We move forward toward some items designed to aid your vanity. A magic curling wand. How nice it would be to just wrap your hair around the wand and say a magic word to make the curl stay until you release the hair from its obligation.

Other items are more practical. A set of self-cleaning dishes captures my eye. They would make cleanup after dinner so easy, but the pattern is hideous. The light green plates are covered in a glaring orange and blue tropical design. The starting bid is high, and I doubt they'll get any bidders. Too bad. I'm sure the owner will be disappointed when the dishes return home. Next I admire an elaborate magical brass fire starter. It would be so convenient for someone who uses candles frequently or has a fireplace.

My eyes alight on a tall, crystal-footed perfume bottle with a delicate handle, a small pour spout, and a beautifully shaped stopper. Its curves are captivating, and its placard says it magically preserves contents from UV damage and age spoilage. This would be perfect for my homemade oil mixtures. Many of the more delicate oils will not keep in a clear container due to UV damage, but I do love to see the colors of the oils. Right now I keep my oils in amber jars. Excitement thrills through me as I write down my bid. It's the first bid entered on this item, and I hope I'm the only one interested.

Jack seems taken with some magical strategy games, so I wander over to the glass cases. They're filled with jewelry, weaponry, and other high value items. I see nothing of relevance in the first case as it's filled with chainmail gloves, hoods, and small weaponry.

In the second case, a soft, thrumming vibration captures my attention. It's not as strong as some of the other vibrations I sense, but it gives off a wider spectrum of frequencies than I've felt before. My eyes alight on a necklace made of small metal pieces linked together in strands that connect at a choker and fan out in all directions. If the necklace were worn, the cascading strands would lie all over the shoulders and dip down to cover the sternum. The choker has no clasp, and it is labeled "Belladonna Necklace, Properties: Protection against magic." I shiver when I look at it. It's both alluring and menacing at the same time, and the intricate web of vibrations exuding from it tells me of the great power it contains.

An older gentleman with a bald head and a distinguished beard has just approached the case next to me. He leans toward me and says, "It's fantastic, isn't it?"

I feel a sense of delight coming from him. He's enchanted by the piece, but his delight is somehow repugnant to me. He continues with a twisted little smile on his face. "What's amusing is it's lauded as a piece for protection. Now what do you think would happen if someone who had a magical gift wore it?"

I'm startled at this thought. Why, their magic would probably be suppressed. The necklace would be like a prison.

I feel a vile joy build in the man as he contemplates this and looks at me sharply. I feel uneasy about this conversation and quickly turn to see Jack watching. When Jack approaches, I'm relieved to see the stranger move on to examine some items in another case.

Jack puts his arm around my shoulders and leans in to me. "There are some amulets in the last case on the other side. Let's take a look."

I move with him, momentarily grateful for the security of his presence. In the case Jack leads me to are a few amulets but none as old as what I'm looking for. Jack releases my shoulder and tells me he'll be at the next case over. I look closely at the contents of the case in front of me. There's an exquisitely designed set of ancient silver mirrors labeled "Scrying mirrors, Properties: Visual and audio communication over distance." A substantial minimum bid is requested, well out of my price range.

A handsome, aristocratic man is bidding on the set. I ask him, "Are the old mirrors more valuable than the newer ones?"

He smiles at me and explains, "Most scrying mirrors are the same, new or old. They allow you to see and listen. But some of the older mirrors have additional properties even the owners aren't aware of. Some allow you to zoom in and out. Others allow you to see the surrounding area as though you are there. I've even seen those that allow you to spy or see things that are otherwise warded."

I puzzle at this. "How can you spy with a mirror set that is clearly used for two way communication?"

The gentleman replies, "Well, sometimes the set is designed so you can turn one on without notifying the other and therefore see and hear what's going on when the other owner is unaware."

"Ohh!" I say, turning a little pink. "I should have guessed that. I'm a little ignorant on the subject. That's quite an invasion of privacy."

The man smiles at me. "Don't be embarrassed. I'm a collector, so I know a good deal more than most. My name is Robert LaRoche, by the way." He holds his hand out in greeting.

I place mine in his and give it a firm squeeze. "I'm Bluebell Kildare."

Robert says, "It's a pleasure to meet you, Ms. Kildare." He holds my hand a tiny bit longer than necessary, but it's not unpleasant. In fact, it's quite the opposite.

Robert is a handsome man, perhaps in his late thirties. He's tall and slender with an elegant stance and handsome face. His thoughtful brown eyes stare intelligently from behind wire frame spectacles. He emanates none of the intense power Jack does but instead holds an easy grace. His hair is a tad longer than it should be, which combined with his spectacles and pale skin gives him the look of a scholar who buries himself in a library too often.

Turning back to the mirrors, I inquire, "How do you know this set has some of the extra properties?"

Mr. LaRoche points to the mirror facing down with its intricate filigree showing on the back. "Do you see the filigree? I can date the work based on my knowledge of the skill level and the popular craftsmanship during different periods. I can date this particular piece at approximately 200 R.A."

I whistle softly at this, and Robert smiles. "To be honest, I can't know for sure if this piece has any special properties, but due to the expense of producing such fine work it was likely made for someone of extreme wealth, so there's a good likelihood of some special properties being imbued. The only way to know with certainty is to take it home and study it."

"What will you do if it's just a plain old scrying mirror?"

Robert smiles again. "The piece is worth well beyond the minimum bid simply due to the workmanship and the age of the piece. If I find I have a standard piece, I can always remove it from my collection by reselling it at another auction."

I glance around briefly and see Jack is still at the case next to me.

Across the way I see the man who had been looking at the Belladonna Necklace glance at Jack, then at me. When his dark eyes collide with mine, I feel a shiver running through me again. I quickly turn back to Mr. LaRoche.

"So, you're a collector?"

Robert nods with the corners of his eyes crinkling in a smile.

"Mr. LaRoche," I say in a soft voice that will not carry. "I have some questions about a particularly old piece I've heard about. Given your knowledge on the subject, would you mind if I ask you about it," I look around as I add pointedly, "at another place and time?"

Mr. LaRoche looks intrigued. "I'd be delighted to help you if I can." He pulls a card out of his wallet and says, "Please call anytime."

I take his card. "Thank you so much, Mr. LaRoche."

He bows his head and smiles. "The pleasure is all mine."

I part ways with Mr. LaRoche and head toward Jack. "Did you hear that?" I ask.

Jack nods. Vampire hearing is great for some things. He puts his hand at my back again. "Let's get some champagne to celebrate."

We head toward the throng, and once again, the feelings begin to press down on me from all directions. Jack grabs two glasses of champagne from a passing waiter and hands one to me, then thankfully skirts the crowd and heads toward the orchestra. He leans close and his breath tickles my ear. "This is a quadrille."

We stop under one of the fig trees and listen to the orchestra play. I watch the baton prancing in the air like a marionette puppet without strings. With the music so loud, it's much easier to tune out the overwhelming emotions afloat in the room. It is all a matter of focus.

Jack holds his champagne without imbibing but refills mine generously until my head is buzzing. Finally, I cover my glass. "Jack, I may be indiscreet if you give me any more. I think that's enough for now."

Jack's lips twitch, and I wonder if that was his goal.

Just then, an elderly woman leading two beautiful young ladies, one on each arm, approaches. The elderly woman has a sharp nose and beautiful, large eyes. Her snow white hair is pulled up in a tightly wound bun. Her companion on the right has sleek, long, dark hair and wears a tight, red, floor-length gown with a slit traveling to mid-thigh. Her companion on her left couldn't be more opposite with blond hair piled high, looking delicate in a pink, silk, high neck gown with tailored lines and a flared skirt.

The elderly woman says, "Good evening, Jack. You've been cloistered in this corner all evening, but Sabrina and Heather insisted we say hello."

The woman on the left looks terribly embarrassed, and I imagine she wanted nothing less than to say hello.

The woman on the right, however, immediately puts her hand on Jack's arm and coos, "Hello, Jack. It's been a while since I saw you at the Rosewood party. Why, you're practically becoming a hermit." Her hand on Jack's arm lingers several seconds too long, and I find myself bristling as she completely ignores me.

Jack's mouth tightens a bit at the corners but he replies easily, "Hello, Sabrina." Then he nods in my direction and says, "This is Bluebell Kildare. Bluebell, please meet Sabrina Remington, Heather Remington, and their grandmother, Vivian Remington."

Heather smiles gently, and I feel a patient kindness coming from her soul. I immediately like her and try to include them all in a sweeping smile, but my smile falters slightly at Sabrina, who is standing much too close to Jack for my pleasure. "It's great to meet you all."

Sabrina's soul feels selfish and greedy in contrast to her beautiful features and stunning smile. She turns to me and says, "What a quaint dress, Bluebell. Who is the designer?"

I feel a blush crawl up my cheeks as I can't say who designed it, and certainly can't say it's borrowed.

Heather comes to my rescue, saying, "Obviously it's an Alexandria with that exquisite silk." Then she turns to me and says, "It matches your eyes perfectly."

I smile at Heather in gratitude and she smiles back.

Jack nods in the direction of a man who looks to be around thirty, with a slightly portly midsection and a kind face, hurrying this way. "Isn't that your fiancé, Sabrina? You've made an impressive match."

Sabrina scowls briefly, then turns around, plastering her stunning smile on her face again. She breaks away from Vivian and steps toward the man. I hear him say, "Sabrina. There you are. I was looking all over for you."

Sabrina says, "Oh, I'm sorry, Bradley. I was just saying hello to an old friend."

Old friend indeed. I wonder what kind of friends they were.

Vivian says crisply, "Well, Jack, I hope you enjoy the rest of your evening."

Heather nods shyly. "Nice to meet you, Bluebell. Good evening, Jack." Then Heather and Vivian turn to greet Bradley.

I breathe a sigh of relief as they walk away. Jack looks at me questioningly and gestures to the dance floor, "Shall we dance?"

I frown as I consider this. Dancing might ward off other "old friends," but the idea of being held in Jack's arms makes me more than a little nervous. "I'm not a skilled dancer, you know."

Jack smiles. "They're about to play a slow waltz. I can lead you through it easily." I like his face when it's lifted in a smile.

As if on cue, the graceful strands of a waltz begin. "Are you psychic?" I laugh.

Jack chuckles. "No, I just have good hearing, remember?"

Jack disposes of my empty champagne glass, and with his hand on the back of my waist, he ushers me to the dance floor where couples are already swirling around. When he turns to face me, he places my left hand on his shoulder and holds out his right hand for me to hold. I place my hand in his hesitantly, and Jack puts his other hand at my waist, pulling me close against him, far closer than old standards would allow. Then he starts dancing with his arm practically holding the weight of my body as he moves us gracefully to the music. I don't have to think at all as I simply place my feet down where Jack moves us. It's a good thing because with my head buzzing from champagne and the wonderful heat of Jack's body next to mine, I've lost all coherent thought anyway.

After a minute I get a feel for the pattern of the steps, and Jack loosens his grip, letting me guide my own body but still keeping me close. I revel in the hardness of Jack's body under the smooth fabric of his suit. The heat coming off him is a magnetic force pulling me in. I catch myself absently rubbing my thumb over the fabric on his shoulder and still my hand. I lean back to look at Jack as he swirls us around, thinking to distract myself from the feel of him by talking. But that is a grave error. His eyes are gazing at me intently, liquid pools of green again. My mouth goes dry. I turn my head to the side and Jack leans his jaw against my hair.

We dance silently, and the room disappears. There is nothing for me in that moment but the feel of Jack holding me, guiding me, surrounding me. I wonder if he feels the same. It seems every nerve in my body is attuned to Jack as though he is the center of the universe. Every place where our bodies touch flares alive with sensation. A tingling current spreads from each of these points and travels through my body, coalescing at the pit of my belly. I tremble at the sheer force of my attraction to him and the effort it takes to control it. Jack asks if I am cold, his breath brushing against my ear and sending another shiver through me. I lie and tell him I am. I'm trapped by my lie when he responds by pulling me closer again. It is all I can do to control my breathing and maintain a semblance of propriety.

Eventually Jack slows our pace and we come to a stop. When the world comes back to me, I realize the music has ended, and I'm standing in Jack's arms, still holding on to him. I can't let go of Jack quite yet because honestly my knees have no strength. I smile at him and say, "Just a moment. I'm a bit dizzy."

I am, but not the kind of dizzy I pretend. I keep my hands on his shoulders for a moment, getting strength from him and taking a few shaky breaths. Once my head has cleared and my heart has calmed, I step back and force a brilliant smile. "Can you point me to the ladies room?"

Jack says, "Let me take you there."

I protest since what I want is a little space from him.

But Jack's eyes steel and he insists. "I have an agreement with Varg. I'll wait right outside. You can take your time."

There is no bending him, so I acquiesce as we head across the room. When I enter the restroom, I go straight to the sink and run the water. The sharp coldness splashed on my forehead, cheeks, and neck clears my head and brightens my eyes a bit. I pat myself dry and meet Jack outside.

"Should we leave now?" I ask.

Jack frowns and replies, "It would be rude to leave before the winners of the auction are announced. It should be soon. Would you like to walk in the garden?"

"That's a wonderful idea." I think the night air will do me good.

Jack holds my arm, and we quietly exit out the French doors leading to the portico and down the steps to the glow stone path that twines through the beautiful garden. The mild evening air of early summer surrounds us. The garden is filled with the chirping of crickets and a symphony of insects that always accompany the Smoky Mountain outdoors. The stars are shining brightly tonight, and the moon hangs low in the sky. We walk deeper in the garden, leaving the sounds of the party behind us.

Jack keeps his hand on my arm until a cool breeze blows by. It causes me to truly shiver, and I wrap my shawl tightly around me. Jack puts his hand on my shoulder and pulls me into his side, tucking me under his arm. We walk slowly, admiring the plants lit by shimmering firefly lanterns. Neither of us speaks a word as we follow the winding glow stone path through the roses, the bulb garden, and the elaborate trellis garden at the end. I'm afraid to interrupt the magical moment with my voice, lest I bring it to an early end. The feel of Jack's warm solid body next to mine is both endlessly enticing and comforting. It feels just right.

Eventually, unfortunately, the path loops around and starts meandering its way back to the mansion. I can't help but feel sad this moment will soon be behind us too. I wonder when I started feeling this way about Jack. Has it always been this way? Or has it crept up over time? I am twenty-three years old, and I've never before felt this wanting for anyone. I have no idea what to do about it.

We are about to ascend the stairs back onto the portico when I feel a small tug on my sixth sense. It is more like an itch, and it's coming from above me. I pause, and Jack pauses with me, dropping his arm. I look up toward the top of the house and let my sixth sense rise. I whisper, "Jack, something's up there. I can't tell what it is, though."

Jack's body stills and his nostrils flare as if he is scenting. "It's a cat. I hear faint meows, and I smell fear and weakness."

I tug on his arm. "Let's find Mrs. Glenwood."

When we locate Mrs. Glenwood in the midst of several ladies and gentlemen, Jack steps in and asks her for a private word.

"But of course," she says and steps away from the group with a concerned look on her face. As we walk with her a few steps away, I see people in the small group she left casting curious glances our way.

I look at her and ask, "Do you by any chance have a cat?"

Mrs. Glenwood's eyes open wide, and sadness and hope both

spring forth. "Have you seen my dear Cleopatra? We've called for her up and down the street every night this week until tonight." She gestures to the room, indicating the party.

"I'm not sure if it's Cleopatra or not, but there is a scared and weak cat in your attic."

Mrs. Glenwood opens her mouth wide, then shuts it, then opens and shuts it once more. "The attic!" she finally exclaims. "I should have thought of that."

With her skirts hiked high, she runs to the hall. Jack and I follow her, and the small crowd tags along.

She runs up the stairs calling, "Jeffrey. Jeffrey. Cleopatra is in the attic!"

I see the same elderly man who asked for my coat now running up the stairs after Mrs. Glenwood, huffing and puffing a bit, but running all the same. My estimation of Mrs. Glenwood goes up immensely since I know she is running up to the attic in a dress that probably costs more than my entire wardrobe. Jack and I stay at the bottom of the stairs, riveted.

People keep milling out of the ballroom into the hall, inquiring about the ruckus. The bald man I saw by the Belladonna Necklace walks up behind us. I turn my back to him and look at Jack, hoping the man will simply pass. Unfortunately, I feel his dark soul close behind me, and I know my wish is not to come true.

I hear him over my shoulder and am forced to turn and face him. "Hello, Inspector Tanner, Inspector Kildare. Are you enjoying your evening?"

His soul does not feel right, and I slip my arm under Jack's while turning to greet him. Jack says smoothly, "Good evening, Mr. Blackwater. The Gala is always a wonderful event." Then Jack turns to me and says formally, "Ms. Kildare, this is Tobias Blackwater, our City Treasurer."

I turn to the man and lie, "It's a pleasure to meet you, Mr. Blackwater."

Blackwater smiles in satisfaction before addressing Jack again. "It's a shame about the boy at the Cock and Bull. Jason, wasn't it? Have you captured the perpetrator yet?"

Jack clears his throat. "Unfortunately, I can't comment on an ongoing case."

Mr. Blackwater narrows his eyes slightly. Jack is being coolly aloof when I expect charm and grace from him. He could have at least acknowledged Mr. Blackwater's concern.

Mr. Blackwater puffs himself up a bit. "Well, as an elected official of this city, I am concerned for all our citizens."

Jack replies smoothly, "Of course." Then a heavily pregnant silence follows, and I continue studying their faces curiously. Jack's face is irreproachably calm and emotionless, and Mr. Blackwater's face is painted with a smug smile that doesn't quite match with the repressed rage rolling off him.

Blackwater finally says, "Well, I must say hello to Mr. Abrams. Good evening to you, Inspectors."

Jack nods in acknowledgement, and Mr. Blackwater saunters off in the direction of the crowd milling by the ballroom entrance.

I am about to ask Jack what that was about when Mrs. Glenwood appears on the second floor landing cradling a white and silver pointed cat to her breast. She seems oblivious to the considerable amount of dust on her dress as she comes down the stairs and heads directly to me, all the while cooing, "I've got you, girl. Don't worry. I've got you now. And we are going to have a nice big meal for you in just one minute." I feel overwhelming joy coming from Mrs. Glenwood now.

When she gets to me, her eyes are brimming with tears. "Thank you so much, Bluebell. If there is anything I can ever do for you, please let me know. I'm in your debt." When she's finished, she doesn't wait for me to respond but leans in to give me a quick peck on the cheek and heads off, murmuring to Cleopatra, "Let's get you something to eat and drink, my precious girl."

Jack looks at me and asks, "How did you know something was up there?"

I don't really know myself, so I reply, "I just felt like something was tugging on my sixth sense. I usually can't feel animal souls, so I'm not sure what brought my attention to it."

Just then we hear someone broadcast the auction winners are about to be announced.

"Shall we?" asks Jack.

I put my arm in his and we return to the ballroom.

Later, on our way home, surrounded by the smell of leather in Jack's car, I reflect on what a wonderful evening it's been. Jack won a magical chess set and generously donated it to the orphanage. Once you start the game, the pieces can't be jostled out of place and can only be moved in turn. If you cheat, the board loudly announced you as a charlatan. And I couldn't be more pleased with my prize because I hold my beautiful crystal decanter in my hands.

CHAPTER 23

EVIDENCE OF ENTRY

BLUEBELL KILDARE

MAY 28, 2022, RED AGES

ack pulls up in front of my building, and before I can blink he opens the passenger door. Taking my hand in his, he helps me out saying, "I'll see you to your door."

When we arrive, I nervously reach for my keys in my handbag. Should I invite him in? Will he ask for a kiss? Do we pretend like nothing unusual happened tonight? My keys snag on the clasp of my purse, and drop to the floor in front of the door. I feel my face flush with embarrassment as I quickly reach down to grab them.

When I stand and begin to put the key in the lock, I feel Jack run his thumb over my bare shoulder. That's all it takes for my nerves to thrum to life again. My shawl has dropped, and my birthmark is exposed. I look behind me and see he's examining my birthmark, tracing it round and round with the tip of his finger. Shivers of pleasure run through me. My birthmark is a circle with a dot in the middle in raised pink flesh. Outside of the circle lies another circle in darker pink with wavy edges. This simple touch of fingertips on my bare skin makes my knees melt. I lean back slightly into Jack's hard body behind me.

Jack says in a husky voice, "You have a birth mark."

"I've read it's a symbol of the sun and the sacred circle of the Goddess of Light."

Jack rubs his thumb over it again, making my insides feel like molten lava. He whispers with a catch in his voice now, "It's also the symbol of fertility, rebirth, and the soul." Jack reaches around me, his arm burning me like a brand as he gently takes the keys from my hand that I now realize has dropped uselessly at my side. He opens the door.

As the door swings inward, Jack sniffs and quickly pulls me behind him. He enters, approaching Varg who's sitting in the middle of the living room. From where I stand, all I see are two glowing yellow eyes.

"Someone has entered," Jack announces as he turns on the light. He nods toward Varg and a small pool of blood on the floor in front of him. Next to him, my coffee table lies on its side and the jar of scented oil I used earlier today is reduced to a pile of shards covered in a wet, oily mess. The scent of lavender and mint overpowers the room.

Varg looks relaxed and satisfied, so I guess the threat has gone, but still I feel shaken and extremely angry. Someone was in my apartment! This is my home, my first haven from the world. No one has a right to enter without my approval. I feel violated.

My eyesight dims as I send my sixth sense out, looking for the presence of another soul just to be sure the intruder has gone. From Jack's direction I sense the intense glow of his soul. I've never opened up my sixth sense around him like this before. I'm stunned by the depth and power of his soul's light. I can feel the border of black taint from Lilith's mark hovering around the edges of his essence, trapping it. It infuriates me. But beneath that, from the core of his soul, I feel a strong sense of compassion and mercy. Oddly enough, I sense in equal measure their oft adversary, justice. I could discern more with time, but I'm keenly aware I'm infringing on his privacy.

I force my sixth sense away from Jack, and encountering no other souls in the apartment, I give my attention to the lingering emotions. Stepping toward Varg, the feeling of rage and frustration hits me like a blow. Beneath that, I feel in small portions both fear and pain. Interesting that the intruder's rage and frustration superseded the pain of his injury from Varg. It smacks of an unbalanced mind when frustration wins over self-preservation. I circle the area, feeling the outer edges, but encounter no sign the trespasser moved beyond the center of the room.

I take a few steps toward the sliding glass doors and smack into a feeling of such intense lust and passion, I feel a burning at my core, radiating out though my entire body, making every nerve tingle yet again. Holy Plane of Fire! Immediately I snap off my sixth sense, letting the reality of the room soothe my senses. I know who was standing in this spot earlier today. A warmth starts to creep up my neck and into my cheeks, which I quickly try to control as I watch Jack do his work.

He's become a blur of motion, checking the perimeter of the apartment, scenting and searching.

I call Varg to me to make sure he isn't bleeding. When he stands, I find a piece of torn cloth that had been hidden under his paw. Varg submits to my inspection with dignity and seems perfectly hale and hearty. I breathe a sigh of relief that he's not harmed.

When Jack finds nothing, he returns to us. I get my work pack and lift the torn cloth gingerly from the floor with my gloved hands, looking at it closely from all angles. It's a fine, woven black fabric with a seamed edge. "I think it's a piece of trouser."

Jack sniffs it and growls in frustration. "I can't smell anything under the scent of the oil."

Sighing, I place it in an evidence bag anyway, and we look about the room for other clues.

Jack moves more slowly, scenting around the perimeter of the room, trying to find the point of entry. He takes his time before turning to me. "Whoever it was did not break in. They portaled in. There's no scent on the boundaries of the room."

"I know. I have the entire exterior of the place warded."

Jack starts methodically searching the rest of the apartment. I call out to stop him. "Jack, there's no one here. I would feel them."

"I know. I'm checking to see if he went anywhere, but it looks like he portaled into the middle of Varg's lap and left immediately."

His brow is furrowed when he returns to me. He announces, "I think I should stay here tonight." Then he adds firmly, "On the couch." He looks coolly at me, and it feels like a slap in the face.

A flash of anger goes through me. I might have wanted him to stay ten minutes ago, but only if he wanted to be with me. Not because he feels like he has to protect me. He really needs to learn to take me seriously. Plus, perhaps irrationally, I feel I've just been rejected.

"Absolutely not!" I say as I throw my handbag down. "I already told you no. I have weapons. I have a wolf that has already scared whoever it was away. Plus, I sense souls, so no one can surprise me." I march toward the door and open it for him. My invitation for him to leave is glaringly clear.

Jack nods and silently leaves. I slam the door after him. "Don't let the door hit you in the ass on your way out." I mutter.

CHAPTER 24

SILENT VIGIL

JACK TANNER

MAY 28, 2022, RED AGES

I chuckle as Blue slams the door behind me while muttering some very unladylike things. She definitely has spirit. With a sense of relief, I pull in a deep draft of fresh air. Her sent is so strong inside it practically drives me wild. To smell it all around me all night and know she was just a few feet away would have been slow torture.

My blood turns cold again as I think of an intruder entering her apartment. The threat is significant. Obviously there is no question about whether or not I'm watching out for her tonight despite her protests. The only real question was where I'd be watching from.

I drive my car a few blocks down and run back toward the building. I see Blue and Varg emerge from the doorway, taking their nighttime walk. I follow them from a few blocks behind, keeping to the shadows. Varg is aware of my presence and glances back occasionally, but he's unconcerned. I'm reminded again to be grateful she found the beast.

When they return to the apartment, I scale the building. I pause on the wall outside Blue's kitchen, and the feel of her nearness calls to me. I splay my right hand over the brick and lean my forehead against the wall as a deep longing to touch her washes over me. Instead, and with great willpower, I continue to the roof and case the perimeter of the building.

Everything seems quiet on the street below. The sound of Blue pouring water and sprinkling something hard into a bowl filters through the roof. She is feeding Varg, no doubt. She patters to the bathroom, and a short time later the soft rustling of her bedding tells me she has slipped under the covers.

I lie down on the roof over Blue's bedroom and focus my senses on the sounds from below. She tosses and turns, moving restlessly in bed. A small thrill courses through me at the idea that she might be thinking of me as I think of her. The memories of the evening drift through my mind. Her desire tonight was clear. I recall how her heart raced when she first saw me and again when I asked her to turn around in her dress. I remember how her skirt lifted as she spun and how it softly floated down around her beautiful legs, legs I would love to see parted and wrapped around me.

The sensation of her peaked nipples brushing against my chest while we danced is burned into my mind. The smell of her arousal filled my senses and played havoc with my sanity. I remember how her womanly scent filled me again at the door as I traced her birthmark. Then her knees gave way and she leaned limply back against my chest in the heat of her desire. The intoxicating scent of her blood as her head fell against my shoulder rushed through my senses, and my desire for her was so great, it took all my considerable control to resist her. There is nothing I wanted more than to lean over her and taste her beautiful neck.

Her lack of experience is obvious, though. She is so unsure and apparently oblivious to how beautiful and alluring she is. I should be thankful because if she used her considerable power over me, I'm not sure I'd be able to turn her away. I smile at how the champagne affected her so easily, yet she was still quiet and shy on our garden walk. Scowling, I recall how the mass of people made her heart rate speed up and her skin turn pale. I shouldn't have brought her there. My scowl deepens at the memory of Sabrina's games.

Listening through the roof, I hear Blue's breathing slowing down now. Finally, I can tell she's completely drifted off into peaceful slumber.

During the night as the cold air blows in from the north, pushing the last of the warm air up the mountains, a light rainfall comes. The cold pellets hit my face and soak my clothes. Still I lie on the roof, welcoming the light shower, hoping it will distract me. Water pools in spots on the roof and runs in rivulets in others, racing down the scant slope and out the gutter system. I watch the water run in tiny streams over the pebbled tar near where my head lies. Still I think of Blue.

I can't help the thoughts entering my head, wondering how it would be to lie next to her, feeling her silky skin throughout the night. I try to push those thoughts away, as that should never be, yet they insinuate themselves with a stubborn refusal to leave. It will have to be enough that I can keep her safe.

The night wears on, and when the rain finally breaks and the sun peaks over the horizon, it reveals that I am still positioned prone on the roof over Blue's bedroom. Still I remain, alert but as silent as the moss that grows in the shadows of the roof's ledge. When I finally hear Blue rise and begin to move about, I stand and climb down the side of the building, reluctant to leave her behind.

CHAPTER 25

The Yellow Sea

BLUEBELL KILDARE

MAY 29, 2022, RED AGES

It is a comfortable seventy-four degrees with a mild breeze blowing and the sun shining as I head to the office. Before I pull away from the curb, I take a moment to appreciate the mist lazily hanging on the green mountain peaks despite the vivid blue sky.

As I head down the main thoroughfare in Rowan Park toward Windsor Avenue, the traffic slows to a snail's pace. I'm stuck behind a large, obnoxiously turquoise truck. I unroll my window and crane my neck, but I can't see beyond the wide bumper in front of me. Traffic coming from the other direction is sparse, but it's whizzing past at a normal pace. I hear a slight din in the distance, but the source remains obscured.

When I spot a right turn coming up, my foot starts anticipating the opportunity to use a little gas. Maybe I can go down a street or two to avoid the hang-up. Finally I reach the corner and take a quick right. I sail free down the entire block then take an easy left. Sure enough, I'm able to zip past the last few blocks to Windsor Avenue. When I get to the stop sign at the corner, I look to the left and see cars packed tight as sardines past Windsor, so I decide to stay on the road less traveled and continue to skirt traffic. What in the world is going on?

A block to the right of the main thoroughfare, I continue on about half a mile, thinking to cut over at National Street. But suddenly I see the source of the traffic jam. Right in front of Mr. and Mrs. Glenwood's mansion, there's a slew of Dilectus Deo in all their yellow-robed glory, shouting threats while simultaneously quoting the Bible. Criminy! They're everywhere. How many breedists are in this city?

It looks like the main protest is in front of the Glenwood Mansion, and people are congregating on the sidewalk and all through the street, completely blocking traffic. They must be a thousand strong. The throng is so large people have milled down to the east side of the block, hanging in clusters.

As I approach the end of the block and am about to make another right to further avoid the crowd, I hear some shouting coming from behind a couple of hawthorn bushes close to the corner. I think nothing of it until I hear a thud followed by a very distinct moan. Holy smokes! Someone's getting beaten up over there.

I stop my car and flip open my chimerator. I perform a quick chant to contact Jack, and when his face shows up on the pearly surface, I say, "I'm in front of the Glenwood's. Someone's getting beaten up behind a bush at the Dilectus Deo protest. I'm going in, so please send back-up and an ambulance." I see his brows scrunch up, then I flip the ring closed before he can deter me.

As soon as I jump out of the car, Varg jumps in the front seat and hurls himself through the open window after me. I hear sickening thuds, the obvious sounds of flesh impacting flesh, as I race across the lawn. When I round the corner, I see three men surrounding a figure on the ground, one of them crouched over with his fist raised.

I pull out my Glock and yell in my loudest and most authoritative voice, "Hands in the air. I'm with the Supernatural Investigation Bureau and you are under arrest."

All three heads spin and gawk at me simultaneously. One man freezes and the other two run. Varg takes off, chasing one of the men, and after about thirty feet I see him fly through the air and jump right on the man's back, forcing him down with the strength of the impact. The man wriggles and struggles, yelling and crying in fear until Varg clamps his jaw loosely around the man's neck. The man mercifully shuts up and stills. A wise choice, I'm sure.

We've gathered the attention of a few protestors on the outer edges of the street, and from them I sense a bewildered curiosity. The din is so loud, the crowd so thick and agitated that the main part of the protest goes on unaffected.

What I feel from them is a massive wall, huge and dense, full of anger, hate, and fear. I remember Jack told me the time and location of the Gala was confidential. Now I know why. Clearly the Dilectus Deo take issue with a large-scale transfer of magical items. While I'm taking this in, I busily cuff the first guy and drag him toward the metal railing on the mansion's front stoop.

Once I have him secured, I run toward the victim. He's a young man, about my age or slightly younger, wearing jeans and a jersey t-shirt. His face is bloody, and he's curled up on the ground in the fetal position, breathing noisily. As I lean over him I see his eyebrows are bright pink. Assuming he is Gifted and not just in an attention-seeking stage, I feel for his magic. It's just under the surface, and I can tell it's a gift relating to communication, but I can't say exactly what.

I try to engage him by saying, "An ambulance is on the way. Where are you hurt?"

He starts to talk, but it turns into a cough and I see blood speckles form on his lips. Cripes!

I lean over and say, "No, don't talk. You're injured too badly. Stay still, and we'll get some help."

I rush to my car and grab Varg's blanket in the back seat. I gently lay it over the man, and at that moment Jeffrey, the Glenwoods' butler, joins my side.

Jeffrey says, "Oh my God. Is he going to be okay?"

I snap at Jeffrey. "Don't look to God to see if he'll be okay. It's so-called men of God who put him here." I take a deep breath and finish in a more reasonable tone. "I'm sorry, Jeffrey. I called Jack, and an ambulance is on the way."

Jeffrey looks sheepish and says, "I called the police and an ambulance as soon as it started, so there may be two coming."

"Jeffrey, do you have any rope?" I ask as I gesture to where Varg is holding on to the second perpetrator.

Jeffrey stammers, "Oh, right. Of course." He rushes in the side entrance. As I watch him go, I see two pairs of eyes staring out from behind the blinds next to the front door. Mr. and Mrs. Glenwood, I assume.

A few minutes later Jeffrey appears with a length of rope. I use it to tie the hands and feet of the second perpetrator and anchor him to a tall ash tree in the yard. As soon as Varg lets go of the man's neck, the man starts spitting out a string of cuss words that would make Maud roll over in the grave plot she hasn't purchased yet. I ignore how much the man of God hates me and how the Beloved of God wants to see me cut into tiny pieces with a dull, rusty serrated knife because as I truss him up the first ambulance arrives.

I run over to the ambulance where Jeffrey is already giving the medics the scoop. It seems Jeffrey was able to get a view of the whole thing from the office window.

Varg is staring avidly at the mass of people shouting in the street with a low growl rumbling from his chest. I can see he feels cheated because one man got away. I feel cheated as well. The crowd is a sea of identical yellow robes, and there is no way I could find the third perpetrator on my own. I look at Varg, and Varg looks at me.

I prompt, "Varg, where's the third guy?"

Varg takes off in a flash and runs into the crowd, breaking up the masses, leaving me a narrow wedge of space through which to follow him. We move quickly through the crowd until one man grabs on to my arm and yells, "Get out of here, Aberration."

Before I have a chance to think, my gun is in my hand, but it's not necessary. Varg spins around and lunges savagely at the man. The man lets go as he backs away from Varg, and we immediately take up the chase again.

Our sprint through the crush is causing even more of a ruckus as people start yelling obscenities, threats, and epithets at our trail. Our perpetrator must know we're after him, because I see a wave of yellow gowns moving out of the way of one gown in particular as he runs ahead of us. I catch a glimpse of his head, but all I see is a mass of thick, dark hair. We have pushed and shoved our way through about two-thirds of the crowd by now and are nearing the far end of the block when Varg gets an opening and darts between some legs to grab on to the man's ankle.

The man goes down face first, and Varg stands on his prey with forepaws on his back and a vicious growl in his ear. The man screams, "Get him off! Get him off!"

I pull my gun out and aim it at the man. I hear someone near the edge of the circle surrounding me shout, "She's an Aberrant."

Suddenly, I feel the full force of hate, anger, and fear of this crowd center on me, and it doesn't take a genius to see this is about to get even uglier.

I try to diffuse the crowd by yelling, "I'm with the Supernatural Investigation Bureau, and this man is under arrest for beating an innocent bystander."

Somehow this title does not garner the degree of respect I'd hoped it would, and the angry voices escalate. I hear a woman shouting, "She's probably lying."

Voices get angrier and the words get uglier.

"She's a freak."

"One of the unnaturals has one of God's Beloved."

This last statement raises the mob madness to an unprecedented level. I sense violent intentions from dozens in the circle around us, which are reinforced by the first soft mutterings of "Get her." and "Bring her down."

The circle starts to tighten, and I move my gun off the man now, relying on Varg to secure him. Instead I point it at the crowd.

I spin in a small circle, looking each yellow robed figure in the eye with a great deal of boldness. "Step back," I yell. "This is a matter for the law."

They aren't listening, and the circle is tightening. I glance back at Varg and see him growing before my eyes. He stands with his head low and his hackles raised from head to tail, claiming his prey but ready to pounce on the crowd if need be.

I hope the mob backs off for its own sake because Varg is huge. Everyone's eyes are on me, so I don't know if they notice him. As I'm about to start shooting at the ground near the feet of the crowd to push the circle back, he raises his muzzle and howls eerily. The sound echoes off the large mansions lining the street. Everyone's eyes swivel to him, and a collective gasp comes from the horde.

Just then I see a dark blur fly over the heads of those nearest me and land in the center of the circle. It's Jack. He pulls out his sword and starts whirling it around the crowd in a dizzying display, driving it back at all points of the circle and widening the space around us. Some of the anger dissipates, turning to fear and frustration. Jack moves faster than their eyes can see, and they know his sword will cut indiscriminately. Jack doesn't waste time with announcements or words; he simply continues to widen the circle by stepping nearer and nearer to the crowd as he extends his sword its full reach, daring anyone to encroach on the circle of death he's created.

I hear shouts of "Police! Police!" followed by a voice over a loudspeaker saying, "This protest is over. Disperse or be arrested."

A large percentage of the crowd moves off immediately, but a few hateful eyes pinned on me are more reluctant to leave than others.

Ernesto pushes through the thinning mass and cuffs the man under Varg's feet. I say, "Ernesto, you should question Jeffrey at the Glenwood Mansion. He saw that man and the two others I've already secured attack the victim."

Ernesto says, "I certainly will, Señorita. You got yourself in quite a tangle today. I'm glad it came out okay."

I smile gratefully. Then with a whistle I call Varg over to me since he seems reluctant to give up his final prize. The police are in full force now, moving people down the street and waving them to their cars. With satisfaction, I watch all three men get shoved into S.I.B. cars.

Not until the entire area is clear does Jack put down his sword and turn to me. He asks with daggers in his eyes I know are meant for others, "Did anyone hurt you?"

I shake my head and reply, "One man grabbed my arm, but Varg scared him off."

Jack's eyes flick to Varg and then back to my face. He says in a grim tone, "You may not have been hurt, but another minute or two and you could have been dead."

I lift up my chin and respond steadily, "All in the line of duty, Jack. I did what was right, and if you know me at all you should never expect less."

I holster my gun and walk, head held high, back to my car with Varg trailing behind me and Jack watching my back.

CHAPTER 26

NEW LEADS

BLUEBELL KILDARE

MAY 29, 2022, RED AGES

I enter the office accompanied by a feeling of tremendous relief. Rubalia, who's intently gazing at her computer screen, pulls her eyes away to greet me. "Good morning, Blue," she says. She flicks her eyes downward. "I see you still have the beast with you."

I'm slightly shocked it's still morning since I feel wrung out already. However, I reply with an understated calm, "Good morning, Rubalia. I still work in homicides and it's still dangerous. He saved my life yet again this morning. Do you have any messages for me?"

Rubalia raises her eyebrows doubtfully responding, "I don't have messages, but some documents have come through." She hands a few sheets of paper over the counter while glaring at Varg. Varg looks innocently back at her, completely unfazed.

"Thank you," I say as I sift through the documents. "Could you get me the name and number for the president of the local Rotary Club, please?"

Rubalia nods, "I'll bring it right in."

"Is Jack in yet?"

Rubalia's eyes turn troubled and glance down the hall. "Yes. He must have had a hard night. I don't think he slept at home because he was here running the shower when I arrived. Then both he and Ernesto rushed out of here like bats out of the Eternal Fire. A few minutes ago Jack comes back and Ernesto brings three guys up the back way in cuffs to the interrogation rooms. They're being questioned now."

"Hmm," I respond. "Please tell him I'm writing a report and I'm here if he needs me." Those are the words that come out of my mouth, but the words running around in my head are quite different. Did he spend the night in some other woman's arms since he clearly had no interest in mine? Sabrina at the Gala seemed eager for a piece of him. A streak of jealousy runs through me that's impossible not to recognize. As I walk to my office, I glare down the hall toward Jack's office, wishing my glare could penetrate the door and set something on fire.

I sit down at my desk and look around my comforting office. Varg stretches out by the floor-to-ceiling window, apparently enjoying the view. It is not as grand as Jack's, of course, but it's tastefully furnished like the rest of the unit and brightened by a few personal possessions. I love my lush green fern the most. It sits in the corner next to the window, thriving in the cool shade of the air-conditioned room. I splurged on it for my one year work anniversary. It makes me feel somehow connected to this place, and I'm proud I've kept it alive and flourishing.

I organize my thoughts and type out a report about today's mob incident. Additional paperwork is required for every Dilectus Deo incident. They aren't officially considered a cult but are on our watch list. A separate form must be completed to document hate crimes against the magically Gifted. I have to include the nature of their magical gift and what their mark is. I don't have all the information yet, so I'll have to complete an addendum report later. At this point I don't even know the victim's name. The extra work is no hardship because I really want to visit him in the hospital anyway to make sure he's okay. He obviously had internal bleeding, so he could be severely injured. When I'm done, I zap the paperwork to Rubalia and Jack in an email for them to review and route as necessary. Then I take a minute to let my anger at the Dilectus Deo seethe.

After internally raging long enough, I look at the profile sheets for the owners of the Meteor Shockwave. Leroy Zevin looks defiantly at the camera in a photo that's obviously from a previous arrest. He has a record of breaking and entering, home invasions, and battery, and he's been in and out of prison. Hector Martinez has some speeding tickets and a juvenile record that is closed, but nothing notable for the last twenty years. Agnes Zadwaski only has a driver's license photo and no record at all besides one ticket for expired registration on another car she owns.

I dial up Gambino.

"Gambino," he answers with a little more roughness than usual.

"Hola, this is Blue. What have you got on the three car owners?"

Gambino lets out a sigh of frustration that is clearly audible through the line. "The bartender doesn't know any of the three, and every one of them has an alibi."

I echo his sigh with one of my own. "Let me think about it, Gambino. I'll call you back."

I stare at the three sheets for a moment, particularly at Agnes' sheet because something isn't sitting right with me. Finally, I click on my intercom and buzz Rubalia. "Rubalia, can you come in here for a moment? I want to run something by you."

Rubalia enters, and I gesture her to the chair opposite my desk. "Rubalia. I'm going to tell you about a car, and I want you to guess if the owner is a male or a female."

Rubalia says, "Sure," and by the set of her shoulders, I can see she takes the question seriously.

"Okay," I say. "A 1968 Meteor Shockwave in the color pewter green."

Rubalia lifts up her chin and answers confidently, "A man, of course."

"Why do you say that?"

She explains, "First of all, it's old as dirt and would cost too much to repair if you couldn't do it yourself. Sad to say, but there aren't many women who know how to fix a car, except for my second cousin Jovita Glover." Rubalia pulls her glittering glasses down to the tip of her nose and gives me a look. "She can make a junkyard car purr like a pussycat, but that girl is talented and rare." Then she settles back further in the chair, though never letting her back actually touch its back. I'm not sure I've ever seen Rubalia touch the back of a chair.

"Second of all," she continues, "a Meteor Shockwave that is gray-green has 'man' written all over it. Now, if it were repainted red I'd think twice. But not only is the inside big and uncomfortable with that long bench seat in front that you have to slide across, but what woman wants her complexion to be seen next to a gray-green color? It is a man's car, through and through."

"I completely agree with you, Rubalia." I hand her Agnes' sheet. "Can you find out if Agnes Zadwaski has a husband or another man living at the house?"

Rubalia nods. "I sure will." She stands and hands me a slip of paper. "And here's the information on the Rotary Club president and vice president. The president is on vacation right now, so you'll have to call the vice president."

I watch Rubalia walk out gracefully in her slate gray skirt suit, closing the door gently behind her. I sure wish I had her wardrobe. Maybe then Jack wouldn't have been so cold to me last night and possibly spent the night in some other woman's arms.

"Ugh!" I slam my hand down on the desk. He can have all the women he wants. He can have an orgy of women if he wants. What's it to me?

I practically injure my fingers punching in the phone number for the Rotary Club vice president while scanning the paper. The President is Victor Edmundovich, the mayor. How interesting.

"Dunfield Realty," a young, bored-sounding female voice answers.

"This is Inspector Kildare calling for Sigmund Dunfield. Is he available?"

"Hold, please," the voice says, sounding quite a bit sharper now that I've announced myself.

After a minute the phone picks up again and I hear, "Sigmund Dunfield here. Can I help you?"

"Hello, Mr. Dunfield. This is Inspector Bluebell Kildare from the Supernatural Investigation Bureau. Do you have time for a few questions?"

Dunfield replies in a professional voice, "Of course. How can I be of assistance?"

"I understand the Rotary Club sponsored the Sun Flare Celebration Fireworks and Magic Show this year."

Dunfield answers enthusiastically, obviously eager to share information on his philanthropic work. "Yes, we did. We do every year, as a matter of fact. Not just the Fireworks and Magic Show, though. We sponsor the entire celebration. The city picks up the tab, of course, but we do all the organization of the vendors, entertainment, and local talent."

Hmm, I wonder if they get kickbacks from the vendors they select. Not my problem, but I wouldn't be surprised. "That sounds like a lot of work."

He boasts, "It certainly is, but we feel it's part of our civic duty. We divide and conquer, with a different Rotary member taking the lead on the different events that take place."

"Who's the lead for the Fireworks and Magic Show?"

Dunfield answers easily, "Oh, that's Fire Department Chief Gerald Mack, since of course fire is his specialty, and he needs to be involved from a safety perspective anyway."

"Thank you so much, Mr. Dunfield. You certainly do provide a great service to the city with your work."

"You're very welcome Inspector Kildare. But may I ask what this questioning is about?"

"I'm sorry, Mr. Dunfield. I'm not at liberty to say as it is part of an ongoing investigation. However, I can tell you that right now I am just doing a little background research."

"Oh, I see. Well, I hope I was helpful," Mr. Dunfield says, a salesman to the end.

"I really appreciate your assistance."

When I hang up, Rubalia knocks and enters. She hands me a new profile sheet with the photo of a ruddy-looking man in his fifties with a receding hairline and sagging, weak blue eyes.

Rubalia says, "Paul Zadwaski is her brother and listed her address as his place of residence at his last arrest. He looks like a sorry man. No other names come up under that address."

I beam at her and feel like things are truly looking up now. "Thank you so much, Rubalia. You are a goddess of research." Rubalia smiles back and starts to close the door.

"Wait. Rubalia?"

Rubalia opens the door wide again with an expression denoting boundless patience. Goodness knows she needs it with us.

"Can you do a little side research? Nothing urgent, but I'd like to know who's responsible for checking on suspected city corruption. Please keep it on the down-low as I just have a suspicion, nothing concrete."

Rubalia gives me an ear-to-ear grin and her eyes get very mischievous. "I'd be more than happy to."

I feel blessed to be the recipient of true glee from Rubalia, so I give her a pure, beaming smile right back. "No rush, Rubalia. No rush."

She closes the door softly and I read the sheet she just handed me. Paul Zadwaski, age fifty-four, currently has a DUI and a suspended license. He was driving the Shockwave when he was arrested for drunk driving. This is our guy. I can feel it.

I dial Detective Tony Gambino using normal pressure on the keypad this time. "Gambino." I say excitedly when he answers, "I think I've found our man. Agnes has a brother, Paul Zadwaski, who has a DUI and a suspended license. He was driving the car when he was arrested for the DUI, and he listed her address as his own."

Gambino swears, "God damn it! I told my detective to give me everyone at the addresses where the cars were registered. I should have known he didn't do it when he came back with only three sheets."

I disregard this, as his internal issues are not my problem. "Gambino, I'd like to be there for the questioning. Can we meet at Agnes' house in an hour?"

"Sure thing," he says. "See you there."

I quickly add, "Hey Gambino, by the way, I have a new police dog companion."

Gambino laughs. "Nice one," he says and then hangs up.

I look at the phone in my hand. What, he doesn't think a woman would have a dog? What is the deal?

CHAPTER 27

POSITIVE REPORTS

JACK TANNER

MAY 29, 2022, RED AGES

A moment after I hear Blue hang up her phone, she runs down the hall to my office. Who in the city government does she suspect of corruption? If I ask her she'll know I overhear all of her conversations. When she pauses outside my door, I place a file on top of the report I'm reading and call out, "Come in."

She wears jeans paired with a soft blue tee that hugs her body with excruciating closeness. Her light shimmers around her as though in tune with her obvious excitement. She slides through the door with a radiant grin on her face. Her faithful companion comes in after her and sits next to her feet. She stands in the middle of my office, biting her lip and wiggling her boots, totally unconscious she does that around me.

Her voice is lively, full of light tones, as she asks quickly, "Did you finish your interrogation of the perpetrators from this morning?"

"I'm letting Ernesto handle that since he questioned Jeffrey and has a line on the Dilectus Deo. That's not what you really want to talk about, is it?"

Blue shakes her head and says, "Jack, I think we found our perpetrator. One of the registered owners of the matching cars in this area has a brother living with her. He was recently arrested for a DUI while driving the car. I'm meeting Gambino in an hour at the owner's house."

I was leaning back in my chair as she told me this, but I sit forward now, smiling. "Excellent news, Blue. That is a wonderful break."

She says, "Rubalia did the research and found him." How nice of her to give Rubalia credit when deserved.

"Let me know how it pans out."

She nods at this, her excitement still palpable. Then suddenly she starts biting her lip again as though she feels awkward. "Well," she says, "that's all I have."

I say, "While you are here . . . I'm sending Michael Radskif over to redo your wards. He'll be there tomorrow at two. He can ward your apartment inside and out so no one can portal in again. The department is covering the cost since the need is in relation to a case."

She frowns slightly at this and looks down at the toes of her boots. When she raises her eyes to me she says, "Alright, I'll plan to be there. I'll also let you know how things go with the case."

"Thank you. Remember, earlier reporting is better."

She nods and leaves my office with Varg following behind.

How has she grown into such a beautiful woman with such a good heart? And to top that off, she's my most tenacious Inspector, solving cases with her gift, her passion, and her considerable intuition. Today scared the living daylights out of me, though. I need to think about hiring a partner for her. An image rises in my mind of a man riding around all day with her in a car. My gut aches at the thought, but it would be safer for her.

A few moments later I find myself still staring at the door she walked through. I shake myself and pick up my cell phone, dialing up voicemail. I hit replay on my latest message. Dragomira's unmistakable voice says, "Jack, I met the Illustrissima. Please stop by, for we have much to discuss."

I frown and play it again.

"I met the Illustrissima." And again and again and again. "Illustrissima. Illustrissima. Illustrissima." I slam my hand down on my desk. She must be mistaken.

CHAPTER 28

FLY TRAP

BLUEBELL KILDARE

MAY 29, 2022, RED AGES

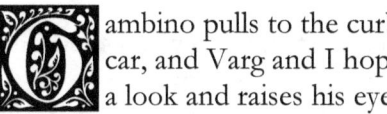ambino pulls to the curb on Agnes' street in his marked car, and Varg and I hop out of mine. Gambino gives Varg a look and raises his eyebrows at me. I nod back at Gambino to confirm he's with me. Gambino tilts an amused smile that miffs me. Varg deserves considerable respect in my humble opinion, and Gambino is not, as of yet, giving it. Humph. Gambino will learn soon enough.

Agnes lives in a blue, one-story cottage trimmed with white shutters and yellow daylilies. It's humble but pleasant and well-cared-for. Gambino rings the bell, so we wait to see who appears.

Agnes opens the house door but leaves the screen door conspicuously intact. She looks in her fifties with light brown, wispy hair flying about her shoulders. As soon as she sees Gambino, she frowns. "I thought I answered all your questions already."

Gambino smiles amicably, gesturing toward me. "This is Inspector Kildare with the Supernatural Investigation Bureau. I'm sorry to bother you again, but we have a few more questions."

Agnes squints her eyes and crosses her arms under her ample bosom, nodding reluctantly. "Okay, I guess, but you can't come in right now. My house is a mess. What do you want to know, anyway?"

Gambino smoothes his suit lapel as he asks, "Is your brother Paul home?"

Agnes looks disgusted. "No. He's probably at the damn pub, getting sloshed again." She tilts her head as though thinking, and then asks curiously, "Why? Do you think he had anything to do with it?"

Gambino's brow furrows and he glances down at his shoes. "We can't answer that question. Right now we're just gathering information.

The pub you mentioned, is that the Cock and Bull Tap?"

Agnes shifts on her feet and answers with a mixture of shame and resignation. "Yes. That's where he always is."

Gambino asks the crucial question. "Do you know where Paul was on May 26?"

"No," she says with a huff. "Remember I was visiting my parents in Hickory Creek? I've not got him in my pocket, have I? He was probably doing what he always does: hanging out at that pub or sleeping it off."

Gambino seems to think he's gotten all he can and moves to leave with a "Thanks, Ms. Zadwadski."

I quickly step up to the screen door to ask a few questions in my own way. "Is that your pretty blue Sunray in the driveway?"

Agnes pushes through the screen door to look where I'm pointing. The sun shines down lighting up the brightly patterned apron tied about her waist. She gives her car a loving glance and answers with pride, "Yes, it is."

I walk to the driveway and circle the car as I admire it. "It is a beautiful car." I trail my fingers down the hood. "I've heard it's very comfortable and that it's great with the top down."

Agnes steps out further toward the car and smiles. "I always wanted a convertible. I saved up for years to buy it."

"Well," I say, "I think it was worth the wait."

She nods at this, and a little of the pinched grimness of her lips softens. Seeing this, I ask, "Where's the Shockwave? I drive past this way to work, and usually see it in the mornings. It's hard to miss a classic like that."

Agnes frowns, "That was my father's car. It's a beauty, alright, but not my style. Paul had a fender bender and is having it repaired right now."

I stand back to admire the car in full. "So Paul usually drives the Shockwave?"

"Yes. It's too awkward for me with that big front seat. And besides, it's that awful green color." She wrinkles her nose.

I laugh, thinking back to my conversation with Rubalia. "I can understand that. Well, thank you so much for your time. I'm sorry we had to bother you again."

Agnes' thin smile stretches across her face. "I'm sorry I couldn't be of more help." Then a sad and worried look passes over her face. "I sure hope Paul wasn't involved in anything bad." Then she walks quietly back in the house.

Gambino looks at me curiously. "You have some skills, Inspector."

"I have some special talents that help me out." I look Gambino in the eyes with what I hope is an earnest expression. "I believe her that Paul isn't here. I can tell when someone lies, but if you need me to, I can circle the house looking for another soul."

Gambino gives a shake of his head. "That won't be necessary."

"What's interesting is she's apparently completely unaware that her brother has a DUI. She answered that question so easily and with no fear at all. I take it when you questioned her, you didn't give her any details. She feels honest about everything she said. She truly doesn't view her brother as a bad man, just a pathetic one."

Gambino looks to the side with faraway eyes. "Most of us have someone like that in the family."

I wonder what his family is like. I've never asked him, and suddenly I feel quite self-centered. For now, though, I let that comment slide, as there is business to get to.

"Back to the Cock and Bull Tap then?"

Gambino nods firmly. "Yes. I'll meet you there."

A few minutes later, when I arrive at the Cock and Bull Tap, I look at my watch and see that it's approximately 11:06 a.m. Ha! "Approximately." I chuckle thinking back to Officer Warren at the crime scene.

Gambino and I push through the heavy doors of the Cock and Bull Tap together and they swing closed heavily behind us. Light streams through the leaded windows, creating a soft glow on the warm wood furniture filling the room. The lunch crowd has yet to arrive, so the place stands practically empty. We scope out the occupants and see a uniformed man sitting by himself at one of the long trestle tables. Two more men sit apart from each other at the bar with their backs to us. One seems further in his cups than the other if the way he uses the bar to prop himself up is any indication. A soft blues melody plays over the speakers, filling the air with a soulful mood.

The bartender sees Gambino and I and lifts up his hand in greeting.

One of the men on the bar stools notices and spares us a glance. His eyes widen into twin round, bloodshot globes when he sees us. With a yelp and a spryness I wouldn't have credited him with, he jumps off his stool and runs out the side exit.

The bartender yells after him, "Hey. Your bill!" At the same time, Gambino and I take off after him with our guns pulled. Damn it! I should have known better than to leave that exit uncovered.

We exit the building and spot him across the street. I start to run after him, but Gambino jerks me back, and I skid to a halt, watching as the first of several cars whizzes past me just inches away. How stupid could I be? Varg comes bounding around the corner of the bar, apparently having heard our exit and wanting to join in the fun. When the cars finally pass, we hightail it across the street, eager to catch our suspect.

Paul had entered the alley across the street, but now he's nowhere to be seen. Blast it! We pound down the gravel alleyway as fast as we can, hoping for a glimpse of him hiding on either side. Even so, it only takes a second for Varg to race ahead of us at top speed. We look left and right, but the buildings are packed tight as sardines, leaving no place to veer off. Still, we see no sign of him. I am more than fed up with disappearing men.

Gambino pulls ahead of me with his longer legs, but when I make it about halfway down the alley, I come up to Varg, who is issuing a low and dangerous growl toward the base of a dumpster. I open up my sixth sense and confirm there is a soul inside. Gambino pauses when he realizes he's running alone and retraces his steps toward us. I catch his gaze and nod at Varg and the dumpster. Gambino nods back in understanding.

I point my gun toward the lid of the dumpster, and Gambino kicks it, yelling, "This is the Crimson Hollow Police. Put your hands in the air and come out slowly."

We stand there patiently for a moment, nothing happens. I nod again to assure Gambino. He gives it another try, this time allowing more force and rage in his voice. "We know you're in there. Come out with your hands up. Now."

Finally, two shaky hands poke out and begin to raise the dumpster's lid. Gambino flips the lid back, exposing Paul's ruddy head. Slowly he stands, and his stained, t-shirt-clad chest comes into view above the dumpster rim.

Gambino asks, "Paul, now why did you run?"

Paul speaks in a piteously slurred and whiny voice that makes me wince. "I was scared."

You don't need a gift to see this is true with all the shaking he's doing. On second thought, a good part of that could be the alcoholism talking.

Gambino trains his gun on Paul and orders firmly, "Climb on out of there. Don't make any fast moves."

Paul grabs the side of the dumpster and tries to stand on a stack of garbage bags to get leverage, but he slips back, falling on his rump in the gross muck.

"Oh, for Christ's sake," Gambino swears. Thrusting his gun in his holster, he leans over to grab Paul's arms, pulling him out effortlessly.

Paul swings his legs over the edge, and instead of catching himself, he slops to the ground like a sack of pudding. I can see and smell that he's wet himself. Yep, a good portion of that shaking is real fear, not just alcoholism.

Gambino shakes his head at the pathetic ruin of a man. He pulls his gun again and says, "Lie flat on the ground, Paul, face down, and put your arms behind your back."

Paul is blubbering now and still trembling, but he lies down and obediently puts his hands behind his back. I honestly don't think he has any gumption left in him. The fact he even ran in the first place is surprising. Gambino quickly slaps some cuffs on him and reads him his rights.

As we walk a very stinky Paul back to Gambino's squad car, Gambino asks "Paul, where is your Shockwave?"

Paul slurs, "M'fred Robby's houz."

Gambino gathers the rest of the details as best he can and calls on his radio to have the car impounded for evidence.

When Gambino finally closes the car door on Paul, he turns to me. "Well, I'm glad we were able to wrap this up, and your wolf sure came in handy." I puff a little at his praise of Varg, but I see that Gambino's feeling some premature success.

"Gambino, Paul isn't the man who grabbed me behind my

apartment. He isn't tall enough. He couldn't have aimed as well as the man who shot at me behind the Cock and Bull Tap. Look at his hands shake. Nor does he have the skills to break into your evidence locker. He's not Gifted."

Gambino scowls as he recognizes the truth.

I continue, "I think he's only a part of the picture. I have a little leg work to do while you process him and he sobers up. How about I stop by the precinct later on to see how questioning is going?"

Gambino looks a good deal less happy than he did a minute ago, but his shoulders are still strong, and he looks determined to soldier on. "Sure thing."

I head back to the Cock and Bull Tap and approach my friend Steve Jamison. I extend my hand for a shake, and Steve accepts it warmly. With a nod toward the door he inquires, "You got him?"

"Yeah, we got him."

Steve pulls his hand back and whistles softly while his eyes rest lightly on me. "That sure was hot to watch."

His honest appreciation for my physique is clear in his eyes but has no effect on me. I brush it off and lean against the bar. "So, was that the same man who wore the red cloak on the day I came in here?"

The bartender says, "No, Ma'am. That's Paul. He's one of our usual barflies. He's here all the time. The guy in the red cloak had never been here before and hasn't showed up since."

I look at him closely, squinting my eyes, giving him warning to be square with me. "Are you sure?"

Steve purses his lips. "I am abso-fucking-lutely sure."

I sigh. "That's what I thought. Thanks, Steve."

I head out, but as I approach the door, I throw over my shoulder, "Keep remembering his face. I might be back."

CHAPTER 29

EMPATHETIC SOUL

BLUEBELL KILDARE

MAY 29, 2022, RED AGES

I pull my car into the visitor section of the Crimson Hollow Fire Department. No sooner do Varg and I stroll through the administration door than a smoking hot fireman walking in my direction asks, "Can I help you?"

If I were another woman, I would surely answer that with, "I'm on fire. Can you lend me your hose?" However, since I am not another woman, I pull out my badge and say, "I'm Inspector Kildare here to see Chief Gerald Mack." I sure wish I were another woman sometimes.

The fireman points down the hall. "Third door on the right."

Varg and I continue forward and pass two more handsome, well-built guys. This place is just crying for a fireman calendar. Chief Mack sure keeps them in shape.

I restrain myself with all my virginal dignity and instead knock calmly on the door that reads "Chief Gerald Mack" on the outside.

He calls out with a deep, smooth voice, "Come on in."

I open the door and the first thing I see is a beautiful Dalmatian sitting on a plaid dog bed under the window. The Dalmatian jumps up and starts doing the doggy happy dance around Varg. Varg stands at my side and does a little sniffing but remains aloof and dignified. I think he's playing hard to get. I open the door further and see a wide oak desk with an older gentleman sitting behind it. His lanky form is obvious even as he sits in a casual and relaxed position.

He smiles at me gently and gestures at the chair opposite his desk. "Make yourself at home."

I step in and sit down at his desk. Varg parks himself by my side, and the Dalmatian lies at Varg's feet, rolling over to show her belly.

"Hello, Chief Mack. I'm Inspector Kildare of the Supernatural

Homicide Investigation Unit."

Chief Mack inclines his head slightly with a smile still on his lips.

"I'd like to ask you a few questions."

Chief Mack inclines his head slightly more and says, "Sure."

So far Chief Mack has hardly moved, his face has been nothing but kind, and his voice is smooth and rich as spiced rum. I am getting a feeling about Chief Mack, and it's a good one so far. He has medium brown skin with curly black hair that's cut close and graying at the temples. The age spots that speckle his face are all but eclipsed by the intelligence shining out of his observing eyes.

"I understand you lead the committee that oversees the Sun Flare Celebration Fireworks and Magic Show."

Mack nods at this and watches me as I continue.

"I understand there was a talent interview on Phantom Island. You were interviewing volunteers."

Mack nods at this as well.

Clearly Mack is not going to chat it up, so I'd better ask direct questions. "Did you do the interviews?"

Mack says in his slow as molasses cadence, "Well, I did the early interviews, but I got called out on a big fire in the Warehouse District about midway through. The rest of the committee finished."

I pull out the missing person's photo of Jason. I lay it on the desk and push it toward Chief Mack. "Was this boy at the interview?"

Mack looks at the photo carefully and then looks up at me with a troubled look. "Sure was."

"What can you tell me about this boy?"

Chief Mack closes his eyes for a moment as though he's pulling a picture of the boy up in his mind. "The boy was real talented. He was selected for sure. But he never showed up to the practice sessions."

I look closely at Chief Mack and say, "Jason was kidnapped. Your interview was the last anyone saw of him before he disappeared. He was found murdered twenty-eight days later."

A look of sadness passes over Chief Mack's face in concert with the feelings coming from inside him. Mack is a man full of great empathy for the human race. I feel that. That must be why he chose this job. Mack looks past his furrowed eyebrows at me and says slowly, "I'm real sorry to hear that. Truly, I am."

He is sorry. Mack is feeling pain for the boy and telegraphing it. I feel it swell inside me and pinch my chest tight.

"Did you see Jason leave with anyone?"

Mack looks thoughtful as he rubs his chest as though it feels too tight. "No, Ma'am. He was still there when I left. The selected candidates were held till after the interviews so we could give them the rundown."

I can see the wheels turning in Mack's head as he processes everything I've said and then some. I have a feeling that as quiet and slow to speak as Mack is, nothing gets past him. He is the sort of man who thinks a lot but shares just a sliver of what he's learned.

"How are the interviews conducted, and how is the location secured?"

Mack thinks on this a minute, then replies, "Well, we do it on Phantom Island because that's where the fireworks are set off for the show. The surrounding water provides some protection for those onshore. Because we're dealing with an unknown quality in the candidates, we keep them on the mainland and call them over the bridge one at a time."

"Chief Mack, would you mind putting together a list of everyone who was on the island, both those who attended the interview and those who judged it? I'd like to know who was accepted and who was rejected. I'd also like to know which committee members wanted Jason and which didn't."

Mack rubs his lips with his forefinger thoughtfully, then says, "I sure can do that, but I can tell you now all the committee members wanted Jason. There's no question about that."

I stand and hand Chief Mack my card. Then I offer him my hand.

He puts both of his long-fingered hands around mine, and I feel the warm, callused strength envelop me. "You take care, Inspector Kildare." Chief Mack looks into my eyes, showing me he means it.

I smile. "Thank you, Chief Mack. You do the same."

Chief Mack's eyes remain deeply troubled as I depart his office with Varg following behind me. The Dalmatian makes to follow us too, but Mack gives a soft whistle and she turns around to sit on her bed again.

I sure like Chief Mack. He's good people. No doubt about that.

CHAPTER 30

BEES AND HONEY

BLUEBELL KILDARE

MAY 29, 2022, RED AGES

When I arrive with Varg at the precinct, the clerk in the sallyport informs me I'm expected and escorts me to the interview area. Detective Gambino is standing behind the one-way mirror watching Detective Schmidt question Paul when I approach.

Gambino turns at my arrival. "We had to wait for him to sober up, so we only got started about twenty minutes ago."

"How's it going?" I ask as I watch Paul stare mutinously at Detective Schmidt.

Gambino smiles wryly. "Not well. I wanted to observe, but I'll have to take over."

I watch for a few minutes as Detective Schmidt asks Paul if he ran over Jason, and Paul responds by covering his eyes. Schmidt accuses Paul of beating and starving the boy. He sneers at Paul and insinuates Paul likes young boys. Paul keeps his cuffed hands over his eyes through all the derision and accusations, repeating, "I didn't do it. I didn't do it." Detective Schmidt is getting nowhere with Paul, and his ploys are ridiculous.

I watch Gambino too. Disgust rolls off him, but I can't tell if it's aimed at Paul or Schmidt. If I had to put money down, it would be on the latter. His scowl deepens as the interview progresses.

I pull out my sixth sense and feel a significant amount of hate in the room, but it's not coming from Paul. Rather it is coming from Detective Schmidt. I recoil from sensing him and sift through those feelings to narrow in on the feelings emanating from Paul. Paul is scared out of his wits. He's pathetic, but there's no evil in him. There is a great deal of guilt, though. I don't see how someone with a soul that mild could have tortured that boy in the way he was tortured.

I pull in my sixth sense as Detective Schmidt exits the interview room, slamming the door on his way out.

I look at Gambino and ask, "May I question him?"

Detective Schmidt snarls, "Like you can accomplish shit."

Varg gives a low warning growl to Schmidt, baring his teeth. I ignore Schmidt, briefly hoping he will make Varg angry enough to attack, but then chastise myself for the thought. Instead I look to Gambino. Gambino inclines his head minutely. That's all I need.

As I enter the interview room, I see Varg put his paws on the mirror frame to keep an eye on me. I sit across from Paul and say in a soft, warm voice as though I'm greeting an old friend, "Hello, Paul."

Paul jerks in surprise, obviously expecting Schmidt again. He lifts his eyes over his fists and lowers his hands. "Hello."

"So," I say conversationally, "I met your sister Agnes today. She seems really nice and has a beautiful car." As I'm speaking I open up my sixth sense to feel Paul's emotions. He lightens up at the mention of his sister and nods. Encouraged by this, I continue. "So how long have you been living with her?"

Paul's mood shifts to sadness. "Since my wife Hannah died about six years ago."

I look Paul in the eyes and say in a soft, empathetic voice, "I'm sorry to hear about your wife, Paul. How did she die?"

Paul nods, and I can see that he internalizes my empathy. He takes a deep breath before speaking. "She died of breast cancer. It was horrible to watch."

I nod at him gently, still pouring as much of my empathy at him as I can. It's easy to do as I can feel his pain, still terribly strong after all of this time. "I know it was. I imagine that's when the drinking turned really bad." I try to make it sound like it is totally reasonable to become a drunk after watching that. And who am I to judge? Maybe it is totally reasonable. Being a drunk isn't a crime.

Paul looks down at his cuffed hands on the table and nods as he fidgets with his fingernails.

"So," I say, "your sister took you in and has been really good to you even though you have a drinking problem."

Paul nods again and waves of shame and guilt fill the air.

I continue speaking gently. "Here's the thing, Paul. We know the car hit Jason. We have evidence from the car on Jason's body. Paint chips were found in his skin and the grill pattern of the car was marked on his body. We also found pieces of the headlights and windshield glass smashed on the ground and embedded in his forehead. So we have no doubt the car hit the boy."

Paul quietly listens to this, picking at his cuticles but not responding.

"Did you hit the boy with the car, Paul?"

Paul covers his eyes with his hands and shakes his head. He says, "No, no, no."

But I sense something when he covers his eyes. He isn't covering his eyes to block his view of me. He isn't trying to hide from me. He is covering his eyes to block out an image or a memory. His "no" isn't really an answer to me either. His "no" is self-denial.

I look at Paul and lay my hand gently on his shoulder, patting it a few times. Then I play my hardest card yet. "Paul. It's okay. I understand. I know you didn't do it."

Paul uncovers his eyes and looks at me in confusion and disbelief. He thinks he just got a "Get Out of Jail Free" card, and he isn't sure what to think of it. His feeling slowly shifts to one of shock and perplexed amazement.

I ignore him completely. Turning my back slightly, I pick up my phone, pretending to dial Gambino. With a sigh into the phone, I say "Gambino, the car is registered to Agnes. Paul says he didn't do it, and I think I believe him." I pause a moment as though listening. Then I say, "I think he's protecting Agnes because she took care of him for so many years." I pause again and sense alarm coming from Paul. "Yep. All the evidence points to her. You'd better go get her and lock her up for manslaughter."

I have my head resolutely turned from Paul the whole time, but I feel his alarm escalate to utter and complete horror and guilt.

I flip the phone closed now and stand up, still not looking at Paul. I hear him start to sob softly and whisper, "I did it. I didn't mean to do it. It was me. It wasn't Agnes. Please don't hurt Agnes."

I feel like a total heel, but I have to do this. I affect a perplexed look and sit back down again. I keep my voice soft and reach my hand out across the table toward Paul without touching him. I allow question and confusion to enter my voice. "Paul, what happened?"

Paul has his mouth covered with his hands as though he wants to hold back the words, but he stares on my outstretched hand, and he talks. He talks between his weeping with tears streaming from his eyes.

"I was drinking at the Cock and Bull Tap. Just before the police shift started coming in, I ducked out to my car and took a nap. When I woke up, I started to drive home, and as I left the alley this naked boy runs out of nowhere. I couldn't stop in time."

Then Paul's soft sobs turn into tormented, racking sobs. I hear the horror in his voice and feel it in his soul. Paul looks me in the eyes, but he doesn't see me. He sees the image he's been trying to block out the whole night. He's seeing the thing he wants to deny.

"I saw the boy's face hit the windshield. I saw his eyes. He was looking at me through the windshield. He looked straight at me and saw me when he hit it. He was alive and had this hopeful look on his face."

Paul pauses and looks at me and stresses this thing that is causing him more horror and pain than anything else. "He was so full of *hope*. Then the expression of hope went right out of his face when his head hit the windshield. All I could see was blood smeared around his face and his eyes staring at me. His dead eyes!"

Paul's emotions are so powerful, they rip through me—painfully. I can feel everything he's feeling. He is an excellent projector, and as luck would have it, I am an excellent receiver.

I could leave now, but I'm not done yet. I take several deep, fortifying breaths and then lay my hands on Paul's cuffed hands, holding them gently. This is a man who feels great empathy, guilt, and pain. He feels intensely, and I need to use that to help him the little bit I can. But I have to hurt him more to do it.

I say, "Paul, I know you didn't mean it. But you know you shouldn't have been driving a car after drinking. You know your reflexes are not right after drinking. If you had been sober, you might have stopped in time." Paul sobs harder, but I keep going because he needs to hear this. "This boy is dead because of you. So we have to press charges because you deserve a strong consequence for this. The boy will never get a chance at the rest of his life. He will never get a chance to find and be with his Hannah."

Paul nods at this as pain wracks his body and shakes his shoulders.

He keeps his head down and gasps for breath between sobs.

Then I finally say, "Paul, your wife doesn't have a chance at the rest of her life. This boy doesn't have a chance at the rest of his life. But Paul, you do. You have a chance at the rest of your life. And you need to decide how to use it. Would your wife have wanted you to use it this way? Drowning yourself in alcohol? Avoiding responsibility for your actions? Spending your life dulling your pain?"

Paul shakes his head as he continues to weep. I can hardly watch. But since I'm putting him through it, I have to watch it. Not only do I watch it, but I feel it. I feel everything he's feeling, and I'm cutting him deep. I cut myself just as deep.

With a thickened throat, I finish it. "Okay then. Detective Gambino is going to come in and ask for a written confession. And then you need to start thinking about the right way to live your life from now on. Good luck, Paul." Then I release his hands and leave quietly.

When I enter the observation room, I lean against the door frame. The tears I'd been suppressing leak out silently. I swipe them away and take several deep breaths.

Gambino watches me thoughtfully in his quiet, intelligent way. When my breathing calms down he says, "Excellent work, Inspector."

At the same time, venomous hatred is spilling out of Schmidt even more powerfully than before. He spits out, "That was sorry fucking work. You are way too soft and pathetic. You only got a partial confession. What about the kidnapping and torture?"

Gambino's cheeks start to turn red, but he keeps his back to Schmidt and raises one eyebrow to me.

I return the look squarely while ignoring Schmidt. "Paul didn't do the rest. I'm sure of it."

Schmidt snickers at this. "What? Don't want to blame your lover boy? I saw you fondling him."

Gambino ignores Schmidt and nods at me slightly. The telltale splotches of red appear on his ears now, and a blood vessel in his temple pulses as he grinds his teeth. He keeps his gaze averted from Schmidt and wrestles to remain composed. He finally turns to Schmidt, speaking through tense lips that brook no argument. "Get a warrant for Agnes' house and search it. Take two other officers with you. I want Franks to be one of them."

Schmidt looks at me as if he just won a round and leaves victorious.

After Schmidt slams the door, Gambino turns his grimacing face to me. "I believe you, but we have to follow procedure, and I want other officers there as a witness to what he does or doesn't find. Franks is fair."

CHAPTER 31

A BIG MESS

BLUEBELL KILDARE

MAY 29, 2022, RED AGES

I glare at the last set of stair treads leading to my floor. Only a few more steps till home. I think longingly of my soft comforter and pillows. It's been a long, exhausting, emotionally trying day.

When I ascend the stairs, Varg and I proceed down the hall to my apartment. The hallway is spacious with little receiving tables outside each door. The walls are plaster and painted in a pleasant taupe. The ceilings in this building are high and set off with elegant white crown molding. Alexis' apartment door is at the beginning of the hall and is painted with what used to be a bright red. The door across from my apartment is a vivid blue, but that apartment has lain vacant since my arrival. I assume it must be large because there are no other doors on that side. The years have taken their toll on the door paint while the rest of the hallway is kept in great condition.

As we approach my worn and scuffed emerald painted door, Varg starts growling viciously, baring his fangs. Thus warned, I push my sixth sense through the door, searching for life in the apartment. I sense no living souls, but still Varg snaps and growls. A growing sense of unease fills me.

I insert my key in the deadbolt without turning it, then pull out my Glock. I turn the key very softly until I hear the click. I give a quick twist at the knob and a kick to the heavy oak door, which slams into the wall behind it. A furiously snarling Varg charges in and disappears within the darkness. I put my back against the solid door and hold my gun forward, tense and afraid. I extend my arm and flip the light switch on.

Holy cripes! My apartment is completely trashed. I tentatively step inside and turn to deadbolt the door behind me. Varg is doing a perimeter check, growling every step of the way. I join him with my

Glock, ready for action. As far as I'm aware, the only being that would not register a soul is a Dark Vampire since their souls have already joined Lilith. I try to leap over the sofa cushions that have been thrown on the floor, but when my foot hits the floor it goes flying out from under me. I land with a thump right on my butt. Stunned, I sit there quietly until the stinging recedes, reflecting on the fact that ballet lessons as a child might have served me well. With a glance around, I surmise that my foot landed on a book that slid forward when I put my weight on it. Dozens of my precious books, with pages torn and spines split, litter the floor under the sofa cushions by my feet.

Holy smokes! I realize I'm still holding my Glock. Luckily I didn't accidentally set it off when I went flying. Reasoning that if someone were going to jump out at me, they would have done it already, I carefully slide it back in its holster. With considerable stiffness I stand up and gingerly rub my jean-clad left butt cheek. Cripes! I'm going to have a whopping bruise tomorrow. I carefully step over the remaining books and cushions until I make it safely to the other side of the living room. Checking the remainder of the apartment yields nothing—nothing but a big, fat, huge, monolithic mess.

My couch is tipped over on its front as though someone had been examining the spring works underneath. I flip it on its feet, throw the cushions back on, and collapse in an exhausted heap. I drop my head to my hands and absorb the disaster. Piles of my beloved books lie around in various stages of destruction. I absolutely love those books. They are my treasures, found at garage sales and picked neatly out of resale shops, fragile with age. Exhaustion threatens to overtake me. I'm tempted to ignore the mess and bury myself in sleep. Inviting as it sounds, the mattresses are upended and the pillows torn to shreds. I have to deal with this now.

I stare at my chimerator with reluctance, knowing I must inform Jack. He would be furious if I didn't call. On the bright side, perhaps he can arrange for an earlier appointment with the ward specialist. I bite my lower lip in consternation. Ugh, this is not a call I want to make. With a sigh, I flip open my chimerator and chime his line.

Jack's handsome visage comes into view. "What's wrong?"

I let the words tumble out of me, the quicker the better. "Jack, my apartment was ransacked with no sign of entry. Is the ward specialist available tonight? My apartment is becoming a public thoroughfare, and the novelty is wearing thin."

Jack's eyes narrow, and even through the tiny chimerator I can see he's furious. He finally speaks in a low, hard voice. "I'll see," he says, and he closes the line.

I sigh at his abruptness and then force myself to stand and start putting things to rights. My books come first. I pick them up one by one, straightening their covers and unbending their pages to place them back in the bookcase as carefully as I can. Three heartbreaking shelves and eleven unsalvageable books later, I hear a knock at the door.

"Who is it?" I call.

Alexis' strong voice answers through the door, "It's me. I've got the deworming meds for Varg."

I jump over the piles of books still remaining to open the door. Varg butts his head through before I can get it fully open. Alexis' eyes open wide at the sight of the apartment behind me. Stepping back, I allow her entrance, waving my arm at the mess. "Welcome to my very, very humble abode."

Alexis demands, "Now what in God's green Earth took place in this apartment?"

"I won a contest and got a free home makeover."

Alexis tilts her head at me and squints her eyes in disbelief.

"I had a huge party, and it got a little out of hand?"

Alexis raises one perfectly arched eyebrow at me while pursing her lips and plants a hand on her curvy and cocked hip.

"Okay, it's the case I'm working on. I think one of the perpetrators did this. They're looking for something."

Alexis looks at me questioningly. "Did they find it?"

"There's nothing here they'd want."

She looks around and squares her shoulders. "Well, let's get to it. This mess isn't going to clean itself."

"You don't have to help me."

Alexis gives me a sideways glance, and this time she raises both of her eyebrows, clearly meaning I have no say in this. How could I possibly say no to a pair of arched eyebrows? Obviously I lost this battle before it even began.

She smacks the bottle of dewormer on the table and says, "Give him a tablespoon with his food once a day for two weeks."

I nod obediently.

She plops a bag on the table. "I also brought you some banana bread and peanut butter canine cookies for Varg."

I break into a grin. I love banana bread. Suddenly things are looking a bit brighter. "Thank you so much."

Alexis takes a deep breath and says, "I'll take care of the kitchen since you probably don't even know what you have in there anyway." She forges off and starts washing the pots and pans and silverware that are all over the floor. Self-cleaning dishes would be great right now.

I turn back to the bookshelf to continue trying to rescue my books. After a few minutes I glance over and see that she's filled up an entire trash bag with broken cups, plates, and glasses. On the top of the pile I see the remains of a broken ceramic cheese and cracker dish shaped and painted like a penguin. Yep, I definitely don't recall having that.

It's amazing how much easier it is to tackle this work when a friend helps. Before Alexis finishes the kitchen, I complete the living room, and I move on to the bathroom. Just as I'm done in the bathroom, I hear another knock at the door. As I approach the door I feel a roll of intense rage flowing through it. I ask, "Who's there?"

A deep, growling voice yells through the door, "Jack."

My heart does a little flip, and I open the door. It's very unusual for me to feel Jack's emotions at all, so I'm surprised by the amount of rage coming from him. He pushes past me and without preamble does a perimeter check. His nostrils flare and his gaze is thunderous as he sees the mess still in the bedroom. He turns to me. "Was anything taken?"

I shake my head. "Not that I'm aware of."

Jack gestures toward the bedroom and asks, "Was it all like that?"

I nod.

Still staring at the bedroom, Jack spits out, "They were looking for something small."

I look at the ripped open pillows and feathers littering the floor and have to agree. However, his statement makes me nervous that he's going to say something in front of Alexis that he shouldn't. I quickly intercede. "Jack, please meet my good friend Alexis."

At that, Alexis steps into the living room, which is all of five steps away from where she was. She smiles slyly and gives a little wave.

Jack nods and greets her shortly, hardly giving her a glance.

I could kick him for his rudeness. He's such a Neanderthal sometimes.

Jack looks back at me with narrowed eyes and somehow manages to spit out between his clenched jaw, "The ward specialist can't come until tomorrow morning. That's the best he can do. He has another big job right now. I'll sleep on the couch."

I start to protest, but at the look of steel in Jack's eyes I can see it's useless. I sigh and move to the kitchen to help Alexis finish up.

Alexis nods toward the other room where Jack is still examining the damage and mouths, "Hot."

I nod back and mouth, "Neanderthal."

When we've finished cleaning up the last few things Alexis announces loudly, but with a sly wink my way, "Well, I need to get going. I have some prep work I need to do for tomorrow."

It's clear she's purposefully leaving me alone with Jack. I'm not sure if I should smile at her or kick her. I settle on giving her a hug. After all, you can't really be mad at the bearer of banana bread. That balances most evils.

"Thanks for the dewormer and the banana bread and the cookies for Varg. And a big, huge thank you for helping me out."

Alexis hugs me back. "I really approve," she says, shifting her eyes toward Jack, "of the name Varg, of course. Excellent choice."

I quirk a smile, and Varg and I see her to the door, dead-bolting it behind her.

"I need a break." I announce to Jack. I plop down on the sofa, stretch my legs out, and pat the sofa next to me. "Come sit with me and I'll give you my updates."

Jack sits down at the far end of the sofa, stretching his long legs in front of him. His body is deceptively languorous, but his eyes are the deep shadowed green of a rainforest at dusk and are filled with a gleaming, hard glint. His face looks steely and distant. He reminds me of a panther, savage and silent, waiting to spring. Jack gets so angry he scares people sometimes, but for an unexplainable reason I trust unequivocally that he will never hurt me.

"We caught the guy who hit the boy with his car. He's at the precinct signing a confession now."

A little brightness returns to Jack's face. I can see the thoughts flickering behind his eyes as he works out what this means. He says, "So a different man is looking for the amulet or they were working together."

I shake my head. "I felt this guy. He's a drunk who has made a string of mistakes in his life, but his soul doesn't have the capacity for the sort of evil the torturer must have."

Jack accepts my judgment without question and replies, "A second man, then."

I nod.

"I have another lead. Jason's best friend remembered Jason was going to an interview to volunteer for the Sun Flare Celebration Fireworks and Magic Show. His friend said Jason's gift was one of amplification. He could make any magic stronger by multiples just by being present."

Jack whistles and shakes his head, making his gold curls shimmer slightly with the movement. "That's a powerful gift."

I nod in agreement. "Fire Chief Mack leads the Fireworks and Magic Show committee. He was there for part of the interview and remembers seeing Jason there. That makes the interview the last place Jason was seen alive."

Jack nods slightly at this, the implications clear.

"Chief Mack is getting me a list of everyone who was at the interview, both the committee members and the candidates."

"Excellent news."

I consider how nice it would be to just reach over and run my fingers across the hard, angular planes of Jack's face. Instead I launch myself off the sofa and declare "Back to work." as I head to the bedroom.

I pull back the curtains that separate the bedroom alcove from the rest of the apartment. When Jack steps through the doorway to help, it suddenly feels very intimate to be in my bedroom with him. Thankfully I have a huge disaster to distract me. First, Jack and I right the mattresses. Then I get a large garbage bag and start stuffing torn pillows and feathers in it. I look over and see Jack dubiously eying the pile of clothes on my floor, particularly my lacy, pink, black, satin, bowed, and animal print underthings.

I laugh and say, "Why don't you get the feathers and I'll get that."

Jack looks slightly embarrassed but very relieved as we switch spots. I chuckle to myself because finally someone saw my fantastic underwear, but not quite how I imagined.

I heap handfuls of my frilly underthings on the dresser and start folding them one at a time. After finishing a few, I suddenly feel Jack behind me, only inches away. His emotions are more muted now, but I still feel them softly. Waves of concern radiate out from him, intertwined with lust and rage and some other subtle emotion. I can feel the heat of his body behind me. I'm in the middle of folding a pair of red satin panties with lace side panels, but I pause and slowly lower my arms. Is he going to kiss me? What will he do?

Suddenly hundreds of feathers drift over my head, sticking to my hair and face. I whirl around, and Jack steps back with laughter in his eyes. He stands there holding an empty pillowcase.

"Jack!" I glance around, seeing nothing close at hand but my lingerie. I fold up a pair of panties and whip them at him.

Jack easily snatches them in mid air, smiling.

"Hey, now that is not fair."

I scrunch up a bra and whip it at him. While he unfolds the panties to admire them, the bra hits him in the face. He picks that out of the air as it bounces off him. Seeing my strategy needs to be altered, I take a whole armload of underthings and throw them at his face. Jack laughs and fends off the flying lingerie with his hands. Then I lean over the bed to grab another torn pillow and shake it at him, but the feathers fall in a miserable heap at his feet, so I ball up the rest of the pillow and throw it at him.

"Hey!" he laughs.

I grab another pillow and jump on the bed. I reach inside the rip to grab handfuls of feathers and toss them up in the air over Jack. Feathers stick out of his golden curls, and I start laughing as he makes a game out of trying to catch individual feathers in the air. I laugh so hard I am out of breath, and I plop down on the mattress. Jack smiles and sits next to me with his hands on his lap.

We sit there silently for a while. Jack's warm body just inches from mine is so tempting that I have to forcibly keep myself from leaning into him. To break the awkward intimacy, I say, "From the moment I came into the apartment I sensed a violent rage and frustration. It covered every inch of the apartment, and I don't like feeling it. Unfortunately, that's all I could glean."

Jack turns to me and asks, "You okay?"

I reach out and gently squeeze his hand and look into his shimmering green eyes. "Yes. I'm much better. At least the bedroom is filled with a feeling of fun now. Thank you." I give his hand one more squeeze, then hop off the bed and start picking up my lingerie again. With Jack's Vampire speed, we quickly put the room to rights.

By the time we are done, my stomach is rumbling. I look at Jack and ask, "Do you eat at all?"

Jack smiles and says, "Not food. But you are starving. I can hear it from here. Let's get you something to eat."

"I don't have any bagged blood for you. I'm sorry."

Jack twitches his lips as though laughing at a private joke. "That's fine. I had some before I came over."

I wonder what he's laughing at. Ohh! To him I *am* bagged blood. I should be more careful of what I say.

I head to the kitchen with Jack and Varg following close behind. I put a small amount of kibble in the bowl and pour some of the deworming medicine on it. Varg seems to like the taste because he wolfs it down. When he's done, I give him a small cut of beef from the freezer. Varg happily brings his treat to the rag rug in the living room, which is a relief because there isn't enough room in my narrow galley kitchen for Jack, me, and Varg.

Jack leans against my kitchen wall, watching me, and says, "It's good you give him meat."

"He's a wolf. I figure he needs more than kibble to feel satisfied. I consider it an insurance policy."

I look in my fridge and pull out some vegetables and chicken. Jack reaches over me, grabs a knife, and quickly cuts up the meat while I clean and cut up the vegetables. A splash of olive oil goes in the pan with the heat turned on high. Just as the oil starts to waver, I throw all the meat and vegetables in, stirring it quickly. Jack searches my cabinets, and using Vampire speed, he sprinkles some spices in so fast I can't see what he's using. When the food is done, I sit down at the table, and Jack somehow manages to fold his long legs under my table too.

I look at him. "Isn't this awkward for you, watching me eat?"

Jack's lips twitch again as he watches me. "Not at all. I'm enjoying myself."

I don't know what else I can do. I have to eat, so I dig into my chicken, broccoli, asparagus, and mushroom stir fry, and the savory flavors fill my mouth. "Holy smokes! What did you put in here? It is so unbelievably good." I look up at Jack in surprise.

Jack smiles devilishly. "It's a secret." I give him my very best pouty lower lip, but he only smiles wider and refuses to budge. I vow I'm going to search through my spices to figure it out.

So I dig in. And I dig and dig and dig until only two bites remain on my plate. I push my plate away in finality. "I can't eat another bite. I want to. It was so delicious. But I can't." Jack chuckles and stands up, taking my plate and utensils to the kitchen. While I clear the rest of the table, Jack quickly washes the dishes.

I sneak a peek at him while he stands at my sink drying my plate. His tall form leans into the counter, and his big hands gently do the work. I can see the hard curve of his butt cheeks through his trousers. My belly does flips. He's so handsome and strong. It's nice he can be domestic too. I never would have thought he was like this. My heart joins the party by giving a little squeeze and pitter-patter. Jack looks at me curiously. I look back at the table I'm wiping, feigning nonchalance. I'm sure I do it about as well as Jack does. Did he hear my heart go pitter-patter?

Chapter 32

Belfry

Bluebell Kildare

May 29, 2022, Red Ages

t is getting late by the time we're done cleaning up, so I ask Jack if he wants to come with me to walk Varg. He obliges, and together we head out my green painted door.

The evening air has not yet cooled the mountainside down, but a fog has rolled in. We walk through the white mist quietly together. Varg takes the lead, and we follow behind. As we take in the foggy scenery, Jack asks, "How do you like living here?"

"I love it," I respond. "I'm close to Alexis and Maud, and it's just a few minutes' drive to work. Plus the building is old and has character, which I adore."

Suddenly I realize I know very little about Jack, so I ask, "Where do you live?"

"I have some land in the country not too far from here."

My mind's eye conjures up the vision of a lonely farmhouse on some acreage.

As we continue walking, a peaceful silence enshrouds us more tangibly than the mist. The night air is filled with only the sounds of my boots, Varg's nails softly tapping on the sidewalk, and the occasional song of a city bird. Sometimes we hear a car go by and both Jack and Varg lift their heads to inspect it. Two fearsome warriors walk next to me, and I've never felt safer.

After a few miles, Varg starts to lead us back toward home. When we get close to the apartment, I ask Jack, "Do you want to see the amulet?"

Jack tilts his head as he considers this and says, "Yes. I think I do. But I don't think we should visit it again after this. Tonight the mist will hide us, but whoever is looking for it may be watching you, and we don't want to lead him to it."

I nod, as it makes good sense.

We walk up the wide, white cement steps and enter the narthex of St. Michael's Church. No one is there, so I peek into the nave. Father O'Brennen sits on one of his pews as is his wont, writing rapidly in a notebook. I stand there for a moment until he feels our presence and looks up with a smile.

"Hello, Father. This is my boss, Jack Tanner. Jack, this is Father O'Brennen."

Father O'Brennen stands up and clasps hands with Jack in a warm embrace. He says, "It's good to see you again, Jack." Then he looks at me. "We know each other, though it's been a long time."

"Yes, it has," Jack affirms.

This surprises me. Though I suppose Jack is so old he must know generations of Crimson Hollow residents.

Something unspoken passes between the two men, and Jack says, "We want to take a look at your bell room."

Father O'Brennen smiles. "Sure. I'm about to retire. Please leave through the front and lock up behind you when you're done."

We say goodnight, and then I show Jack to the bell tower door. The mist obscures the moonlight as we climb, so it's very dark in the stairwell. Jack walks behind me and puts a steadying arm on my waist. With no light, the heat from his hand feels even more intense than usual.

After a moment, Jack gently pulls me to a stop and says, "We're at the ladder." His deep voice softly reverberates through the stairwell and through me.

I nod. "It's just above."

Jack turns toward Varg, who has been patiently trailing behind us, "Guard the landing."

I hear Varg settle down close to the ladder.

Jack puts my hands on the ladder. "You first," he instructs.

I proceed, acutely aware of Jack just behind me. He certainly has an eyeful of my backside.

When I pull myself up to the bell room floor I scoot over, and Jack climbs nimbly up after me. The moon reflects off the shifting mist, giving us a low light to see by. I pat the floor next to me and scoot over to where the rock is. Jack sits so close his knee touches mine. It's a tiny space for two grown people, and his nearness ignites a smoldering flame in my body I try unsuccessfully to ignore. A quick peek at his emotions tells me he has them tamped down securely now.

I count out loud so Jack knows exactly where the amulet is. "One, two up. One, two, three over."

I grasp the edges of the rock with my fingertips and slowly start to shimmy it loose. Once Jack sees what I'm doing, he reaches over my lap and places his hands on the top and bottom of the rock. As he does this, he leans over me, and I inhale his musky male scent. He smoothly pulls the rock out and sets it on the floor before leaning back again. I reach behind the rock next to the opening, feeling around for the bag. I manage to pinch a corner of it and carefully pull it out.

"This is it," I announce as I hold the bag up.

Jack looks at it closely, examining the front and the back. He looks at the thread, and he opens the bag and sniffs it. When he's done he hands it back to me and says, "The craftsmanship is stunning."

I'm not a connoisseur of fine metal craft, but even I can tell it's magnificent. I carefully replace it and push the rock in again.

Jack seems satisfied. "That's a good spot for it."

Then he stands and offers his hand to help me up. I take it. When we're both standing I lean over the half wall, place my elbows on it, and look out over what I can see of the city. The neighborhood is shrouded in mist, shifting and gliding over buildings, gathering thick in some places and thin in others, an ever-changing monochrome of misty city.

Jack stands next to me and asks, "So, how well do you know Father O'Brennen?"

This question takes me by surprise because I'd thought to ask the same question of him. "When I came of age and had to leave the orphanage, Father O'Brennen let me stay in my apartment for a few months rent-free until I got my first job."

Jack asks, "Are you very religious?"

I laugh softly. "No. When I lived at the orphanage we would come here to church, and at every opportunity I would escape services to come up here to the bell room."

The memories bring a sadness that I try to swallow down. I face away from Jack and stare out at the rolling mist.

"You probably remember me telling you about when I was younger how the kids at the orphanage thought I was an evil Witch because of my birthmark and my gift. The housemothers called Father O'Brennen in to evaluate me at one point, so at some level they must have believed it could be true."

When I say this, I feel Jack reach out his hand and tenderly stroke my hair. I'm trying to keep my emotions in check, but his kindness makes tears spill silently from my eyes. I keep my head turned so Jack can't see. "He said I was perfectly normal." Despite my efforts my voice comes out broken.

Jack holds my chin and gently turns my face toward him. He sees the tears, and I feel an overwhelming flood of emotion coming from him. It's like he's kept himself in constant control, and now I am finally seeing the truth of him. He pours out empathy and kindness toward me. He gently wipes the tears on my cheeks with his thumbs, and he pulls me to him. I willingly lean into his chest.

Jack murmurs, "Don't cry, Blue." And he gently kisses the tear tracks on my face in a rain of tiny kisses. His kindness is so overwhelming and his empathy so real it undoes me even further and I start crying all the more. I lean my forehead into his chest, and Jack folds me in his arms, holding my gently shaking shoulders. I feel his large, comforting hands caressing my back soothingly as he murmurs, "Don't cry, beautiful. Don't cry, beautiful Blue."

I feel the warmth of his arms surrounding me and the comfort of his solid chest and consoling hands. Slowly, I let my old hurt and sense of betrayal flow out of me. Jack keeps his arms around me, calming me, and my sobbing subsides. It's an old pain. I've never told anyone about this, not even Maud.

As I calm down I realize my arms are about Jack's waist. Jack gently pulls me back, and looks at me with such tenderness. He leans down and softly kisses one eyelid and then the other. Then he goes back to the first eyelid and rains tiny kisses all along my lash line from one corner to the other. His kisses are tender and as light as falling snowflakes, yet they leave a trail of warmth in their wake. He has one arm around my waist, holding me against him, and his other hand twines through my hair as he leans over me.

His lips feather over my other eye in the same manner, covering it in tiny, beautiful kisses, full of warmth and kindness. I savor the feel of his lips against my skin and his arms around me, and I ache for more. The heat of his mouth touches the tip of my nose and dips lower, until I feel his warm breath hovering over my lips.

My whole body stills in anticipation with every nerve singing, focused on the warmth of his lips over mine. Slowly, he lowers his mouth, kissing one tiny corner and then the other with kisses as light as a butterfly. He brushes both of his lips over my upper lip, gently, tracing its outline. He moves to my lower lip, brushing it so softly with his in the same manner, setting off a wild tingling sensation and cascade of warmth that leaves my breast heaving for air.

Jack pauses with my lower lip lightly snagged between his, and I dare to open my eyes. I see bottomless, vivid, green, swirling eyes looking into mine intently. He opens his mouth and slowly, deliberately draws my lower lip into his mouth, sucking gently, watching my eyes all the while.

I feel a rush of heat and liquid fire deep, low in my core. Jack inhales roughly and groans. The realization comes through the fog of my mind that he can smell he is making me wet with wanting, and he likes it. A low unbidden moan escapes at that thought, and I reach for Jack's shoulder as my knees go weak. Jack pulls me against him, and I feel the hard length of him pushed up against my belly. I relish this evidence of his arousal and the knowledge that I am causing it. Jack's lips and tongue tease at the seam of my mouth, and I willingly open up to him. His tongue immediately claims my mouth, explores it, delving gently into every crevice, caressing me from inside out.

I am filled not only with Jack's tongue and am surrounded not only by his hands and his body, but his desire fills up the space around me soaking through me. I can feel his desire and his pleasure at my touch as I feel my own pleasure, and it makes me desperate for more. Crazy for more.

I run my hands rapidly down Jack's back and over his buttocks. His limbs are steel hard under the fine fabric of his trousers, but I'm frantic to feel his skin. Jack pulls me to the side and presses me against the stone pier between the arches. His lips break from kissing my mouth then a fiery trail of kisses follows down my jawline and my neck while holding my hips against him. I desperately glide my fingers up his chest, searching for an opening in his shirt. My untrained hands feel his chest, and my right hand runs across his nipple. Jack gasps in response, and I hone in and do it all the more, drinking in his desire, feeling it escalate with every stroke of my fingers. But I lose all thought as Jack slips his hands under my shirt and deftly finds my nipples.

"Oh my God," I moan as he rolls them between his fingers and flicks them with his thumb.

Then he pulls my shirt completely off me and his mouth is on the curve of my breast. I want, I want, I want so much. He slowly pulls a bra strap down, running his finger under the edge of the cup, lowering it. He takes my nipple fully into his mouth and gently suckles it. Oh my God. Liquid heat rushes between my legs. I try to reach out for Jack's shoulders, but my arm is trapped by my bra strap. Jack pulls the other strap down, trapping my other arm, and suckles my left nipple.

I am moaning incoherently, what I don't even know. I have no knowledge of where I am or how I'm even standing. There is only a disembodied me, every thought is anchored on Jack. I must touch him; I must get closer to him. I press my hips against his hard shaft and hear him groaning and cursing. I rub myself against him and beg, "I need more, Jack."

Jack lifts me up, and I wrap my legs around him. He presses his manhood into me in an undulating rhythm, rocking into me, pressing into me, so gloriously, but it is not enough. I reach up and kiss his mouth with hunger, with an open-mouthed starvation.

Then out of the blue I hear a great fluttering sound inches away from head. It penetrates though the whirl of my senses, and I turn opening my eyes in time to see a black crow flying away.

Jack suddenly clamps down on his emotions, become perfectly still. It's like I was in the midst of a lush forest and have been transported to a barren desert where I'm left parched and thirsty. The air is vacant and forlorn without his emotions filling it, the emptiness sucks the joy out of me as though I've entered the Abyss. The world comes back in a painful rush. Jack still holds me, and my legs are still wrapped around him, my body still throbs and weeps for him, but he does not move. He pulls his mouth away from mine. His eyes are still molten green, but they are now behind shuttered eyelids. The realization causes my heart to twist.

He says gruffly, "It was just a crow."

I let my legs relax, and Jack slowly lowers me to the floor, still holding me close. He steps back a bit, taking his hips away from me, and I feel utter desolation in their absence. My only consolation is the tightening of his arms around me, holding me still against his chest.

As my mind returns to this world, I hear my breath coming in heavy gasps. Jack carefully pulls my bra straps back up, one at a time, slowly and tenderly but dispassionately. He hands me my gray t-shirt. With his low voice cracking he says, "I'm sorry. I shouldn't have done that."

Somehow I steady my breath and nod while grasping my shirt to my chest. I'm grateful he still holds me because my knees are weak and unsteady. After a few moments, when I feel the strength return, I pull back, and Jack slowly, almost reluctantly, releases me.

I pull my t-shirt on embarrassed, and move to the half wall, leaning on it again with my elbows. I say, "Jack, I felt your emotions so strongly, then I felt you close down. I've never felt anyone do that before. It's different with you. I can only feel your emotions when they're strong."

Jack says quietly, "It's part of my training. When I was a young Vampire, I spent some time training in China at a Mahayana Buddhist Temple in martial arts. We were trained to control our minds and emotions as well as our bodies. My whole life is about control."

I accept this and look out into the mist. With what little dignity I can muster I whisper, "I'm sorry I broke down like that. I shouldn't have burdened you with my sob story."

Jack remains silent, and I feel the slightest brush of his fingers against my hair and nothing more. After a few more minutes Jack says, "We should head back."

I turn, and Jack descends the ladder ahead of me and helps me down. In the stairwell he lifts me easily in his arms. I thrill to have his arms around me again, but he carries me down the stairs like a man carries a little girl, not a woman. He gently sets me on my feet at the bottom of the stairs, and he and Varg push through the door as I follow behind.

We exit the church, and Jack locks the door behind us. We trek up the three flights to my apartment without speaking. When we arrive, Jack and Varg do a perimeter check again while I pull down some sheets for the sofa, figuring Jack doesn't need much.

Jack says, "I'll do the sofa. Why don't you get ready for bed."

I nod at him and hand him the pile of linens. Selecting my most modest nightgown, I head to the bathroom and jump in the shower. As the warm water runs down my body, I remember the way it felt when Jack touched me. I soap up my hands and wash my face and arms. When my soapy hands travel over my breasts, I think it's odd that with my hands I feel nothing, but with Jack's hands I feel the world. The memory of his hands on me is raw and powerful, but so is the pain of his cool demeanor. I finish my shower with my body still trilling from the feel of him.

I exit the bathroom with my robe pulled tightly around me, Jack is reclining on the sofa. He looks up at me, and I think his eyes flare brighter for an instant, but he doesn't get up. His eyes flick over me, but his face stays expressionless. His deep voice, scratchy now, asks coolly, "Shall I turn off the light?"

"Sure. I'm ready for bed now."

Jack turns off the light. "Goodnight, Blue."

"Goodnight, Jack."

I slip behind the sheer curtain that makes up my bedroom, and in a few seconds I am securely under the covers. Varg butts his head between the curtains and comes in to take his usual position by my bedside.

I'm pillowless tonight, so I pull the corner of the comforter up to cushion my head and try to wrap the rest around me. When my toes peek out I curl my knees to my stomach and sigh. I can feel Jack's presence in the other room, and I like it. Confused, lonely, and filled with longing, I surprise myself by falling asleep quickly.

CHAPTER 33

BEAUTIFUL VIGIL

JACK TANNER

MAY 29, 2022, RED AGES

I lie in perfect stillness and listen to the sound of Blue's breathing evening out, then slow to a deep slumber. Her presence, just a few feet away, tantalizes me in a bittersweet irony. The one whom I should not have is the woman I want the most. Her scent permeates the entire space, I smell the heart of it coming from her body in bed. By scent alone I know where she is, both from her fragrant skin and the rich aroma of her sweet blood. I see the soft, bluish white glow of her aura lighting up her bedroom. I can't take a breath without being filled with her scent. I don't need to breathe to survive, so I stop to ease the torment. But it leaves me feeling hollow. I take a deep breath in and savor it this time, accepting the sweet agony.

In the middle of the night, when I can stand it no longer, I silently enter her bedroom and stand at the foot of her bed. Mesmerized by this beautiful, forbidden treasure of mine, time flies away. Her aura softly illuminates her skin and every curve. In sleep, her eyes are so peaceful, the eyes I adore. Even now I want to brush my lips against her eyelids. I love the fall of her long, dark lashes against her cheeks. Her limbs are scattered and limp, the same limbs that wrapped around me with all the passion of a burgeoning young woman. I don't deserve something so lovely and so filled with good.

I recall her stories of the orphanage, and it rips me apart because I brought her there. Any hardships she endured are no one's fault more than mine. How could I have abandoned a young child with a group of strangers without knowing what it was like for her on a daily basis? I should have watched over her more closely. I should not have let that happen.

I wrestle myself away from her side and return to the sofa. I lie down and close my eyes, letting the visions of her in my arms flow through my mind like a slow-motion movie. When dawn comes and Varg starts to move about, I knock on the wall outside Blue's bedroom.

Blue opens her eyes and sleepily says, "Jack?"

"Blue, I'm headed into the office now. I'd like to get an early start."

"Okay," Blue says with a yawn. "I'll be there before noon."

"You need to lock the door behind me. The ward specialist should be here soon."

Blue opens her bleary eyes and reaches for her robe. She throws the covers back, and her long, white limbs poke out from her nightgown as she sets her feet on the bedroom rug. She stands, pulls on her robe, and follows me to the door. I shut it behind me and stand outside until I hear the lock click. For a moment I lean my shoulder on the green doorframe, reluctant to leave her. Then I steel myself and head to the office.

CHAPTER 34

The Alley

BLUEBELL KILDARE

MAY 30, 2022, RED AGES

I impatiently fiddle with the handle of my second cup of tea as I watch the ward specialist finish up. He's been chanting and casting wards for over an hour. I'm totally unfamiliar with ward art, so I let him do his business. He's a short, stocky man with glyphs and tribal designs tattooed all over his arms and face. With sparkles from nose and eyebrow piercings, and his short, spiky hair, he looks fierce, and I'm not sure I would want to cross his ward uninvited. But he seems skilled and good-natured.

When Michael Radskif finishes a particularly complex set of movements and chants, he brings his arms down and turns toward me. "I'm all finished here."

I look around and ask him, "Is there anything I need to know?"

Michael smiles and says, "This ward has a very simple entry requirement: you have to want the person to enter. No magic word or special chant will get someone in. No one can enter without you. Let me be clear about that—no one can portal in or occupy a single inch of space unless your heart desires them to be there with you."

"That's it? I just have to want them here? What if I want someone in, then they do something while they're here, and I don't want them in any longer?"

Michael shrugs. "It doesn't count. You already granted them entrance by wanting them in. When they leave, you get to decide if you want them in again. But once they're in, they're in."

So I'd best be sure about someone before I let them in.

Michael packs up his things. Then he pauses and asks, "Do you know where a good herbal shop is around here?"

I smile. "I sure do. My neighbor owns one, and she's very good at her craft." I think about how to tell him to get there, and then decide it's easiest to show him. "Why don't I walk you out and show you where it is? Where are you parked?"

Michael says, "Oh, I got dropped off. How far is the shop?"

I grab my jacket. "Not far."

Michael and I start to leave, and as I close the door, Varg tries to join us. I block him and say, "Varg, stay. I'll be right back."

Michael frowns at that. "You know, you don't need him to guard the place."

"I know, but I'm just going a block with you. I don't want to bother with the leash."

Michael shrugs and we walk down the three flights of stairs. I take him through the alley, and at the end of it I point two blocks over. "See that red brick building? Take a left there and then go two block and take a right. It should be three blocks down."

Michael smiles and thanks me. I watch him cross the street and make sure he's headed in the right direction before I turn back to the alley.

I've never gone through this whole alley before today. It's quite lengthy. Old, tall buildings stand on either side, lending long, deep shadows even in the morning light. There are many alcoves and doorways with decrepit signs hanging askew. Others are completely nondescript. How would you know which was your door? As I walk, my boot heels echo off the building walls, and small pebbles under my feet crunch with each step. I hear the sound of gravel scraping like a foot scuffing the ground up ahead.

I lift my head, and see a shadow flit by the building two down from mine. I stand still, my heart pounding. The location where I thought I heard the sound is still several buildings away. I look to the left and see a large garbage can. Maybe an animal got in it? But no, I am sure the shadow was on the right. I look at the tall buildings on that side seeing nothing. I walk forward, quietly this time, with eyes and ears open. I curse that I didn't bring Varg with me. After three agonizing paces, a squirrel abruptly runs across a clothes line from one side of the alley to the other. I startle, then breathe a huge sigh of relief and relax. I must have an overactive imagination today.

I reminisce about how nice it was to have Jack in the apartment last night. I should quit my job so I can ask him out. I laugh at myself. That is ridiculous, of course, because I love my job.

My musings are interrupted when I sense the unmistakable feeling of someone's extreme rage just ahead of me. The emotion is strong and violent, but I don't see anyone. They must be hiding in the alcove. I am almost at the building where I saw the shadow. I reach for my gun and find I didn't put my holster on before stepping out. Panic sets in.

I look behind me and see the long line of buildings between me and the other end of the alley. It's a long shot. I spin on my boot heel and run back through the alley. I hear footsteps behind me but don't bother to look back as I'm running as fast as I can. Whoever's behind me is fast and getting closer.

I look around for somewhere to block myself off, to protect myself, maybe a piece of wood to use as a weapon, anything. Nothing!

Suddenly someone grabs my arm snarling, "Aberrant."

I'm jerked back against a building. I look up and see Schmidt's furious face.

"You little bitch. You think you can come in on my case and take over." He raises his arm and smacks me across the face.

I'm dumbfounded. I hold my hand to my face. "What are you talking about, Schmidt? It's Gambino's case."

"He would be working it with me, if you didn't wiggle your slutty little self into it. That's why he pays attention to you, ain't it? You're giving it to him, aren't you?"

Schmidt has gone over the edge, and I'm in a real situation now. His face is red, blood vessels at his temples are popping, and muscles twitching.

"I'm not giving it to anyone, Schmidt. You're pissed you were wrong about Paul."

Schmidt snarls and plows his arm into my gut three times to punctuate each word he says. "You. Fucking. Bitch!'"

I try to protect myself with my arms, but he's a trained street cop and much larger than I. I double over in pain coughing, trying to regain my breath. I look up at him and say his name to get his attention, and then lift my knee going for the groin. Schmidt blocks me with his leg and gives me a fist cuff to the face. My vision goes wonky.

"I've had enough of your sluttiness, you little cunt. You want to whore yourself out to Gambino, I'll give you some too." Then he grabs my shirt and rips it open down the front.

I try to push past him, but he holds my upper arm in a vice grip. He pinches my nipples, grabbing my breasts like an animal. I claw at his face because I can't seem to do anything else. He hits me on the other side of my face. I go for the eyes, but Schmidt grabs my wrists and pins them at my sides. He holds me against the building and starts ripping at my jeans. I struggle, but his weight is blocking me, holding me against the building. I feel my button give and my zipper shred. I feel his sick hands grappling with my panties. And suddenly, when I think it might be too late, he's gone. The air fills with snarling and the sound of his screams.

I slit open my eyes and see Varg, who appears twice the size he was this morning, shredding Schmidt's arm. Schmidt's face is streaming blood. Varg has knocked him to the ground now, but he manages to get up and run. Varg follows him out of the alley, biting and snarling at his heels.

I sink down to the ground and rest a moment. Varg returns and sits by me, licking my face. I put my arms around his neck and say, "You're such a good boy. I promise I'll never lock you away from me anywhere, ever again. I promise."

When the tears and stars clear from my eyes and my breathing calms down, I gather my strength and heave myself up, using the brick wall for support.

I hobble toward the apartment and attempt the stairs. My side hurts so bad I have to stop a few times, but eventually I make it to my apartment. The door is still locked. How did Varg get out? I head straight for the bathroom and vomit. I vomit again. I vomit until my stomach is empty. With my head resting on the side of the tub, I wearily turn on the faucet, running the water hot. Then I drag myself up and sit on the toilet lid to take my clothes off. I slip into the tub and scrub myself raw. At some point the sound of the phone ringing breaks through my consciousness, but there is no way I'm getting out of the tub until I feel clean. I scrub myself all over again, then lay my head back against the back of the tub, still feeling dirty and slimy.

Pictures of what happened flash through my head. Maybe I should call Gambino and report Schmidt. But Varg did tear him up pretty good. Then I cringe internally, thinking if I don't tell Gambino, then Schmidt could do this to other women, women who don't have a wolf. I'll have to tell him, but I'll do it later. A vision of how that conversation would go flashes through my head. "Hi, Blue. How are you?" "Oh, I'm great, Gambino. Thanks for asking. Would you like some coffee? By the way, Schmidt assaulted me and tried to rape me."

With a sigh I decide to worry about this tomorrow because I'm so tired.

CHAPTER 35

NOT REMEMBERING

BLUEBELL KILDARE

MAY 30, 2022, RED AGES

I must have fallen asleep because the next thing I know, Jack is pulling me out of the water, and I vaguely discern a towel being wrapped around my body.

"Blue, wake up. Blue, you have to wake up."

I look up at him, puzzled, and ask, "What are you doing here?"

Jack carries me to the sofa and growls, "Blue, you're covered in bruises. Who did this to you? If it was Michael Radskif I'll kill him. I'll twist his bloody little neck."

I start to shake my head, but pain splinters through it, so I say, "Schmidt. In the alley. Varg got him good, though." Then I close my eyes.

Jack shakes me again. "Blue, you can't sleep. You were hit on the head pretty bad. You could have a concussion. You have lumps on your head and a bloody one in back." I lift my hand to the back of my head, and sure enough, I feel a huge, tender lump.

"Must have been when he slammed me against the brick wall," I mumble.

Jack growls again, low and savagely. He props me up on the sofa and orders me, "Don't move. Don't go to sleep."

He goes into the bathroom. I lever my right eyelid open. I order my left one to open too, but it doesn't comply. It feels swollen shut. But one eye is all it takes to see Jack return with his face in a black, murderous rage. He snarls, and his fangs descend, "Your clothes are torn, and I smell his filthy hands all over them."

I see trouble coming. "Jack," I say, "no death by bloodlust. Promise me."

Jack says nothing but holds his mouth in a grim line. He pushes me down on the sofa and starts feeling all over my body and smelling me.

"Jack," I shriek, and push at his shoulders. "What are you doing?"

"Lie still," he demands. "I'm checking for internal injuries. I can smell if a blood vessel burst."

"Oh, okay." I'm not sure why this is okay, but it sounds reasonable, and I'm in no position to argue.

When he's done examining me, he says, "No burst blood vessels, and he didn't rape you. Varg got to him in time." He sounds hugely relieved.

I slap Jack's arm and glare at him with one eye. "I know that, you big dolt. You could have asked."

Jack says, "We should take you to the hospital."

"No!" I protest.

I'm embarrassed enough as it is, being an Inspector and letting that sleazeball get to me. I don't need to advertise it.

Jack sits down next to me and asks, "Do you want me to give you my blood? It would heal you completely."

I still for a moment at the offer, then say cautiously, "Won't that turn me into a Vampire?"

"No, over half of your blood would need to be replaced with Vampire blood to turn you. A small amount of blood will heal you completely. Have you ever taken Vampire blood before?"

I answer softly, "No."

He says, "Well, then it wouldn't harm you, but over time if you get many small donations of blood, some blood stays in you and eventually you will turn. It doesn't have to be one big donation at once. So you should be cautious."

I think about it a minute and then say, "No. I don't want to risk it. My injuries are not that bad."

Jack frowns and says, "Well, I don't smell any internal bleeding. If you stay awake and let me put ice on your injuries, it should be okay."

With relief, I say, "Deal."

Jack orders me again, "Stay awake," and he steps toward the kitchen.

He comes back a moment later with two bags of frozen peas and two towels. He wraps the bags in the towels and places one on the lump on the back of my head and the other over my eyes.

"Blue," he says, "I want you to count out loud for me so I know you're awake. You have to count for five minutes."

For crying out loud! He is such a fussbudget. All I want is to go to sleep, but instead my head is freezing, and he wants me to count. I start counting. "One, two, three . . . "

I try to sit up, but my gut protests. "Jack, there is no way I'm counting for five minutes with my eyes closed without falling asleep. I'll tell you what, how about I put the frozen peas on my left eye, the one that is swollen shut, and look at you with the right eye so you know I'm awake. You tell me when five minutes are over and I'll switch."

Jack sighs but agrees.

We do this for about thirty minutes, switching eyes, until I put the now-soggy frozen pea bag down and say, "That's enough. I can open both eyes now, so that is a big improvement. Besides, my brain is about to freeze."

Now I can also see that the towel is not covering me very well. I move to stand up, and I get dizzy.

"What are you doing?"

"I need my robe," I say. "It's on the hook in the bedroom."

Jack retrieves it for me.

"Would you help me up slowly?"

Jack easily lifts me up and carries me to the end of the sofa, setting me down on the arm. Then he holds the robe open for me so I can slip my arms in it. I drop the towel and close the robe while Jack averts his gaze.

Suddenly I'm freezing, and I start to shiver. "Jack, I'm cold. Would you mind terribly making some tea?"

"Not at all," he says. He helps me into a sitting position on the sofa once again. Then he leaves me for a few minutes, returning with a large mug of tea that he sets on the coffee table. I gratefully take the mug in my hands and savor the warmth. I glance up at him.

"Don't you have to be at work today?"

Jack says, "There is nothing that can't wait."

I look down into the depths of my tea again and ask, "How did you know something happened, anyway?"

Jack sits next to me. "Michael called me when he finished the job. You didn't show up at the office, so I called you. You didn't answer your phone, so I came over."

"Oh," I say. "I heard the phone, but I was trying to scrub the feel of his slimy hands off me." I grimace. "I couldn't stop. I'm sorry. I didn't mean to make you come over here."

I shiver, partly from being cold and partly at the thought of Schmidt's hands on me. Jack puts his arms around me and pulls me back to his chest.

I lean my head on his shoulder and say, "Mmm. This is nice. You're warm like a radiator."

Jack starts rubbing my arms vigorously to stimulate my circulation. He moves up to my shoulders, and I think again how nice it is. His hands are wiping the memory of Schmidt away. I shiver again. Jack moves his hands down to my hips and kneads the muscle there. His arms are around me, and I feel nested in his warmth. I don't know when it happens, but suddenly I realize his arm movements have turned sensual. I turn my head so I can see him. I lightly kiss his neck. Jack stills and stops touching me.

"No, please don't stop," I say. "You're erasing the feel of him. I don't want to remember him touching me."

Jack turns his eyes to me. They burn green, and his mouth twists in fury.

CHAPTER 36

A LIGHT TOO BEAUTIFUL

JACK TANNER

MAY 30, 2022, RED AGES

lue murmurs to me, "No, please don't stop. You're erasing the feel of him. I don't want to remember him touching me."

I think about her remembering Schmidt's hands on her body, and it brings a rage so black and so deep my vision tunnels. I feel her kiss my neck again, and her soft lips bring me back. Her aura's white light shimmers softly about her. My throat catches at the loveliness. I look at her bruised face and swollen eyelids, and through it all, her soft eyes gaze at me tenderly. This woman endlessly surprises me with her capacity for kindness.

I kiss the side of Blue's head and move my hands over her hips again. She settles back against me and sighs. She winces when I glide my hands up to her sides, so I skim over the area. I move to her arms again and caress her in slow, warm strokes. Her lips part, and I can see her nipples pebble under her robe. I kiss the top of her hair and breathe in her scent. She smells fresh and clean and Blue. Like no one else smells.

I lightly skim over her breasts, and her nipples rise even further. Jesus Christ, she is so responsive to me. I rub lightly back and forth over her taut peaks through the fabric. Blue rolls her head, and her lips part even more. I drink in the look of her moist lips with their rounded edges. She lightly bites her bottom lip unconsciously. I dip my head down and pull her earlobe into my mouth, gently tugging. Blue moans, and I harden even more at the sound. God, I want this woman. But this is not about me right now.

I grasp her hips and pull her back against me tightly, reaching my hands around her and flicking both of her peaked nipples with my thumbs. Blue opens her eyes, and I see tenderness, complete trust, and raw wanting.

"Are you sure?" I whisper in her ear.

Blue keeps her gaze firmly on mine and nods. "Please," she says softly.

She completely undoes me with her soft plea. My heart tightens as I realize I've never felt more for a woman.

I untie her robe and slip my hands inside to slowly explore every curve and dip of her body. My hands memorize her breasts, softly circling and teasing her. She arches her back slightly but winces and drops back down.

"Lie still," I whisper. "I'll do all the work."

I draw circles around her nipples until they are tight and swollen, then I roll them slowly and tenderly between my fingers, watching their color deepen. Blue's eyes close, and her lips part again as her breaths come in little puffs. Looking down, I see her beautiful, pale skin beneath my hands and the rosy tips of her breasts between my fingers. Suddenly the air fills with her womanly nectar, and a feeling of utter satisfaction envelopes me. I breathe her scent deep into my lungs, hungry for a taste.

I control myself and pull her more tightly against me until I feel her bottom pressed firmly against my shaft, nestling me. I suckle lightly on her ear some more, tasting her salty skin. The scent of her rich blood flows so close to my mouth, tantalizing me. Blue turns to me and steals a kiss. I tease her lower lip tenderly, careful to avoid her swollen upper lip. Then I move my mouth away and kiss the top of her head, afraid of hurting her.

I take turns gently pinching both nipples with one hand, and I slip my other hand between her thighs, softly teasing her dark curls. When Blue shifts her hips toward my hand, I slide my fingers in deeper, slipping over her slick flesh. I thrill in the lushness of her soft, wet skin. Lightly, I tug at her thighs, and she opens up to my hand like petals to the sun. I can see the dark, curly hair between her parted thighs glistening with moisture. I watch, riveted, as I dip two fingers between her creases into her wet, pink folds. Blue jerks her hips up toward me. She is so warm and open to me, but I hesitate a moment, holding still. Then, slowly, I move my fingers up and down, caressing her swollen womanhood.

Blue groans and her mouth opens wider, searching for me like a hungry bird. She kisses my neck and my jaw, all that she can reach. She hungrily kisses and sucks on my skin, apparently no longer feeling the pain of her swollen lip. I move my fingers deftly over her silky flesh, and she opens up more, lifting her hips to me. I find her bud and gently stroke it.

A shudder and a soft moan escapes from Blue's mouth as she thrashes her head. I keep rubbing and circling, spreading her honey all over her beautiful little clit.

Blue is moaning and chanting now. "Oh God, don't stop."

I feel her muscles tightening in her thighs and her flesh becoming taunt under my fingers. I am so hard I'm pulsing and gently rocking against her. My desire courses through my veins, and every glance at her, at any part of her, fuels that desire. She is so beautiful, this woman I hold in my arms. I wrap my left arm around her and pull her firmly against my throbbing shaft. Then I move on to her breasts once more, going back and forth between her nipples with my left hand, nibbling her ear, while I caress her sweet center of pleasure all the while.

I feel the tension in her body continue to rise. Her moaning is coming at a frantic pace. She searches for my lips again with hers. I tilt my neck to give her access. I fill her mouth with my tongue and stroke more firmly on her bud as she tightens her thighs around my hands. I keep stroking as she clenches around my fingers, tightening and releasing in a beautiful rhythm, coming in glorious waves.

In this moment she opens her eyes and looks at me. Her striking blue eyes seem to pierce right to my soul, and at the same time I see the beautiful light of her aura spread out in a bright burst. Her light fills the room and flashes, setting it ablaze, going well beyond the walls. It covers me and sifts through me and fills me with her essence. It is too much. The look of her eyes, the smell of her arousal, the scent of her blood, the sight of her body, the feel of her warm liquid flesh clasping my hand, the tenderness of her lips, the caress of her soul, the joy of her light.

Filled with her being, my control shatters. I shake and jerk underneath her as my body explodes and my mind fills with the brilliant light of a million points of pleasure, all centered around Blue. Each point of pleasure is a little spark in my mind rising up through the dark sky, joining together, collectively creating enough light to glow like a small bright sun. Then the points of light burst outwards again dispersing, drifting slowly back down, leaving streaming trails behind them. As we float back to Earth I am so happy to feel Blue in my arms, trembling like a fine string instrument, as I tremble with her.

I am truly shaken to the core of my being. I've never felt anything so wondrous in all my centuries. I kiss her head reverently, and she kisses my neck gently. Then she closes her eyes. I whisper, "No sleeping, Blue."

She opens her eyes again, smiles at me, and sighs happily. "Let me close my eyes for a few minutes. I'll hum a little so you know I'm awake."

She hums a sweet little tune, a lullaby, I think.

I watch her lying in my arms, and my view of the room and the world starts to open a little. Her tea sits there, cold by now. Her broken books still sit stacked on the floor by her bookcase. My eyes drift back to her, still lying against my chest, wrapped in my arms with her robe spread out to her sides.

I murmur against her head, "When you came, your aura shot a light so bright it filled the room."

I frown. I see my aura, a deep blue, tinged with the black smut of Lilith's mark, mingling with her beautiful, blue-white light. A wave of self-disgust rolls through me. I can't believe I am letting my smut mix with her beautiful light. All the joy seeps out of me. I should not have done this. She is the most pure thing I have ever seen or felt, and I am poisoned.

Blue stops humming, so I look down, and her eyes seem troubled.

She says in a stronger voice, "Jack, I want to get up now. I think I'm okay to move around."

I gently help her to a sitting position and then pull her up. She closes her robe tightly around her middle and says, "I think my ribs are bruised, but not broken."

"I checked already. They're not broken."

She walks around a little and looks at me with puzzled eyes. She heads to the bathroom, and I hear water running.

When she returns she says, "I'm good. I think I want to see Maud."

She walks to the bedroom and starts pulling clothes out of her closet. She ignores me completely and pulls on her underwear and bra, some loose jeans, and a t-shirt. She sits down and tries to lean over to tie her sneakers but winces. Then she slips on some flip-flops instead and grabs her purse and keys.

"Blue," I say, "should you really be going anywhere right now?"

Blue looks at me with a hard, bright light in her eyes. She says, "I'm fine. I'm bruised and sore, but I'll survive."

Then she lifts her chin to me and says softly, "And I'll never remember Schmidt again after what you did to me."

Somehow she does not seem relieved by this. She calls Varg and walks out the door, leaving me standing in the middle of her living room, wondering what in the Plane of Fire just happened.

CHAPTER 37

FOILED AGAIN

BLUEBELL KILDARE

MAY 30, 2022, RED AGES

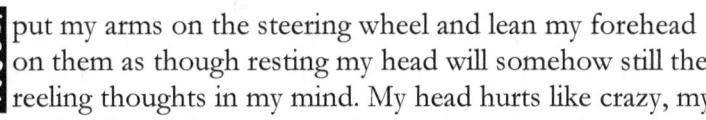 put my arms on the steering wheel and lean my forehead on them as though resting my head will somehow still the reeling thoughts in my mind. My head hurts like crazy, my ribs ache, and my face is swollen and sore, but my heart—my heart is worst of all. It feels sliced and shredded. He looked at my light and felt disgust. Disgust! No wonder he keeps in control of his emotions. No wonder he fought his attraction to me. My aura disgusts him. My soul disgusts him. I'd cry now, but honestly I haven't anything left. I'm wrung out. There can't possibly be any direction but up from here.

In the space of a few hours I've had the worst day, the best day, and the worst day of my entire life again. Except for maybe the day my parents died, and I don't remember that. I pummel the dashboard, then grit my teeth, putting the car in drive. With little regard for speed limits or yellow lights I drive blindly to Maud's house and arrive in no time.

When she answers the door, she exclaims, "Lord Almighty! What happened to your face?"

"Unpleasant story," I say, and Maud lets me in.

"Well," she says, "an unpleasant story is best told over a nice, cool mint julep, which is just what I happen to have."

I kiss her cheek with my fat lip. "You are the best. That is exactly what I need."

When I'm comfortably seated at her kitchen table, I ponder the garden while Maud fixes us two tall glasses and places a few fresh mint leaves in them. "Where did you get the mint leaves?" I ask.

Maud smirks and says, "I went into the garden yesterday."

"Ohh! Really? What brought this on?"

Maud sits down across from me and nods her head toward the

infamous Harry Pickets' house. Her green eyes, vivid next to her flaming red hair, sparkle with life. "Harry had a party yesterday, a barbeque."

"Do tell! Did he invite you?"

"Of course. And of course I told him no. I told him I was busy shampooing my hair that evening." Maud fluffs her hair lovingly as she says this.

I chuckle softly. "The bright red is very becoming, by the way."

Not to be distracted, Maud continues with her story, "And boy am I glad I didn't go. You would not . . . *believe* . . . what he did." A look of total affront covers her face. "He played jazz all . . . night . . . long. He had speakers in all four corners of his yard, and the music was so loud over here I went to investigate. And what do you think I found?"

"I can't even begin to imagine . . . "

Maud leans back in her chair and angles her head toward the neighbor's house with narrowed eyes. "Of course you can't. It is unheard of. The speakers that were against my fence were actually pointed at *my* house!"

"You've got to be joking."

Maud shakes her head. "It's true. I had to listen to jazz until midnight. I couldn't sleep a wink."

"So what are you going to do about this?"

Maud gets up and opens her pantry door. She gestures me over. I ignore my pain and get out of my chair to see what she has in store for poor Harry Pickets. A dozen shiny rolls of aluminum foil are stacked neatly on the bottom shelf.

My curiosity is definitely piqued. "What are you planning to do with *those?*"

Maud smiles her mischievous smile. "We're going to foil his car, of course."

I laugh hard and deep, and I have to hold my ribs because they hurt so bad. "So when are we going to do this?"

She responds in a hushed voice as though Harry might have spies trying to eavesdrop on her plan. "After I see him turn down his lights for the night." She purses her lips. "If you're feeling up for it, of course."

"I think I am," I respond with a smile. "But how will he know for sure that you did it?"

"I made some banana bread today. I'll wrap it in foil and send the neighbor boy over with it in the morning."

I smile at this and sit back down at the table. Maud gets out some lemon sugar cookies and we snack for a bit. After a few minutes, Maud finally asks, "So what happened to your face?"

I sigh. "It was a guy from the precinct. He was jealous of my success and blamed me for his lack."

Wanting to quickly dispel her pity, I gesture to Varg. "Varg got him good, though. I'm sure he came out worse than I did."

Maud nods firmly. "That's important. You have to give as good as you get. Then you can hold your head high."

After giving this sage advice, Maud leads us to the living room to relax while we await our midnight adventure. As we sit comfortably together through the evening, I contemplate how lucky I am to have Maud.

Eventually, Harry's lights go out. Maud gives me a black robe to put over my clothes, and she slips on a black dress and a hat to cover her red hair. When properly outfitted for our nefarious deed, we sneak over and plaster his car from top to bottom in aluminum foil, shiny side out. After it's covered, we press it down into every crease to show the fine details like any great piece of art. For an extra bit of fun, Maud ties an aluminum foil bow onto his antenna. It makes quite the racket and I'm surprised he doesn't wake up. The prank is so good that I enjoy myself despite my pain.

Finally, when the car is one bright, shiny, silver, beautiful mess, I give Maud the thumbs up. She winks back as she appraises the results. With the prank set, we sneak silently around the block to her house and reconvene in her living room. As soon as the door is closed we have a good laugh.

I hug Maud goodnight, and then Varg and I head home. The incident with Jack still twists in my gut, my ribs still hurt, and my face still stings, but now I feel like I've been comforted by the home nest.

CHAPTER 38

A MUTUAL UNDERSTANDING

JACK TANNER

MAY 30, 2022, RED AGES

Hunting brings out the wild predator in me. I feel like a jungle cat, one who hunts and seeks, then lies in wait with patience and stealth, exercising infinite control with lethal intention. I know with absolute certainty I will meet success because I am faster, quieter, more accurate, and more in control than any of my prey.

But that is not how I feel right now. Not on this hunt. If success is the ability to reach my prey and decimate him, I can absolutely succeed. If success is my ability to control and restrain myself from killing in bloodlust and drinking him dry, then things may go awry. Never have I wanted to bring death to someone so badly. Never have I so desired to suck the life out of someone, to feel his soul slip away. I'm standing outside Schmidt's bedroom window, and hear him breathing inside. His very breath is an affront to me. Each inhale and exhale makes me rage anew.

I must remain in control. If I turn into a Dark Vampire, Blue will have no one to watch over her. Also, Lilith is an evil, soul-sucking demon, and I refuse to give her my soul. She doesn't deserve it. As I say this to myself, I feel my old stubbornness rise up and some small measure of sanity regained.

I noiselessly move to the opposite side of the house. With deft fingers I break the aluminum window frame off the guest bedroom and slide the glass out. In one quick movement I'm over the windowsill and headed for Schmidt's bedroom door. It's open, and he lies in bed, breathing erratically. I stare at him for several minutes from the doorway, measuring my control and awaiting his recognition. He's huddled, shaking under the covers, and the smell of a significant wound, tainted with infection, permeates the air. My appreciation for Varg rises to a new level. Schmidt doesn't appear to have cleaned his wounds or sought medical attention yet. It's such a shame.

Suddenly he looks up, and I know he can see my eyes glowing in the dark. I see him fully, in the minutest detail, and I despise every ounce of flesh making up his puny, weak body. I want to annihilate it, destroy it, wipe it out of existence. He moves his left hand under the covers. I wait expectantly. A small metal object tears a hole through the comforter, tracking toward me. Even without my quick movement, I'd never be hit with that shot, as it is widely off course. Before the bullet reaches the same plane I was standing in, I've moved to the side of his bed.

I cover his lips with one hand and pinch them closed in an iron grip. At the same time, I grab his other hand through the covers and crush it with the slight flex of my fingers. The small bones of his hand shatter with a wonderful crunch, offering a small measure of satisfaction. I release his hand, and the gun falls to the floor with a thud. Muffled screams come from behind his pinched lips.

I lean over him and scrape my fully extended fangs over his neck. His muffled screams turn to whimpers. My fangs ache with the desire to rip his flesh to shreds and suck the lifeblood from him. I feel the evilness of Lilith's mark teasing me and taunting me to go on, to do more. Even as I tremble with fury, I resist and instead continue my business, whispering slowly, "Schmidt, right now my fangs are poised over your carotid artery. My rage for you is so immense I am on the verge of killing you in bloodlust, be damned my soul. But that's too easy a death for you. I want to peel the skin from your body inch by inch, in strips, and dance in your blood. I want to delight in the sound of your agonized screams."

I pause a second as I smell and hear Schmidt urinating on himself, which the dark stain spreading over the comforter confirms. I continue whispering, "I want to drive chisels up your fingernails and peel them off one by one. I want to cut your eyelids open and tie you to a rock and watch the ants devour your eyeballs."

Sweat pours down his face and his heart beats so fast I think he might have a heart attack. But I'm not done yet.

"I want to slice open your gut and hold a bucket of hungry rats to you, letting them eat you inside out. But I'm not going to. I'm going to leave you alive today. I'm only going to do this because Blue asked me to. But I'm only going to accommodate her if you promise me a few things."

He starts to nod his head, but when he feels my fangs against his neck again he stills.

"I'm going to remove my hand from your mouth and let you open it, only so I can hear if you agree." I pause a moment to make sure he understands. I say it with a cool matter-of-factness. "If you scream, I will kill you. And I do want to kill you. Blink if you understand."

Terror fills his eyes. He understands quite well, but I await confirmation. Finally he blinks, and I release his lips.

I continue, "I want you to promise you will never show up for work again. Your days of pretending to be an officer of the law are over. If you do show up at work, I will sever your spine. Do you agree to this?"

"Yes," he whispers.

"If you ever come close to Blue, within a mile of Blue, I will torture you the way I want to, the way I described to you. I won't sever your spine because that's too easy. Oh, it would be much too gentle and much too kind for you. You. Must. Stay. Away. From. Her. Do you agree to this?"

"Yes," he whispers again.

"Good," I say. "We have an understanding."

I blur out of the room and slip through the window again. Only the silver moon and the twinkling of stars mark my exit, and I wonder if anyone will ever know how grand my accomplishment was today. Today I left him alive.

CHAPTER 39

OFFICE IN DISARRAY

BLUEBELL KILDARE

MAY 31, 2022, RED AGES

I open the office door and see the file cabinets emptied on the floor. With stiff joints and sore muscles, I walk in to the vision of Rubalia on her knees in her cream and black houndstooth woven suit with her back to me, slamming scattered papers on top of a pile in front of her.

"What happened?" I ask.

Rubalia stacks some more papers and raises her voice. "This place is going to the Plane of Fire! That is what's happening. The office is a wreckage. Jack apparently hasn't slept at home for the last three nights. He keeps showering here." Rubalia looks up. "And what in the world happened to your face?"

I remember my bruises and feel my face heat up in embarrassment. "I had an altercation with someone, and Varg won."

Rubalia sniffs and says, "Well, maybe that good-for-nothing is good for something." Then she looks at Varg with her sharp eyes and says, "Next time win the altercation faster."

Varg lowers his head and slinks away. I've been on the receiving end of Rubalia's stares many a time, so I know how he feels.

I look around and see the entire office is a disaster. "So, what really happened here?"

Rubalia keeps slamming papers on the stack as she explains. "Jack called me at six a.m.—just after dawn, mind you. He tells me the place is a mess because it was broken into and searched and asks me to come in early. Well, of course I was already up and dressed by then."

I smile slightly at this. Of course she was up and dressed by six a.m.

"It is quite a mess now," Rubalia says, "but you should have seen it when I arrived. And your office isn't much better. They got all the offices."

"All? Mine, Ernesto's, Xavier's, and Jack's?"

Rubalia nods.

"What in the Great Abyss?" I exclaim. It must be the guy who is after the amulet. He must be getting desperate if he's willing to search our office. This is not good.

I peek in on Ernesto. His office is neat as a pin except for a small pile of papers on his desk. The only other item out of place is the skewed painting he's straightening on the wall.

"Rubalia told me all the offices were trashed. How come yours is hardly touched?"

Ernesto turns and his gaze scans my bruised face and swollen eyes. "Good morning, Señorita," he says. "Trees are too grand to waste on the animals we investigate, so I hardly ever use paper."

Then Ernesto gestures toward my Glock and looks at me seriously. "Do you know how to fire that?"

I know he's suggesting I didn't defend myself well, so I respond to his real question. "I didn't have the gun with me at the time. That was my fault. But to answer your question, I could use some time at the shooting range."

Ernesto nods and says, "We should go together. Also you need to practice with the crossbow and be wary after dark. Dark Vampire activity has been picking up."

"Jack told me about that. Did you find the perpetrator for the killing outside the Heifer grocery store?"

Ernesto says, "Yes. We let him be judged by the sun. Now I'm working on a homicide case in Collins Gardens. I suspect the Dilectus Deo are involved, but I lack evidence."

"Good luck with that."

I wearily walk down the hall and check on Xavier. Files are strewn all over the floor. Office equipment has been thrown around. Even the picture frame has been taken apart. Xavier uses tons of paper, and his office was a mess to begin with, but this is ridiculous. I'm afraid to see my office now. Xavier is talking on the phone and absently straightening a few things around him. He seems at home in the mess. He points to my face and points to his eye, obviously referring to my black eye, and frowns.

I mouth, "I'm okay."

He nods and smiles.

I head to my own office and take a look around. It is not as bad as Xavier's, but worse than I'd hoped. My files are dumped all over the floor like his, but fortunately I have fewer. The entire contents of my desk drawers have been tossed around the room. My chair is upside down. My plant has been dumped out, and dirt is scattered around. I look at it lying on its side like a dead corpse. Everything else I can deal with, but I love my fern. I slam the door behind me, wincing as the movement hurts my stomach.

I take a deep breath, then stoop to the floor, grunting in pain from my ribs on the way down. I sit on my butt and start shoveling dirt back in the pot. Varg comes over to sniff in interest then lies down in his usual spot by the window, unconcerned with the mess. I scowl at him. Of course he's unconcerned. He doesn't have to clean it up.

Once I've scooped as much loose dirt as I can, dumping it into the pot, I place my fern back in. After patting the dirt around the plant, I sit back to look at it. It's a little limp, but it's still standing erect, which makes me feel much better. I dust my hands off and scoot over on my butt to the papers on the floor and start gathering them into piles. To avoid the pain in my ribs, I scoot around the floor and slowly manage to pile up most of the papers.

Jack walks in. I tilt the skewed chair up so it's sitting on four legs again and stack the pile of papers on top of it. Then I hoist myself up by using the arm of the chair to avoid using my stomach muscles. But the blasted chair tips precariously, and the files start sliding off the edge. I scramble to straighten it just in time and catch the files as they slide off. I stack them on my desk and sit down in my chair in an exhausted huff.

All the while, Jack is standing there watching me with his lips twitching.

"What do you want?" I grumble.

Jack closes the door behind him and sits down in the offending chair. He says, "I didn't expect you to be in today, Blue. You can take the day off if you need to."

I wave my hand. "I'm fine. Just sore and bruised. Besides that, I'm a new woman."

Jack frowns at that.

Then I say, "Plus, I have a case to solve. They certainly are making the rounds looking for the amulet."

Jack shrugs and says, "Hopefully now that they have searched both places, they will be done. But to be sure, I'm sending the ward specialist over to everyone's house today."

"That's an excellent idea. Are you having him do the office?"

"It's already done." Jack nods as though satisfied with the arrangement.

Then his eyes soften as he looks at me. "Blue, do you want to press charges . . ."

I raise my hand to cut him off. "No. I'm not ready to think about that."

Jack nods then gets up to leave.

I have one more thing to say. "Jack."

Jack turns around.

"I should probably get some self defense training, hand-to-hand combat, and more skill with weaponry."

Jack looks closely at me. "A smart decision," he says. "I'll think about it and come up with a good recommendation."

"Thanks, Jack. And by the way, I didn't tell you yesterday, but I had shut Varg in the apartment while I showed the ward specialist how to get to Alexis' herbal shop. If Varg had been with me, this," I gesture to my face, "never would have happened. He had to break out to get to me."

Jack looks at Varg and says, "He's a good guard for you, and you should always keep him with you, but you need to learn how to depend on yourself as well."

I nod. "That's what I think, too." Then I look down at my papers and start sorting through them. Jack leaves and softly closes the door.

CHAPTER 40

IS THE DOG RABID?

BLUEBELL KILDARE

MAY 31, 2022, RED AGES

I groan and sit down again in my chair as I grab painkillers out of my purse. I shake out two little red pills as I survey my office. It is about half picked up now. I wash the meds down with bottled water.

Rubalia buzzes me. "Blue, Chief Mack is here to see you."

"Thanks, Rubalia. Send him in."

Chief Mack ambles in and rolls a keen eye around the office. His eyes quietly examine the two shiners I have as well as my fat lip. He sits down quietly and places a document down on my desk. He makes himself comfortable by leaning back in the chair, stretching his long legs out, and clasping his hands on his lap.

I look at the document and ask, "Are you sure you got everyone on the list?"

Mack's lips stretch in a lazy smile. "I'm sure."

"I'm very grateful for this," I say. "I hope it wasn't too hard to put together."

"It wasn't too hard." After a brief pause, he continues. "Now, would this list have anything to do with what is going on in your office today?"

I smile. "Maybe."

Mack asks, "Would it have anything to do with those two shining beauties you've got there?"

I crinkle my eyebrows. "No, that is another matter entirely."

Mack asks in his same laid-back, even tone, "Do you need any help with that other matter?"

I gesture toward Varg and say, "No thank you, Chief. Varg here already settled that matter."

Mack ponders on this for a space, then says in his deep, smooth intonation, "If a dog attacks because it doesn't know its place and you put it in its place, then it will likely stay there. If a dog attacks because it's rabid, no matter what you do, that dog will keep on attacking. The trick is to know what kind of dog you're dealing with."

I lever myself out of the chair and walk to the window. What Mack said shakes me. I hadn't considered that Schmidt might continue to be a problem. I suddenly feel very unsafe. I look past the manicured lawn to the street beyond where unknown people ride in cars, passing at regular intervals. I watch them wondering where Schmidt is now and if he's out there lying in wait. I turn to Chief Mack, "You're right Chief Mack. I'll keep that in mind."

Mack says, "Now, about this list."

I ease myself back in the chair.

"The five who were conducting interviews are listed at the top," Mack continues. "All five of us are members of the Rotary Club. I lead the Fireworks and Magic Show Committee every year. The rest of the spots are filled by whoever volunteers that year."

I look and see the following people listed:

Gerald Mack, Chief of Fire Department

Hilda Gunderson, Owner of Zen Spa and Salon

Milton Goldberg, Owner of Goldberg Jewelers

Tobias Blackwater, City Councilman, Treasurer

Hank Fletcher, General Manager of Mountain Paper Mill

I ask, "What do you know of the four volunteers?"

Mack says, "Milton is the only one I really care for. I bought my wife's pearls from him. He has a joy about him that I think would be hard to corrupt. I run into Tobias at the city council meetings on occasion and at budget time. I can't say that I like him much. He seems cold and greedy. But as treasurer, he controls my budget, so I'm biased against him. The other two I don't know much of, besides what I see of them at the Rotary Club meetings."

"And what do you see of those two at the Rotary Club meetings?" I ask.

Mack contemplates this for a moment. "Well, they're always on opposite sides of any debate. That's all." He leans forward and says, "Well, if that is it. I should head back to my men."

I tap my pencil lazily on the desk and ask slowly, "Chief Mack, did you tell anyone you were asked to put together this list?" Mack's slow talk must be contagious.

Mack says, "No, Ma'am. I wrote it up myself."

I say, "Thanks, Chief Mack, for stopping by. You have been a big help."

Mack's smile reaches his eyes. He nods his head graciously and says, "It was my pleasure." Then he languidly stands up and strolls out.

He would have made an excellent Chief of Police too. I'll bet nothing gets past Mack.

CHAPTER 41

SOLIDARITY

BLUEBELL KILDARE

MAY 31, 2022, RED AGES

ith the sound of the shutting door still echoing in my mind, Rubalia buzzes me. "Detective Gambino is waiting to see you."

"Please send him in."

Gambino opens the door and winces when he sees my face. He's wearing a charcoal gray, pinstripe suit today, but is clearly unshaven. During the time I've taken to observe him, I've noticed his eyes keep straying to my face, and his cheeks turn a blotchy red. I gesture toward the chair and he sits down.

Gambino leans to the left of the chair and spreads his right arm over its back, taking up as much room as possible. Gambino says, "Jack called me in. He told me what happened with Schmidt."

I pick up my pencil and draw some squiggles on my pad. "Ohh?"

"Yes. He also said I shouldn't expect Schmidt back at the office."

I spin the pencil in my fingers and tap the eraser on the pad, watching it bounce off and vibrate. "Did he, now? Did Jack also happen to say if Schmidt was alive when he left him?"

Gambino grunts at that. "Jack said that he crushed Schmidt's hand while Schmidt was shooting at him to immobilize his firing hand. He said beyond that, he didn't harm him. He had a talk with Schmidt, and they came to an understanding about repeat offenses."

"Hmm," I say.

Gambino looks out the window and says, "I know Schmidt is alive because he called in sick today."

I think back to the moment in the alley when I saw Varg's teeth tearing into Schmidt's arm. I remember the blood streaming from his face. "I expect he did. I'm glad he's still alive."

Gambino grunts noncommittally. Funny, so much can be said with a sound. Gambino's grunt says he wouldn't care if Schmidt were dead, except then he would have to arrest Jack. Gambino may look like an Italian gangster in his pinstripe suit, but he is more self-actualized than most people I know. We sit quietly for a moment.

I push myself out of the chair to look out the window again, an effort that takes a bit of leveraging.

Gambino asks, "Are you okay? Do you want to press charges?"

"I want to know if Schmidt is a rabid dog or just a stupid dog."

Varg growls, and Gambino asks, "What?"

Still looking out the window, I respond, "Never mind. There is no evidence it was a hate crime so it would be handled in regular courts. How many breedists would be on the jury? Even if convicted, what is the worse he would get? An assault charge with a slap on the wrist? It's more likely that the judge would throw it out for lack of evidence. You could push for a small suspension from work, at most. And what would happen to Varg? If Schmidt countered with his own charge, Varg could be ordered put down."

Then I turn around. "If Schmidt doesn't show up at work again and doesn't bother me again, I won't press charges. So far, Varg got him, Jack got him, and he's off the force for good. If he does it again, at least he won't have his badge to protect him." *And he won't screw another case up like he did this one*, I think. "It's more than I'd get going the official route. Now what did you find when you searched Agnes' house?"

I see the truth reflected in Gambino's eyes as he answers with another grunt. "We found nothing. Slab-on-grade. No other structures were on the property. Neither Agnes nor Paul own any other properties. We checked with the bartender at the Cock and Bull Tap, and it seems Paul was there for several hours before the boy died. He left about an hour earlier, right before the police shift arrived. That was typical for him."

"So the bartender's story matches Paul's."

Gambino nods. "I don't think Paul had anything to do with the kid's kidnapping and torture."

"I believe the other party is after the amulet," I explain. "The wards in my apartment were breached, and every room was trashed." I gesture around my office. "I assume Jack told you we had an uninvited visitor here last night as well."

Gambino nods grimly.

I sit down again. "What I say next needs to be handled delicately."

Gambino's face hardens.

I buzz reception. "Rubalia, can you ask Jack to join us in my office?"

CHAPTER 42

Suspect List

JACK TANNER

MAY 31, 2022, RED AGES

When I enter Blue's office for the second time today, her presence still hits me like a jackhammer, complete with visions of her softly moaning while lying in my arms yesterday. At the same time, my gut twists from seeing her fat lip, black eyes, and battered face. I steel myself and affect professionalism. Now is about getting the job done.

Blue furrows her brow and squints a little while pressing a finger to the side of her temple. Then she clasps her hands on her desk and turns to Gambino.

"First I'd like to get you up to speed," she says. "Jason's best friend gave me a tip that Jason had intended to interview as a volunteer for the Sun Flare Fireworks and Magic Show. Jason's gift was the gift of magnification or amplification. He could magnify the effect of any power by at least ten times. An extremely powerful gift, which could be sought after and abused for countless reasons. My guess is someone sought it to find the amulet, the rest of the key, and the book. I hope only the amulet has been found so far, but we should consider all possibilities." Blue takes a breath. "I'm getting ahead of myself a bit here."

I can see the wheels turning in Gambino's brain. His eyes get shadowed and he looks like he is trying to find a word that eludes him. "Wait," he says, "can you tell me about this book? What exactly does it do?"

Blue gives me a sideways look, deferring to my judgment on this one. I speak for us. "The book is an important magical artifact, but its purpose is privileged information. It is essential it doesn't get into the wrong hands. I can't tell you more."

Gambino gives me a brief, hard stare, and the air in the room thickens with his unspoken questions and doubts. I return his stare levelly. He decides to accept this gracefully and turns to Blue. "Please go on."

Blue clears her throat, then presses her finger to her temple again. "The Rotary Club sponsors the Sun Flare Celebration each year. They provide the manpower to organize it while the city pays for it. The lead of the Fireworks and Magic Show Committee is always Fire Chief Gerald Mack. I met with Chief Mack, and he confirmed Jason was at the interview on the day he went missing. That makes it the last place he was seen prior to the kidnapping."

Blue sweeps both of us with her startling blue eyes. She winces when she turns her head. I am about to stop her from continuing on while in obvious pain, but she speaks again, in a softer voice now. "There were five people on the Fireworks and Magic Show Committee doing the interviews. Chief Mack was one of them. He said he had to leave early because he was called out on a fire. I don't believe Chief Mack was involved, just because of the person I feel he is." Blue pinches her nasal bridge then looks at Gambino. "But I assume you can easily check his whereabouts so we know we're doing our due diligence?"

Gambino shifts in his chair and absently rubs his cleft chin. "I agree with your character assessment, but I'll definitely confirm."

Blue taps her pencil eraser on her desk, and the next words rapidly tumble out of her mouth. "The other four people are Milton Goldberg, the owner of Goldberg Jewelers; Hilda Gunderson, the owner of Zen Spa and Salon; Hank Fletcher, the General Manager of the Mountain Paper Mill; and Tobias Blackwater, the City Treasurer. All are prominent business people, with the exception of Tobias Blackwater, who is on the City Council."

She winces again and starts squeezing her fingers while simultaneously watching our expressions.

"Blue, do you want to reschedule this meeting until tomorrow?"

Blue looks surprised but lifts up her chin in determination, "Absolutely not. Let's get through it."

I scowl and turn to Gambino. "What issue will you run into if we question the councilman?"

Gambino settles back in his chair and answers carefully. "Tobias is in control of the entire city budget. He could cause problems. He is also closely connected to the mayor, so we could get pressure to stop the investigation."

I can't stand politics. The simpering and sly maneuvering is pathetic. I stand and prowl the room as my distaste gets the better of me. Unfortunately, Blue's office is too damn small. I turn to Blue and Gambino. "Then we will have to question the other three first. Hit Tobias last."

Gambino, in a calmer state than I, gives his take. "If we question the three, word will get back to Tobias quickly. We won't have much time to move."

I pound on the window frame in frustration. A soft sound escapes Blue's mouth. Immediately contrite for making the noise, I turn to her. She must have a headache. I wish I could sense her like she can sense people.

"Blue, do you think you could question the three covertly to try to pinpoint their whereabouts after the interview? You would need to confirm through a second party, if possible."

Blue looks excited, like she thinks this could work, despite her continued finger fidgeting and brow furrowing. "I could use my sixth sense to validate what they tell me. I'll need to be creative, but, yes, I'm sure it can be done." She turns to Gambino and says, "I'd like you to participate so you can give me your take and you stay in the loop."

Gambino looks happy to have a plan. "Sure. It's a good way to start."

"Great," Blue says. "I have some more research to do on the amulet. Can you meet me here at, say, one o'clock tomorrow?"

"No problem," Gambino says.

"Good. Dress casually." Then she looks at both of us, and with her finger poking into her temple again, she says, "Thanks for playing, boys. Now, I have a stabbing headache, so I'll call this meeting to a close."

CHAPTER 43

SOLICITING ASSISTANCE

BLUEBELL KILDARE

MAY 31, 2022, RED AGES

My declaration of pain quickly rushes Jack and Gambino out of my office. Thank goodness for small miracles. As soon as they leave, I reach into my purse and with trembling hands, shake two painkillers out of the bottle, and swig them down with some water.

After a few slow breathing exercises, I dial Robert LaRoche. A butler or assistant or whoever rich people from old money have answering their phone picks up and gets Mr. LaRoche on the line.

A robust, pleasant voice says, "Good afternoon. Mr. LaRoche speaking."

I, trying to sound casual, say, "Hello, Mr. LaRoche. This is Bluebell Kildare calling. We met at the Glenwood Charity Gala last Friday evening. Is this a good time for you?"

Mr. LaRoche says, "Certainly. How are you, Ms. Kildare?"

I wince at his enthusiastic voice. The noise goes straight through my head. Then I lie, "I'm great, Mr. LaRoche. It's such a beautiful day today." The truth is I can't even remember the temperature this morning. I glance outside to make sure it isn't storming or gray or anything else that will give me away as a liar.

"I was wondering if you'd mind if I stopped by to tell you about the special piece I mentioned."

"I would be delighted to discuss it with you. When did you have in mind?"

"Would tomorrow morning be terribly inconvenient for you?"

Mr. LaRoche says, "I have some time at nine a.m. if that works for you."

I poke my finger into my temple, trying to create a point of pain outside my head to distract me from the greater pain inside my head, and I gush, "That would be perfect. Thank you so much, Mr. LaRoche. I really appreciate it."

Mr. LaRoche says, "It's my pleasure. I'll see you then."

Acting like a brainless twit has me feeling like a brainless twit because I feel myself blushing despite my headache. "Awesome! Thanks, Mr. LaRoche." I hang up the phone and then practically vomit in my mouth. Awesome? Did I really just say awesome to an attractive, scholarly man? It must be the headache. I would vomit, but it'd hurt too much.

I flip open my chimerator and chime Alexis' line next. She comes into view with a bright, happy "Herbal Enchantments."

"Alexis," I beg, "can you please try to talk softly? I have a terrible headache and I called to ask you if you can hand deliver some products to me this evening."

Alexis whispers, "Sure. What do you need, and what in the unholy fire happened to your face?"

I whisper back, "I need something for a splitting headache from a knot on my head. I need something to reduce bruising and swelling on my face. I also need something to help with sore muscles in my body. I'm willing to pay any price you require. But I also want to know if I can borrow something to wear for a meeting tomorrow with a high society gentleman."

Alexis is silent for a moment, then says, "Well, that depends. Did this high society gentleman have anything to do with the knot on your head, the bruising and swelling on your face, or the sore muscles all over your body?"

"No," I whisper.

Alexis whispers back, "Then I guess I do. But it will cost you full details about the bastard who's responsible. I'll come over as soon as I'm off work."

I gush, "Thank you Alexis." And this time I mean it.

CHAPTER 44

COVERT SENTINEL REVEALED

BLUEBELL KILDARE

MAY 31, 2022, RED AGES

*ing donnnngggg.*

Shoot, I guess I have to move now. "Coming," I shout toward the door.

Striking pain assails my head behind my eyes at the sound of my own voice. With great effort, I lever my body from its prone position on the sofa into a sitting position. The dull throbbing in the back of my skull decides to join the melee of unwanted sensations by becoming not so dull. I grimace pushing myself up into standing position, sort of a hunched standing position.

Diiinnngg doonnnnnngggg.

I yell "Hold on!" wincing at the pain generated from my own voice. I move stiffly in the direction of the door, and I slowly straighten my spine out. For crying out loud, this sucks!

Finally I reach my goal. Varg is already there wagging his tail. When I open the door, Alexis stands there with a look of ghastly interest on her face and two bags on her shoulder, one green and one white. Her beautiful chocolate skin shines, but her large, dark eyes pop as round as donut holes.

I whisper, "Come in."

She whispers back, "Oh, you sure did get worked over good." She's savoring my injuries the way most people enjoy a fine wine.

I wave her into the kitchen and whisper, "Yes, yes, I know. I'm a Healer's delight. You probably have erotic dreams about wounded people showing up at your door."

Alexis chuckles and greets Varg with a good back rub, then puts the green bag on the table and starts pulling things out of it. She gives me a small blue bottle and says, "Drink all of this right now. It will help your headache immediately, and will reduce inflammation to help your head and your puffy eyes and your swollen lip."

"Way to make me feel beautiful." Then I greedily grab it and toss it down. Ugh, it makes me want to spew. I sputter and grimace. "Is that made of dead rats?"

Alexis says solemnly, "Yes. Dead rats and snake tails."

I look at her suspiciously. "You are kidding, right?"

Alexis puts her arms on her hips. "Of course. Don't be ridiculous. Snake tails are way too expensive."

Hey, now she's speaking at a normal volume and I'm not cringing. This is a positive development. "What about the rats? I hope they're too expensive too."

She ignores me and gives me a tiny red bottle. "Heat up some tea and pour half of this in. It'll taste strong but pleasant, like spiced tea. Drink one cup now and one before bed. This will help with the bruising."

She pulls out a jar and continues. "This is a salve for your muscles. It smells like eucalyptus. Use it morning and night over all the stiff areas." Alexis pauses and says, "Well, that's it. Let's get the kettle boiling." She heads to the kitchen to do just that.

I attempt to follow her, but she says, "No, no, go put the salve on, and I'll have tea ready when you're done."

I nod obediently and shamble off to the bathroom with my salve. When I finally emerge, I smell like a minty eucalyptus tree, but the salve is sinking deliciously deep into my muscles with a cold heat, loosening them up. Alexis is sitting quietly on the sofa, sipping her tea with a cup and saucer for me on the table beside her. This is the part that I dread: the talking about what happened part.

I sit down beside her and say, "I feel much better already. My head is clear and my muscles feel so much looser."

I warm my hands with the tea and smell it. A fragrant aroma of cinnamon and cloves with a hint of pepper fills my nose and makes my mouth water. I take a small sip and the taste is similar, except with a stronger sense of hot. Not black pepper—maybe cayenne? It is peppery and spicy and delicious.

Alexis leans back on the sofa and lifts her eyebrows. "Now for my payment."

I put my tea down and sigh. "Okay, but don't get all emotional on me because you'll make me all emotional."

Alexis agrees, but I know better.

I pick up my tea again and stare into its depths of swirling spices and spill the story. I tell her about Schmidt's name calling, his abuse, and his attempted rape, all while looking down at my tea. I feel her empathy, sadness and anger floating over me. Then I tell her how Varg rescued me. Not until then do I look up. Her eyes are big and watery, and her full soft lips are turned down in a frown. Shoot! I knew it. She's using the trick I use on my perpetrators when I question them.

Her empathy twists up my gut, and all the emotion I had bottled in, all the scared little girl, all the helpless anger, come rushing up. I can handle anything but that empathy. And I cry. Not just crying but bawling, sobbing, great heaving shoulders, soul-ripping, snotty, ugly, face-twisted crying. Alexis pulls me into her arms and squeezes me, and I hug her back.

When my sobs finally quiet down, she asks, "So what's going to happen to Asswipe Schmidt?"

I say, "Jack found out and paid Schmidt a visit afterwards. Schmidt won't bother me again if he values his life. Jack said he wouldn't be going back to the police force either." As I say this, I pull myself together and lean out of the hug, reaching for my life preserver teacup.

Alexis says, "That's good. So that's why Jack is camping out on our roof."

I choke on my tea and sputter, "Camping on our roof?"

Alexis looks at me queerly. "Yes, I saw him up there when I came home. Didn't you know?"

I'm flabbergasted, floored, stunned, then a slow, burning irate. "I certainly did not. He's got some nerve."

Alexis gives me another one of her keen looks and says, "Actually, I think it's sort of romantic."

I protest, "Romance has nothing to do with it. Jack has absolutely no interest in me whatsoever. He as much as said so." My voice sounds somehow deflated even to my own ears.

Alexis says, "Humph. I don't care what comes out of his mouth. I've seen his eyes when you're nearby. I feel like a peeping tom just being in the room with you two."

I think about it a minute, and my anger, even if it is mixed with a little pleasure, is still stirring. "Still, he has no right to stalk me like this."

Alexis asks, "Is he stalking? Or protecting?"

I wave her words away. The difference seems negligible to me at this point. "Regardless, I'm going to have a few words with him about it, for sure."

Alexis says, "Well, that is between you two." Then she changes the subject. "Have you seen the news about the Dilectus Deo? They're staging protests all across the country against Vampires and the Gifted. And yesterday a college couple was found dead in the girl's dorm at the university. They were both Gifted."

"No," I say. "I ran into a few protests here recently, but I had no idea it was a national issue. I need to catch up on what's happening . My incident with Schmidt sidelined me quite a bit for the last two days."

Alexis nods understandingly and updates me on the happenings at her shop. Then she asks, "So what's the deal with your meeting tomorrow?"

"I have to interview a man about a piece of evidence we found. He's a wealthy man, comes from old money. I'm trying not to be obvious about asking him questions regarding a case, though I'm not lying to him either."

Alexis pulls her white bag up on the sofa and says, "I think what I brought will be perfect, then."

She pulls out a beautiful, white silk tunic with a mandarin collar surrounded by little blue and gold flowers made of embroidery and beading. The wide cuffs of the sleeves have a matching ring of embroidery around them. Then she pulls out a matching set of loose, flowy pants.

I hold up the tunic and admire the handiwork, and finger the silky smoothness of the rich, white fabric. "It's exquisite."

Alexis says, "It can't be machine washed. Bring it to me dirty. I have a special charm to clean it safely."

I nod absently, still tracing my fingers over the delicate little flower pattern.

"Well," Alexis says, "I should let you rest, I have some more cooking to do tonight."

I follow Alexis to the door and hug her again. "Thank you for everything," I say. "You are truly a good friend."

Alexis smiles and walks down the hall to her apartment. I shake my head. That woman, she never stops working. I wonder if my parents were like that. I sure wish I'd known them.

Chapter 45

A Confusing Illumination

Bluebell Kildare

May 31, 2022, Red Ages

I close the door on Alexis and sit down to finish my tea while I ponder Jack. We did have that beautiful moment. And he is very protective of me. But I know he felt disgust. On the other hand, he is standing guard on my roof.

Oh, for crying out loud! I get up and do the only thing that will help me resolve this mess: I go talk to Jack. As I leave, I hold the door open for Varg, but he is sitting placidly on the rug, apparently not taking sides. "Traitor," I say, then walk down the hall to the stairwell leading to the roof.

Before I open the door, I take a few deep breaths. I'm going to be calm. I'm going in with Zen emotions.

I open the stairwell door and walk up the staircase. It's dark except for the light shining through the cracks around the door to the roof. I arrive at the top landing and open the door. The roof opens up to the evening sky with stars shining around Jack, who leans casually against the half wall, watching me. His broad shoulders make a striking outline against the deepening blue-black of the night sky. A small light over the door illuminates his face and he's giving me his half grin, slightly crinkling his beautiful green eyes.

I tilt my head to look at him and sashay over. I place my elbow on the wall a few feet away from him. "Fancy meeting you here. Do you come here often?"

Jack casually replies, "I'd be lying if I said it's my first time. The views are exceptional."

Clever man. I take this in stride and ask, "Have there been a rash of homicides on my roof you've failed to inform me about?"

Jack stands straight now and says, "I consider my presence here more proactive than reactive."

I tilt my head up to look him in the eyes. "Are you concerned about Schmidt or the mysterious portal jumper?"

Jack shifts on his feet, "Actually, both parties deserve concern."

I lean over the wall and look down at the sidewalk. "Can this proactive protection detail be done in my apartment rather than on the roof?"

Gently, Jack says, "I think it would be best if I stayed out of your private space."

Ohh, the rejection rips another hole in my heart and Zen evacuates my mind. I push away from the wall and snap, "Fine. If my aura disgusts you so much, then stay on the roof all night. Enjoy the cold." I rush toward the door.

But before I take two steps, I see a blur, and Jack appears between me and the door. He leans over me, his eyes shining like brilliant green lights. Jack asks, "What in the world makes you think your aura disgusts me?"

I shoot daggers at him, "You forget what I am. I feel strong emotions. I know you were disgusted yesterday. I could feel it when you told me what happened to my aura."

Jack reaches a hand out and tenderly traces my jawline. My whole body shivers from his touch.

Jack's deep voice washes through, "Blue, your aura doesn't disgust me. Your aura is an extension of your soul, and it's the most beautiful sight I've ever beheld—except for perhaps you, but it's part of you. From the first day I met you I've found it beautiful. It shines a shimmery bluish white light that feels clean and holy. I believe it's the only thing in this world that is truly clean and holy. It draws me to you like a buttercup tracking the sun. I can't seem to turn away."

My whole body is trembling now, and it's all I can do not to lean into his touch as he continues to trace my jawline back and forth. I try to lighten the moment to get control of my emotions. I ask, "Jack, did you just compare yourself to a buttercup?"

Jack drops his hand and steps back with a self-deprecating laugh. "I guess I did."

Then I ask hesitantly, "But why did you feel disgust? I know I felt it coming from you."

Jack looks away and a pained expression crosses his face. He says, "Blue, it's you who forgets what I am. I am Vampire. I carry the mark of Lilith. I see my own aura as well. Yesterday when your aura was shining so bright and beautiful, I saw my aura, dark blue and ugly with its taint of black from Lilith's hold on me. It was mixing with yours, smearing her filthy black through your aura." Jack looks back at me with regret and anger in his eyes, but these emotions are not directed at me. "I'm tainted. I'm marked by evil. No matter how I live this life, in the end, I'm going to the Plane of Fire. My road is chosen. I'm not going to harm you in the process."

I'm shocked. "I had no idea you felt that way," I say, "but that's ridiculous. First of all, I'm no holy being. I'm just a person. Secondly, you didn't choose to be Vampire. You haven't killed in bloodlust. You aren't going to harm me simply by being with me. You certainly aren't going to taint me by sleeping on my sofa instead of the roof."

Jack moves so quickly again that he disappears and reappears with his arm around my waist, bending me over backwards, holding me over thin air. His chest almost touches mine. It's close enough I can feel his heat. My heart beats rapidly. His mouth is so close to my neck I can feel the brush of his breath. Maybe I should be frightened, but I'm not. I'm thrilled.

Jack speaks very softly, and his voice thrums through my mind and my body like night fills the midnight sky. "Again, you forget I'm Vampire," he growls. "I live on a knife's edge, fighting temptation. Yesterday I was a hairsbreadth away from killing Schmidt, and I'd have enjoyed my vengeance wholeheartedly. I would have relished every scream of his pain."

Jack moves his mouth slightly so that his breath now tickles my ear. "I am most dangerous to you. My eyes are sharper than yours. When you put that oil on your skin, to my eyes it glitters like a million diamonds beckoning me. My nose is stronger than yours. I smell your scent rushing through your veins, wafting from your skin and your feminine core. Your scent calls to me, telling me you want me, alluring me, begging me to taste you, beckoning to me as though you were designed specifically to taunt me."

I gulp because I do indeed want Jack at this very minute, but I am a fool to do so. Jack drags his lips across my neck now and murmurs, "How much harder do you think it is in your apartment where your scent permeates every fabric and lingers in the air?"

Jack pauses, and then as if it takes great will, he gently straightens me, releases me, and steps away. "The only thing that keeps me from taking you even now is that beautiful white glow surrounding you, enveloping you, announcing you as too perfect to ruin."

The space between us feels huge after having him so close to me. I lift my arm to him. He steps back further away and I drop them mournfully. With deep heartache I say, "I'm sorry. I'm so, so sorry."

Jack smiles wryly. "Don't waste your pity on me. Just don't tempt me. I'll stay here and do the necessary and you should go back to your apartment and live your life. I'm Vampire. I don't need sleep. I don't feel cold. Don't even think of me. I am nothing but a boss keeping an eye on an employee who is working a dangerous case." Then he steps aside and gestures toward the door. "Go. Forget all about this."

My mind is reeling. I don't know what to do with all this new information so fast. I slowly walk toward the door. I feel like a rubber band is stretching from Jack to me and the further I go, the greater the tension. I am almost sure it will snap and bring me back to him despite my exertions. With great effort that has nothing to do with my sore body I make it past the door and follow the staircase down to my apartment.

Forget all about this? Not freaking likely. The things Jack said will surely be seared into my brain for all eternity.

CHAPTER 46

CONVENING

JACK TANNER

JUNE 1, 2022, RED AGES

I walk into Dragomira's shop, and the familiar book stacks and shelves of gadgets meet my eye. Nothing much ever changes here. Dragomira stands at the counter, absorbed in one of her textbooks as always. Her softly waving hair frames her still arresting features, and her elegant hand turns a page. She finally looks up, her eyes lightening as she takes me in.

"Jack," she says in her mesmerizing voice, "I see you received my message."

"Of course."

She looks a bit put out. "I see you were in no hurry." She comes out from behind the counter, quickly turns the deadbolt in the door, and flips the closed sign outwards. "Come," she says. "We have much to discuss."

She ushers me into the back room, which is an extension of the store filled with even more books, gadgets, and dust, but no windows, sunshine, or spying eyes. The room softly glows with firefly lanterns. "Would you care for a drink?" she offers.

"No, thank you."

"Well, I'll have one." Dragomira moves her finger in a small pattern, and a cabinet door opens obediently to reveal a decanter filled with a deep amber liquid. She fills a glass with what I identify by scent as finely aged whiskey. Glass in hand, she sits in one of a pair of comfortable wingback chairs next to the stone fireplace. I take the other.

Dragomira says, "Illustrissima came to me. Why didn't you tell me you were sending her?"

I frown. "I didn't. She found her way on her own."

Dragomira's eyes open wide, looking for a moment absolutely

nothing like a being of her great age. Then she nods as though snapping pieces of a mystery together. "She called herself Bluebell. I didn't recognize her at first as the one you call Blue. Does she know who she is yet?"

This makes me very angry. "Dragomira, you don't know who she is yet. You are jumping to conclusions prematurely."

Dragomira's eyes suddenly spark with a bright yellow light. "I am not the one biased here, Jack. I have been studying this for two thousand years. Over that time I have met countless people, and never have I come to this conclusion. So I am most certainly not 'jumping' to anything."

I feel ashamed. "Please accept my apologies." When Dragomira nods briskly, I ask, "So what makes you so sure?"

Dragomira swirls her whiskey in the heavy cut crystal glass, letting the aroma waft up to her face. "Her light, of course, is so obvious. But that is not enough. I tried to delve into her mind, but failed."

I sit forward, enraged. "You delved into her mind!"

Dragomira takes a generous sip of her whiskey and leans back as she says, "I *tried* to delve into her mind. As I said, she is blocked. She has a thick wall around her. I couldn't get in quickly, which is . . . something. And you should have seen the Fairy dust swirling up to greet her when she entered. It was as though every particle was alive."

I shout even louder, "Fairy dust! You are making decisions based on Fairy dust? Are you out of your mind?"

Dragomira huffs, "Clearly you do not understand the significance." Then she sets her whiskey down and leans toward me.

"Jack, you have been watching after her so long. Have you forgotten the why of it? Pretending she isn't who she is will only make the danger to her more grievous. You must come to grips with this. She has a role and purpose that have been foretold for two millennia. You can't stop it by denying it."

I stand, raking my fingers through my hair. I think of all the hopes and denials and fears that have been drifting through my head for the last twenty-odd years I've been watching over her. She is not the right one. The Shining One will not come while I still hold on to my soul. Perhaps she is the Light Bearer, but she will fail. Or, worst of all, I will fail her. All of my doubts and fears race through my head. The one I can most easily voice rips itself from my gut. "She is too young yet!"

Dragomira looks at me through slitted eyes "We do not choose the time of our calling. Had I a choice, I would have chosen it as a tender hatchling of fifteen years rather than waiting two millennia."

I'm still not convinced. "I need more proof. Can you get more proof?"

Dragomira picks up her whiskey again and swishes it, examining its amber depths. I stand there with my heart in my throat, awaiting her decision.

She finally looks up at me, "I can give her a test. Have her come to me in two days' time."

A weight lifts off of my chest and tension drains from my shoulders. Surely she will fail the test. Surely Dragomira is wrong. She is just a girl with a white aura. It happens. It must happen. Just because I've never seen it before doesn't mean it doesn't happen.

Dragomira stands up and pierces me with her flaming eyes. "Jack, when she passes the test, you must face reality."

All my lightness fades away. I run my fingers through my hair again and say with more confidence than I feel, "I will consider the value of the test, so make it true, and don't hurt her."

"Of course," Dragomira says.

I wonder what she will do if Blue is the one and her millennia of waiting and studying comes to an end. I wonder what I will do.

CHAPTER 47

A SAGACIOUS GENTLEMAN

BLUEBELL KILDARE

JUNE 1, 2022, RED AGES

I step toward the LaRoche mansion through the beautifully landscaped front lawn with my loose, silk tunic and pants blowing gently in the mild mountain breeze. I feel so much better today. My muscles hardly ache, and my fat lip is entirely gone. My bruises are so light a dab of concealer made them disappear. Most wonderful of all, my headache has not returned.

The entrance to the grand stone building ahead is marked by an arched double door painted in red. It's framed with white trim and etched sidelights. I straighten my back, remembering Maud's words about posture, and try not to look intimidated. Varg brushes up against me, a comforting feeling.

The butler must have seen me walk up because the door opens as I arrive. The distinguished man raises his bushy eyebrows at Varg. I answer his unasked question, "He's my constant companion and well behaved."

"And you are?"

"I'm Bluebell Kildare. I have an appointment to see Mr. LaRoche." The butler nods in a businesslike manner, "Very well, then. Mr. LaRoche is expecting you."

I follow the butler through a large hall with a gleaming, polished wood staircase leading up, and checkered marble tiles guiding us forward. Midway down the hallway, the butler ushers me into a room. He announces, "Ms. Kildare here to see you."

I enter and see Robert LaRoche leaning back in an enormous office chair behind an elegant, carved wood desk. The room is bordered by long, arched windows, and to my utter delight every space between them is filled with bookshelves. The inside walls are lined floor to ceiling with books. A small staircase leads up to a loft that holds glass-enclosed cabinets and shelves, which I assume display collections of magical artifacts.

I step up to the desk, and Mr. LaRoche rises to greet me. He's more handsome than I remember, perhaps in his late thirties, lean and bookish, with spectacles and a certain grace about him. He's wearing a tailored, tan linen suit that looks elegant and rich but endearingly wrinkled. It fits perfectly with his slightly too long brown hair falling about his face.

I offer my hand, which he shakes with a firm, warm grip. He notices Varg and accepts him graciously.

We appraise each other in a friendly manner then Mr. LaRoche smiles at me. I wink at Mr. LaRoche in return and say, "You *must* have secret passages behind those walls. You don't have to tell me, of course, because then it wouldn't be a secret. But if I had a room like this I would definitely have secret passages."

Mr. LaRoche laughs outright. "Please sit down," he says with a genuine smile.

I take the seat across from him. It's a sleek, black leather upholstered wing chair with curvy, carved mahogany arms and feet. If ever a chair were sexy, it is this chair. Varg sits quietly at my feet next to the sexy legs of the chair.

Mr. LaRoche looks around his study thoughtfully, "Yes, I can see why you'd think there were secret passages. It does sort of have that look, doesn't it?"

"Yes, it does. Your home is quite old and grand." And I think to myself I'd bet my last dime there's a vault behind one of those bookcases.

Mr. LaRoche is pleased at the compliment. A smile crinkles his eyes behind his wireframe glasses. He could be a real ladies' man if he wanted. He says, "It's been in the family for almost five centuries. We've been fortunate to hold it through the worst of times with the Vampires."

I whistle. "Not many families managed that. How did your family do it?"

Mr. LaRoche taps his knuckles on the wood desk and says, "It was a bit of misfortune that worked out for us. My great uncle from centuries ago, Reginald LaRoche, was turned against his will. When he came home to the family, the family welcomed him instead of casting him out. He was the third born son. Shortly thereafter, a Dark Vampire caught Jacques LaRoche, the first born son, in the garden and almost killed him.

Reginald LaRoche heard the noise and exterminated the Dark Vampire. Since then, we've had a few more family members turned, resulting in a continuous chain of Vampires to protect the first and second born sons."

I think about this. Since Vampires live so long, the family only needed a few Vampires to cover the span of five hundred years. "That's an impressive story. You took a bad situation and turned it to your advantage."

Mr. LaRoche nods, "Yes. While the rest of the country was at odds with Vampires during the Bloody Era, we had some measure of protection on the estate."

I make a mental note that Mr. LaRoche's comments are understated and to watch for this in the future. Things were so bad during the Bloody Era before the human and Vampire agreement, many people reverted to living in caves and deep in the woods.

He finishes, "We came across the ocean from the Near East in 1200 R.A., so we had owned the estate for three hundred years by the time of the Bloody Era. But the house was lost in a fire and rebuilt in stone five hundred years ago."

I ask, "Is that how you became interested in ancient magical artifacts? Because your own estate held some old magical pieces?"

Mr. LaRoche says in a pleased voice, "Brilliant deduction. I inherited the family's collection, which has grown over the centuries. I like to think we've become increasingly knowledgeable over time. My specialty is semiotics. But enough about me and mine. I understand you're intrigued by a particular piece yourself. Why don't you tell me about it?"

I say, "Well, you must first promise that my questions and description of the piece will be held in the strictest confidence."

Mr. LaRoche answers easily, "But of course, Inspector Kildare."

I'm sure my jaw drops because Mr. LaRoche laughs at my surprise, "Did you think I'd fail to do a little research on you when you are here to speak with me for that exact skill?"

I pick at the beaded embroidery on my cuffs and say with chagrin, "Well, I guess I didn't think you would be that interested. I was honestly afraid you wouldn't want to talk to me if you knew." I look at Mr. LaRoche with a wry smile. "And please call me Blue."

Mr. LaRoche gives me his crinkly eyed grin, "Only if you will call me Robert. And the rest is stuff and nonsense. I promise I have no reason to avoid the law."

I smile at that. "Excellent to hear, Robert. Then I'll tell you the questions I'm about to ask pertain to an investigation surrounding the murder of a teenage boy. The investigation is ongoing, so I can't give you many details. I have a sketch of the piece for you. It's an amulet that's quite old. I'd like to hear your version of the history of the piece to see if it matches what I've heard elsewhere."

"I'll do my best," Robert says.

I hand him the sketch. He looks at it and draws a deep breath. Then his face becomes serious as he studies the drawing in detail. He seems to have forgotten I'm in the room as he examines the picture of the back of the amulet and nods to himself.

Finally he glances up, "First of all, this amulet is missing a piece: the eye. Without the eye, the amulet is ineffective. Joined with the eye, the amulet is the key to opening the ancient *Grimorium Cantionum Spiritualium*."

I shift a bit in my chair and say, "That much I've learned already."

Robert asks, "And do you know what the book holds?"

I shift a bit more. Talking about the book makes me antsy. "My understanding is that it carries instructions for calling demons and spirits from other planes."

"Yes, it certainly does that. But that's a very casual understanding of its purpose. It's designed not just to teach you to summon but also to teach you to manipulate and control all spirits and souls."

I furrow my brows as I think about this, and after a minute I say, "I don't quite understand the difference."

Robert says gently, "Blue, you and I have souls. The underworld is a pit of spirits and demons and souls controlled by Lilith. Imagine the power to control all the souls of the living, the dead, and the undead. Imagine the power to determine if someone's soul stays in their living body or departs for the Plane of Light or the Plane of Fire. Imagine the power to determine if the spirits and demons of the underworld stay in the underworld or are beckoned here to walk amongst the living. Imagine the power to control Lilith herself."

I sit back in my chair with my mind reeling, "Oh, I see. That is quite different. So why would Lilith have allowed Patersuco to keep the book if it could be dangerous to her?"

Robert says, "I see you've heard the tale, but not completely. Lilith did want the book; however, Patersuco meant to bargain with the sacrifice of his son and his own soul, but never the book. Fortunately Lilith was tied by the bond of the calling and could not take it unless Patersuco gave it up as part of the bargain. As corrupt as he was, even he knew not to give his most powerful weapon to his most powerful enemy. The Birth of Vampires was Lilith's revenge on Patersuco for denying her the book. She wouldn't have helped Patersuco out at all, but she devised a way to turn the gift into a curse to get her vengeance on Patersuco and all mankind.

"The book had not always been in Patersuco's possession. He stole it from a small Pagan temple in ancient Ireland that some say was built for the express purpose of hiding it. After he turned into a Dark Vampire, the book was recovered from his possessions. It's unknown how he became aware of it or how he obtained it originally. But clearly after the theft it could no longer be contained in that place. Since it held the power to control Lilith, it could not be destroyed. It was too valuable a tool, but it needed to be held for only the direst need. So the book was separated from the key, and the key was broken in two. All three items were hidden in separate locations."

"Do you know where these locations are?"

Robert shakes his head firmly. "No. And should the knowledge be under my nose, I would not seek it. That is a bounty I prefer not to harvest." Robert pauses, then adds, "However, I'd not want the wrong person to find it either."

I think a moment, then say, "Let's suppose someone were looking for these three items. What sort of person would want them?"

Robert takes a deep breath and pauses before speaking. "Someone who hungered for incredible power at any expense. This book brings great power over the living, the dead, and the undead. But it comes at great expense, as Patersuco found out."

I rub my temple in frustration. I was hoping for something to lead me closer to the perpetrator. Instead I have more questions. "Thank you very much for this information. You have certainly enlightened me."

Robert says, "A dark topic, indeed. I'm glad I could help."

An idea springs to mind. "Can I ask you another question? It may be easier to answer and perhaps even more useful."

Robert says, "Of course. I shall do my utmost."

"I'd like to give you a list of five names, and I'd like to know if you're aware of any of these individuals having an interest in magical artifacts, just from the circles you're in."

Robert looks a little relieved, "I can certainly do that."

I think he's as weary of the morbid topic of the book as I am. I quickly pull out a note pad and write down the five names.

Gerald Mack, Chief of Fire Department

Hilda Gunderson, Owner of Zen Spa and Salon

Milton Goldberg, Owner of Goldberg Jewelers

Tobias Blackwater, City Councilman, Treasurer

Hank Fletcher, General Manager of Mountain Paper Mill

Robert takes my list and goes over the names. "Chief Gerald Mack purchased an item from me. He was looking for a piece to help him with fire investigations. I had a pair of enchanted glassicals that acted like infrared detectors. When you put them on, they render the user capable of seeing remnants of heat up to a week old. It was a very interesting tool but not very valuable, and I had no use for it. However, it was extremely useful to Chief Mack for pinpointing the origin or pattern of a fire that had already died out.

"I saw Milton Goldberg at the Pemberton Estates auction last spring. He won a few pieces of jewelry that were imbued with certain magical characteristics. One item was called the Truth Ring. It was charmed to turn red if the wearer was lying. It was a distasteful piece in my opinion, and I can't imagine requiring a loved one to wear it." Robert stops and looks at me speculatively. "But a useful piece for an Inspector, I would think."

The possibilities flow through my mind. "Indeed."

Robert continues, "Another piece, a beautiful teardrop pendant actually turned color to match the wearer's dress, but slightly more brilliantly. It's a much more enjoyable piece, in my opinion."

Robert pushes his chair back and steps out to walk a little while he continues. "I've seen Tobias Blackwater at many auctions, private and public, though I've never seen him win a bid. I suspect he's a voyeur of dark magical objects." Robert looks sharply at me, "That's just speculation, mind you."

I assure him, "Any information you give me, even your opinions or speculations, will be helpful. I will treat speculations as speculations, I promise. Now, do you remember specifically any of the items he's looked at?"

Robert looks like he's pondering a puzzle. "He was at the Pemberton Estates auction and showed interest in the Truth Ring Milton won. Last year at the Lawrenson's Estate Auction he spent some time looking at a scrying mirror. He also attends the Glenwood Charity Gala each year. You could ask Mrs. Glenwood if he's won any items."

"I may do that. The scrying mirror he was looking at, was that a single mirror or a pair?"

Robert frowns at this and says, "It was a single mirror, which indicates it was more of a spying mirror than a two way communication device."

"And Hilda Gunderson or Hank Fletcher? Have you any knowledge of them?"

Robert says, "No, I've never met them or seen them in my circles."

I sit silently for a minute to see if he can think of anything else. When nothing ensues, I say, "Well, thank you so much, Robert. You've been an enormous help. I really appreciate your time."

Robert smiles, "It's been my pleasure." Then he rings the butler bell on his desk.

I rise, and Robert steps forward to take my hand. He raises it to his lips and gives me a soft and pleasant kiss on the hand, saying, "Until we meet again my dear, beautiful Inspector Blue."

I feel my face heat up, and feel a bit tongue tied. After standing there awkwardly for a beat, I say, "If you ever decide to give tours of your secret passages, please give me a call."

Robert tilts his head back and laughs throatily. "I most certainly will."

The butler arrives to show me out, and I throw one more glance back at Robert, who has a twinkle still in his eye. I give him a wink, and he returns it with the flourish of his arm in a miniature bow.

I laugh my way out the door. I really like Robert. He's a fun guy and handsome to boot. Not sexy and dangerous like Jack, but pleasant and companionable. I try to shake this thought as it enters my head. I really need to stop comparing people to Jack.

On my way to the car, I notice my outfit still looks fresh. Not one to waste a valuable loaned resource, I decide to see if Mrs. Glenwood is receiving today.

CHAPTER 48

VACANT GENEROSITY

EXPOSED

BLUEBELL KILDARE

JUNE 1, 2022, RED AGES

I arrive at Mrs. Glenwood's estate and reflect on how peaceful it looks without the swarming mob of Dilectus Deo around it. The drive leading to the mansion is lined with magnolia trees. I decide to leave Varg in the car because I haven't tested him against cats yet, but I leave a window unrolled so he can jump out if needed. It would be ironic and just my luck if I called on a favor for saving Mrs. Glenwood's cat just to have Varg eat the cat instead.

At the door I give my name and card to the butler and ask if I can have a few moments of Mrs. Glenwood's time. Jeffrey leaves me on the stoop and returns a few minutes later to show me in. He says, "Mrs. Glenwood is in the gardens enjoying a late breakfast. She would be delighted if you would join her."

Jeffrey ushers me through the house and out onto the patio. Mrs. Glenwood sits at a beautifully dressed table next to the bulb gardens. Memories of the Gala night with Jack come flooding back, and my heart squeezes a little bit. If only it could have lasted forever. I push those thoughts away as I have important business to attend to right now.

Mrs. Glenwood waves me over, "Blue. I'm so glad you came to visit. I was just having a late breakfast. Please join me."

Just as I'm pulling out a chair, Varg appears from the side of the building, looping gracefully toward us. Mrs. Glenwood smiles at him. "Who's this handsome fellow?"

"I'm so sorry. I left him in the car, but he seems to be rather attached to me. This is Varg. Is Cleopatra anywhere around? I don't know how he'll do with cats."

Mrs. Glenwood beckons Varg, ruffles his neck fur and says, "I'm sure he'd be fine. Cleopatra is confined to my suite as she's still recuperating. We'll have to introduce them another time. Varg certainly is quite large."

I laugh because he is only at his large dog size now. "I know. He's massive. But he's come to my aid a few times, so I appreciate his size."

Mrs. Glenwood pours some tea in a fresh cup Jeffrey just set out. Jeffrey looks a little miffed she didn't wait for him to do the honors. She looks sternly at him and says, "Jeffrey, you're hovering again. I can handle serving tea to my guest. I'll be fine." Jeffrey leaves, none too happy for it.

Mrs. Glenwood whispers to me, "They think because I'm wealthy and a woman that I must be frail and incompetent." Then in a normal voice she continues, "How do you like your tea?"

"With sugar, please."

Mrs. Glenwood plops two sugars in my tea and pushes it toward me. She waves at the overabundance of food on the table, "Please, help yourself."

It looks gorgeous: poached eggs, sautéed asparagus in hollandaise sauce, and toast, all served on fine china. I reply, "Just tea will be fine, thank you. I've eaten already."

Mrs. Glenwood laughs, "Of course you have. Not everyone is as slow to wake up as I am."

"So how's Cleopatra doing?"

Mrs. Glenwood leans back and says, "Well, she was severely dehydrated and very scared. The vet gave us fluids to administer to her twice daily. She perked up a bit yesterday, but she's still spending most of the day under my bed."

"Well, I'm glad she's getting better. I imagine it will take time. Are you sure she was locked up by accident? Do you have any new staff with a disliking for cats?"

Mrs. Glenwood frowns at this and says, "I hadn't even thought of that. I'll have to do some investigating. We do have new staff, but I can't say I'm aware of any specific issues." She ponders this for a minute, then comes to some private decision and closes the subject off in her mind for later. Her face is remarkably transparent. Then she fingers my card on the table and asks, "So, to what do I owe the pleasure of your company?"

"Well, I'm conducting an investigation, and I'd like to ask you some questions. However, the person I need to ask the questions about is a prominent political person, and I need to know if I can ask the questions in confidence."

Mrs. Glenwood grimaces. "What's the nature of the crime?"

I reply with as little drama as possible. "It regards the torture and death of a young man, a boy, really. I'm not at liberty to give further details as the crime is still under investigation. I must ask you to keep even that little bit in confidence."

Mrs. Glenwood looks emotionally disturbed at this news. I feel empathy tinged with sadness flowing from her in strong waves. Her face turns down and her eyes grow sad. She says, "Well, of course. I will do anything I can to help. We can't have torturing, murdering thugs running around, even if they wear the finest tuxedos."

"My thoughts exactly. On the day of the Gala, Tobias Blackwater was in attendance."

Mrs. Glenwood's face turns to one of distaste, and her emotions turn a bit cold. She says, "Yes, he was. He's always invited. Though why I invite him I don't know. A stingier man I've never met."

"Why do you call him stingy?"

"Because he bids so low at the silent auction that he's never won an item."

"Well, surely a great many people bid on items they don't win, right?"

Mrs. Glenwood purses her lips and says, "Well, true, but he bids absurdly low. For instance, if an item is marked with a minimum bid of two thousand dollars, he bids two thousand and one dollars, even though there are clearly several bid slips collected for the item. Surely he must know he won't win. I've decided he bids so the other members at the Gala think he's charitable, for his political career's sake."

I dig into this a bit further. "So you think he bids without ever having the intention of buying an item?"

She nods, "I can't prove it of course. But that is my guess from looking at the bid report last week."

I light up. "You keep a report of the auction bids?"

"But of course. How else would I determine who to invite? My goal is to collect as much money for the orphanage as I can. Though some people, like Mr. Blackwater, I invite more for social considerations."

I ask eagerly, "May I have a copy of that report?"

Mrs. Glenwood hesitates, "Normally I wouldn't share it, but it isn't protected legally. So I ask you to exercise the same confidentiality you have asked of me, unless a particular detail is required for your case."

I am practically dancing for joy. This is an excellent piece of news. I eagerly give my oath.

Mrs. Glenwood nods in satisfaction, then rises. "Just a moment, dear. No time like the present." She disappears into the house.

She returns a few moments later with a report in hand.

I wave toward the butler bell and tease. "Aren't you supposed to ring if you need something?"

Mrs. Glenwood exclaims, "Oh, poppycock! I'm chubby as it is. If I had people wait on me hand and foot like they want, I'd be rolling down the hill. Have you looked at what they serve me for breakfast?"

I laugh. "It is quite a feast."

Mrs. Glenwood sniffs. "Indeed."

I quickly peruse the report. It's a matrix with the names of the items in rows and the names of the bidders in columns. Where the name of the bidder and the item intersect is the bid amount. Across the bottom is a total of bids for that person and percent of the aggregate minimum bid the bidder made. Tobias Blackwater bid an impressive 8,753 dollars' worth, most of which he placed on several items with high minimum bids. His percent of minimum bid was 100.02.

"So Tobias only went over the minimum bid price by .02 percent on average?"

Mrs. Glenwood says, "Exactly! And the columns below indicate the numbers of bids made and the number of bids won. As well as the total funds raised from winning bids for each individual."

I nod, "So he bid four times and won zero times, thus no funds were garnered. This person three columns over only bid once and only for six hundred dollars, but his average annual bid was three hundred percent of the minimum bid."

Mrs. Glenwood says, "Exactly! So the charity earned six hundred dollars on his bid, far more than should have been received for that item."

"I see. Well, I'm embarrassed I bid so low and didn't bring much money in for you compared to the other bidders."

"Nonsense. You were Jack's guest, and Jack was very, very generous."

I'm puzzled. "But this list says he only bid six hundred dollars, and that's on the low side compared to some of your other bidders."

Mrs. Glenwood said, "Well, that's because he chooses to donate directly without bidding. It was unusual for him to bid at all. He donated twenty thousand dollars this year for the Gala."

I gasp. "Ohh! I didn't realize. That *is* very generous, especially on an inspector's salary."

Mrs. Glenwood looks at me strangely. "Blue, Jack is quite rich."

I look up at her. "He is?"

She pats my hand and says, "Yes indeed."

"Hmm. I had no idea. I mean, he has a nice car, but a lot of men put themselves in the poorhouse to have a beautiful car."

Mrs. Glenwood sighs, "Jack could buy enough sports cars to line the entire ridge of the Blue Ridge Mountains."

I raise my eyebrows in surprise. Where did he get all that money? Did he come from money? Did he own oil?

Mrs. Glenwood smiles, "He is quite a catch."

I scoff at this. "I can't imagine any woman 'catching' Jack."

Mrs. Glenwood gives off a peal of laughter. "Quite right you are. I imagine that's the only reason he's been single these many years."

I laugh with her for a moment. Then feel guilty laughing over tea while a torturer is running around free.

"I really must get going. Evildoers rarely stop for tea, and I can't let them get ahead of me. Thank you so much for helping me today. Now you should consider us even."

Mrs. Glenwood shakes her head, "I'm afraid I can't do that. Today I was simply doing my civic duty. You did me a personal favor, one I won't forget. Plus you just cleared the protest from my front yard, and helped that poor man. I am still in your debt, and you must let me pay it back."

I say graciously, "If I ever need something from the upper echelons of society, I will come straight to you."

Mrs. Glenwood nods seriously, obviously knowing her value in that area. "Please see that you do. And feel free to drop in any time, even when you're not chasing evildoers who are doing dastardly, evil deeds."

I laugh at this. "I will. I promise."

Then Varg and I skirt around the building to head to the office.

CHAPTER 49

ARTFUL DECEIT

BLUEBELL KILDARE

JUNE 1, 2022, RED AGES

I walk into my office with Varg trailing behind and some documents I'd requested from Rubalia in my hands. I stop when I see a beautiful, huge, dark brown leather dog bed surrounded by three bolstered sides sitting next to the office window. I pivot right around and ask, "Rubalia, do you know who put this beautiful dog bed in my office?"

Rubalia pushes her glasses down to the tip of her nose, then looks out of them at me. "Of course I do. I did." Then she returns to her paperwork.

I move forward and lean over her counter while she studiously pretends I'm not there. "Well, it's absolutely lovely. Thank you. It must have cost you a fortune. Can I reimburse you for it?"

She looks up at me and says, "No you can't reimburse me for it. First, it is not for you. It is for the beast, since he was kind enough to intercede on your behalf the other day. Second, I did not *purchase* it. I made it."

Then she lifts her glasses and looks at Varg through my doorway. We both watch him sniff the bed and lie right on it. With the sunlight streaming through the window, hundreds of pieces of his fur are visible flying through the air, swirling around with particles of dust from the ventilation movement.

"Rubalia, both your work and your taste are impeccable, but you were exceptionally clever to make it leather. Now it can be wiped right off."

Rubalia puts her vibrant red, sparkly cat eye specs back on the tip of her nose, making a lie out of her somber face as she says, "Exactly! You will find the polish in the upper right hand drawer of your desk." Then she returns to her work, with the corner of one side of her mouth drawn up, a smile refusing to be completely suppressed.

I set my papers down on my desk. I sit down for no more than the amount of time it takes to check my drawer for the polish when Rubalia buzzes me, saying that Gambino is waiting to see me.

Gambino walks in, today wearing a black suit, a crisp white shirt, and a gray silk tie. It goes well with his graying temples and dark hair. He looks fantastic and dignified, but he obviously forgot I asked him to dress casually. I chuckle at how he's going to pay for that.

"Good afternoon," Gambino says as he sits in my chair, spreading out to take up as much space as possible.

"Well, it's been a good morning. The jury's still out on the afternoon."

Gambino laughs, "You look much better today. Did you get any good info?"

"I did. But before we get into that, let's narrow down the probable suspect list."

"Sounds like a plan. How do you want to go about this?"

"Let me handle Hilda Gunderson first. This one should be easiest."

I look at the documents Rubalia gave me, and I dial Zen Spa and Salon. I put my finger to my mouth to shush Gambino and put the phone on speaker.

A bright sounding woman's voice answers, "Zen Spa and Salon. Rebecca speaking. How may I help you?"

I say, "Hi, My name is Rose Smith, and I want to make an appointment."

Rebecca asks, "Who do you usually see?"

"I usually see Hilda."

"Excellent. She has an appointment available on Tuesday at three o'clock. Would you like that spot?

I say with as much ditz in my voice as possible, "Actually, I always get my hair cut exactly five weeks apart. You know, otherwise it gets unmanageable. But I forgot to write down the date of my last appointment. Can you see if my name is on the books with Hilda for five o'clock on April 28?"

Rebecca says, "Sure, let me check." A minute goes by and she says, "No, it must have been another day."

"Hmm, I was almost positive it was that day. Are you sure you don't have an appointment for Rose Smith, or Rosalie Smith. Oh, or check Brittany Smith, that is my middle name. It could also be under Rose Phelps. That's my maiden name."

Rebecca sounds rather annoyed at this point, "Unless your first name is Darryl and you were looking for a chest wax, I'm sure your appointment wasn't at five o'clock with Hilda on April 28."

I affect dismay and say, "Oh, I wonder if I have the wrong week. Let me look at my records again and call you back. Thanks so much."

Rebecca says with a very tight voice, "No problem. Have a Zen day!"

Gambino's face is beet red, and he's covering his mouth, trying to hold his laughter in. He finally lets out a burst of noise that sounds more like choking. I wiggle my eyebrows at him.

Amidst his laughing, he barks out, "Very nice work."

I flip him a smile, "Hopefully Hank went back to work after the interviews and this one will be easy too."

Gambino holds up one finger and says, "Give me a minute to recover."

I do a quick internet search on Mountain Paper Mill where Hank works and the local recycling plant to gather some intel. When Gambino's face reverts to a healthy pink tone under his otherwise olive complexion I set my plan in motion.

I dial, and a gruff male voice answers, "Mountain Paper Mill."

I say, "Hello. Can I talk to receiving?" The phone clicks abruptly and I must have been transferred because I hear ringing again. A voice answers, "Receiving."

I say, "Hi, this is Susie from the billing department at the Earth Center Recycling Plant. I'm looking at a shipping receipt from my driver dated April 28. Do you show receiving a shipment from us on that day?"

The receiving clerk says, "Hold on." Then after a moment of silence, she says, "Nope."

"No? Shoot. Well, you know, this is a serious issue. My shipping receipt definitely says April 28 at five p.m. for a truckload of baled cardboard, but I don't show a copy of the original purchase order. We've been having problems with this driver, so I need to verify this before we take disciplinary action. We also need to stop the billing process. Can you check which floor manager was on duty at five on April 28?

A very annoyed clerk says, "Hold on." After another moment of silence, she says, "It was Hank. He came on at five. I'll transfer you."

I say, "Thanks." Then as soon as I hear the ringing again I hang up.

Gambino, who has managed to maintain his Italian coloring this time despite his Irish ways, says, "You are slick."

I appreciate his appreciation of my skill of artful deceit for the greater good. "Thanks. Now, Goldberg Jewelers is going to be a bit more difficult." I stand up. "We're going to have to see Milton in person."

CHAPTER 50

AN EMBARRASSING PRETENSE

BLUEBELL KILDARE

JUNE 1, 2022, RED AGES

I stop by Rubalia's desk and lean over it while Gambino waits at the side. "Rubalia, your ring is costume jewelry, isn't it?" I suspect it is because she wears different jewelry every day to match her outfits.

Rubalia huffs, "Of course. Do you think I could afford fine jewelry on what the Bureau pays me?"

"No. That's how I guessed. I can't afford real jewelry either. Do you mind if I borrow it for the rest of the afternoon?"

Rubalia peers at me from behind her specs. "Why do you need it?"

"I need to pretend I was told it was a real diamond while I question a jeweler."

Rubalia tilts her head down and peers at me over her glasses, "If you don't bring it back, things will be very unpleasant for you."

I throw up my hands, "I promise. I'll bring it back. If I don't, I'll buy you two to replace it."

Rubalia reluctantly hands me the ring, and Gambino, Varg and I head to the jeweler's in Gambino's unmarked car. As he drives, he glances over at me quickly and asks, "So what's your plan for the jeweler?"

I look at him and say, "Well, you're going to be my father."

Gambino opens his mouth, closes it, opens it again, closes it again, and finally yells, "Your father!"

"Well, I told you to wear casual clothes, didn't I? Otherwise you could have been my boyfriend, or friend, or my brother."

Gambino tightens his fists on the steering wheel and his cheeks redden a little.

I ignore his stress and continue. "My boyfriend gave me an engagement ring, and we suspect it's fake. We're checking it out. I'll get him to confirm it's fake. Then I'd like you to direct him toward verifying if he was in the store on April 28 at around five o'clock when the ring was supposedly bought. You can say you want to make sure one of his employees didn't sell it."

Gambino nods.

When we arrive a few minutes later, I ask, "Can you please park directly in front of the jeweler's window so Varg can watch from the car? Otherwise I'll have to let him come in."

I watch as Gambino's jaw relaxes a little and he says, "Sure."

Varg hops up to the front seat as soon as we vacate and watches as Gambino and I enter the Goldberg Jewelry Store. A tall, very fit, and almost too pretty to be handsome man waits behind the counter. A woman is working at the jewelry bench. I walk straight toward the man.

"Hello, are you Mr. Goldberg?"

The man says, "Yes. How can I help you today?"

I stand awkwardly with my hands in my pockets and say in a low voice, "I'm Stephanie Fisk, and this is my father, Timothy. This is very embarrassing, but my boyfriend gave me this engagement ring, and I'm not sure it's real. He said he bought it from you and showed me a receipt dated April 28. Can you tell me if this was your ring?"

Mr. Goldberg says, "Certainly. Let me have a look."

I hand him Rubalia's ring.

Mr. Goldberg looks at it and immediately frowns. He goes to his drawer and pulls out a jeweler's eye loupe. He puts it against his eye and squints at the stone.

He puts the eye loupe back and turns back to me. "Stephanie, this certainly isn't our ring. It's cubic zirconium in a gold plated setting. We do not sell gold plated jewelry or cubic zirconium. We only sell precious jewels and metals."

I put on a sad face, "I was afraid of that."

Gambino says, "Mr. Goldberg, when we tell him we know the ring isn't real, he'll most likely say you or one of your employees ripped him off. Can you confirm who was working that day at five o'clock?"

Mr. Goldberg ponders the idea one of his employees might be

running a scam, then seems to dismiss the notion and says, "Certainly." He opens up his phone and checks his calendar. "My assistant Julia worked until five, as I had some personal business earlier in the day, but I came on at five and let her go."

"Well, it definitely would have been after five since he works at the paper mill until then. And I don't think you ripped him off. This certainly has been enlightening. I appreciate your time, Mr. Goldberg."

Mr. Goldberg smiles and warmly embraces my hand, "No problem. I'm glad you came in to check. I would hate to have it thought I sold that piece. I hope we see you here again under better circumstances."

I smile and say, "You just might."

Gambino holds the door for me as we exit and head back to the office.

CHAPTER 51

TARGETING THE SUSPECT

BLUEBELL KILDARE

JUNE 1, 2022, RED AGES

When Gambino, Varg, and I trail back into the office, I hand the ring to Rubalia and ask, "Is Jack available?"

Rubalia checks his phone light, "It looks like it." Then she hands me some papers. "These are the documents you requested earlier."

I peruse them briefly and thank her.

Gambino, Varg, and I walk to Jack's office, and as I raise my hand to knock, Jack says, "Come in."

I laugh at myself. I did it again.

Jack is lounging back in his chair feigning nonchalance as usual. His catlike grace is always on the verge of action. His long fingers gently clasp the arms of his chair. His eyes quickly flick over me. My mouth goes dry. I take the seat across from him, and Varg lies next to me. Gambino sits on the other side.

Jack says to me, "You're looking better."

"Alexis really helped me out."

Jack nods and turns to Gambino. "Welcome, Gambino." Then his eyes sweep both of us. "So what do we know now?"

Gambino fills him in. "Blue called the businesses of Hank Fletcher and Hilda Gunderson under false pretenses. We visited Milton Goldberg. In each case we were able to verify they'd returned to work by five o'clock on April 28. So unless they took Jason with them, it's unlikely they were involved.

Jack asks, "Do you think they suspected anything with your questioning?"

Gambino inclines his head toward me as he says, "No. She's pretty gifted at this type of subterfuge."

Jack lips twitch at that. "And what about Gerald Mack?"

Gambino says, "I verified he was called to the fire and that he was there."

Jack nods. "So that leaves us with Tobias Blackwater."

Gambino inquires, "Are you sure it wasn't any of the participants in the interview rather than the interviewers themselves?"

I interject, "To answer that, let's review what we know."

Both men turn to hear what I have to say. "Jason was killed. His killer is not likely to have been the one torturing him because he was seen at the pub just prior to the killing. A man in a dark red cloak was seen at the Cock and Bull Tap just after the murder and was not seen there at any time prior. His description is tall, about six foot; neatly trimmed, full, dark brown beard; prominent, long nose; and thin face.

"Jason was found with a dark red thread caught under his fingernail, and the amulet has a similar dark red thread caught in its clasp. The amulet was found close to Jason. Someone has been searching quite aggressively since, including while Paul, the killer, has been incarcerated. So that someone could not be Paul."

Gambino says, "Agreed. There are definitely two parties: the party who killed Jason and the party who is searching for something. Because the evidence locker was the first place searched, we can assume the searcher was looking for something we consider evidence. But since none of the other evidence was taken, we can guess the purpose of the searching was not to remove evidence. I think as far as the searcher is concerned, any evidence we have linking the death to Paul is a good thing. The only other thing they could be searching for is the amulet."

"That's a very good point," I say. "Now, we know there was a second individual. We can assume it's this man in the red cloak. The person who's been looking for the amulet has the ability to move through portals, as the places he's searched were heavily warded on the exterior. This person wears finely made trousers as evidenced by the scrap of fabric found in my apartment during the first attempt on my place. So this is a man of wealth or position or both.

"Now, the amulet itself is the key to a book of extraordinary powers. The person searching for such a key would be someone with a desire for power. Jason had a desirable power. He had the ability to magnify magic. So any magic someone wanted done would be magnified with Jason's help."

Jack's green eyes flicker first to me, and then to Gambino. "That is a highly desired power. I've done a little research on this, and only a few people in history have had such a power. It is definitely motive for kidnapping."

Gambino thoughtfully rubs his chin at this. I let him ponder for a moment before I continue. "Jason was tortured and running naked through the streets, so I assume he was not conceding to whatever was asked of him. I believe he had the amulet on his person when he was hit by the car, and it flew out of his hand and into the bush. This amulet has been hidden for centuries, and suddenly it is found in the hands of a boy with the ability to magnify magic."

Jack sits up straight and looks at me keenly. "What do you think this means?"

"I believe that Jason's particular brand of magic was required to locate the amulet and the man seeking the amulet had been looking for just such a power for some time. I think the interview was one of several screening methods he used to find a power that could be used to locate the amulet. When he saw Jason's power displayed at the interviews, he knew he could use it to meet his ends, so he kidnapped him."

"I don't believe those who participated in the interviews were in a position to see the powers of the others because they were not called to perform together. They were called to perform one at a time with only one interviewee on the island at a time. The only people who would have seen Jason's power in action were the interviewers."

I pause for a moment and watch as Gambino and Jack take that in. Then I pick up one of the pieces of paper Rubalia gave me earlier and flip it over on Jack's desk.

"This is Tobias Blackwater. As you see, he is wearing a deep red cloak with a suit underneath in this photo. You can also see he has a blackish-brown beard, neatly trimmed. He fits the description of the man in the Cock and Bull Tap."

Gambino doesn't even look at the photo. I assume he knows what Tobias Blackwater looks like from seeing him at city meetings. His eyes widen in recognition of the truth when he comes to it. He looks back at me with a grim expression.

I pause a moment, then I say, "He's been watching me. I've seen him twice."

Jack sits up and growls menacingly, all pretenses of nonchalance flees. His eyes rake me up and down as if to make sure I have no new damage. He demands, "I saw him talking to you at the Gala. When was the other time?"

I tilt my chin up a bit and say, "On the day I found Varg. He was the man who grabbed me behind my building. I knew I recognized his soul at the Gala, but I didn't recall from where until Chief Mack gave me the list of names. Then I started to piece it together."

Varg growls at this. There seem to be a lot of growling males in this office.

"I've had the distinct feeling of being followed, but I can't say for sure if Tobias or Schmidt was stalking me."

I continue, "We're looking for a man who's greedy for power. Tobias is a man who delights in power over others. I got that from him at the Gala as he looked at the Belladonna Necklace." I shiver at the memory.

Jack pounds his fist on the desk and says, "We don't have any evidence as to where he took Jason, or that he did take him."

"We do have the thread from his cloak. But I agree. We need more." Then I frown and say, "But there is more. I'm just not sure it will lead us to the evidence we need."

Gambino says, "Well, let's have it."

I say, "LaRoche recalls him at the Pemberton Estates auction looking at a Truth Ring. Milton Goldberg ultimately won that. At the Lawrenson's Estate Action, LaRoche saw that he was interested in a single scrying mirror."

I explain the difference between a single scrying mirror and a pair for Gambino's benefit. "He was also at the Glenwood Charity Gala and Silent Auction looking at the Belladonna Necklace, as I've already mentioned."

"I had a conversation with Mrs. Glenwood, who believes Blackwater goes to auctions for the purpose of looking at items but not bidding. She provided me with a report of his bids. He bids so low he's sure not to win. He's essentially combing auctions looking for the correct item but not buying it."

Gambino frowns and asks, "How does this help us?"

I say, "I believe he may not be winning the items in bid, but he's still obtaining them. He peruses the auctions and selects the items he wants. He places a very low bid since he was observed looking at the item. He watches to see who wins the item, then uses his portal ability to obtain it. This single scrying mirror could possibly be the tool that, along with Jason's magnification ability, allowed him to find the amulet that had been hidden for so many centuries. LaRoche assured me that the amulet was so carefully guarded it must have been heavily warded from scrying, but with Jason's help, I believe Tobias finally found it."

Gambino says, "That is a lot of conjecture with no evidence."

"Yes. I know." Then I turn to Jack and ask, "Since these are all magical artifacts, if they were stolen would they have been reported with the Supernatural Investigation Bureau or the precinct?"

Jack says, "Unless there's evidence of Supernatural activity in the perpetration of the crime, they would be under jurisdiction of the precinct, though that should change. Clearly the precinct is unable to evaluate a pattern in the theft of magical items since they don't have a good understanding of the items' capabilities."

Gambino nods in agreement. "Let me call the precinct and ask for a list of all magical items reported stolen in the past few years."

While we wait, Jack nods at Varg, "I wonder what he is exactly."

I pat Varg on the head, "He is obviously a wolf."

Jack scoffs, "He's more than a wolf. He appeared out of nowhere just as Tobias was attacking you. He knew to keep Tobias away from you. He keeps you guarded at all times. He seems to understand at least some of what we say."

I consider this. "True, but perhaps he is just exceptionally intelligent and protective."

Jack looks thoughtful.

Then I say, at great risk of my reputation, "There *is* the fact that he grows when he fights."

Jack swivels his gaze to me and raises his brow. I shrug my shoulders, neither able nor willing to explain more.

Rubalia comes in with the fax from the precinct. Gambino reads it, and it's his turn to raise his eyebrows. "Last September, a single scrying mirror was reported stolen. Last April, a lie detector ring was reported stolen. Yesterday, the Belladonna Necklace was reported stolen."

Silence fills the room. We know he's our man, but we lack evidence for the torture.

Gambino says, "We'll have to check with the owner of every item on this list and determine if the item was purchased at an auction or otherwise displayed publicly before it was stolen. Then we'll have to confirm that Blackwater was present at the public viewing. That is just to start."

Then Gambino looks up sharply. "Is the amulet still safe now?"

"Yes," I say. "It's in the original location I placed it. It's on holy ground so he cannot scry it or portal there."

Gambino looks satisfied.

Jack says, "This corroborates what we suspect, but it doesn't provide evidence for Jason's capture or a clue to the location where he was held."

I agree and lay out my next step. "Tomorrow I'm going to return to the scene of the crime to see if I can get any ideas."

Gambino looks at me with a puzzled expression. "It happened a week ago. What evidence could still be there?"

"The location and the surrounding area. Can you run a search for properties owned by Blackwater?"

Gambino says, "A search like that would set off too many alarms and might get us shut down."

Jack says, "I can have Rubalia run that search on our system. I'll have her use stealth mode, though I highly doubt Blackwater has any insiders in the Supernatural Investigation Bureau."

Gambino gets up. "I'll get started on my part as well."

I nod. "I'll see you tomorrow morning, then. Hopefully we'll find something."

I get up to leave with Gambino, but Jack clears his throat and says, "A moment?"

I sit back down and face him as I hear the door swing shut behind Gambino.

Jack says, "You know, Blackwater has his eye on you because he thinks you have the amulet."

I fidget with my hands in my lap. "I know."

"What are you doing tonight?"

I look up at him. "I'm visiting Maud, and then I'm spending the rest of the night at home."

Jack nods. "Good."

I still don't know what to say to him about last night. I think he doesn't want me to say anything. So I don't. I quietly leave with him watching me all the while.

CHAPTER 52

LEMONADE

BLUEBELL KILDARE

JUNE 1, 2022, RED AGES

As Varg and I walk up to Maud's house, I notice the marigolds remain and lament the loss of the zinnia. Maud opens the door, still sporting her bright red hair. Instead of pairing it with black, though, she's wearing a bright pink dress with peek-a-boo shoulders and an A-line skirt. Her shoes are green strappy sandals, and she looks fantastic as usual.

I kiss her cheek and ask, "All ready for summer?"

Maud kisses me back. "The summer fun has already begun."

We gather at the kitchen table as is our wont. Maud pours lemonade and sits down. Then she positions herself to watch out the glass patio door toward the wild jungle and beyond.

I look out to see what she's watching. A car pulls up in front of Harry's house. A woman gets out and walks up to the front door. Other people walk or drive away. A minute later, the woman who just walked up walks back to her car. Another car pulls up.

"What's happening over at Harry's?"

Maud smiles deviously. "Yesterday someone knocked on my door with Chinese delivery. I never ordered it. It was from that stinking Harry."

I say, "No." and almost afraid to ask, I ask anyway. "So what did you do?"

Maud says, "I placed an ad in the classifieds. It gave Harry's address and said there was a bottom dollar basement sale on items from a closed down electronics store with TVs, stereos, laptops, things like that."

I laugh. "Maud, you are a treasure and a terror."

Maud nods distractedly, "Of course, dear. Now, hush, I'm enjoying the show."

The two of us watch for a while. We see one man leaving with an old tube TV. Maud mutters, "I don't believe it. He's actually letting them have his stuff." After a little while longer we see Harry go outside and pound a sign in his front yard.

The next people who drive up read the sign and drive away.

I turn to Maud, "Hmm, what do you think the sign says?"

Maud raps her pink painted fingernails on the table. "I don't know, but you're going to find out for me."

With that extremely subtle hint, I decide this is a nice time to take a hike around the block and scope it out. When I return, Maud ushers me in. With her eyes wide and excited she asks, "Well?"

I tell Maud with as straight of a face as I can, "The sign says 'Sale over, all sold out.'" As soon as I see the twinkling in Maud's eyes, we both burst out laughing.

"Smart man," Maud says. "When life hands you lemons, make lemonade."

"You know, Maud, maybe you should give him a chance."

Maud sighs, a smile playing on the corners of her lips. "Maybe. He's persistent, all right. I'll give him that."

CHAPTER 53

BAD OMEN

JACK TANNER

JUNE 2, 2022, RED AGES

I keep staring at the reports of Dark Vampire sightings, but by damned, the numbers are not changing no matter how hard I pierce the papers with my eyes. Dark Vampire sightings are at record highs. Ernesto has been busy non-stop for weeks. I need another Dark Vampire hunter on my team. But what I want to know is why this is happening. I must track down the source.

The phone rings interrupting my thoughts. I look out my office window, wondering if it's later than I thought. No, dawn is just breaking over the tree line. Well, whoever it is, it can't be worse than these numbers.

"Hello?"

The voice on the other line says, "It's Gambino. I've got news."

"I've got ears."

"I've had a guy tailing former officer Dean Schmidt since you told me about Blue. So far my guy has been planted outside his house. We hadn't seen so much as a light switch flicker and were beginning to wonder if he moved his locale before we arrived—until this morning, that is."

Gambino pauses and I prompt, "Well, what has changed?"

Gambino takes a deep breath, obviously not wanting to say what he's about to say. "Well, about thirty minutes ago, Schmidt's garage door opens and he takes a drive across town. My man thought he was drunk with the way he was swerving over the road. He finally parks in front of the Dilectus Deo headquarters, the Center for Enlightenment." Gambino gives a bark of laughter that is full of irony.

"Well, then Schmidt emerges from his car, and my guy says he's like death warmed over. His arm is swollen to twice its normal size. He can hardly walk, but he makes it up to the Center. Then, just as they open the door, he collapses on the stoop. They end up dragging him in."

"Gambino, that is the absolute worst place for that man to be. He is a viper now, but they'll turn him into a monster."

"I know. Anyway, I'm pulling my man off of him. Tailing a man protected by the Dilectus Deo isn't wise unless we have evidence he's committing more crimes. Are you sure Blue doesn't want to press charges?"

"I don't want to speak for her, Gambino. She said no. But it wouldn't hurt you to ask again. Maybe a little time has changed her perspective."

"Will do," Gambino says with a bit more hope than I'd grant his cause.

I hang up and pound my fist on the desk. I look down at the report I'd been staring at. I was wrong; this day, maybe this entire decade, just got worse.

CHAPTER 54

PHANTOM ISLAND

BLUEBELL KILDARE

JUNE 2, 2022, RED AGES

I drive deep into the Warehouse District and arrive at the Cock and Bull Tap on Industrial Drive. Varg is eager to get out of the car. We stand in front of the tavern and look across the street as I consider the warehouses on the opposite side. Could he have been held in a warehouse? I should have Rubalia research the warehouses in the area.

I walk until I arrive at the corner of Industrial Drive and River Road, then head down River Road with Varg at my side. I stop at the alley where Jason's body was found. I picture how his broken limbs were splayed across the asphalt. My gut wrenches.

I think back to what I learned at the medical examiner's office. He was found on the right side of the street, face up at the alley entrance with his head pointing toward Half Moon River. Paul must have been driving the car down the alley and hit the boy as he turned left on River Road. Jason must have been coming from that direction.

I walk further down the road toward Memorial Lane. Memorial Lane runs parallel to the river with Red Wood Cemetery on the other side. The cemetery is located on higher land that slopes toward the river. It's not visible from here, but the sound of rushing water is clear.

I wonder where a naked boy could be kept and tortured so no one would hear. Would the river noise hide his screams?

At the corner of River Road and Memorial Lane, I see a dead end sign, quite appropriate for a road ending in a cemetery. Varg and I cross the street, and the river sounds grow louder as we approach. At the edge of the cemetery, River Road terminates in a turnaround. Between the cemetery and the river is a strip of wild brush that dips down the bank.

I stare at the cemetery again from this vantage point, and peer down Half Moon River. As the crow flies, or as the river flows, it's not far from here to Phantom Island where Jason was last seen before his abduction. Varg and I walk back to the car. I need to visit Phantom Island.

A few minutes later I park my car at the library, and Varg and I stroll over the lawn to the bank of Half Moon River, which borders the property. A steel and stone bridge crosses over from the library's manicured lawn to Phantom Island in a tall arc. The island is a small mass of green land sitting in the middle of the river where it runs wide and shallow. The riverbanks around the island and a large part of the front has been landscaped into a beautiful park, but the center of the island has been left wild with a dense forest and thick canopy of leaves casting deep layers of shade. I imagine those shadows are how it gets its name. People often spread out on blankets on the manicured portion of the island, reading their books. But this morning the island is quiet and deserted.

I carefully examine the riverbank by the bridge on the mainland and wander about one hundred yards in each direction. I'm not seeking anything in particular; just hoping for a clue. The island bank is indistinct because the river is so wide here.

Grasping the steel handrails tightly, I climb the high, arcing bridge with Varg following close behind. The further I get from land, the more the dank air fills with the smell of muddy water and decaying vegetation. At the top, I glance up the murky river toward Red Wood cemetery about a mile ahead and consider its proximity again. A steady breeze carries the rich river scent to us as we stand suspended over it on the bridge. I gaze at the sky where large white clouds with heavy silver linings threaten with the foreboding of rain. We descend on the opposite side, and I walk the shaved lawn along the perimeter of the small island as Varg happily explores the landscaping, sniffing and marking territory as he goes.

There are two wooden slat park benches close to the bridge, facing an island bed of bright yellow daylilies and brilliant blue irises. I follow the strip of flat green lawn around the island away from the library side of the mainland. Across the river, I see the rear of a row of shops with a narrow alley running behind them. I stop frequently to inspect the lawn and landscaping for any article which might have fallen during a struggle. Varg stays close, sniffing all around with avid interest.

Continuing around the other end of the island, the expansive strip of manicured grass narrows to a path between the river and the dense forest crowning the island center. Walking this close to the forested area,

I delight in the dapples of sunlight spotting the forest floor as rare rays of sunshine seep through the canopy of leaves. As I move past it, the sunlight and various shades of gloom shift eerily within the forest. After rounding the bend, I'm on the final stretch of the length of the island that lines the library side.

The grass widens again here, and the view of the library is partially obscured by a single row of small, ornamental dogwood trees with the slight remains of fallen blossoms littering the ground. They would have been in full bloom a month ago. The row continues along the library side of the river all the way to the bridge. I bet in full bloom they'd have completely concealed any struggle on this side of the bridge.

"Varg," I call as I head toward the bridge with a heavy feeling of defeat. Varg, who's sniffing on the outside edge of the forest, gives a low yip and goes a little further in. I head back down the dogwood lined path, angling toward the forest to see what holds Varg's attention. The hair on the back of Varg's neck is raised, and he's standing at attention sniffing the air.

As soon as I reach him, he moves further into the forest and I follow cautiously. The trees have high trunks and not much brush, but the trunks are densely spaced. The dappling of light filtering through the canopy of leaves becomes sparser with each stride. Incessant insect buzzing and clicking creates eerie background music to the forest. With each step, the light alters, mingling with the dark, creating an ever-changing kaleidoscope of grays becoming ever dimmer as I step forward. The root system on the ground is thick, bulging out of the earth, making little pockets of different levels of footing. After about fifteen feet I glance back, but can barely see the park landscaping through the thick of trees. I hope Varg doesn't go much further because it's really spooky in here.

The thrumming of the insects builds to a crescendo, effectively cutting me off from the rest of the world. My heart pounds in my breast. I yank my leather vest close around my body and wrap my arms around my middle. My adrenaline spikes , and irrational panic sets in. I try to breathe slowly to calm myself down.

Then, out of the corner of my eye, I see something move in a quick blur. I move my head in that direction and the movement stops. I stand stock-still, staring at the space from where the movement came, waiting tensely, peering keenly, and listening closely. Then, in a rush, out of an area of deep darkness, a large black bird flies off a tall branch and swoops down between the trees heading straight toward me. I watch as it looms closer and larger with every moment. I throw my hands over my face and cringe, squatting down to the forest floor.

I stay there, crouched and cowering, but after a few breaths I realize nothing bad has happened. I slowly peek between my fingers and am heartened to see nothing in front of me. I carefully stand and lower my hands, peering into the gray veil of shadows that surrounds me. The blackbird is sitting on a tree branch on the other side of me, choking down an insect. Holy smokes! I feel so foolish.

I cast around for Varg and see he's just ahead. The hair along his back ridge is still raised, and he growls unhappily at something blue lying on the ground.

I move toward him, and after a few paces, realize the something blue is a backpack. I nearly drop to my knees in relief. This forest has me a nervous wreck. Oh, I hope against hope this is Jason's and it holds a clue.

I grab a strap that's sticking up and try to pick it up. It's heavier than I expected, and as I move my boot back to brace myself, my foot catches on a root and my ankle twists painfully. I throw my weight forward again attempting to keep my balance. I reach for a branch to steady myself, but it offers insubstantial support, and I drop with an "oomph!"

Shoot! My leg is twisted underneath me. I hold my weight with my arms and slowly stretch my leg out in front of me. It moves well but painfully. Once I have it stretched completely out, I gingerly rotate my ankle, and it feels okay. Relief washes over me as I realize I'm not greatly injured. The forest ground is dirty, but I decide to plant my butt to examine the pack while I get my bearings.

Scooting over on my butt, I stretch my arm out until my fingers reach the straps, and pull it to me. I remove my own pack and take out a fresh pair of gloves and evidence bag. With gloves on, I unzip the pack and pull out a textbook: AP Chemistry. I open the front cover, and on the sign-out sheet is neatly printed "Jason O'Connell." My fear leaves me and my heart sings.

I flip open my phone and dial Gambino. "Gambino," I say when he answers. "I just found Jason's backpack in the woods on Phantom Island. Actually, Varg found it."

Gambino's voice is filled with a smile. "That's fantastic! I'll be right there." I hear a click and close my phone.

I rummage through the backpack while Varg sniffs around, growling occasionally at some scent he runs into. I flip through tattered notebooks, but at first glance they're only filled with school notes, so I put them aside. I pull out two more textbooks and check to see if anything is inserted. I feel at the bottom of the pack, and my hand runs into a pile of small objects; loose change, pencils, an eraser . . . I would love to dump the backpack out to examine the contents more closely, but not here. I check the front pocket and pull out a copy of the flyer for the Sun Flare Celebration Fireworks and Magic Show. I carefully place it back and zip up the pack. Full examination will have to wait until I have a clean space.

It seems time to brave standing, so I pivot until I'm on my knees and then lift to one foot. Pushing off my bent knee, I slowly attain standing position. I shift my weight between my ankles. My right ankle hurts a bit, but doesn't appear to be sprained. I swing one pack at a time to each of my shoulders and slip carefully back the way I came. Varg is still interested in the area, but a whistle brings him looping toward me. With eyes peeled to the forest floor, I safely reach the edge of the woods.

With great relief I leave the woods and amble onto the manicured lawn. I see the library parking lot between the trunks of the dogwood trees, and Gambino is just exiting his car. I wave my arm wildly at him, he waves back, shouting, "On my way."

Varg hears his voice and takes off running. In a flash he's over the bridge headed straight toward Gambino to greet him.

Once my feet are planted safely on the path leading to the bridge, I dial Jack. His warm, deep voice reverberates through me like the sound of a harp being strummed. "Jack," he answers.

"Jack, it's Blue. I found Jason's backpack." As I'm speaking, I suddenly feel a terrifying wave of maliciousness coming from the forest. Gambino and Varg approach the bridge. I spin around to the forest, looking for the source of that terrible impression.

Jack says from my phone, "Excellent work. Where did you find it?"

I peer into the woods. My eyes seem to be playing tricks on me because the air appears to shimmer. I turn my attention back to the phone. "On Phantom Island," I say. "I'm here now."

I look backwards again toward Gambino and he disappears from my line of sight on the other side of the bridge. The air behind me thickens with the scent of evil, so I twist toward the forest again. A shape begins to solidify just at the tree line, and the roiling feeling of viciousness screams at my senses. Tobias Blackwater emerges in solid form, jumps from the trees, and grabs my arm.

"Tobias is here!" I shout into the phone as I shove my shoulder into Blackwater with all my might.

My backpack falls off with a thud. Blackwater still has my arm in a painful grip, so I drop the phone and swing the other backpack at him with my left hand. It hits him, but he refuses to let go.

Holy Plane of Fire! Was he waiting for the very moment Varg left me? I yank and pull away as hard as I can. Unexpectedly, my vision starts to dim. I faintly hear Jack's voice roaring through the phone as it lies on the ground, "Blue!" At the same time I hear Gambino's louder voice from the top of the bridge yelling, "Stop!" and Varg's vicious growl threatening pain and death.

The graying of my vision relentlessly increases. The world goes completely dark.

At first I feel I'm blinded, and I thrash around for balance, but no solid form meets my hands or feet. I feel suspended, alone in space, but I can still sense Tobias Blackwater's presence as a nasty, sticky sweet insanity nearby. The air around me fills with a whooshing noise. I feel confused and nauseated, as though my insides are being sucked out by a vacuum. The air rushes by me as I stand still. I hold out my hands, and my fingers trace through insubstantial air. My heart races and sweat pours down my temples. Then, suddenly, I feel wonderful, hard ground beneath me. I fall to my knees as the turmoil stops. It's dark here, but I'm in the world I know again, and Tobias Blackwater still holds my arm.

Blackwater drags me forward, taking long steps as I stumble behind him, attempting to stand. He hauls me a few feet through the darkness. We turn a corner as the shock wears off me. I see light ahead. We are in some sort of cave or tunnel. I am *not* going wherever he's taking me.

I shout, "Let me go, you sleaze bucket." I dig my heels into floor, which feels like impacted dirt.

Still pulling at me, Blackwater turns his head and speaks over his shoulder in a singsong voice, "A little further, my dear Bluebell."

What in the Great Abyss? He's freaking crazy. Trying to stop our advancement any way I can, I jerk myself backwards. Blackwater's grip bites cruelly into my right arm, so I reach behind me with my left arm trying to grab my gun out of my holster. My left hand fumbles the Glock and it slips to the ground. Blast it! I drop all my weight on the ground so Blackwater doesn't pull me away from the gun. He still has my right arm, and I stretch out, reaching for the gun with my left. My fingers are inches away. I'm straining, but I just can't reach it.

He moves to stop me, but his movement gives me blessed slack, which is exactly what I need. Stretching my arm to its fullest, I finally grasp the handle of my gun. But as I do, Blackwater jumps on me and pins my left arm under his right. He twists my wrist, and the pain shocks me into dropping the gun again.

Holy smokes! Now I'm really in trouble.

I'm sprawled on a dirt floor, and Blackwater is on me, holding my right arm and my left wrist. His twisted face sneers in amusement. I flash back to a vision of Schmidt pushing me against the wall and ripping at my clothes. Fresh anger seethes through me, and I wiggle and fight Blackwater madly now. I pull up my knee and hit him in the groin; amusement drains from his face as I keep kicking and kneeing him.

Blackwater releases my left arm to grab at his crotch, and I rake my fingers down his face. He lifts a hand to protect his face as I try to poke his eyeballs out. He grabs my wrist again, and I wriggle and writhe to get away from him. He plants all his weight on one knee in the middle of my abdomen, crushing me beneath him. Then he holds both my wrists over my head and ignores my now ineffectual kicks and blows.

He picks up my gun. I look in his eyes and see nothing but malice and insanity. I'm sure he's going to kill me on the spot. I twist my arms again, still trying desperately to free myself. I think about Jack and Maud with longing, realizing I may never see them again. But Blackwater surprises me by spinning the butt of the gun toward me and slamming it into my skull. I feel a shock of pain rip through my head, and my vision is washed with red. I feel myself go limp, then my vision tunnels and narrows to a pinpoint, and finally I see nothing more.

Chapter 55

Searching Desperately

Jack Tanner

June 2, 2022, Red Ages

I stand up behind my desk, and my chair goes crashing behind me. The desk phone is still in my hand, and her voice still echoes in my ears. *"Tobias is here!"*

Black rage flows up through my body like oil fills a drum, the pressure mounts and mounts until it explodes. I explode! I roar my rage, so dark, so dense, a pain like nothing I've ever known.

Ernesto enters my office in a flash with sword in hand. When he sees it's just me, he lowers his sword and stands just on the other side of my desk, but he is still wary, as he should be. I feel crazed.

"What is it?" he asks. He's in a defensive stance, ready to jump me should the need arise.

I notice the desk phone remains in my hand, and I'm slowly crushing it.

Xavier opens the door and steps in, gun drawn. Seeing no one but Ernesto and I, he puts his gun down but keeps behind Ernesto.

Then Rubalia appears. "What is going on?" she demands shrilly; her face a mask of fear.

My senses are at their highest, and the tangy scent of my colleagues' blood fills my nostrils and hits with force. My fangs descend.

Somehow, with Rubalia's demand, I find my voice and am able to growl, "Tobias Blackwater has taken Blue. I need to call Gambino."

I look dumbly at the phone in my hand and see it has been pulverized by my grip; its plastic shards litter the carpet. My blood still pounds in my temples, making it difficult to think straight.

Xavier says, "Use your cell phone in your holster."

I feel for my cell phone and dial Gambino. When he answers, I hear Varg in the background alternating between vicious grows and haunting howls. Gambino's voice sounds rough. "I'm at Phantom Island. Blackwater portaled out with Blue just as I arrived."

I wince to hear what I'd feared voiced out loud, making it real.

"Stay there. I'm on my way."

Ernesto has relaxed his stance a little. Perhaps he has more faith in me than I do.

I close my eyes, reaching deep inside for some clarity of thought and self-control. My heart screams "Blue!" but my mind says, "Think of a plan. What should you do?"

I turn to Rubalia, who is a ghastly shade of gray beneath her brown skin, and her eyes are unnaturally shiny. "Rubalia, I want a list of all properties owned by Tobias Blackwater or any of his family. Chime me as soon as you have it. Call Mike Kramer, the head of the Western Appalachian Supernatural Investigation Bureau and let him know one of our colleagues has been kidnapped by a murder suspect and is in great danger. Tell him the suspect can portal, so we have to operate covertly, without reinforcements. Tell them we may need some support for our regular case load depending on how long this takes. We will keep them updated. I'm going to need you here as Command Central."

Rubalia nods. I add, "Please have a car packed with food and bags of blood in a cooler in the parking lot of the Cock and Bull Tap. If we haven't found Blue by evening, we'll need it."

I turn to Ernesto and Xavier. "You're with me. Meet me at the car."

I look around the room. No one has moved. They're all staring at me like a still frame: Rubalia with her lips pinched and a quivering chin, Xavier with a look of shock, and Ernesto with wariness and concern.

I've managed to speak calmly for a full minute, but my insides are a swirling tempest of rage, battering me, wearing at my control. I need Xavier and Rubalia to leave my office because the scent of their blood is too enticing while I'm in this state. My fangs are still fully descended, and my throat is thickening. On the brink of losing complete control, I raise my voice again, "Leave my office. Now!"

Rubalia startles and Xavier winces, and thankfully they scatter like rabbits. Ernesto leaves as well, but I smell him outside my door. He knows I'm tottering on the edge.

I reach into the fridge under my desk and pull out four bags of blood. I sink my fangs through the plastic of each consecutively, mechanically, drinking but tasting nothing. It's a precautionary action because my rage is too strong and my instincts are besieging my mind. The last thing I need is to let hunger take control.

When done, I toss the bags in the garbage can and go to my closet. I assess my arsenal and choose my sword and scabbard, two semi-automatic pistols, and a long knife. I strap on my holsters and knife sheath and carry my sword and scabbard out.

Ernesto is indeed standing sentinel outside my door, sword in hand. I'm glad he is keeping watch over me. If ever I needed a friend to keep me in check, this is the moment. He follows me through the reception area where Rubalia furiously types on her computer with tears silently streaking her face and her mouth set in a grim, determined line. I wish I could give her comfort, but I have none to give. We pass her silently heading down the hall to the stairwell. I whisper quietly under my breath, for Ernesto's ears alone, "Friend, my control is weak."

Ernesto looks at me with wise eyes full of sorrow and whispers back, "I know, mi amigo. You are like I was when my Rosalie died. I will watch you until you are yourself again."

I smack his shoulder in approval.

We arrive at the car; Ernesto takes the passenger seat and Xavier the back. I'm flying down the road to Phantom Island, the scenery a blur, before their doors are even shut. I'm singing a song of death in my mind, and the song has Blackwater's name in every chorus.

When we peel into the library parking lot, Gambino is standing outside his car with Jason's backpack on his hood. He flips his phone closed as I get out. His face is red and scowling as he says, "Varg took off. I have three men from the force joining the search. I've alerted the chief who's alerted the mayor." His eyes grab mine, and I see a degree of my pain reflected in his. "We shouldn't have let her go out alone."

I bark with rage, not at him, but at myself. "I know, damn it!" The guilt sits like a huge boulder in my chest, pressing down on me.

Then my chimerator tightens, and I flip open the lid angrily. Rubalia says without preamble, "He has a family estate on the corner of Lawrence and Wilson Street. 53 Lawrence Boulevard. His other properties are all out of state."

"Thanks Rubalia. File the emergency entry paperwork. Hold on." I look at Gambino, "Did you put a BOLO out on his car?"

Gambino nods.

"Did you notify airport security?"

"It's automatically part of the BOLO."

I speak to Rubalia's chimera. "Rubalia, can you check to see if he owns a private plane?"

"Of course."

I flip the chimerator closed and open it again, chanting a familiar name. A wild, melodious voice answers as an image comes into focus. "The Dragomir Magical Artifact Shop."

"Dragomira, it's Jack. Blue has been taken. When someone has the gift of portaling, how far is the range?"

Dragomira drags in a sharp breath, and then she says, "Usually no more than two to three miles."

Then her voice softens and she says gently, "Jack, I think this may be your test. I am truly sorry."

I flip the chimerator closed again, and my heart silently cries out. A test I've surely already failed. I run my fingers through my hair, still staring at my chimerator while I get a grip. Two, maybe three seconds pass; that is all the reprieve I'll allow myself. Then I look at Gambino. "Blackwater lives at 53 Lawrence Boulevard. Park a block away, and wait for our approach. If she is there, I do not want him moving her."

Gambino nods. I run to my car and take off to Blackwater's residence with Ernesto and Xavier.

We arrive in an old neighborhood with, large elegant homes, sprawling yards, and tree-lined streets. I park a block away from the property line, and my team gets out.

"I'll take the roof. You two guard each entrance, but stay hidden. I'll work my way down and whistle when you can enter."

We move silently forward. The house is an old brick Tudor with plenty of entry points for persons of our skills. Xavier takes position in front of the house behind a large black maple tree. Ernesto crouches below the window line and slips around back. I go to the side of the house and scale it quickly, gripping the bricks and timbers, listening for noises in the house. Nothing but the normal squeaks of a house moving and air flowing through vents greets my ears.

I break the wood frame of a small attic window and edge the glass out. When I slip through, I noiselessly place the glass on the floor and proceed through the attic. It's thick with dust as evidence of its neglect. I assess that it's used for storage only and that it's empty of human life. A brown bat colony keeping vigil on the roof beams shudders and trembles when they smell my presence.

I descend down a rotted wood stairway to the second floor. The landing door opens to a wide hallway lined with bedrooms, seven to be exact. I smell no life, or death for that matter, but I do smell the lingering scent of Blackwater and two other distinct human scents. The place reeks of the stale scent of fear, but nothing of Blue. How I ache for the scent of Blue.

I descend the stairs to the main level in a flash. So far I've heard not a whisper or a breath in the house beyond the bats and a few mice inside the walls. My heart grows colder as each second makes it clearer Blue is probably not here. I tour the six main rooms downstairs to confirm there is no life. I open the front and back doors and whistle Xavier and Ernesto in. Gambino has joined Xavier in the front and comes in as well. An unmarked car sits across the street with back-up for Gambino.

As they enter the house, I say, "She's not here. The house is empty, but we need to search for clues. We're looking for files listing properties or associates, hidden safes, anything."

Xavier says, "Let's start in the office." I follow his lead because he's my expert in this area.

Xavier unlocks the large, ornate desk taking center stage in the room. He shifts through files in its drawers as Ernesto heads to the file cabinet. I go to the fireplace and grab a long piece of kindling and wrap one end in newspaper. I use my fangs to pierce my hand and drip blood about halfway down the stick creating a rough fire stop. Then I set the newspaper on fire with matchsticks from the mantel. As soon as the wood catches, I knock the newspaper into the fireplace and close the flue. Then with my handmade torch I carefully examine the interior walls of the room.

I wave the smoking torch next to the walls and bookcases and gently blow it into cracks to watch it languorously curl its way back into the room, proof there is no air seepage. When I get to a large mahogany panel between two massive bookcases covered with hunting trophies, the smoke slips in the crack between one bookcase and the panel to disappear. I check the other side of the panel and the same thing happens. My excitement rises. "We have a hidden door!"

Xavier jumps up to examine the panel. Using his intuition he grabs the deer antlers on the rightmost side of the panel and gently pulls it down. The entire head of the deer levers down as though on a hinge and then clicks in place. The panel springs open and bumps Xavier's foot. Thank the Holy Light I brought Xavier along. "Good work, Xavier."

Xavier nods, fully absorbed in his task. He lives to meet the challenge of every locked space as though claiming no one can keep secrets from him. He pulls the panel door open all the way to reveal a massive steel door with an old-fashioned combination lock. Xavier pulls a tool out of his pack. I gather it's some sort of listening device as he presses it to his ear then presses the other end to the vault just to the left of the lock. He turns the lock to the left, then to the right, then to the left. His movements seem to be in excruciatingly slow motion. He spins a large wheel on the vault door to open the latch. I hear creaking and scraping of the metal works, and finally the door swings toward us.

It opens to a chamber lined in glass shelves filled with ancient magical artifacts of all kinds. My hopes come crashing down in an instant. My chest tightens with a stabbing pain. I slam my fist on the top of the safe doorway so hard the massive iron frame dents with the shape of my fist and the sound reverberates through the house like a sledgehammer, breaking windows as it goes.

When the fine tinkling of shattered glass quiets, my ears pick up the faint sound of voices and my hope flares again. "Someone is here, below us somewhere."

Xavier steps away from the safe with a huff of disgust, "Look for other hidden doors. If he has one, he will likely guard other secrets this way."

Xavier and Ernesto quickly assemble their own handmade torches and take off to other parts of the house. Gambino steps in the chamber with broken glass crunching under his shoes. He looks around grimly. Two red spots rise to his cheeks as he says angrily, "I'll be damned. I bet half of the items stolen in the last five years are here."

I couldn't care less about stolen items, so while Gambino calls in his back-up, I continue searching the interior walls of the room. As I'm finishing, Xavier yells from across the house, "Jack. We've found something."

I follow his voice, and Gambino follows me. Xavier and Ernesto are in a large mudroom off the kitchen, looking at a tall, floor-to-ceiling bench with coat hooks on it. I blow smoke around the back panel and sure enough, it disappears.

Ernesto hands Xavier his torch, and using brute strength he wrenches the bench away from the wall. A stone doorway emerges with a staircase twisting downward. I descend, using Vampire speed and eyesight, blowing my torch out with the strength of the air rushing by. Ernesto follows with sword drawn. The stairway is narrow and made of crumbling stone, walled in on both sides. It twists several times, then ends in a long hall that slopes down further still.

As we reach the end of the hall we turn right. It opens into a large stone room with a low ceiling. At the back of the room are two iron barred cells. One holds a man and a woman, a Latino couple, clasping each other desperately on a small cot, looking toward us blindly in the darkness. The woman softly sobs and shakes with fear. Their clothes are plain and worn but clean and neat. I see a slight body on a cot in the other cell. I rush to it and see it holds an emaciated young Latina girl, unkempt in rags, lying on the bare pallet with only a single threadbare blanket. She's making soft whimpering noises.

Ernesto says "Dios mio!" and starts talking rapidly in Spanish to the couple.

Xavier steps up to their cage and removes a tool from his pocket to break the lock. I notice a key ring hanging on the wall, grab it and toss it to his feet. Xavier picks up the key ring sheepishly. He unlocks the door, and the woman flies into Ernesto's arms, speaking urgently in Spanish all the while, holding him like she will never let him go.

As Ernesto comforts her, he says over her shoulder, "They do not speak English well. They were kept as domestic slaves. Blackwater held their daughter here as blackmail to keep them."

Gambino joins us downstairs now and steps aside to radio for an ambulance.

I am glad we found this family, and I want them to have the care they need, but my need to find Blue is desperate. So I press Ernesto, "Ask them if they saw Blue."

Ernesto talks with them a moment. Both the man and the woman shake their head as they reply to Ernesto. My heart drops again.

Ernesto confirms, "No. Blackwater locked them in here yesterday and hasn't allowed them out since. Normally he lets them out in the morning and locks them up at night after the housework is done. They have not seen a young woman in the house in the last few days."

I turn to Gambino, "Do you have anyone who speaks Spanish? I need Ernesto with me, and they need to talk to someone."

By now Xavier has opened the door to the little girl's cell. Ernesto gently extricates himself from the woman's arms, and together they kneel down on either side of the girl's cot. The man, meanwhile, keeps thanking me in both Spanish and English. Shortly, he joins them at the cot and gently strokes his daughter's hair. Ernesto speaks softly to her. The girl tries to lift up her head but then lies back down in exhaustion. Ernesto holds her hand and says something tenderly to her again. She nods slightly. Ernesto gently lifts her up in his arms. She practically disappears behind her long dark hair. She is so slight, she reminds me of a tiny sparrow with broken wings.

We ascend the stairs and wait for the ambulance at the front door while the mother and father keep speaking in Spanish to Ernesto and their daughter.

"What are their names?" I ask.

Ernesto looks at the couple and says, "This is Claudia and Jose Herrera." Then he looks down compassionately at the little girl. "This is Evita. She is sixteen years old."

I'm shocked. She is so small and looks twelve years old at most. "How long was she kept down there?"

Ernesto's face turns dark with fury, and the girl sees it and starts whimpering again. Ernesto schools his face and murmurs gently to her. When she seems to relax, he looks up with a world of pain in his eyes. "Over five years. She has not been out of that cell in over five years."

I curse under my breath. Three ambulances arrive, and Ernesto gently lays the girl down on one of the gurneys and whispers to her again. Her parents are able to get in the gurneys on their own. The girl is obviously distressed when Ernesto steps away, but one of Gambino's men steps up and starts speaking to her in Spanish. She quiets down, but she watches Ernesto all the while, obviously afraid to let him out of her sight.

Neighbors are gathering in front of their homes, watching what is happening and gossiping heatedly.

"Ernesto," I say, drawing his gaze away from Evita. "We need to go back to the Warehouse District by the Cock and Bull Tap."

Every second passing ticks through my mind. I turn to Gambino. "Can you have someone look through the rest of the files here and call me if something comes up?"

"Yes. I'll stay here and supervise for tonight. We'll check the rest of the interior walls using your method."

I put out my hand, and Gambino grips it firmly. "Thank you, Gambino."

Gambino says, "Good luck. I'll call you as soon as I know we have everything we can get from the house."

I glance back at the house as Gambino's men put the crime scene tape across the large stone doorway. I look toward the neighbors again. A lot has been found in this house, and I don't think the neighbors will ever view it the same way.

I call Xavier over, speaking quickly. "Xavier, we're going to search every warehouse in the district, and I could definitely use your special expertise."

Xavier puts his hands in his pockets, grins, and then frowns, apparently momentarily forgetting the gravity of the situation in his joy of the challenge. He remarks, "Obviously you don't have enough time to file a right of entry permission for every building there. Do you have enough cause to invoke the emergency entry right?"

"Absolutely. Based on Jason's condition we have every right to fear for her life. I'll call Rubalia and ask her to submit the paperwork."

Ernesto shifts his stance, his agitation obvious. I can see Evita affected him strongly. "Señor," Ernesto asks, "are you going to call in for another unit to help?"

"Ernesto, I wish I could. But bear in mind that Blackwater can portal Blue out at a moment's notice if he knows we are close. We *must* work quickly and move stealthily, and calling in a big team would make that impossible."

Ernesto nods. "I agree. I was concerned about that."

Xavier says, "We have the skills to do this quickly. Let's get to it."

With that, we hurry to my car, and I floor it to the Warehouse District. While I'm driving I call Rubalia. "Rubalia, have you found any evidence of a private jet?"

"No, Sir. I called all the private hangers in a two hundred mile radius and told them to be on the lookout for Blackwater. I faxed a photo of him to each and gave your number."

"Thanks, Rubalia. Great thinking. We're about to search the Warehouse District, building by building. Can you submit the emergency entry special license paperwork?"

Rubalia says, "Of course. I have a few prepped already. I'll just enter the location."

"When you're done with that, I'd like you to switch tracks and start looking for any business dealings he had with anyone who owns property in the Warehouse District. Also, generally keep looking for any local properties at all."

"Yes, Sir."

"And Rubalia, call Mike Kramer and tell him I want a team assigned to help you with research. You're to lead it. Don't let him arrange it any other way."

"Yes, Sir."

"If he gives you any problems, send me a text and I'll call him myself."

"Yes, Sir!"

I click the phone closed, concentrating on the rapidly passing suburban streets, hoping she comes up with something, anything. Rubalia is a master researcher. If there is something to be found, she'll find it.

CHAPTER 56

AN INTRODUCTION TO PAIN

BLUEBELL KILDARE

JUNE 2, 2022, RED AGES

I wake up drowning in freezing water. Choking and gasping for air, I try to swim, but I can't move my arms. I open my eyes and see the long, thin face of Tobias Blackwater grinning at me, with an empty bucket in hand. I try to wipe the water from my face, but my arms are restrained above my head. They move a little but not far enough. I sputter and cough. The cough sends a blast of pain through my head. Aside from the biting edge of cold water and pain, my mind feels dull and slow.

I keep my head still and the blast of pain settles to a great throb in the spot Blackwater hit me. I observe that I am in the middle of a dark room with rock walls and a dirt floor. A firefly lantern hangs from a hook on the wall, casting a long shadow on the opposite side of Blackwater. I feel air all over my body. Without moving my head, I know he's stripped me naked. Blackwater's leering face comes one step closer. I lift my leg to knee him, but my foot is restrained as well. I try my other foot with the same luck.

Blackwater laughs softly. His nasty, perverse joy fills the room.

Risking an escalation of pain, I slowly tip my head up and see my arms are shackled, the chains attach to one of several large timber ceiling beams. I look down and see my ankles are shackled to chains cemented in a square block beneath me. I school my features not to show desperation, and I face Blackwater, who seems inordinately pleased with the situation.

"Ah, Bluebell," he sneers, "so good to finally meet you under more civilized circumstances."

I respond as calmly as possible. "Where am I?" Speaking drives another streak of pain through my head.

Gleefully, Blackwater responds, "Somewhere you can scream as loud as you want and we will remain undisturbed."

His voice hurts too. I can feel his soul dripping in evil, invading my sixth sense.

"You hit me hard. How long was I out?"

"Only a bit, my dear."

"What do you want?" I ask.

Blackwater frowns. "I want the amulet, of course."

"What amulet?"

Blackwater claps his hands together. "Wonderful!" he says. "I thought you would say that. I already know that you know too much. I understand my uniquely acquired magical artifacts are now being researched within the precinct. My job as Councilman is now over, thanks to you. Not that I mind. It was a tedious pretense."

He wants to talk and enjoys bragging. I'll go along with it to give Jack and Gambino more time.

I prompt him further. "What magical artifacts are you talking about?"

"Why, the ones you are wearing, amongst others."

I'm surprised at this. I tilt my head down, and with a dawning horror, I see a fine mesh collar around my upper chest and shoulders: the Belladonna Necklace. I wiggle my fingers and toes and feel a heavy ring on my left hand.

Blackwater smiles slightly. "Yes, the Ring of Truth. I can tell when you lie, so don't bother. And the Belladonna Necklace prevents you from using magic. Not that a Sensitive is much threat. Where is the amulet?"

Strange, I don't feel any different. I reach inside, and my sixth sense feels normal. I sense the malevolent thrill Blackwater is getting from having me at his mercy. The baseness of his greed and the evil at his core, is like a black, oily pit centered around his body where his soul should be. The necklace isn't working, but of course I don't tell him.

Blackwater slaps me across the face, snapping my head back. Lightning streaks through my brain. When I can see again, he's standing in front of me with that mad smile on his face.

"Bluebell, we are wasting time. Where is the amulet?"

I hope if I keep my responses as questions, the ring will not reveal my lie. I ask, "What amulet are you talking about?"

Blackwater reaches behind his back and pulls out a whip with a long leather braid. He holds it up, waving it gently, letting the long thong undulate back and forth. Shivers go through me that have nothing to do with the biting cold. Things have gotten very serious very quickly. I can feel Blackwater's enjoyment, and I have no doubt he would use the whip. In fact, I can feel his anticipation. But I also know I cannot let this man get closer to a book that would let him control demons, spirits, and souls. I cannot allow him to have the power to wreak havoc on the world, not with his evilness.

Blackwater asks, "Do we need to use this? Where is the amulet?"

I grit my teeth and say, "What amulet?"

Blackwater's smile lights up his eyes. "I'd hoped you would play, at least a little."

He moves behind me, and as he does I notice he has a slight limp. "Why are you limping? Did my bullet find you under the semi?" I ask innocently.

Blackwater snarls. "You'll pay for that too."

I hear the brief rush of air a second before I feel the strike in the middle of my back. I clench my muscles and jump. Then I feel another strike across my left shoulder blade. It feels like fire. My back muscles are all clenched. My eyes are clenched. My mouth is clenched. Then another strike, and my body jolts. Then another strike, and I realize my body is no longer mine to control.

Blackwater pauses and cajoles, "Where is the amulet, Bluebell?"

I am breathing heavily now. It would be so easy to give in. I harden my resolve, and I say through panting breaths, "What amulet?"

Blackwater cackles with glee. I try to prepare myself. I understand now there will be no relaxing. The pain is too great. My back is already on fire. Blackwater whips me again. I try to go somewhere else in my mind. I remember an afternoon at the orphanage spent on the lake with sunshine and cool water. I attempt to breathe evenly.

Blackwater lays the whip down harder now, and with each stroke my whole body jerks. The next stroke pulls me out of my thoughts and back to the room as the whip hits the necklace and the chains dig into my skin. I desperately try to retreat in my mind again. I imagine cool water rushing over my skin. The whip falls again and again, and I jolt and spasm under it. The pain is so great the urge to cry uncle pressures my brain. Two more lashes and Blackwater pauses.

He asks, "Where is the amulet?"

This time I don't bother to answer.

Blackwater coaxes from behind. "Bluebell, just tell me where the amulet is and this will all be over. There is no need for more pain. Be a good girl."

I continue my silence, trying to breathe evenly, taking every second of solace.

Blackwater comes around to my front. He reaches his hand out and draws it across my breasts almost lovingly. I shrink from his hand, but I can't move far. He fondles one breast, then another. He asks, "Why ruin such lovely skin, Bluebell? It seems such a shame."

I laugh inside that he is trying to appeal to my vanity. I spit in his face. A big glob of it runs off his forehead, and he wipes it off his brow distastefully with his sleeve. He sets his mouth in a grim line and walks behind me again. I feel the familiar rush of air as my warning. He whips me with all his strength now. I recognize the scent of iron in the air from my own blood. I can't catch my breath and am heavily panting. Each lash that rains on me drives lightning shots of pain and fire up my back and into my brain. My previous pain from the gun handle is long forgotten. I can't imagine how the human mind can receive so many pain signals at once.

I try to keep silent, but as the lashes fall, my skin splits and shreds of it are being peeled from my back. I scream in my mind so loudly I can't tell if I am screaming out loud. I can't count the strikes. At some point I feel warmth rush down my leg, and I realize I urinated on myself. But I'm well beyond feeling shame.

Later, though I don't know how much later because every second lasts an eternity, I realize my whole body is just dangling from the shackles. My legs can't hold me. The whip still rains on me. Then blessed darkness comes.

CHAPTER 57

WAREHOUSE DISTRICT

JACK TANNER

JUNE 2, 2022, RED AGES

We pull up to the Cock and Bull Tap and exit the car. I point to the first warehouse on the street, a short, steel structure, looking squat against the darkening sky with the last pink rays of sun streaming behind it. "We'll start here and move all the way up the street, then circle back."

Xavier takes a look down the long street. "You want covert, right?"

"Yes."

Xavier looks back at me. "How about I go ahead and start gaining access to the back doors. I'll disable any security systems along the way, and you two can follow behind and do the searching."

Ernesto says, "I should come with you to scout for security guards." He looks at me with a calm I wish I could feel. "If there is a guard, I will place three stones by the back door so you know not to enter that way. Then I'll place another three stones by a window or vent or other location we open up instead of the back door."

Evening is on us, and I am anxious to start. "Let's get going."

Ernesto turns to me, looking resolute, and grasps both my forearms in his own. "We will find her, mi amigo."

I take strength from my longtime friend's support, but it gives only a weak glimmer of light in the abyss of darkness I'm stranded in. I can only say, "We will get every building. Let's not leave one undone."

I run to the back door of the first warehouse. Xavier runs after me, his ebony skin melting into the shadows. Ernesto gracefully circles around the building, listening and smelling for life. He must hear no sign, as he gives Xavier the nod. Xavier's excitement is palpable. There is nothing he enjoys more than the challenge of covert entry. He deftly unlocks the door, and I slip in as Xavier and Ernesto are on to the next building.

I do a quick run through of the entire building. It's a one floor open warehouse with a small office. I smell every crate, thankful each time I do not smell Blue in it. I press my ear to the floor and listen for signs of life below. Then I move on to the next warehouse.

This one has three stones by the door. I find another three stones under a vent on the roof. I grasp the ridging of the steel walls and easily climb up. The vent lid is loose. I remove it and peer in. It's a fifteen foot drop. I hold on to the vent lid and silently drop inside, landing with ease. The security guard is in a small office with a window facing the main aisle that is flanked by shelves and shelves of boxed goods. I use the corner of the back wall to climb to the roof. Then I swing from steel beam to steel beam until I have viewed and scented the entire open space.

I drop noiselessly in the front corner of the warehouse out of view of the security guard. Crouched down, I make my way below the office window, quickly scanning my senses through the wall for life. I only smell and hear the security guard. I cross to the other side, climb the wall, then scale the ceiling beams to the back of the building. I lever myself through the vent hole. Then, grasping on to the ridges of the building again, I replace the vent and drop back down.

I continue on to the next building, and the next, and the next. At each large crate I come across I am filled with hope that Blue is not inside. At the end of each building my heart plummets that we haven't found her yet. When we are done with over thirty warehouses on this street, we move on to the next street, and then the next. The night wears on, and my hope becomes dimmer and dimmer.

Finally, when every building has been searched and the night has grown old, we reconvene at the Cock and Bull Tap. Ernesto looks grim, and Xavier worn. I want to scream into the night air, howl my frustration at the stars. Instead I open the car that Rubalia had parked here and toss several bags of blood to Ernesto, taking my own fill. Rubalia packed more earthy sustenance for Xavier, and he enjoys it ravenously.

We head inside the Cock and Bull Tap near closing time. Xavier heads toward the men's bathroom. I order a beer and sit quietly with Ernesto. The noise of the bar, loud men and women laughing and slurring their words, grates on me. How can they not know such a precious person is lost and in trouble? How can they enjoy their lives when all joy is gone from mine?

When Xavier returns, he nods, and I hand him the beer. I head toward the men's bathroom, pass it up, and continue on to the "No Entrance" door beyond it. I open it and ascend the staircase to the upper floor of the Cock and Bull Tap. It's a residence, clean, comfortable, and small. I quickly do a check and find no life here.

Damn it! I need to find her. She is in trouble. I know it.

My chest aches, and my insides are cold. I lean against the door and remember her as I saw her yesterday. She was sitting in the office, going over the logic of why it must be Tobias Blackwater who tortured Jason. She spoke intelligently and vivaciously, so full of life and quiet strength. She is a veritable warrior, digging and poking until she finds the truth. She spoke with such logical reasoning and determination that fits perfectly with her beautiful face and soul. She has no idea how beautiful she is, inside and out.

I repeat her name in my head, letting it echo around. *Blue. Blue. Blue. I should never have left you alone.* With this last thought, I push myself away from the door. Missing her and hurting for her will not help her now.

I return to join Xavier and Ernesto downstairs, shaking my head at the outcome of my search.

Xavier has dark circles under his eyes and is slumping in his chair. "Xavier, you should rest and join us tomorrow morning."

Xavier yawns, "Sorry, I wish I could go on endlessly like you, but I'll be better help after some shut-eye."

I give him a half-hearted smile. I can't quite muster the whole thing. "I know. Use the car that Rubalia left us? Stock up on blood for when you meet up with us tomorrow. We're heading back to the island to do some more searching."

Ernesto asks, "What is next, mi amigo?"

"We are going to search up and down the river. We are going to find her."

CHAPTER 58

INTO THE DARKNESS

BLUEBELL KILDARE

JUNE 2, 2022, RED AGES

I gradually awaken from searing pain in my back and biting pain in my arms. My body hangs from my arms, which are still above my head, held in place by the shackles around my wrists. The iron cuts into my numb hands from the weight of my body.

But that is nothing compared to the pain in my back. My back is a living fire! Every small movement sends another rush of muscle spasms through my back. I smell a strong metallic scent in the air, and know it's from my own blood, pooling on the floor. I recognize the heavy, acrid scent mixed with the scent of iron. It comes from the urine pooled around my feet. My inner thighs and legs burn where it sat on my skin for hours, and the soles of my feet are damp from it.

Ohh, no! This is exactly what happened to Jason. He had calluses on his wrists and arms from these shackles. His feet were rotting, and the smell of human feces and urine covered him. My feet will be rotting soon too if I don't get out of here.

I stop thinking as another wave of muscle spasms rips across my back. The horror begins to set in my mind. My back is like Jason's. I am where Jason was. How did this happen to me? I was supposed to capture Blackwater, not get captured by him.

I slowly stand so my legs support my weight, and a thousand pinpricks fill my hands as blood gradually returns. My mouth is parched, my lips cracked. It's completely dark in here, and freezing too. I'm shivering and I am feverish, but more than that, the air is simply cold. I feel small and lost in the darkness; my panic rises again. I push those feelings away and instead focus on how grateful I am that the solitude announces so loudly the absence of Blackwater.

I wonder where Jack and Gambino are. I wonder where I am.

Where can you scream and have nobody hear? I wonder if they'll find me in time. How much time has passed? How much time do I have? The questions stretch on endlessly, but not as far as the darkness.

Knowing this line of thinking will drive me mad, I resolve instead to investigate the darkness with my senses to see what can be learned. I hear a light but distinct plop, plop, plop sound behind me to the left and up high. Is that water dripping? I close my eyes and listen carefully. I hear a softer and duller dlop, dlop that sounds lower to the ground. I think the sharper, higher noise is water dripping onto the protruding edge of a rock on the wall, and the softer noise is water dripping onto the earthen floor. All of the water drops seem to be coming from behind me.

I smell the air. Behind the scent of urine and blood is the rich, decaying scent of moist earth. I open my eyes again. There is no light to be seen. Not even a crack of light, not a single ray of sunshine. I'm in complete darkness. I remember the beam above me, but I don't recall the ceiling behind the beam. What is the beam attached to? Cripes! I should have been more attentive.

So the sounds—is it raining somewhere, or am I just near water?

My legs are cramping with cold. I shift my weight to ease the worst of the cramping, and a roll of excruciating pain washes through my back again. I hold still and breathe evenly until the pain subsides.

I close down my senses and open up my sixth sense. It flares to life stronger than ever before. The Belladonna Necklace definitely isn't hurting my abilities. If anything, it's helping them. I sense my own fear and pain permeating the room, and the vile, malicious madness that is Blackwater's signature.

Beyond that, I feel remnants of terror and aloneness still remaining from Jason. He was in this room. Little wisps of emotions linger and waft toward me like scents blowing past me in a breeze. It's unbelievable I can feel this after so much time. I catch his quiet strength, so weak now it's hardly there. But it *is* there.

I push my internal sense further outward, hoping to find the souls of people. I push past the boundaries of the room, seeking at all sides for some sign of others. Nothing. No, not true. There is something. I can sense several tiny souls, oblivious and ravenous, from behind the walls. They are down the tunnel, perhaps. Some small hungry creatures live down here with me. I am stunned and elated I can feel the souls of animals now, but at the same time, my mind shudders from the thought of the hungry creatures and the blood at my feet is surely calling to them. I am immobile. A new horror at my situation begins to set in, but I push the thought away. Fear will not serve me now.

I slowly withdraw my sixth sense and let my regular senses rise to concentrate on the sound of the darkness again. The agony of my back and cramping in my legs return to me. My arms hurt so bad from holding them over my head for so long. And my fingers . . . well, I have no feeling in them any longer.

I try to keep my mind off my body. The plopping noise of the dripping water is coming more quickly now, and the lower dlop, dlop, dlop noise has become continuous. I feel a drop of water hit my head. Then one hits my shoulder. Then several more hit me on my cold and fevered body. I feel it stinging my back, but my back is so pain-filled it hardly registers. My skin feels clammy and feverish all at once. I shiver with cold.

I stand quietly and feel the endless dark around me as I push the pain out of my mind again. I let the sound of the water and the feel of its drips, cold, sharp, and biting on my skin, fill my mind completely. I meditate on it. I become a part of it. I let all fear slip from my mind and envelop myself in the music of the rain and the darkness.

After some time, I slowly become aware again, out of my self-induced trance. My stomach feels sick from lack of food. How much time passed while I was absorbed in the rain? I should stop asking myself that. It's a useless question. The rain is now dripping so heavily from the beam overhead that my hair is drenched. Water courses down my arms. I put my mouth to my shoulder and lap at what water I can get. Then I open my mouth and lift my head to take in the water that drips from the beam. It tastes richly of earth. It's cold, and I am cold to the bone. I hope it helps to clean my mangled back.

I wonder what Maud is doing. Has she had another round with Harry? Will she ever admit she likes him? What color is her hair today? I hope I don't end up dying here because then Maud would be alone. I want to hear more about Harry and laugh with her over their pranks. I hope she isn't worried about me now.

I think of Alexis and her shop. The kitchen is so cozy, and Alexis is so fun and bossy. She makes the most amazing things. I wonder what Varg is doing. Did Gambino take him? I hope he's okay without me. My heart aches for my friends.

I decide to blank out my mind again and feel with my inner self. This time instead of pushing it out, I imagine it softly expanding away from me. It lightly disperses and effortlessly fills the space around me. I let it drift through the darkness of the room, beyond the walls, out over the small souls, and beyond. It seems like it's going further than ever before, but it's hard to tell in the boundless darkness. I feel all around me at once, and encounter the souls of many, many small creatures. I let my fear go, and instead recognize them as small balls of light. I try to direct my sixth sense one way so it travels further and further. I search for any sign of people; stretching first in one direction, then another. But as far as I can reach, I only find the tiny balls of light from the small mammals inhabiting the earth around me. Where could I be that there's no human life around?

I pull my sixth sense in again. The room is here, freezing me. My pain slams into me, and I nearly choke at the sudden onslaught. I realize that while I was using my sixth sense, the pain and the sense of my body faded. Good. I will use that when I need it.

The rain must have stopped. The water drops are coming less frequently now, even irregularly. If this is the same rain that threatened the sky on Phantom Island, then it's likely that it's nighttime on the same day, or early morning. I listen carefully, and between the sounds of the occasional rain dripping I perceive a low rushing noise. I must be by the Half Moon River. I'm underground. I wonder if I'm at Red Wood Cemetery. I feel a rush of hope. Then it fizzles out. What good does knowing where I am do me if I can't move?

I try pulling on my arms again. I let my hand muscles go limp and round and try to slip them through the shackles, but they prove too tight. I try to pull at my feet, but the shackles are even tighter there. I grit my teeth against searing pain as I stretch my left foot as far as it will go and try to wiggle the chain. Blast it! There is no movement in the bolt cemented into the block I stand on. I breathe quietly for a while until the pain subsides. Then I try the right foot. Same result.

How long until Blackwater returns? I don't want to think about it, but I must. What do I need to learn the next time he comes? I need him to bring the light so I can examine my shackles. I need to examine the beam my shackles are attached to. I want to see the roof over the beam. I want to check the bolts in the floor and the size of the cement pad I stand on. I need to check the chain links for any spots of weakness.

I think about Jason and wonder if he did all of these things. He had no shackles on him when he was found. I wonder how he escaped. I must get Blackwater to tell me. I also need to learn about the amulet and what he wants with it, in case I make it out alive.

As I think all of these thoughts, the fever gets stronger and stronger. I finally let my mind rest and slip away into a darkness of my own making.

CHAPTER 59

THE RIVERSIDE

JACK TANNER

JUNE 2, 2022, RED AGES

Ernesto and I get out of the car at Phantom Island. "The boy was kidnapped from here. He was found in front of the Cock and Bull Tap. Half Moon River runs from one location to the next. Blackwater can portal, so he may not have used the river, but he may be anywhere along the river."

Ernesto stands in his casual blue linen suit, his elegance and grace belying his predatory nature. He looks up and down the river, sniffing the air, cocking his ear to hear. He says, "Then we must search all along the river and every building between here and the Tap to start. We should search three houses deep on each side."

I nod and add, "We should search every structure on the properties, not just the houses, and listen to the ground near the structures. We don't know if the center point is Phantom Island or the Cock and Bull Tap, so we need to search south of Phantom Island and north of the Cock and Bull Tap. He can portal two to three miles, so we will need to go that far. But I think the stretch of river between the island and the Tap holds the most promise, so we should start there."

Ernesto looks at me closely for a moment and says, "I know she is very important to you, Señor."

At his words, all the feelings I've been keeping at bay in order to function come flooding into me again. My throat thickens. I turn away from Ernesto and try to control my emotions. Then I look him steadily in the eyes and say simply, "She is my light, nothing more and nothing less." I take a deep breath. "We must find her. I'll take this side; you take the other side of the river. We will go three miles past where it hits the Red Wood Cemetery."

Ernesto and I move at an impossible pace, searching up and down the river all night. We look for tracks, scent the ground by the river, and check the perimeter of every structure for scent or sound. We listen to the earth. We pause only to be sure of the scents we run into. We check both sides of the river with Ernesto on one side and me on the other.

    With every unsuccessful minute that passes, I'm ripping further in two. We must find her. We must find her. Her name swims in my head like a beautiful chant. *Blue. Blue. Blue.* It taunts me and tantalizes me, urging me on. When I start to feel desolate, I think of the glow of her beautiful light the day I held her in my arms, and I feel hope again. That's what she is to me. She is my light and my hope.

CHAPTER 60

STRENGTHENING THE SOUL

BLUEBELL KILDARE

JUNE 3, 2022, RED AGES

I wake up gasping for breath again with cold water dripping down my face and running in rivulets between my breasts. This time, at least, I don't imagine I'm drowning. Blackwater stands in front of me grinning with an empty bucket again.

My shivering is uncontrollable, and I can't tell if it's from the cold water, the cold air, loss of blood, or an infection setting in. I speak through a chattering jaw, "Have you come to taunt me?"

Blackwater sets the bucket down and straightens. Clasping his hands together in front of him, he rocks back and forth on his heels like an excited schoolboy. His thin, bony face seems almost jovial in a perverted way. His cruel mouth twists into a semblance of a grin as he says in a singsong voice, "Taunt is such a negative word. I like to think of it as plucking the juicy fruits that life throws my way." Then he leers up and down my naked body with his gaze lingering long at my breasts. "And you are a very juicy fruit."

Another wave of chills runs through my body, this time for an entirely different reason. I want to cower away, but there is nowhere to hide. I avoid Blackwater's gaze when it finally makes its way toward my face, and I look beyond him instead. The firefly lantern is hanging on the wall reminding me I need to take advantage of the light. I tilt my head back. That small movement causes my back to move, and pain rips through me. I grit my teeth and pretend I'm trying to let the water run off my face.

There are several beams across the ceiling. My chains are attached to the beams via a wide band of iron going around them. A large closed loop is attached to each band, securing the chains. There are no bolts in sight, so they must be on the ceiling side of the beams. My chains are made of thick loops of iron, not soldered, but so thick it would be impossible for me to loosen them. What I wouldn't give for some superhuman Vampire strength right now. The beam is supported by the rock and dirt walls, and it in turn supports loosely fitted, rotting boards that make the ceiling. The boards keep the dirt mostly at bay but let water through. I wonder how far underground I am. Far enough for no screams to be heard. But how far is that? A few feet? Ten or more? Screams. He was afraid of screams, which is why this place is underground.

I'm still pretending to shake water off my face when suddenly I see water flying at me again. This time, because my head is tilted up, the water goes down my nose and into my lungs. I whip my head down and curl over, coughing and hacking to get the water out of my lungs. Pain surges over me with each cough because my entire body has to move. When my lungs finally clear, I stand straight again, which comes at no small price, and glare at Blackwater from under dripping hair. "What was that for? I'm already awake."

Blackwater sneers, "You stink."

"Of course I do. You've left me no option but to pee myself. Leave one of your buckets by my feet and I'll use that."

Blackwater looks at me askance. "Do you think I am a chambermaid to carry your slop out for you?"

I look at his fine trousers and white dress shirt with gold cufflinks and the odd brilliance in his eye. I can sense his emotions permeating the air. He exudes irrational fearlessness and can hardly contain his excitement. Is his excitement about getting the amulet or about hurting me? Perhaps both. His soul taints the room with a cloying, black choking feeling that is twisted and unnatural. I wonder how he can be so sick and still keep up appearances.

I retort, "Do you expect me to be alive long enough to fill it to overflowing?"

I can see Blackwater's dark eyes glinting as he ponders this. I wait expectantly for the answer.

He says, "Very well then."

I bite my lip as I now realize how limited my days are. Should I just give him the damn amulet and try to get it back later? No, he didn't free Jason when Jason found the amulet for him. I am so cold, and my back hurts so much, but my survival instincts require I push on. I study the stone walled room then the face of Tobias Blackwater with his maniacal demeanor and crazy gleam in his eyes. I wonder if these are my last days and this is my grave.

"Tell me, how were you able to use Jason to get the amulet?"

Blackwater's eyes dance merrily and the air fills with the waves of his madness as he answers, "Jason had the ability to amplify magic. I can portal, and I had a very powerful scrying mirror. Very simple recipe."

I decide to try to stroke his ego in an attempt to get information. He seems bright, but he is clearly not right in the head. "That's impressive, finding the tools to locate the amulet, especially since it was so carefully hidden. No doubt hundreds of powerful sorcerers have tried to find it over time. So what went wrong that Jason was able to escape?" This is a lot to say with my body shivering. I'm almost thankful for the cold as it has a numbing effect.

Blackwater laughs mockingly, catching onto my ruse. "He escaped in a way you couldn't possibly accomplish, my dear Bluebell. He used his amplification powers to grab on to my portal magic while I was finishing a shift, and it carried him out of here."

I feel another nail in my coffin. I obviously can't use Jason's method of escaping after all.

Blackwater's laughter trails off, and his face turns unnaturally dark as his mercurial mood shifts yet again. He mutters, "He was quite a talented boy. It's a shame because I had planned such great uses for him."

Then Blackwater steps up to me and raises his arm. I flinch, but I can't move far. I watch his eyes squint and his mouth purse in a scowl as he hauls off and hits me. My head snaps to the right at the force of his arm.

Blood flows down my nose freely. I lift my head and look him in the eyes. "What was that for?"

Blackwater rubs his temples like he has a headache and frowns. "I was not happy about losing Jason."

I feel the mood in the air shift, and Blackwater's spirits lift as he turns taunting again. "Your dear Vampire lover and that dago detective you have wrapped around your finger are looking for you." Blackwater laughs softly. "They aren't even close, and because I jump here, there is no way for them to follow me. Even that damn animal of yours can't sniff a trail to us. But isn't it so good to know your loved ones are trying so valiantly and so uselessly to find you?"

He's trying to hurt me. I won't give him the satisfaction. I say, "Yes. Thank you, Blackwater. How kind of you to let me know I'm missed."

Blackwater scowls and says, "Now, let's get down to business."

He circles around me, pausing at my back, which causes me to flinch. He comes back to face me, "You passed out last time and I had to stop. No enjoyment that way, certainly." Then he starts speaking clinically as though I am a hunk of meat. "Your back is a swollen mass of black bruises with eleven gashes where the skin has been ripped off or split."

He reaches behind his back for the whip and waves it in my direction. I watch it shimmy through the air, undulating back and forth, mesmerizing me like a snake. "Bluebell, are you ready to tell me where the amulet is?"

Every time he asks me, I feel like I have a new chance to tell him and get out of here. But I remind myself there will be no getting out of here by his hands. "Why do you want the amulet?"

Blackwater grins maniacally, making his bony cheeks and long nose stand out, and his mood elevates again to elation. His rapidly oscillating mood swings tell a tale of his madness louder than a herald. His voice rises to a higher pitch, and his sing-song voice says, "Imagine a world where the natural order is restored, Bluebell. Where the magically Gifted, who are now scorned and ridiculed, rise up and take power from mediocrity. Imagine a world where Vampires are controlled and are no longer a threat to the magically Gifted."

"That is a grand dream, Blackwater. How will this happen?"

Blackwater raises his arm to me and brings it down even harder this time. He shouts in fury, "We will make it happen!"

My neck jerks back as I feel first the shock of pain, then the wet, thick oozing of blood that drips straight down to my mouth. I tilt my forehead forward, hoping the blood will make it to the floor. I scream inside my mind in frustration. I can't even wipe my face.

Then Blackwater smiles a sickly sweet smile. "Your time is up, Bluebell. Where is the amulet?"

I close my eyes, knowing the agony that is about to come, but I keep in my mind's eye the fact that my flesh and will are all that stands between this man and the death of millions of innocent people. I wish I could ignore this fact, but I can't. In my mind I see thousands of strangers, people who I've passed on the street or seen in a shop. It could be any of them, all of them. He could hurt small children, the sick, the elderly.

I open my eyes and look steadily at Blackwater as I ask softly, "What amulet?"

Blackwater's eyes flash with savagery as he spits out, "You intend to play that game again, do you? Well, I'm happy to oblige."

He is angry again. I've lost track of how many times he has switched between angry to gleeful in the past five minutes.

He once again walks around to my back. "Let's see how many you can take tonight."

I take a deep breath as questions and answers swirl in my mind. Should I tell him? Maybe if I tell him he will set me free. No, he will not let me live, and he will hurt many people if he gets the chance. I can't do it. I'm not going to tell him.

I hear the whip move through the air, and it lands on my back, tender, enflamed, and broken from the night before. I arch in pain.

"One!" he shouts gleefully.

He strikes again.

"Two!" This time he's counting the lashes out loud. "Three! Four!"

I keep thinking of where the amulet is as if that is my salvation, but I'm so delirious with pain I'm afraid I might accidentally tell him. So I rip my mind away from that thought and start repeating my mantra in my head. *What amulet? What amulet?*

The whip keeps falling, and I arch with each hit. My muscles are so swollen from the last set of lashes that each hit now ruptures muscle cells. I can feel my flesh being pulverized.

"Five! Six! Seven!"

The whip has broken all of the scabs that formed overnight and is now meeting raw muscle with blood flowing freely.

"Eight! Nine! Ten!"

I'm surprised I have any skin left on my back, but pieces of skin are being torn off with each lash. The pain is so great I can't tell where a hit lands anymore.

What amulet? What amulet?

Blackwater comes around to my front. "Where is the amulet?" he asks.

I whisper with all the strength I have left, "What amulet?"

Blackwater purses his lips, but a tiny smile starts to lift the corners of his mouth. Then he moves behind me again. His anger at me for denying him what he wants is now warring with his twisted joy at causing me pain.

"Eleven! Twelve!"

I'm gasping for breath. My eyes are squeezed shut. My teeth are clenched. The pain racks through me as the whip laces its course across my back.

"Thirteen! Fourteen!"

I still fear I might shout out the location of the amulet the next time Blackwater asks, so I keep desperately chanting my refrain in my head: *What amulet? What amulet?* I repeat this litany until these are the only words I can remember. The lashes keep raining down.

"Eighteen! Nineteen! Twenty! Where is the amulet?"

I hang limply from the chains like a rag doll now and whisper, "What amulet?

So Blackwater continues. "Twenty-one! Twenty-two!"

The pain is so great my mind can scarcely understand it all. The electric impulses ripping through my body to my brain are coming so fast my brain can't decipher one lash from the next.

"Twenty-seven! Twenty-eight!"

I let my sixth sense float away from my body so I can bear the pain. I feel the filthy, cloying mass that is Blackwater's soul, and instinctively draw away from him. I expand my sense forward. I reach for the small animals behind the walls and down the tunnels. They are starving, but their souls are bright and good. I am so weak.

"Twenty-nine! Thirty! Where is the amulet?"

I hear the question as if coming from a dream. I feel my physical self barely breathe out, "What amulet?"

I realize my body hangs limp in the chains, struggling for breath under the wrath of the whip, but my real self seems to be the part that is exploring for light, searching for strength. I wrap myself around the soul of a rat and hold tight, seeking comfort and fortitude in its light.

Then I sense a much greater source of light above.

"Thirty-four! Thirty-five!"

I expand through the dirt, past the surface of the ground. I feel so thin now. My soul is weakening due to the failing body it's still attached to. I'm ravenous for that light. I can't reach it; it's so high up in the sky. So I call to it. I beckon it with my soul.

"Fifty! Fifty-one!"

With a tiny part of my mind I realize Blackwater hasn't asked about the amulet for a while. I feel a small amount of light from the source in the sky reach down and meld with my own. I pull a little bit of that light down into my essence. I feel myself burning brighter as it strengthens me. I don't hear Blackwater counting anymore. He must be done.

I am loath to turn off my sixth sense because I know the pain will be immense. But I know I must. It's risky for my soul to be so separate from my body when I'm in such danger of dying. I pull myself into my core and feel myself snap back into my body.

My senses come alive, and I'm suddenly aware of my body again. I gasp and throw my head back in a scream, but before the sound is even out of my mouth, my brain is so overwhelmed by the pain that darkness takes me immediately.

CHAPTER 61

AN ERRANT WOLF

JACK TANNER

JUNE 3, 2022, RED AGES

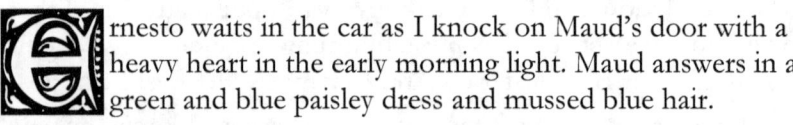rnesto waits in the car as I knock on Maud's door with a heavy heart in the early morning light. Maud answers in a green and blue paisley dress and mussed blue hair.

Maud looks surprised to see me and says, "Hello, Jack. What are you doing here?" Then she puts her hand to her mouth, and I can see her face filling with a profound grief and horror. The only other time I knocked on her door was when I told her that her husband had died in the line of duty.

Quickly I say, "No, Maud. We don't know that yet."

Maud steels herself and says, "What do you know, Jack?"

"Blue was taken by Tobias Blackwater. He's the perpetrator in the crime we're investigating. He portaled her away, but we don't know to where. This happened yesterday morning. We've searched all day and night and will continue to search until we find her."

Maud takes a moment to digest this, her skin pale with shock. Then, apparently remembering her manners, she says, "Would you like to come in?"

"I don't have time. I wanted to ask if she told you anything about the case."

Maud steps back a little, and I see her hand shake as she holds the door. She says, "No. Blue is always silent about her work. She only told me she had a case where terrible things were done to a young boy."

I nod. Maud knows the bare minimum, which only tells me Blue was conscientious about following the rules of a case. I would expect nothing less from Blue.

Maud looks up at me and says, "How can I help?"

I think about it for a moment and then say, "Varg was with her, but

Blackwater only took Blue; he didn't take Varg. Varg stayed with Gambino for only a few minutes, and then he took off. I believe he must be hunting for Blue. Varg may have some special powers of his own. I'm not sure it was an accident he happened upon her in the alley the other day. If I am right about his special powers, he may have been looking specifically for her."

Maud looks at me with intelligent eyes. "And if he found her the first time, he might find her again?"

"Yes. I can't chase after him myself, but I think it would be worthwhile if someone did."

Maud nods. "I'll find him. You concentrate on bringing Blue back. Let me have your number and I'll give you mine."

Maud runs into the house, and when she returns she hands me a slip of paper with her number on it. I hand her my card, then turn quickly to leave. As I do, I hear Maud whisper from over my shoulder, "You had better find her, Jack Tanner."

CHAPTER 62

RUNNING IN CIRCLES

JACK TANNER

JUNE 3, 2022, RED AGES

Ernesto and I pull in the library parking lot to meet Gambino and Xavier.

I look to Gambino and ask, "Did you find anything?"

Gambino's face is drawn, and he looks unusually pale. "No, damn it. We found nothing but some properties out of state. I still have a guy sifting through the files for any signs of other local property."

I walk over to a tree next to the parking lot and pound my fist on it. The tree shakes root to leaf, and thousands of blossom petals float lazily down to the ground. I pound my fist some more. Then I straighten and take a couple of calming, deep breaths. I don't need to breathe, being a Vampire, but it does help relax the body. When I turn around, I see Xavier and Gambino staring at me with looks of concern and grief on their faces.

I flash my eyes at them in anger. "Don't grieve her yet."

Gambino realizes he'd been doing just that, and an abashed look comes over his face.

"Gambino, I know you want to be on the ground with us searching, but that's not the best place for you. We are far better suited for finding a scent trail than you are. But while we're busy here, we need a real detective going over Blackwater's files, searching for any clues."

Gambino says, "I know. We have half the force looking out for Tobias Blackwater by car. If we find him, we find her. There are enough men on the ground."

I watch as Gambino turns toward his car. He obviously did not sleep last night and is tired and worn.

I turn and address Xavier. "We're going to search the city, house to house. But we are not entering, so I don't need your help right now.

What I do need is for you to go into the office and keep it running while Ernesto and I are out here. We can't leave it unattended for days on end. Call Mike and ask for some assistance with the Dark Vampire cases. He will send someone out to take over for Ernesto while we are engaged here. Also, check on Rubalia to make sure she got the assistance she needs to do her research. Brainstorm with her and keep working any aspect of this case you can think of. She's an invaluable asset."

Xavier looks disappointed he can't come with us but also proud I'm asking him to step in like that. He nods and says, "I've brought a cooler of blood. I'll move it to your trunk."

"Thank you."

I pull out my city map and place it on the hood. I draw a three mile radius around Phantom Island. I show Ernesto and Xavier. "We'll start here. You take the east side, Ernesto, and I'll take the west side. We're going to hit every structure in this area. Circle around each building looking for Blue's or Blackwater's scent. Listen for either of their voices. Go block by block. We will start on the south end and work our way north. When we are done, we'll go to the Cock and Bull Tap and start over there. But first we need to replenish ourselves."

Xavier takes his cue and pulls the cooler out of his car. I transfer it to my trunk. Handing four bags to Ernesto and keeping the same for myself, we drink it quickly as Xavier pulls out of the lot.

CHAPTER 63

USING THE LIGHT

BLUEBELL KILDARE

JUNE 3, 2022, RED AGES

I feel myself drifting awake, but the pain is so great, I will myself back to oblivion. I can't face it. I drift in and out with the pain both rousing me and making me unconscious as I become aware of it. One time I think I feel something gnawing on my foot. I feebly try to kick at it. I drift away again. Again I feel pain in my foot. I kick again.

A sharp pain in my foot finally drags me to a consciousness I'm loath to enter. I flare out my other sense at it. There are three small souls gnawing at my feet. I push against their souls, beating them with my light, driving them back. I drift back into dark again, but this time it's a real sleep, not unconsciousness. They do not return.

I wake dripping in icy water again. I stand weakly in my chains with my head bent, my legs hardly able to hold my weight.

Blackwater says, "Bluebell. I wish I had more time to spend with you, but I'm afraid you have to leave me today."

I lift my wobbly head to look at him, curious, but not hopeful. No, I know better than that.

"I brought a present for you." Blackwater mocks as he pulls a gun from behind his back. "Look, your gun. How kind of you to give it to me yesterday."

Then he snaps the whip with his right hand. His tone changes and becomes sharp and angry. "Today is going to be your last day, Bluebell. But since I'm generous, you have a choice of deaths. You can tell me where the amulet is and die by your own gun. Think how poetic that would be—a familiar friend ending your torment. Or you can die by the whip."

I can sense anger from him, but also fear and panic. I can't sense any delight this time.

I ask with a trembling voice, "What has changed?" I can't quite make the sounds come out of my throat the way I want. I am just too weak, I think, from fever and loss of blood.

Blackwater says defensively, "What do you mean?"

I whisper, "On the outside. Suddenly you are hurried and desperate. You're on the run. What has changed?" I breathe heavily after saying that much. My knees falter and I start to slip, but I steady myself.

Blackwater says, "I have people to answer to Bluebell. You've made things difficult for me. Your lover and your dago partner have also made things difficult. I'll have to change things today, and that, my dear, means that we will be ending our little affair first. Either I will have the amulet and you will die relatively pain-free, or I enjoy one last therapeutic session with you and then you die. Either way, you are not waking to the next sunrise."

I nod and answer, "I'll not seek to hurry my own death. You'll have to use the whip."

Blackwater is furious at this. He wants control, but every maneuver he makes to gain what he seeks glances off me. He can't comprehend why I would seek a death of lingering pain over one of speed. It appears he thought there was no chance I would deny him.

Blackwater says, "Be that as it may, I will lie the gun by the wall." He sets it down about eight feet in front of me. "If you call on me to stop, as long as you tell me where the amulet is, I'll switch weapons at any point."

I say politely and softly, "Thank you, but you needn't have bothered." I muse at how I have answered him with no more emotion than if he had offered me a cup of tea. I must already be disengaging from this life.

Blackwater says, "I'm curious Bluebell. What drives your choices?"

I whisper slowly, "I walk the path of light. I will not divert. You walk the path of darkness. You will not understand. You want to control the Vampires by their mark of Lilith?" I pause and take several breaths, then continue on. "But you've already been marked by Lilith for some time now, Blackwater. I see the stinking, oily black muck on your soul. How much more does she own you, who earned her mark so willingly by your own deeds, than the Daylight Vampires who had her mark foisted upon them? Their mark is external, but your mark comes from the center of your soul."

I pause again as my breath comes in short pants. "It might be true I will die by your hands today, Blackwater. If so, today you will reaffirm your place with Lilith in the Plane of Fire."

I see something deep flash in Blackwater's eyes, and uneasiness flows from him, then doubt, and finally denial rises in him. As I expected, he is too mad, too corrupt to see the truth or change his course.

Blackwater walks behind me. I feel the first lash cutting across my raw, exposed muscle and slicing through me. It registers as a new streak of pain racing across my back and into my brain, screaming louder than the rest of the signals of pain, but not alone. It is a chorus of pain. There has been no end to my pain for so long now.

I don't wait this time. I push my other self out of my body. I know my soul is connected too thinly to my body because I move out of it too easily. I expand outward, desperately looking for strength. I reach up to the light, sending tendrils of my soul's light toward the sky. I narrow my light so my reach can go further and further. The thin stream of light pours up to the sky and beyond. That tiny, thin thread of light passes the moon and the stars heading upward toward the glow until they join as though meeting in a welcome embrace. Energy shoots back down the thread and starts filling my soul back up. My soul glows brighter. What was once a thin veil of light becomes a great glare.

I look back over the room, and can see myself separated from my body except for a thin strand of light connecting my body to my soul. My soul, my real self, floats in the corner of the room as I watch Blackwater. I can feel his fear and anger as he drives the lash into me again and again. I can see the blood coming off my back, splattering Blackwater's arms and body.

I turn toward the light in the space beyond the sky again, and I think about Maud and how much I will miss her crazy hair and her crazy stories. I think about Alexis and how kind she's been to me. I think about Jack, who is so hard on himself. I regret losing the promise of what had been evolving between us, a promise like a brilliant green shoot popping out of brown earth in the spring.

As the light from the place beyond the sky continues to fill me, my light grows brighter and brighter until I can hardly see the room anymore. I feel so filled with energy and light. I think of all the people I am protecting. I think of the countless babies and children who will live a relatively safe life because I am dying. I think of the mothers and the fathers who will continue being mothers and fathers. I think of all the Vampires who are without blame and how their torment will not grow worse here on Earth because of me. I accept my losses and I willingly trade them for these gifts.

CHAPTER 64

CRYPT

JACK TANNER

JUNE 3, 2022, RED AGES

fter searching most of the three mile radius around Phantom Island, we have moved slightly south of the Cock and Bull Tap. Large silver clouds reflect hidden sunrays, and a storm gathers in the air. The sun is setting to my left. Red streaks the sky as the final rays of light dip behind the house-lined street. The houses are sparser here with multi-acre lots dotted with obscure structures. There are plenty of barns, sheds, chicken coops—a lot of places to hide a small woman. Animals are harder to deceive than humans are, which makes navigating the country setting in stealth more challenging.

A call comes in while I'm in the middle of scenting the perimeter of a large, old farm house about twenty blocks from the Cock and Bull. My phone is on vibrate, but still the hound dog sitting on the porch hears it, then catches my scent. He starts barking and howling as he bounds for me.

I run a few blocks away as I press the phone to my ear.

"Jack," Maud says, "we spotted Varg heading north on Swain Road. He was at the corner of Swain and Gilson. We lost him when he crossed some properties, and it's getting dark now. I'm sorry we didn't find him earlier."

"You did great, Maud. I'm headed that way. I'll see if I can catch up with him."

I head west, then north, running between old homes and over large yards with my sword softly bouncing across my back. I jump over a stone wall and keep going.

After a minute my phone rings again, and I click it on while I run.

Gambino's voice holds a hint of reserved hope. "We found some old files in Blackwater's family archive. The family owns several plots at the Red Wood Cemetery. Of course half the town owns plots at that cemetery. But it was close to where Jason was found, so it might be worth checking out.

"Thanks," I say, not wanting to think of Blue and burial plots at the same time. "Text me the numbers of the plots."

Gambino says, "I'm already on my way, so I'll point them out for you."

Just then, Rubalia chimes me. I pop open the cover to open the line.

"Jack!" she says excitedly. "I called the local cemeteries and found that he owns a few plots at Red Wood. A large, gray mausoleum sits on one of those plots."

My heart lifts at this news. It can't be coincidence they both called me at the same time about the same thing.

"Call Ernesto and have him meet me there." I flip the ring closed and take off running at great speed toward the cemetery.

As I close in on the cemetery, the final rays of sunshine disappear. I see a thin but brilliant bluish white beam of light shooting out from the ground toward the sky. I would know that light anywhere.

I race to the place where the light shines out of the ground, and the implications stun me. There is nothing but dirt there. Surely she's not buried?

My heart screams as I frantically look around. There are many mausoleums, and I don't know which one is Blackwater's. With no other viable options, I desperately start digging at the earth where the beam emerges. I feel like I'm losing my mind at the horror of wondering if Blue is buried alive. With my bare hands I start heaving up huge chunks of dirt when some headlights drive right up on the cemetery grounds.

Gambino steps out of the car. "Jesus, Mary, and Joseph!" He runs to me.

Just then a brilliant flash of lightning strikes, illuminating the cemetery, and a movement catches my eye. Varg's shiny fur reflects the lightning with an unearthly glow as he runs across the cemetery toward us. I keep digging, unwilling to slow down, but keep one eye trained on him. His nose is low, and he is tracking at high speed. He stops at a large mausoleum and claws the door snarling. That is all the clue I need, so I run over to it, tearing the door off the hinges. Gambino pivots and follows us.

Inside are two caskets. I break the seals and throw them open, one after the other. Nothing but the rotten scent of the long-dead remains. I look to Varg. He is clawing at a break in the floor. It's a hatch, so I rip it open and see a stairway to what must be a crypt below. I fly down two flights of stairs at my fastest speed. Gambino follows as fast as he can. Varg is ahead of him.

I run down a long, dark hall, pulling my sword out as I go. A light shines from an entrance to the left. Moving faster than the human eye, I enter the room. The room is awash in a bluish white light. Blackwater has a whip raised over Blue, and she hangs lifelessly in chains. He looks at me, and before he can even open his mouth to scream I have slashed his entire hand off the end of his arm with the tip of my sword. His hand, with his fingers still curled around the whip, drops uselessly toward the floor.

Before it even reaches the ground I have reached Blue. Her heart is not beating. I rip open my wrist and press it to her mouth. I hear Blackwater behind me release a high pitched scream of agony. Then there's a rush of wind as Varg flies through the air toward Blackwater with a savage snarl. I hear his fangs slicing repeatedly through skin and bone, and more snarling and screaming, and I am glad. I am so glad. When silence ensues, I know Varg has finished Tobias Blackwater. I slit my wrist again because it has healed already, and I reapply it to Blue's mouth.

As soon as Gambino enters the room, his eyes run over the chains still connecting Blue to the ceiling and floor. He sees her lifeless body and me forcing blood down her throat. The look of grief returns to his face. He stops and calls an ambulance.

I slit my wrist again, deeper this time, pumping my fist to keep the blood flowing out. Then Gambino walks around Blue as I continue to work feverishly on her. When he sees her back, his face turns ashen and he steps back, bracing himself against the wall. He turns to the side and vomits.

Just then, Ernesto arrives. He rips the chains off the bolts above her arms and legs, careful not to jar her.

I am murmuring, "Live. Live. Please live."

Gambino eventually looks away from Blue and toward Varg and the remains of Blackwater. Blackwater's neck is ripped open, and his face is a lacework of gashes. Varg is sitting by Blue, whining softly now.

All of this is happening, and it is registering faintly in my mind, but just barely. My entire being is focused on getting blood into Blue's system. I slit my wrist yet again, even deeper this time. I must get more blood into her. I am sitting with her in a pool of her blood, spread all over the cement pad beneath us. She has lost so much. I massage her neck, trying to mechanically get the blood down.

When the chains are fully removed, I gently sit her down, careful not to touch her back in any way because there are strips of muscle, barely connected, hanging from her. I continue pressing my wrist to her mouth and massaging her neck up and down. Work, damn it! Work!

I look up and see her beautiful light in the corner. She is slipping away. Something in my heart springs up, and I reject that completely, with every ounce of feeling I have. I will not let her go!

I look straight into her shining, brilliant light, and I start yelling, "Blue. Don't you dare die on me now. Blue. Come back! Come back! Blue, Varg needs you. Maud needs you. Please. I beg you. I need you!"

CHAPTER 65

CHOOSING

BLUEBELL KILDARE

JUNE 3, 2022, RED AGES

Something in the room catches my attention. I see movement and hear a voice shouting a word I know. I know it, but can't remember what it means. It feels like it's coming from down a long, long tunnel.

I move closer to hear. I think that's my name. I think that's what people called me while I was there.

I move a bit closer. I know that voice. It's Jack. Jack is the good one. The one I trust.

I can barely see him through my light. He has his hand held over my mouth. Not really my mouth anymore, but the mouth of the body that used to be mine. It sits on the ground now. Jack is supporting it by the neck. The head is lolled back, and his hand is over my mouth. But he's looking at me. The real me. My light. And he is shouting. He isn't looking at my body. He's seeing my soul up above my body in the corner of the room.

He is shouting, "Blue. Don't you dare die on me now. Blue. Come back! Come back! Blue, Varg needs you. Maud needs you. Please. I beg you. I need you!"

Some of my light fades, and I am able to see the room better. I wonder what Jack is doing with his hand over my body's mouth. I get closer and see he's squeezing blood into it from a wound on his wrist. Ohh, he's hurt!

I get a little closer. Now he is rubbing the body's throat, but he's still looking at me, the real me. He looks straight at me, and I look at him. I look right into his eyes, and he looks pained and happy at the same time. He says, "That's right, come back to me, beautiful. It's Jack. Come back to me, Blue."

I feel a longing to be with him rise up inside of me so I drift a little closer still. Then suddenly the darkness takes me again.

CHAPTER 66

HOPING

JACK TANNER

JUNE 4, 2022, RED AGES

I pace back and forth in the lobby of the surgery ward while strangers try to piece Blue back together. I've seen a lot of carnage in my life, much worse than yesterday, but nothing has ever affected me so much as seeing Blue's skin missing and the insides of her flesh exposed with bone and sinew in clear view. I'd give her my own skin to heal her wounds if I could.

I pull my hands away from my head when I realize not only am I running my fingers through my hair, but I'm actually tugging on it and pulling some out. I tuck my fingers in my trouser pockets.

Strangers with no idea how important Blue is to the supernatural breeds and to all humanity are putting her back together as though she's just another person. Strangers who have no understanding of how my life would rip apart. They would lose two souls if they lost one.

I stand before the window. I vow if she dies on that table, I will hunt down each person in that room and rip them to pieces.

I feel a gentle hand on my arm. I turn and see Maud looking at me with grieving, pale green eyes and her wide lips pinched.

"Any word?" she asks.

I put my hand on her shoulder. "Not yet. They just started."

She turns away from me and sits in one of the upholstered waiting room chairs, wrapping a paisley shawl tightly around her shoulders, looking small and frail and all of her age. Her blue hair has faded to a light pastel color, her nail polish is chipped, and her dress wrinkled. I know her disarray is a measure of her love for Blue. I sit next to her and look at my hands. A few strands of my hair are still stuck to my fingers. I gently pull them off and watch them float to the floor. We must be quite a sight, the two of us.

The hours pass and still we sit together, silently, side-by-side, watching the doorway, waiting for word. A white clock hangs on the far end of the room against a beige wall with stark, black hands ticking interminably forward. Along the wall I'm facing, the paint is old and chipped along the rubber baseboards, three and a quarter inches from the right corner. The floor is made of green and blue speckled linoleum tiles. The third, seventeenth, and fifty-fourth tiles have chips in them and need replacing. I trace their outlines with my eyes, listening to the faint sound of the clock ticking over the much louder sound of Maud's breathing and her rapidly beating heart. Maud smells of roses and lilacs, overlaying the tangy smell of her thinning blood.

As I begin to count the freckles on Maud's arm for the third time, Alexis comes rushing in. "No word yet?" she asks, out of breath.

I shake my head as Maud looks up. Maud reaches out her hand to Alexis, and Alexis comes forward, opening up both arms. Maud stands and silently steps into them. Alexis wraps her arms around Maud, gently soothing her, rubbing her back. After a few moments Alexis pulls back and says, "Why don't we go get a nice cup of tea from the café and maybe a sandwich."

Maud says, "I'm not hungry."

I interject, "Her stomach has growled seventeen times in the last hour."

Maud glares at me, and Alexis nods over the top of Maud's head. Without waiting for a reply from Maud, she pulls her along and out the door.

The clock keeps ticking. I add it to my list of things to destroy if Blue doesn't make it. I'm deep in my fantasy of how I will dissemble and crush the various parts of the object that marked the last hours of Blue's life when I get a surprise visitor.

Dragomira walks in wearing a beautiful cream dress and an exotic, red embroidered scarf floats behind her. Always one for the dramatic, that female. Her eyes are a bright blue today. She takes Maud's chair next to me after surveying the empty waiting room.

"Can you tell me what happened?" she asks.

I wonder absently how Dragomira found us. I never called her. Perhaps she counts clairvoyance among her many skills. "How did you know we were here?"

Dragomira says, "It was on the news."

Oh. I would be embarrassed, but I can't bring myself to care.

"Then you know Tobias Blackwater was the man looking for the amulet?"

When she nods, I go on.

"He had her chained in a crypt and was flaying her to death. He had already torn through her skin and muscle and was ripping into her spinal bone when I finally found her."

Dragomira winces.

"Her heart wasn't beating."

Dragomira puts her hand on my arm.

"She is alive now. I gave her some of my blood."

Dragomira looks up sharply at this.

I say, "Of course I didn't turn her."

Relief washes over her face. Then Dragomira says, "If you are done answering my questions before I ask them, I'd like to know about her light. What happened?"

"Her soul was separated from her body when I arrived, only connected by a very thin strand. Her light was brilliant. She was deep underground, several stories down, but I could see her light through the earth, a thin beam pushing straight up into the sky, going even beyond my eyesight, past the moon. She was leaving this life. I called her and called her, she must have heard me because she moved closer and closer. Then all of a sudden her heart began to beat, and the center of her light popped right back into her body."

Dragomira's eyes shift from vivid blue to deep purple with a fiery red gleam in their depths. "Do you still need a test to know she's the Illustrissima? Do you doubt she's the Bright One, the Shining One we have been waiting for?"

Sadly, I don't. I hang my head. "No."

"You did a wonderful job, Jack. You found her and saved her."

I shake my head and say, "I failed as a guardian. I didn't even kill Tobias Blackwater. Her wolf did. I should never have put her on this job on her own. She should have had a partner the whole way."

Dragomira reaches out and touches my shoulder. "No, Jack. There are parts of this journey she will have to travel on her own. You should be her guardian and partner as much as you can now and watch her closer, but she has much to learn. She will not learn it all under your shadow. Nor will she want to. Just remember, you're the one who called her back. And what is more important, you're the person she returned for."

I look up as she stands to leave. "She will make it, Jack."

"How do you know?"

"I know."

I dip my head back down to look at the speckled tiles again. I don't lift it until Alexis and Maud walk back in with Gambino close on their heels.

Gambino asks, "How is she?"

I stand up and shake his hand in greeting. "No word. She's been in surgery for six hours now."

Maud and Alexis sit across from us. Gambino takes a deep breath and sits in Maud's chair. He looks rough. His jacket is thrown over his arm, and his dress shirt and slacks are wrinkled. His tie is pulled loose.

Gambino shakes his head. "I've never seen anything like that before." He looks at me through puffy eyes. "Her muscle was hanging off the bone in strips. Blood all over the floor. Thank God you were there to give her your blood. Do you think she has a chance?"

"She'd better have a chance."

Gambino asks, "Did you hear that Varg chased after the ambulance as soon as it took off?"

"No. I hadn't heard. But I'm not worried about him. He's found her twice; he'll find her again."

Gambino nods. "Well, we've made quite an uproar at the precinct and the City Council. The mayor is on his way back from vacation. The Chief had to speak to news reporters. The story is all over the country. Human rights groups are crawling all over us, as though owning house slaves is a sanctioned activity in our city. The Dilectus Deo are staging protests all over town, using the opportunity to gain new recruits, and apparently ignoring the fact that two of Blackwater's victims were Gifted. We had a few wackos calling about an alien spacecraft and beams of light. Thankfully, we are also making a lot of people happy by telling them their stolen magical artifacts have been found."

That raises an alarm in my head. "Have you returned the artifacts yet?"

Gambino squints his eyes and looks at me. "No. Why?"

"Because all the items were stolen by a Gifted person and all are magical artifacts. The Bureau should be handling that rather than the precinct. I would have an expert do a complete inventory to make sure none of the elements are forbidden. Then I would put several magical tests to anyone who showed up claiming to be the owner. The precinct isn't capable of handling that. Those objects are likely to be powerful and should not get in the wrong hands. All you will do is check an ID."

Gambino takes this in and ruminates a moment. "I can have the pieces transferred to you."

"Better yet, I'll have my men Xavier and Ernesto pick them up if you could please do the paperwork for the transfer."

Just as I finish speaking, a short doctor with dark frizzy hair and a long nose walks into the room. "Jack Tanner?"

I quickly step up. "I'm Jack Tanner." I can smell Blue's blood all over him, and my gut clenches.

He says, "I'm Dr. Ziggler. I just finished surgery on Bluebell."

I look back at the room and see all eyes glued on us. I turn back to Dr. Ziggler. "You can update us all, Doctor."

He clears his throat. "Bluebell Kildare has made it through the operation. She's in critical but stable condition, which is amazing given the condition she arrived in. She is a fighter. She required an emergency skin graft and countless sutures. She will need more surgeries and more skin grafts, but we need to get her strong now. That is our priority for the time being. She is deeply sedated because if she were to awaken now she would be in unbearable pain. We will keep her sedated for several days. For the time being, she is being cared for in intensive care, but if she does well, she may be moved to the burn ward."

"Why the burn ward?"

Dr. Ziggler says gently, "They have the most experience dealing with skin grafts and missing skin." Then he clears his throat again and says, "I would bring someone back to visit with her now, but we had a very unusual situation occur during the surgery."

I can feel the tension rise in the room, and I start glaring at the doctor.

He says, "No, nothing is wrong with Bluebell, beyond the obvious, of course. While I was doing surgery, an animal, either a wolf or a very large dog—it is hard to tell—walked right in the surgery room. I called a nurse in who tried to coax him out, but every time she got near him, he snarled at her. I couldn't stop my surgery, you understand, so I told the nurse to leave it. He just sat there passively as long as we left him alone. Do any of you know about this animal?"

I think we must have all been smiling a bit because Dr. Ziggler says, "I see you do know this animal."

Alexis speaks up. "Yes. He is Blue's animal, and he's a wolf. He is harmless unless you try to hurt Blue. I think it is a good idea to just let him be near her. He will get back to her even if you manage to remove him."

Dr. Ziggler's eyes open up wide, and I can see he is about to protest.

I say, "We will keep someone with her at all times to watch the wolf."

Dr. Ziggler nods and scratches his head. His frizzy hair bounces to and fro for a minute. "Okay. That will do. Right now only one person can sit with her at a time. If she gets moved to the burn ward, she can have two visitors at a time."

Dr. Ziggler looks at me, "Are you her next of kin?"

I don't know what to say. I look around at the room, at all the people who love her, all the hopeful, shining eyes.

I turn to Dr. Ziggler. "She's an orphan. We're all her next of kin."

Dr. Ziggler smiles. "Well who would like to go first?"

I turn around. "Maud?"

Maud sniffs and wipes her eyes. She pulls her shawl a little closer and stands up on shaky legs. I stride over to her and take her arm. When we reach Dr. Ziggler, she looks up at me and says, "I won't take long."

I nod and hand her off to Dr. Ziggler, who tucks her arm under his and walks through the swinging metal doors.

An hour later when Gambino takes his leave, I am the only one who hasn't visited Blue. I requested to go last because, I don't intend to leave her once I get into that room.

As Dr. Ziggler walks me back he says, "You have been very patient."

I mentally scoff at this because I may have waited, but I certainly haven't been patient.

At the end of the hall we come into a large, sterile room directly across from a nurse's station with glass windows so they can see right in. Blue is lying on her belly with her face turned to the side, and I see Varg's snout and front paws protruding from under the bed. He is a good guard dog, maybe even a better guardian than I am.

I bring my eyes back to Blue, whose breathing is shaky and laborious. Her eyes are closed. Her back is swathed in bandages that have spots of pink marring the surfaces already. I can see them through the slit in the back of the hospital gown. A light sheet covers her up to her waist.

I sit in a small, hard metal chair next to her. I'd rather stand, but here I can see her face better. I have been starving for the sight of her face. I marvel at the curve of her eyebrow and the length of her brown lashes lying on her cheek. One hand is splayed on the sheet, and I trace the outline of her lean, elegant fingers with my eyes. Her nails are always cut short and unpolished. I notice a tiny drip of drool coming out of the corner of her mouth. I grab a tissue from the counter and dab at it.

As I lean in close to her, I breathe in the smell of her rich, living blood, and the soft staccato of her heart fills me with joy. I sit back and wonder how I am ever going to have the strength to let her move forward into this very dangerous chess game laid on our table.

CHAPTER 67

AWAKENING

BLUEBELL KILDARE

JUNE 8 – JUNE 9, 2022, RED AGES

I become aware of the glow of souls around me and voices that seem far away. I concentrate on them, but the clearer the voices get and the closer the souls seem, the more distinctly I feel the throbbing pain in my back. I dive back into darkness.

I again become aware of noises, including a persistent beeping. My back is a constant knife of pain. I feel softness underneath me. I move my fingers slightly. It feels like cotton. I must not be in the room any more. How did I get out of the room? I was sure I would die in that room. I think about lifting my head or speaking, but I am too tired and in too much pain. I seek oblivion again.

I hear noises again. The pain is less now. A light shines through my eyelids. I know the light will be bright if I open my eyes. I'm lying belly down with my face turned sideways on a mattress. I blink my eyes open, but the light hurts them. I close them again. I try to squint them so I can see through the slits. My mouth is so dry. I hear something move slightly next to me. I feel two souls in the room with me. One is a strong soul, solid and good. From that direction comes feelings of pain and shame and love. I recognize that soul, and feel safe. The other soul puzzles me. I've never felt that soul before, but somehow it seems familiar.

"Jack," I croak.

Jack leans close to my ear and says, "Yes?"

"Water?" I beg.

"I can't give you water while you're lying down like that. It will pour onto the bed. I don't think you should move yet. I'll get some ice from the nurse. You can suck on ice cubes."

The thought of ice cubes sounds glorious.

I feel Jack's soul move away, and I mourn the loss. I let my eyes close again. Then his soul reenters the area. "Blue?" he calls softly.

I open my eyes and smile. "Sorry, the light is bright."

"Not as bright as your light."

I puzzle at that. Jack pulls down the shades, then sits down again and gently slips an ice cube between my lips.

I push it to the inside of my cheek and thank him. I'm so tired and weak, but I want to stay awake for a few minutes. There are things I need to know.

"Blackwater?" I say through the ice cube.

Jack says, "Dead."

I grow worried and ask, "Not by bloodlust?"

"No, there was no time. Your heart had stopped. I had to force my blood into you to bring you back. Varg did the honors."

"Thank you. Is Varg okay?"

Jack chuckles and snaps his fingers. Suddenly I see a furry face lying on my bed next to my pillow. The second soul. I smile so hard my chapped lips crack. I want to pet him, but I don't have the energy to lift my arm.

Jack says, "He found the entrance to the crypt when we were looking for you. Then he ran after the ambulance. He made it into the surgery room with you, and has been lying under your bed the whole time you were out except for a few quick trips outside. Alexis has stopped by every day with food and water for him and blood for me."

I smile at this again. Then I lick my lips, still feeling parched. "Ice cube?" I ask.

Jack slips another one between my lips. He lets his finger linger on my bottom lip and traces it back and forth. Then he withdraws his hand.

"How did you know I was at the cemetery?"

"Gambino found out Blackwater owned some plots there. Rubalia called and said there was a mausoleum on one of the plots. I saw a thin beam of light reaching into the sky. It went so high, to the moon and beyond. I would recognize your soul anywhere, Blue. It led me straight to you. Varg arrived and pointed me to the right mausoleum."

I smile and say, "Hold my hand, Jack."

Jack covers my hand, which is right next to Varg's head. He lightly caresses it with his thumb. I look at our hands joined and look over at

Varg's snout lying on the bed and his happy eyes gleaming at me. I say, "You're a good boy, Varg."

Then I look at Jack and say, "Thank you for saving me."

I feel a good measure of Jack's shame and guilt ease. Not enough, but it's a start. I squeeze his fingers lightly and revel in the comfort and closeness of both Jack and Varg. My eyes close as I drift back to sleep.

CHAPTER 68

FRIENDS

BLUEBELL KILDARE

JUNE 10, 2022, RED AGES

I wake with the realization there are people in my room. In fact, I know exactly who's in my room. The energy coming off Maud is a little hyper and restless. She's worried. Alexis is calm and collected. Her energy is more concentrated. Both have good, loving souls that for some reason I can sense without even turning on my sixth sense. Varg's soul glows warm and bright from beneath my bed, shining of loyalty, bravery, and honor. I ponder at the new depth of my gift, wondering what caused it.

My cheek is still squished against the mattress. The pain is bearable now, so I decided to open my eyes. Maud and Alexis are sitting in chairs across from me. I see a machine hooked up to an IV in my arm. Maud is flipping through the pages of a *fashion* magazine, and Alexis is knitting a large, beautiful, pale blue something.

They seem to have their roles reversed. Aren't older people supposed to knit while younger people peruse fashion magazines?

"What are you knitting?"

Both Maud's and Alexis' eyes jump to me. Alexis' face breaks into a smile and Maud's turns into a frown. Alexis says, "A shawl for cool evenings."

"It is a beautiful stitch."

Alexis beams.

Maud, never one to be left behind, says, "You scared the shit out of me, chicky. Making me chase all over town looking for Varg, worried out of my mind for you. I may not look like it, but I'm an old lady. You can't do that to me."

"I'm so sorry, Maud. I didn't mean to worry you."

Maud's face softens at that. "You should be sorry. I called Father

O'Brennen and we had the whole church praying for you."

I wince internally, hoping I don't owe some sort of cosmic debt for that.

"Then I jumped over the backyard fence and nearly broke my hip to tell Harry Pickets I needed his help to drive me around looking for Varg. Thankfully Alexis joined us so I didn't have to spend all day alone with Harry."

Alexis snickers at this and interjects, "I assure you, it was more painful for me than for either of you."

Then she leans in and says, "Harry was more than glad to be her driver. I think he would paint her toenails pink and hand-feed her grapes if he had a chance. But Maud plays him like a puppet."

Maud glares at Alexis and then mutters something under her breath. I hear the words cow, milk, and free mixed in. Then she says sharply, "He asked me into his house while he got the keys. As if I would go in his house. I hardly know the man."

"You have been his neighbor for over twenty years," Alexis exclaims.

Maud snaps, "And exactly how well do you know your neighbors, Alexis?"

I could laugh at that because I'm her only neighbor, but I can see this is going nowhere good. I ask, "How long was I gone?"

"Two days," Maud says gently.

"Oh. I thought it was much longer."

Alexis says, "It was long enough. You were unconscious for another five days and just briefly woke up yesterday." Then she leans back and gestures to the windowsill. "Father O'Brennen brought you flowers."

I look over and see five small vases filled with different types of flowers: lilies, daffodils, tulips, lilacs, and daisies. I look at Alexis and Maud. "Why so many?"

Maud laughs. "He didn't know what you'd like, and several parishioners donated, so he just picked a selection."

Ohh! I hope that is not another cosmic debt. They are lovely. I ask my friends, "Can you get the nurse? I want to turn over on my side."

"Hey there." says the nurse when she enters a moment later. "Mr.

Tanner told me you woke up once. I wasn't sure I believed it. Well, lying on your side is allowed, but you have a lot of damage on your back still. Are you sure? It might hurt more."

"I'd like to try. Can you help me roll over?"

The nurse scoots me over to the side of the bed and places some pillows next to me to keep me in place. As she does this, I notice I am still wearing the Belladonna Necklace. The nurse rolls me backwards toward the center, half on the pillows, and the chains gently clang. She puts a pillow under my head so I am lying sideways with my head supported.

"That's much better," I say. "My muscles were cramped."

Varg decides to join the party by placing his snout next to my pillow again. I look at him and say, "Hey, buddy. You are such a good boy. I missed you."

Varg wags his tail at my coos and hits the stand holding my IV. The nurse glares at Varg, and he sits his haunches down obediently.

The nurse plays with the machine that's next to me. Then she hands me a little plastic button and says, "This is morphine. It helps with the pain. When you feel too much pain, press the button. It will knock you out in no time."

"Okay, thank you." I keep the button close. I've had enough pain.

She hands me another button and says, "Press this button if you need me. The doctor should arrive in a few minutes, so you should get your visiting done now." She nods meaningfully at Maud and Alexis giving them the "you had better skedaddle when he arrives, or else" look. Then she leaves.

I look at Alexis and Maud. "Why am I still wearing the necklace Blackwater put on me?"

Alexis and Maud exchange looks, then Alexis speaks up. "No one knows how to take it off. It's secured with magic and seems unbreakable, even for the Vampires. I guess you're stuck with it awhile."

I frown at this. The necklace is beautiful, and it doesn't work on me, thankfully, but it isn't the most comfortable thing in the world. Maybe Jack knows someone who can get it off. Thinking of Jack reminds me of a question I had earlier.

"Jack said he saw a light over the cemetery, and that's how he found me. Is that true? Did you see the light?"

Alexis shakes her head and says, "No, I can't see auras or souls. Not many people can. If Jack hadn't been searching for you, you wouldn't have been found in time. You know, he wouldn't even leave you alone at the hospital until you woke. I brought bagged blood here every day for him. That man loves you." She nods for emphasis.

"I know," I say sadly. "But he thinks he's tarnished because he is a Vampire. He won't allow himself to be with me."

"How ridiculous!" Maud exclaims. "Why are the world's greatest fools all men?"

"You can kick his butt for me."

Maud says, "Humph. Someone needs to."

We hear a knock at the door. Maud looks over and says, "It's the doctor, chicky. We'll step outside now, but we'll be right here until Jack returns."

Maud and Alexis both kiss me on the cheek and say goodbye.

The doctor is a short, wiry guy with thick glasses, a large nose, and a mass of frizzy, dark hair. His energy is strong, and he feels happy but tired. He introduces himself. "Hi, I'm Dr. Ziggler. How are you feeling, Blue?"

I smile wryly. "I've been better. But I've been worse."

Dr. Ziggler grins. "You sure have. I'm going to examine you briefly. Then we'll talk about your injuries."

When he is done with his poking and prodding, he says, "Well, you're coming along fine—amazing, actually. Do you know how extensive your injuries were?"

"I know I almost died, or I did die and was brought back. Jack gave me some of his blood. But I don't know what damage has been done. I can't see my back."

Dr. Ziggler nods. "Well, I am not sure if you died or were on the verge of death, but by the time you got to us, I couldn't believe you were alive myself when I saw your back. It was bad, Blue. Really bad. Skin was missing from large sections, and the muscle was lacerated down to bone in many places, including in places over your spine. How your spinal cord survived, I don't know. We had to take some skin from your belly and do skin grafts and sew you up as best as we could. But there is significant muscle damage, and you still need more skin grafts. You also had tremendous blood loss. We did the most immediately needed work, but we needed to stabilize you too."

I nod at this.

Dr. Ziggler goes on. "You'll regain some of your muscle strength, but not all of it. You lost a lot of muscle in places. And there will be scarring."

I nod again.

"How are you handling this?"

"I'm okay."

Dr. Ziggler eyes me closely. "I can see you're okay. But how are you okay? No one else would be."

"Did you hear what happened?"

Dr. Ziggler answers, "What I've been told is you were tortured with a whip over the course of days without food or water, warmth or clothing. Your injuries were consistent with that."

I say, "The man who did that to me, he wanted something from me, and if I gave it to him, he would have been able to cause great harm to a great many people. I made a choice. I didn't expect to ever leave that room. I am here now, and he is dead, and he can't hurt those people now. So I'm okay. I am better than I ever expected."

I see a sparkling of tears in Dr. Ziggler's eyes. He nods and pats my hand. "Well, I see then. I'll let you rest now. We'll talk more tomorrow."

When Dr. Ziggler leaves, I decide it's high time to hit the pain button.

chapter 69

Claiming

Bluebell Kildare

June 11, 2022, Red Ages

 open my eyes to a nurse trying to gently move my arm. She smiles down at me. "I need to draw a little blood for the labs."

I try to accommodate her with my eyes closed. I'm so tired, but I can feel her soul strongly. It's a gentle soul, filled with determination and hope. Next to her I feel Jack's soul. Even with my eyes closed I feel how solid and good he is. He is filled with worry, pain, and love. I smile when I encounter Varg's soul beneath the bed. I wonder why I sense so strongly now. I don't even have to reach inside to my sixth sense—the feeling is just there.

When the nurse leaves me alone, I slowly open my eyes. Jack sits in the chair opposite me, and the sun rises behind him through the window. A brilliant pink and orange light filters through the steel gray clouds. Rays of sunshine peek through and light up Jack's curls like a halo, softening the rigid, angular planes of his face.

"Hi, Jack," I say with a slight smile.

Jack crosses his legs and gently caresses me with his eyes, a soft green today. "Hello, Blue. How are you feeling?"

I look at his hand on his knee and wish he would hold mine again. "I'm getting better. I talked to Dr. Ziggler yesterday."

Jack leans forward. "What did he say?"

"He said I'm better than he expected. I need more surgeries for my muscles and to graft more skin onto my back. The muscle will get better, but I'll lose some functionality. He said my back was so ripped up that part of my spine was exposed and that I shouldn't have lived."

Jack looks pained at this and nods.

I say in a puzzled voice, "My hands were injured from the shackles, but there's no sign of the injury now."

Jack says in a quiet voice, "When I found you, you were not going to make it. I gave you some blood. Remember I told you?"

When I nod, Jack continues. "There was a lot of bone exposed, more so than even Dr. Ziggler saw. My blood helped you close up that muscle and start your heart and your respiration. It also closed up the most superficial wounds."

"But I thought Vampire blood could completely heal you?"

Jack sighs. "It would have if I gave you more. But you have to understand, Blue, you lost so much blood and your injuries were so bad, if I would have given you enough blood to completely heal you, there is no doubt I would have turned you in the process. It's the ratio of Vampire to human blood that matters. I gave you as much as I dared at the time."

"Ohh, I see."

I can't stand not touching him, so I stretch my hand toward him. Jack seems to know what I want because he reaches out and gently brushes my fingertips with his and slips his fingers under my palm to softly squeeze it. He keeps his hand there as he continues in a low voice, "Your body has refilled its blood volume naturally now, and it has healed some more. I could give you more blood now. It would heal you, and you would have no scars. Your muscles would be as good as new. You could walk out of this hospital with me today."

I look at him with hope in my eyes. "Would you do that?"

Jack smiles. "Of course, if you want it." Then his face turns serious. "But you need to know, Blue, while I would do anything for you, to help you, I can't be with you." He looks down at his hand holding mine. "I'll gladly give you my blood, but we can't be together. Do you understand that?"

Tears threaten my eyes, but I force them back. Instead I smile a bittersweet smile and trace a finger on his palm. I think carefully about how to answer him, and finally I say, "I understand you, Jack, more than you think. If you help me with this, I will not expect more than you're willing to give."

Jack nods, accepting my answer. He draws out a pocket knife and starts to aim it for his wrist. I shake my head slightly. "I want your neck, Jack."

Jack looks at me questioningly. "But you can't sit up, Blue."

"I don't need to. You're going to lie down. But first scoot me back so you have room."

Jack gently moves me back so I'm close to the bars on the side of the bed but not touching them. Gentle or not, it hurts like crazy. A familiar spasm of pain rolls through my back. I grip his hand for a moment. Jack stills, then asks, "Are you ready?"

I nod. Jack takes off his suit jacket and carefully slides into bed next to me, facing me, on his right side so we are hip to hip. I revel in his body heat and slowly place my right hand against his chest. I so treasure the feel of him beneath my hand.

He kisses my nose, and I look up to his eyes. I watch as he gently bites his lip with his fangs so fat blood droplets form. He draws his face near me and brushes his lips against mine. His lips softly urge mine apart, and I take his bottom lip into my mouth.

I can taste the salty warmth of his blood and a small tingle starts to build. Jack cradles my head and positions me so my mouth is on his upper lip now. I gently pull on his lip with mine, and droplets of blood fall onto my tongue. I feel the tingling expand as a greater warmth washes over my body. Jack groans and gently runs his fingers up and down my arm.

Jack pulls his lip away from me and looks at me with liquid heat in his eyes. He takes my hand and gently suckles my index finger. I feel the soft warmth of his mouth enclosing my finger, pulling and then letting go, pulling, then letting go. He repeats this with each of my fingers until he reaches my pinky. This he twirls his tongue around, evoking a breathless gasp from me. He kisses my nose and looks in my eyes. "Are you ready?"

I nod slightly. That's all I'm capable of doing at the moment.

Jack quickly creates a small slit on his neck with the knife and cradles my head in the crook of his arm, positioning his neck next to my mouth.

I taste him tentatively with the tip of my tongue. The same tingling sensation washes over me again. I wrap my lips around the wound and slowly pull the heady potion into my body. My senses come alive. My nerve endings sing, and my body flushes with a rushing heat. I want him with a wanting I've never felt. I swear I can taste his soul in his blood. It is beautiful and loving.

I arch my hips toward him, helpless, unable to move closer, needing more. Jack sees my need and moves his hips firmly against mine so that we are pressed together tightly. I feel the hard length of his manhood between us.

I suck more strongly now. Jack groans and starts to tremble. I knead his neck with my lips as I take more. I want him. The wanting is so strong that my mind is aware of nothing else. My entire body shakes with desire as I rub against him as much as I can.

Jack murmurs against my hair between gentle kisses to my ear and temple. "I can smell your womanhood so strongly. It calls to me. You are so beautiful, inside and out. I'm so glad you're still with me Blue. I am so glad. I am so glad."

I curl my hand around Jack's shoulder and rub the length of his arm. He gently pulls my mouth away from his neck, catching my lips with his instead.

He rubs his lips softly against mine, imploringly. I open my mouth to him and he kisses me lightly at first, then deeply and sweetly. Our tongues dance for a moment before he pulls away. He pushes in again, then pulls away once more. I kiss the cleft of his chin and the tiny corners of his mouth. Then, feeling more daring, I run my hand down his abdomen, feeling the hard muscles beneath his shirt.

"Jack," I say, "I want to feel your chest."

Jack hesitates. I plead my case with my eyes. He unbuttons his crisp, white shirt quickly, letting it fall open. I place my right hand on his chest, then gently feel around, exploring, getting to know the feel of him, memorizing this moment. I run my fingers across his flat nipples. They harden beneath my hand, and Jack takes in a quick breath. I look up at his eyes, and they are such a dark green they are almost black. I watch his face, and I slowly move my hand down his rib cage, loving the texture and heat of his skin. His heavily hooded eyes peer intently into mine. I feel him suck his stomach in as I go lower and lower until I hit his belt. I try to dip my finger under his belt line, but he stills my arm and gently pulls it up to his mouth. He kisses the palm of my hand and smoothly backs away to slide off the bed.

My whole body feels bereft without him. Only cold air fills the place where he was. Jack leans over and kisses my left eye, my right eye, and then my nose. Then he moves to sit a mile away from me in the darned chair. I sigh my disappointment and sadness.

Jack says, "I am sorry, Blue. If I didn't stop you now, I would have taken you. You're not healed yet."

I don't want to hear it, but I know he's right. It's a small consolation to see it's as hard on Jack as it is me. I hug my blanket close to my body. "How long will it take?"

"A little while still."

"Will you hold my hand until then?"

Jack smiles and reaches over, twining his fingers with mine. Suddenly I feel a blanket of exhaustion fall over me. I struggle to keep my eyes open because I want to keep looking at Jack. But I can't help it. My eyes are so heavy. They close, and I drift away.

It seems like a minute later when I pop my eyes open and try to feel for pain in my back. After discovering no pain, I tentatively use my arms to lever myself up to sitting position. Still no pain. I look at Jack.

"It's amazing! I feel so good."

Jack smiles. It's not the smile of my lover. It is the smile of my boss. My heart clenches at the sight.

"What's wrong?" he asks.

"Nothing. I feel great!" I plaster a smile on to give depth to the lie.

"Can I look at your back?"

I nod my assent.

As Jack moves to the other side of the bed, I notice his white shirt is all buttoned up and his suit jacket is back on. I frown my displeasure. Meanwhile, Jack carefully pulls a corner of the tape and gauze covering my back. Slowly, he pulls more of it down. Then he gently pulls it all off. He turns toward me with a huge grin. "You're all healed. But we should have Dr. Ziggler check you out first."

"I am?"

Jack nods.

I clap my hands. "Good. Then we can get back to work right away."

Jack looks at me strangely as I carefully remove the IV from my arm. "Don't you think you deserve a little vacation after all of this?"

I say firmly, "Jack, there's something you don't know. It isn't over yet. Blackwater was not acting alone. He said he had people to answer to. He said, 'We will make it happen.'"

Jack's face goes deadly black. "Make what happen?" He stands up and starts pacing around my little hospital room, clenching and unclenching his fists.

"He wanted the Gifted to control the world and have power over Norms. He wanted to use Vampires to do it."

Jack hardly flinches when I tell him, but he's overflowing with such evident violence anyone else would be afraid to be in the room. I can feel his fury bouncing off the walls, tangible and absolute. But I am not afraid, because I also feel his pain.

Jack looks at me with bright green eyes and moves toward me purposefully. He gently grabs my face between his two large, warm hands and looks me directly in the eyes. He slowly and deliberately lowers his mouth toward me and moves his lips roughly over mine. He kisses me with hunger, devouring my mouth with his lips. This is no loving kiss or asking kiss. This is a claiming kiss. He is marking me as his.

He lifts me up off the bed and pulls me hard against his body, holds me tightly to him while he fills my mouth with his tongue. He delves and plunges it into my mouth, touching every bit of flesh, filling me as much as possible, moving quickly and urgently. I wrap my arms around his back and rub it soothingly.

Jack suddenly rips his mouth away and holds me closer, encompassing me in his arms, placing his chin over my shoulder, pressing me tightly, rocking me gently, as though he's comforting me, when it's he who needs comfort. He puts his mouth against the hair by my ear and whispers, "I won't let them have you again. I won't let them have you again. Never again. Never, ever again."

In this moment, I truly understand how much pain he went through while I was gone. I can feel it still cuts him deeply. I feel his fear and panic as my own. My heart squeezes with the pain of it and I whisper back, "I am okay. You're okay. We're okay. I promise. We are okay."

Jack finally calms down and pulls his body back from me, but he still holds my arms, and his eyes are actively searching my face.

I say with a sure voice, "Jack. They are not going to get me again."

Jack shakes his head sadly and says, "Blue. There is so much you don't know, so much I have to tell you."

This puzzles me. "What do you have to tell me, Jack?"

Jack grabs my hospital gown at the neckline and tears it about four inches down so it slips slightly over my shoulders. He fingers the Belladonna Necklace and moves his hand to my shoulder. He slowly traces my birthmark with his thumb, and he searches my eyes as if checking to see if I'm ready for what he has to say.

I am getting a little worried now, so I hold his gaze firmly and repeat, "What do you have to tell me, Jack?"

Jack whispers so softly, like the sound of grasses rustling in a summer breeze. "You, Blue. I have to tell you about *you*."

Want More?

Thank you for reading *The Light Who Shines*. I truly hope you enjoyed this novel. Plenty of future adventures await Blue, Jack, and Varg in the next full length novel of the series, *The Light Who Binds*. For those who would love to hear the voices of their favorite characters, audio versions are available. If you would enjoy some history on Varg you can check out *The Binding of the Wolf*, a short story available in ebook only.

Please take a moment to leave a review. I honestly read every one.
Amazon: amazon.com/author/liloabernathy
Goodreads: goodreads.com/Lilo_Abernathy

Support

For those inclined, here are some other ways you can support this book and my future work.

- Recommend it to friends on Goodreads.
- Vote for it on the Goodreads lists.
- Recommend it to your Goodreads groups.
- Post about it on Facebook.
- Tell your circles about it on Google+.
- Recommend it to your book club.
- Tell your friends about it!

Connect

I love when readers connect with me on social media.
My Site: www.liloabernathy.com

Thanks for helping spread the word!

Author Autobiography

I am currently forty-three, but that could differ depending on what year you read this. Unless some fundamental laws of nature change, I expect that number to only get higher. I am half Italian and half Irish. Well, the Irish side is sort of an Irish/German/English/French/Scottish mix, but since I believed I was truly half Irish until my mother's foray into genealogy, I'm sticking to that story.

I live amidst the Smoky Mountains and can sometimes see cloud shadows lying on the mountainside from my front porch. I am not yet snobbish enough to call it a veranda, but time will tell. I'm a great believer in the proof being in the pudding. Sometimes my young adult daughter joins me on the veranda . . . err, porch to admire the view. Often my Australian Shepherd runs around the veranda looking for things to shepherd. Because we are decidedly lacking in livestock, he frequently presents me with slobbery balls to throw. I, in turn, do my best to ignore them.

I started working full time while in high school and haven't stopped since. My illustrious career began with a smattering of service experiences at various fast food and restaurant chains, went on to fine jewelry, slipped into property management for housing projects, morphed into corporate real estate, then ended up in mergers and acquisitions. Please don't ask how that happened as it's still a mystery to me.

My home is a modestly sized ranch, recently purchased and still not completely unpacked. The walls are a boring light beige, but they make the perfect backdrop for my brightly colored Gustav Klimt canvas prints. Van Gogh hopes to join Klimt on my walls soon, but right now the brakes on my Cube need to be fixed, and the washer overflows if I place the water level on super-duper high. Priorities, priorities.

More importantly than all the above, you absolutely must know my favorite color is purple. Not Barney purple, no offense to Barney, but more of a medium eggplant purple. I like to think of it as a "mature" purple, but deep down I know it's really just purple.